I0672903

CARADOC

book three

The Rebel King

Sally Newton

It is AD 47 and the Roman Empire occupies the
south-east of Britannia. Caradoc is now king, but a
king of exiles - king of the free.
In the west Caradoc and his warriors try to hold back
the Roman legions. If they win then their homelands
could be freed. If they lose thousands will die - still
more would be enslaved.
Caradoc is warrior, druid, master of spies and
respected, even by his Roman enemies - but can he
protect the people he loves?

Battles, betrayal, love and the Gods all come together
for this epic conclusion to the
Caradoc trilogy.

The Rebel King
Book 3 of the Caradoc Trilogy
ISBN 978-1-909936-15-7
Copyright © 2019 by Sally Newton

Published 2019
Pendown Publishing
Cornwall, United Kingdom

Set in 11pt Gentium BB

Printed by Lightning Source

www.pendownpublishing.co.uk

Other books by Sally Newton:
The Defiant Prince - book 1 of the Caradoc Trilogy
The Druid Heir - book 2 of the Caradoc Trilogy

Cover: NJM designs

Background Information

Modern dates of festivals
Beltane : 1st of May
Lughnasa : 1st of August
Samhain : 1st of November (this was also New Year)
Imbolc : 1st of February

All of the Caradoc trilogy is a work of fiction woven around a framework of historic truth - and with Rebel King this is truer than ever. Readers familiar with the relevant passages in Tacitus's Annals will recognise that I have followed Tacitus closely, if not to the letter. Some characters and incidents were inspired by archaeological finds.

Further information about the people in this trilogy may be found in the **Author's Note** at the end of this book.

Just about all of the locations in Rebel King are real places. In truth there are far too many to list here without this background note becoming a book in its own right, but perhaps readers who are familiar with the archaeological sites of Britain will recognise them. Check out my blog on Goodreads to see the definitive list.

Note:
In my novels the chief druid of a people is known by the tribe's name, ending in 'os' for a man and 'i' for a woman, whatever their original name was. The chief druid of Britain is known as Britannios, if a woman she would be Britanni. There is no evidence for this as such, it just seems logical.

Caradoc's Britannia, at the beginning of AD 47.

Carvetii

Eire

Brigantes

Ynys Mon

Deciangli
Ordovicis

Cornovi

Corieltavi

Iceni

Catuvellauni

Silures

Glevum

Camulodunon

Dobunni

Verlamion

Londinium

Areas neither allied
with nor conquered by
Rome shaded.

Durotriges

Calleva
Atrebates

Canti

Dumnoni

Gaul

Current names of places

Ynys Mon : still Ynys Mon, or Anglesey
Glevum: Gloucester. Originally a Roman fort in the Kingsholm area.
Camulodunon/Camulodunum : Colchester
Calleva : Silchester, near Reading
Verlamion : St Albans
Londinium: London
Durovernon : Canterbury
Gesoriacum: Boulogne-sur-Mer

Deva: river Dee
Gwy: river Wye
Hafren : still Hafren, in Welsh, or river Severn
Meduwaen : river Medway
Mor: river Mersey
Tamesis : river Thames

One The column

Summer is the usual season for war . . . but we took no notice of that.

I was so cold, sat still amongst the scarps since before dawn, that I worried my feet would not obey me when the time came. We all had cloths around our mouths in case our breath clouds gave us away and by now the damp gathering in the weave was starting to irritate me. Young Tarn joked when he came back from a piss that it came out solid.

But it will be worth it when the Roman supply column comes.

We knew for certain they were coming. As soon as I heard from my usual source I called out my warriors and got us into place. Our horses were hidden, well behind but in reach. I picked a spot where the wind swirled the snow against the rocks and gave us a little more cover. We were all wearing our dullest clothes with hoods up over our hair. I'd even banned everyone from wearing torques, lest they gleam in the sunlight, such as it was. Nothing can ever be left to chance, with the Romans.

Three and a half long years since the legions invaded we'd managed to keep them at the end of a long stick. The eastern lands of the Isle, my own homelands among them, might be part of the Roman Empire – for now – but the menace hadn't spread that far to the west. Thanks to us.

I flicked a glance south to another cluster of rocks and saw my nephew Kynbel stretching a cramp in his foot. He was twenty-two winters by then, a hardened warrior of many battles, but still seemed a boy to me. I could see his hood was slipping so I tapped my own head and pointed. *Wake up, Kynbel.* He got what I meant and pulled up the hood. I smiled at him, before I remembered the cloth over my mouth.

Kynbel ducked back down and I guessed his young ears had picked up the sound of the column on the march. I

5

peered beyond him and fancied I could see a shimmer behind the drifting snow flakes. I was right. The gaudy signum glinted and we saw it a few heartbeats before we saw the soldiers. Behind them were the carts, being dragged up the incline by weary whipped mules. By then my men all had spears and shields ready. I flexed my hands to get the blood back in and loosened the sword of my mother's kin from its scabbard.

Cernunnos, Camulos, Teutates, Epona, protect me and mine, now and always. Give us victory.

They were trudging closer but as we all waited for them to come into spear range the Romans did something infuriating – they stopped.

I saw the officer's hand raised for halt and my heart sank. We had never ambushed right *here* before, but it was a common enough thing, and even with all my precautions they might still have seen us. Machan, to my left, passed me a worried look.

'They could just be resting,' I whispered, but usually they would sit down, eat their dried fruits, and belly-ache. There was none of that today. The officer at the front, an *optio* I think, was scanning his eyes about the hills cautious as a doe.

Wait, I willed my men. *They're not in range yet.*

All the warriors around me followed my unspoken lead but to the south I saw movement – spears, Kynbel's men's spears. Of course *they* were not out of range.

'Come on!' I yelled.

We sprang from cover and sprinted towards the fore of the column just as they heard their comrades' screams and whipped round to defend them. We were yelling like banshees, our bright shields before our hearts. The merest blink of confusion on their part gave us the chance to get near enough.

'Now!'

I threw my spear, getting the *optio* through the throat, and felt the other spears flying round me. About half the enemy were felled immediately but the rest turned on us. I felt a javelin scrape the edge of my owl-eye shield.

'Caradoc!'

Machan's shout warned me just in time – the Roman to my left fell with my sword through his neck. Machan dealt with the one who'd thrown the spear at me. We were doing well, considering the plan had split, but the chaos was spreading. Those enemy at the front who were still alive were hunkering down behind a wall of their shields and those at the far south were doing the same but the middle section were scattering away into the rocks.

'They're trying to get behind us!' I yelled to Tarn, still up high among the scarps. He yanked the brass horn from his belt and blasted out the long note agreed upon, breaking off to defend himself against one soldier who got near. I saw another Roman aiming a javelin at him and smashed my shield into the side of his head. He, and his spear, fell to the ground.

It was too late, any way: Tarn's call had done its work. Colleos and the other men we'd left with the horses were charging in from the west, cutting down the loose Romans like wheat, and hurtling towards those still sheltering behind their shields. The cart drivers were both dead. We now outnumbered the enemy by at least five to one and even the shield-wall didn't feel safe to them – the survivors of the southern group had broken off and were running for their lives into the gorse. The wagons were abandoned.

'Shall we go after them?' Machan asked.

'No,' I said. 'They might be trying to draw us away from the wagons and regain the advantage. We got what we wanted.'

I raised the leather cover of one of the carts and was relieved to find sacks of grain there and not crouching men with knives, despite my words. I sheathed my sword and let my heartbeat go back to normal.

I saw Colleos up on the rocks offering a scrap of cloth to young Tarn.

'You two all right?'

Colleos looked back at me. 'His nose is bleeding – but it's not broken, he'll be fine.'

Well he would know. I turned back to the cart, pulling the dead driver from the seat so that one of my own men could drive it on to Siluria. Machan was checking the next cart along and smiled as he pulled a small, jangling box from beneath the covers. *Excellent.* Gold as well as grain – our Silure hosts will be glad of our presence a while longer.

'My king!'

I spun round to see Hedros, Machan's eldest surviving son, charging my way with a look on his face I knew of old.

'What's wrong? Are you hurt?'

He shook his head. By the Gods – there seemed to be tears in his eyes.

'Go on lad, spit it out.'

'Where is Prince Kynbel, sire?'

Oh Gods.

I looked behind the boy to the southern scarps where Kynbel had been fighting and saw bodies on the ground. Only Roman bodies, as far as I could see, but there could be more among the rocks.

I was running before I knew it.

'Kynbel!'

There was blood in the snow, but that could be anyone's. I saw the edge of an upturned shield poking out from behind one of the rocks and scrambled for it, almost tripping on one of the bodies. I turned the shield over. Two white horses: unmistakably his. I climbed up onto the highest rock and scanned about all the fallen for his face, his clothes, his fair hair.

Nothing. Not even a footprint in the snow I could be definite was his. It was as if he'd been swallowed into a hidden cave.

Oh Gods, oh Gods . . . may my brother forgive me.

'Kynbel!'

Two **The traitor**

Whilst we searched for Kynbel the snow started coming down in earnest, not just the odd flake in the wind, and I was suddenly conscious of the cold again. In so far as we hadn't found his body I must admit I was starting to feel relieved but now, given the snow would cover any tracks, I was anxious to get going.

'Come,' I said to Machan. 'The Romans who ran off must have captured him. We need to get after them before the snow gets too deep.'

Machan had been seeing off the last of the carts towards Siluria and turned to me with a concerned frown on his face.

'My king . . . what if that's what they want?'

A trap. Yes, the thought had crossed my mind.

I threw up my hands. 'What can I do? I promised my brother as he was dying I would take care of all of them and – '

'No.' Machan almost shouted it. 'Stop right there.' Everyone looked to my old friend in shock. He coloured scarlet up to his ears before going on. 'Sorry, my king – but your head has saved us and your own neck many a time and will do so again if you don't, well, if you don't trip yourself up on false guilt. This is *not* your fault.'

I took a big breath. He had a point, but I remembered my instruction earlier to let the stragglers go and stay with the wagons and had been kicking myself for it a while. *Enough*, I told myself. *Deal with the problem at hand.*

I turned to Hedros. 'When was the last time you saw Kynbel?'

He pointed to the rocks where we'd found Kynbel's shield. 'He was fighting two Romans who were trying to corner him in there. He seemed to be doing well and I couldn't help him because I was in trouble myself . . . '

'It's all right, Hedros, I'm not blaming you. Had he been wounded?'

'Not that I could see, my king.'

So, two Romans had cornered him. 'Did they try to separate anyone else away from the rest of you?' I asked and all Kynbel's men shook their heads.

They must know who he is. The thought shot into my mind and I felt sick.

One of our horses stamped in the snow and Colleos quieted him. 'You think they know who he is, don't you?' Colleos asked me.

I sighed. 'It's possible. But how? He was dressed as drab as the rest of us, he wasn't wearing a torque.'

Hedros frowned at that, looking off into the distance as if thinking, and I felt my mood darken still further.

'Hedros, tell me he wasn't wearing a torque, please.'

'I – I think he was, my king. Last night, when we were leaving and he was saying goodbye to Rhian, he was wearing one then. The twisted one he usually wears.'

Cernunnos give me strength. 'Against my given orders!'

Hedros shrank back a little at that and I regretted my outburst, patting him on the shoulder.

'It might have saved his life,' Colleos was saying, 'if they think he is important.'

'Indeed. It also means they can try to torture out of him every plan I ever had, how many warriors we have, where our camp is . . . ' I threw myself up on to my horse and Hedros handed me my shield. 'Let's go. We'd better get back to camp before they get there.'

I should have had more faith that my nephew would be able to withstand torture, or at least I should have showed more faith in front of them, but it was too late, I'd said it.

We passed the area where I had been fighting earlier and I heard a moan coming from one of the Roman bodies. It was the man I'd hit in the head with my shield edge, pretty hard I'd thought. He still had his helmet on and I suppose the broad Roman cheek pieces must have protected his temple. He was now starting to push himself up into a sitting position and didn't seem to realise we were all looking at him, at first, then I saw his eyes go round with fear. His right hand shot towards his sword but Machan's spear was levelled at his chest and he thought better of drawing it.

'Calm,' I said, in Latin. 'Hands on your head.'

He obeyed, looking at me all the while like a cornered wolf. Hedros took the sword from him. 'Bind his hands,' I said to Hedros, in our own language. 'And blindfold him.'

Machan shot me a look. 'He lives? He has seen your face.'

I emitted a grim bark of a laugh. 'If Adminios is still with them then every Roman from here to Gaul knows what I look like, maybe even in Rome. Yes, he lives. We can try to swap him, for Kynbel, and I don't want him to see the way back to camp.'

The prisoner was put on Kynbel's horse and we started for home.

It was a long ride back to our overnight camp through the bleak landscape, my mind pounding like a smith at an anvil every step of the way. I pulled my hood well forward to keep my ears warm but also so my men couldn't see the worry on my face. Kynbel was alive – I had that much faith in the Gods. It was everything else that worried me. Something smelt bad, as the saying goes.

'My king?'

Machan's voice came at the very point a buzzard keened overhead and made me flinch.

'Yes, Machan?'

'We reach the softer ground soon. Shall we take the short cut across it, and hope the snow covers our tracks?'

I looked about me. The snow was still coming down hard, and laying, and my people seemed frozen. 'Yes, take the short cut today, but tell the men to spread out a bit so the prints are not so deep and fill fast.'

Machan nodded and got to it. I kept only the prisoner close to me, Kynbel's mare following my Buanedd dutifully, although even she looked crestfallen. Perhaps I imagined it. Machan seemed to be watching me from the corner of his eye as if I was a tree about to fall. When the smoke from our camp was in sight I called him over to me.

'What are your thoughts, Machan?'

He took a good breath. 'I think Prince Kynbel is alive, sire, but . . . but I am thinking more and more that the whole thing was planned.'

'I agree. That has been turning over in my mind too.' I swept a hand out to our returning warriors but kept my voice low. 'I mean, when was the last time we didn't have a single man killed? The worst anyone got was a nose-bleed.'

'You think they knew about the ambush?'

'I'm not sure.' I shrugged. 'That would mean that they accepted the loss of all those men, the grain, the gold – perhaps a small loss, to them, but . . . I don't know. It seems a huge risk to capture one man.'

Machan shook his head. 'They know you will try to rescue him. They aim to draw you out.'

Well, if it's true then it's a good plan, I thought, *because I won't abandon him.*

We were near the camp now and our people were coming to the palisade to greet us. My wife's broad freckled face lit up with a smile as she saw me alive. I waved back to her before turning again to Machan.

'You are one of my oldest friends, speak now before we are in earshot of all the others – who do you think betrayed us? In your gut, who do you think it was?'

Machan's gaze dropped to his horse's mane, shaking his head. 'I don't know, but I refuse to believe it was any of the men. We have all fought beside you all these years and seen young Kynbel grow. Even Colleos,' he nodded over to our Morini friend, up ahead speaking with the guards at the village gate. 'Even he, a Gaul, he fought at the Tamesis and the Meduwaen, I've never doubted him.' Machan sighed. 'So that leaves the source, the people who told us of the column in the first place. It could be Camulora, or the Sparrow, or both.'

'I don't want to believe it of them, either, but you have a point. Keep this to yourself.'

He nodded. 'Yes, sire.'

As I rode through the gate I was relieved, in my heart, that Machan had not referred to the other person who was under suspicion. The person who had known he would be there at the ambush, known everything I had known. Who appeared to have made it out of the skirmish alive. Who had disobeyed my clear orders by wearing a torque that singled him out. My own nephew, Kynbel himself.

Our overnight camp was a cattle-herders' summer village and pretty bleak in the days approaching Imbolc, but my Nes had a good fire going and dry clothes ready for me. We'd used the smallest house for the night but we'd had it to ourselves, until I had the prisoner dragged in, that is, still tied and blind-folded. Nes and Gladsia watched with eyes round as moons as my men bound him to one of the house poles, as I asked. I waited until they'd left and the door was shut behind them then pulled off the helmet and the rag about his eyes. The Roman blinked a bit at the sudden light, then assumed a terse frown to mask his fear. He had a ruddy face and dark hair with a touch of red in it. At a guess I would say he was about thirty years in age, maybe less.

I crouched to the floor in front of him. 'How is your head?' I asked, in Latin.

No answer.

I looked at the area where my blow had fallen. A bruise was coming, and a bit of a lump, but not too bad. I looked into his eyes, which made him squirm, but I saw what I needed to see – both pupils were the same size. 'I think you will be all right,' I said. 'You can speak, and you shall. Are you thirsty?'

Still silence. Nevertheless I asked Nes to bring me a cup of water. I offered it to his lips, half expecting him to spit it back in my face, but he just shook his head.

'Someone betrayed us. Do you know who it was?'

I'd expected silence but I just tried to gauge his reaction. It was unclear.

'Perhaps you don't know their name, but you would recognise them if you saw them?'

This time I felt sure that he made his face deliberately impassive.

I sighed. 'Listen, I have a mind to swap you for my man who has been captured, but I could just hand you over to the druids if I wanted. Do you know what they do to captives?'

Still nothing.

'What are you asking him?' Nes asked, so I turned back to her and told her all that had happened. When I got to my suspicions Nes looked back to me in horror.

'No,' she said. 'I can't believe it.'

I pulled on the dry shirt she handed to me and got rid of my snow-soaked shoes. 'I don't want to believe it either, but what if they've got to him, somehow? He's never really been happy . . . not for years anyway.'

Nes hugged me. 'He misses his mother and his heart was broken for Airdinna, but he has Rhian now.'

'Does he? She's with Maros often enough as far as I can see. It's not love, whatever else you might call it. What if Airdinna was captured and the Romans have made some deal with him over her?'

'I don't know. It seems so unlikely. He's not like Addy – he adores you, like he did his father.'

'Well, I think you are right, but I'll go to talk with Rhian any way – I've got to be sure.'

Nes frowned. 'Have some food first, at least. Sit back down.'

I obeyed.

All the while our little Gladsia had been pretending to feed her cloth fox stew and babbling to herself. I hadn't really taken any notice of the Roman watching her but now, as she toddled over towards him, fox in hand, and asked him if he wanted any stew, my heart leapt to my mouth. I scooped her up.

'Leave him be, Gla-Gla.'

Nes took her from me, her face as white as mine no doubt was.

'Maybe we should ask Alwona to look after her, whilst the Roman is here?' I said to my wife, and she nodded.

Below, the Roman looked up to us with what seemed like hurt in his eyes.

'I'm a soldier, not a wild beast,' he said.

In our own language, with barely a trace of accent.

Three Negotiations

I recovered from my surprise as fast as I could, without losing too much face.

'Which people are you from?' I barked.

'The fourteenth Legio Gemina.'

Nice try. 'No, really?'

Silence.

'Look, we will be deep in Siluria in a matter of days. If I haven't swapped you for our man then you will be in the hands of not only the Britannios of the Isle – a personal friend of mine – but also the chief druid of the Silures, who is so devout she once threatened me.' I watched him all the while I said this and thought I spied a natural flash of terror. 'So. Start talking. Which people?'

He looked to the floor, his jaw clenched. 'Nervii,' he mumbled.

Nes and I exchanged glances. So he wasn't British, at least. The Nervii, from what I remembered, were from northern Gaul, not far from Colleos's Morini. A people the original Caesar had long since had under the Roman heel, but – if my memory served me right – they put up a fierce fight before the end.

'And your name?'

Again his gaze dropped as if ashamed. 'Lucius Ambix.'

Only two names. Probably not a citizen then.

'Where have your legion taken my warrior?'

Ambix looked back to me with exasperation. 'I don't know.'

That could be true. I rephrased my question.

'Well, where were you heading, when we attacked you?'

He glared.

'There aren't that many likely possibilities – but the quicker we find him, the quicker we can swap you,' I pushed. Again the only sound was my wife preparing the meal as she listened and Gladsia playing with her toys. I turned to Nes with a sigh. 'I may as well get going as soon as we've eaten. You can take the prisoner back to Siluria with you and the guards once you've broken camp. See what Siluri wants to do with him.'

Nesica nodded along, no trace of subterfuge on her face, may the Gods bless her. *I wouldn't really do it, Nes!*

Ambix watched us both, aghast. I could see beads of sweat forming on his brow despite the bitter draughts whistling through this poor herder's hut. My voice hardened.

'Look, soldier: remain a prisoner, or be swapped, it is up to you. Start talking. Who betrayed us?'

'I don't know!'

To be honest I believed him.

'Where were you going?'

He shook his head, refusing to look at me, his chin well down to his chest. 'I won't betray my legion and bring shame on my ancestors!'

I waited for him to raise his head again.

'You *do* betray your ancestors. Every day you march behind the standard of those who enslaved and slaughtered them.'

My point seemed to hit home. The conflict within him marched across his face.

'Help us,' I pushed. 'Regain your honour.'

'You are lying! You've killed all my friends, you'll kill me too, whatever I say . . . '

'Many of my people have died at Roman hands too, don't paint us as any different.'

His eyes flared with fury. 'You threaten me with sacrifice – a flaming death at the hands of savages.'

I must admit I felt shame down to my very bones. *If you knew my story . . .* I exchanged a look with my wife, and took a chance. 'I swear, on my daughter's life, I would never have that happen to anyone, not on my say-so.' Gladsia sidled up to me and I cuddled her. 'But I must get my nephew out alive – you know this, you have heard everything, you know what I fear. You can help us.'

His nose was about to drip so I untied his hands and gave him a cloth. He seemed surprised, but said nothing until, just as I had resolved to tie him back up again, he spoke. 'You speak of swapping me,' he said, his voice choked up, 'but this is madness. I am a simple ranker. Now the men from my tent are dead, the rest of them – they won't give a shit.'

'Join us, then.'

'You mean become a deserter?'

I could see the disgust on his face, but a little uncertainty too, maybe.

'Loyalty is a two-edged thing. You just admitted yourself that they have no loyalty to you.'

At that moment there was a knock at the door. 'Yes?'

Colleos came in, blushing at having to interrupt. 'Just to let you know that Dranis and Leon are back from their – ' he flicked a glance at the prisoner, ' – their task, sire.'

'All right. I will come to talk with them once they've had a chance to rest and eat,' I said. Nesica's great grey dog, Creegan, had taken the chance to come back into the warm, presumably having gone out to relieve himself, and growled as he saw a stranger so close to us. Nes pulled the dog away with soothing words. I turned back to Ambix.

'So, have you decided? Do you want to be free?'

His face twisted into a bitter smile. 'Free,' he spat. 'Free to starve to death among the barbarians and the bare cold rock.'

I raised an eyebrow. 'I shall be 'starving to death' on smoked trout and honey cakes, in a moment. You might be joining me.'

He cast his eyes back down.

I felt he was about to fall one way or the other, like a coin spinning on its edge, and perhaps I had said as much as was useful. I asked Nes to call Colleos back in.

'Colleos, my friend, talk to this man – keep an eye on him. I must plan what we do next.'

It was a relief to get back out into the open air. The snow reflected back the watery sunlight and made the village look hard and bright. I could see young Tarn giving the horses some oats and a rub down before we all got going again. Alwona, Machan's wife, was packing her few things onto her own horse and waved to me.

'Dran's in with Machan, sire,' she said, 'hearing what happened.'

I nodded. 'I'll join them soon. Where's Rhian? I need to ask her something.'

Alwona pointed to round the back and I found young Rhian leant up against the house wall, clutching a cup of dried mint tea, by the smell of it, untouched. Her eyes were red but she was not crying, right then, as she turned to me. If anything she looked angry.

'He *did* take the torque with him, but it is not what you think,' she said.

'How do you know what I think?'

'You think I persuaded him to take it – don't you? To put him in danger like some silly jealous girl. Well I didn't.'

The thought had never crossed my mind.

'What did happen then?' I asked.

'I told him *not* to take it, but he wouldn't leave it with me. He doesn't trust me with it, because it was a gift from *her*.'

Gods help us. I was about to snap something back then bit my tongue – I had once been young and thwarted in love myself, after all.

'Why are you so angry?' I asked. 'Calm down. I am not accusing you of anything. You've always treated me with respect before.'

It was true, though I had always sensed she was wary of me – with good reason, I suppose, given I was uncle to one of her suitors and close friend to the other, and royal, while she was an orphaned peasant Maros's good mother had taken in.

'Go and help Alwona, keep yourself busy,' I soothed. 'I will do everything I can to bring him home safe.'

Rhian just nodded and wiped her eyes on her sleeve.

Dranis, my foster-brother, was in the process of removing a stone from his shoe but got up as soon as he saw me at the threshold, bashing his much-bashed head on one of the house beams as he did so. 'I heard,' he said, hugging me about my shoulders. 'What's the plan?'

Plan? I hadn't even got that far yet. I ran a hand over my eyes and dodged the question.

'I think the Nervii will talk, eventually . . . what did you find?'

Dran sighed. 'We were too late.'

'The Cornovi seat was taken yesterday, sire,' Leon added, his face sallow and worried as ever. 'Even if they'd accepted our help we couldn't have got warriors there in time.'

'Well Uricon threw our offers back in my face twice before, no reason to think he wouldn't have done so again,' I said, though in my heart I still cursed the news. 'Is there any word on Uricon himself?'

'Dead,' Dran said, shaking his head.

Leon nodded. 'We met dozens of Cornovi warriors in dribs and drabs. They all said their king was dead, and his wife too. One of the children, at least, was smuggled out in time – that's the rumour. They – most of them, at least – are heading for the western fort where they believe the child was taken.'

I had visited the Cornovi king twice in the last year to try to build an alliance. He'd been hospitable and polite with me, but as steadfast as Temlyr of the Durotriges used to be in his determination to fight Rome alone, and only then if the legions attacked him first. Suicide, to my mind, and foolish. I remembered two children at his hearth, a girl of perhaps ten winters and a boy of about eight. 'What of the other child?'

'No one knows. It's the daughter they believe is alive. The son hasn't been seen since the attack,' Dran said.

So, another British people fall to the Romans. Why did Uricon not accept my help, Gods?

'There are Roman troops and supplies pouring towards the Cornovi seat from the east, sire,' Leon said. 'Could the stragglers from the column you attacked have been heading there too? They were closer to it than heading back to the Glevum fort.'

Dran nodded. 'The Romans have begun building another new fort, close to the Cornovi seat. We saw it, from a distance. They'd need supplies.'

It did seem probable. 'Right, we'll start from the point that Kynbel is most likely there then, or at the seat itself. We'll get going now. I need to borrow something from you Dran, those chains we discussed – you have them with you?'

At last the plan had formed in my mind.

Four Deception

I got Leon to come with me, but before we'd even crossed the slush-ridden yard Colleos was heading towards us. He beckoned me close.

'The Nervii has said something useful, sire, I think,' Colleos said, in a low voice, before we could reach the door. 'Something strange happened before they left the fort, something to do with the commander's wife – is she one of our people?'

'You mean Aulus Plautius's wife?'

He nodded.

'No,' I said, but my mind burst into flaming thought. *She* wasn't one of my spies, but members of her sometime household were. 'Will he talk to me, do you think?'

'Yes my king. He's talking like his tongue only had a day left now.'

Well, well done Colleos.

We re-entered the relative warmth of the herder's hut. Nes, Gladsia and the prisoner were all tucking into their midday meal. Creegan was settled beside Gladsia, keeping her warm, waiting for scraps. Nes had packed our few things and put them by the door ready for the next move. I saw Kynbel's spare cloak, that he'd left here as we discussed plans the night before, neatly folded among our things, and it brought a lump to my throat. *Hang on Kynbel, we are coming for you.*

I sat down by the fire and accepted the food my wife offered me. The prisoner, Ambix, watching me all the while.

'Do you really think the generals knew we were going to be ambushed?' he blurted. 'When they sent us out?'

I paused, unsure what to say for the best. 'Honestly, I don't know. It seems likely.'

Ambix digested that, the conflict clear in his eyes. 'I will help,' he said at last. 'But my allegiance remains to my friends and to my ancestors. Not to you.'

'Agreed.'

I kept my face calm and impassive but inside I was soaring. We would need him, if my plan to free Kynbel was to succeed.

'Will you tell me what happened with Aulus Plautius's wife? As you told Colleos?'

Ambix nodded, taking a good breath, his gaze flicking to his fellow Gaul. 'Look, it might be nothing, but it was strange . . .'

'Go on.'

'Well she's always been nice to us, you see. Always a good morning, happy Saturnalia, checking we were warm enough, whatever. Then yesterday she just walks past us with not a word, looking straight ahead with tears streaming down her face, straight into the officer's quarters. No servants or ladies with her – which is unusual – and we didn't see her again, not before we left.' He shook his head. 'If she told them anything, well . . . I think it must have been beaten out of her.'

I raised my eyebrows. 'She didn't know anything to tell,' I said. 'Not as far as I'm aware.'

Nesica handed me a cloth to wipe the food from my hands. 'It sounds more like she heard what was going to happen to you all, somehow, and it sat badly with her,' Nes said.

'I think you're right,' I replied, but to be honest another possibility occurred to me: What if the actions of my spy at Glevum, her companion, had been exposed? That would have upset her. Camulora's fate was looking bleak.

Cernunnos, Camulos, Teutates, Epona, please, if she did not betray us, please keep Camulora safe.

Ambix looked from me to my wife as if he knew something was up. 'I agreed to help,' he said. 'But what in Jove's name are we actually going to do?'

I got Dran, Machan and Hedros squeezed in round the fire and laid out to everyone what I was planning.

'No,' was Nesica's first instinct. She looked down at me, with Gladsia on her hip, her face swinging from terror to fury.

'I have to try, Nes. You know I must.'

'It's too risky! They will just put a spear through your chest before you get near!'

Colleos shook his head. 'No. You have value, even more than Prince Kynbel. They would keep you alive to show off, like they did Vercingetorix.'

Yes . . . until they murdered Vercingetorix, right after the parade ended. Nes knew that tale too and her expression darkened further.

'It won't come to that,' I insisted, and it didn't help. Tears were welling in my wife's harebell eyes.

'Caradoc, I beg you – this is madness. Like . . . like throwing yourself on the slaughter man's knife. *Please.*'

'It *could* work,' Ambix said, but that just made Nes suck in an exasperated breath. I made room beside me and hugged her as she sat.

'I can't think of anything better,' I said. 'If I could take less risk, I would.'

Machan was watching us both. 'I can take your place,' he said. 'We are much of an age, and the same height. Close enough to fool any who don't know you well, at least.'

He was right. Machan was more robust than me, with paler hair, but the vast majority of Rome's forces wouldn't know that. If he was captured, though, how long would he survive, before the game was up?

'I can't ask you to do that, old friend . . . '

'But you can speak their language,' he responded. 'It makes more sense for you to play one of the Romans.'

He was right, I could see it on everyone's faces. So, however uneasy I was, I went along with it.

Night still falls fast in the days approaching Imbolc; the light was starting to fail by the time we got back to the battle site. Apart from a layer of snow on all the bodies the area appeared just as we'd left it. Two buzzards flew away with noisy wings as we approached but they did not seem to have done much damage to the fallen so far. Maybe just the eyes.

I flicked a glance over my shoulder to the Gaul. 'You don't need to see this, Ambix. Wait there.'

He shook his head. 'It's all right.'

We approached the bodies, no-one saying a word. I brushed the snow from the optio's helmet and eased it off his head. He looked younger than me, and still a bit scared in his eyes even in death, so I closed their lids. 'Cernunnos, Camulos, Morriga, guide all their souls to the land of youth,' I whispered, but loud enough that all could hear. Everyone started removing the armour, with as much reverence as me – maybe just because they knew Ambix was watching, but I don't think so.

The armour came off easier than I had thought it would. Perhaps the cold slowed down the usual death-stiffness. The officer wore the 'segmentata' type of armour, as they call it, that is metal strips. The others were in chain mail and once we got it over their arms and shoulders it slipped off easy enough.

'What about tunics and shoes?' Dran asked.

'Yes,' Ambix said. 'You'll need all of it.'

I was one of those stripped down to my under breeks on the chill hillside that day, the hairs on my arms all stood up, and not just from the cold. As I slipped the pale woollen tunic over my head I could smell the dead man's scent. The helmet felt heavy and strange on my head, but its original owner had stuck a linen and wool pad onto the inside so it was not as uncomfortable as I thought it would be. Ambix fastened the chin strap for me and buckled the armour.

'Will we do?' I asked.

He looked about us. Colleos, Leon and myself were the three dressed as Romans, being the Latin speakers, and to my mind we would pass. Leon looked too Roman, if anything, given these men had been Nervii.

25

Ambix nodded. 'Just let me carry the signum.' He brushed the snow from it and hoisted it up. 'And I'll go at the front.'

We reached the thick woodland that flanks the Cornovi hill fort just as the sun was sinking. Uricon's fort is on as mighty a hill as one is ever likely to see – or it seems so, where it is, somewhat apart from others of the like. Leon, the first time he accompanied me there, called it a 'volcano'. I had not known what he meant until he explained but then I could see why he called it so. The fires billowing out that day must have added gild to the image. Now, at dusk, it just smouldered.

Without our horses it had been a long walk and I was glad I'd changed back into my own shoes but, given we could stumble upon a Roman patrol at any moment, it was time to change back. I made sure we all passed the inspection of Ambix once again. Now it was the turn of Machan, Dran and Hedros, the three 'prisoners', to prepare.

'Let's get you sorted, before the light goes completely,' I said, and Dran nodded, getting the chains from his bag. He was going to leave the bag on the ground but I stowed it up above head height in the fork of a tree. 'Nothing that can give them the merest clue,' I responded to his questioning look.

Dran and Hedros could stay much as they were but Machan had to have the loan of my latest woad-blue cloak, that Nes had made for me, and the twisted gold torque the Silures gave me whilst I was a boy. They looked well enough on him but it was still strange to see.

'Will I pass, my king?' Machan asked with a smile.

'You just need to perfect the look of perpetual worry on your face,' I quipped back, and he laughed. Next went on the sword of my mother's kin, but not how I normally wore it. The empty scabbard hung on Machan's left, as if the Romans had taken the sword from 'me', while the actual sword was in a different scabbard, belted so that it was hidden beneath the folds of tunic and cloak. 'Try walking,'

I said, and was pleased to see that he could do so without giving the deception away, and that Dran and Hedros were managing too.

Next came the chains. I had asked Dran to make these earlier in the winter, with a mind to deceive the Romans at Camulodunon by smuggling a spy in with some captured slaves, but that idea had never come to pass. Now, after moons of riding about in Dran's saddle bag, they would get to play their part. They were forged from heavy iron, linked with shackles for the wrists like any slave chains, but Dran had made them so they could come undone at will.

'Put your wrists together,' Dran instructed. 'Twist left, pull, twist right.' All three did as they were told but young Hedros's hands stayed shackled. 'Again,' Dran said. 'Slower, Hedros.'

It worked this time, but I could see the concern in his eyes.

'Do it a few more times,' I said. 'Get it to the point you don't even have to think about it.'

'Yes, my king.'

'Good.'

I looked about me, pleased so far. The trees around us were disappearing into darkness and we would soon have to light a torch, but at least we were ready. I could feel the snow melting around my feet and soaking into the sides of my stupid Roman footwear but I could bear it for now.

Once it was fully dark, we would be on our way.

Cernunnos, Camulos, Teutates, Epona, keep my nephew safe, Gods, please. Help us in our task.

'What are you doing?'

The voice came from the trees above.

Five The fall of the Cornovi

We all jumped as if struck by lightning – not least me, given I'd been praying – and we drew swords. Thank Maponos we did not attack. As soon as the feet came dangling down we could see the figure slithering out of the tree was no threat. She stood no higher than my hip but was bundled in layers of cloaks. They made her seem top-heavy, like a beech tree in a gale. A thick plait hung out either side of her hood. As Colleos lit a torch and light fell on her face I recognised her.

'Uricon's daughter,' I said.

The girl nodded. 'Vedica, princess of the Cornovi, daughter of Uricon,' she said, with the slight bow of one royal to another. 'I remember you too, King Caratacos. What are you doing here?'

It was her land, and a fair question, even from a ten year old lass.

'The Romans have captured one of my men, and we think they are holding him at your father's fort.'

'It's possible. It could have happened after I left,' she answered, which was little help but better than a complete contradiction, I suppose.

'What are you doing out here all alone?' I asked of her.

Vedica, it turned out, had not been alone very long. One of her father's most trusted men had hidden her in the tree while he went to talk with some of their warriors he knew to be at a nearby clearing. 'To check they are still loyal, before he reveals me,' as the girl put it. I saw the wisdom in his caution – if the only survivor of the Cornovi ruling family was a ten-summers-green child, as it appeared, then she hung onto that rule with a grip frail as cobweb. I thought of my own niece, Verla, back home. She had been fifteen, when I had to leave her, and that was bad enough.

The man returned and was disturbed to see his young charge out of the tree, with 'Romans' no less, so I had to spend some time calming him down before we made our way to the clearing where some loyal Cornovi had gathered. The fresh smell of raw wood hinted it was a carpenter's encampment before I saw it. The warriors had spread themselves about, leaning on every shaving-horse and log pile, while the carpenter himself served them soup with shaking hands. A woman, I suppose the carpenter's wife, was bandaging one Cornovi warrior's slashed arm. A few paces apart from the rest, in the shadowed edges of the camp, a body lay beneath an oak tree, covered with a cloak.

They all shrank back at the sight of us, grabbing at their spears. I felt Ambix, to my left, tighten like a harp string.

Vedica sprang forward. 'No, no – it's all right. This is King Caratacos, my father's friend.'

'Friend' was overdoing it a bit and I saw looks passed between them, but the spears went back down. I took my own hand from the hilt of the Roman sword as I spoke.

'Cornovi, calm. This disguise is to fool the Romans, not you.'

'Are you here to help us?' one warrior asked.

Honestly, no. Do I risk being honest? 'One of my men has been captured and is being held, either at Uricon's seat or the new fort. I have come with my warriors to rescue him – that we found your princess amongst ten thousand trees must be the Gods' own will.'

It *could* have been that, but even forests have well-beaten paths and chances are we'd just been coming in on one of the main routes out. This clearing, too, must be well known, and I didn't want to tarry long. I wasn't keen to tell them everything, either, but didn't have much choice.

'He will be at our fort, not theirs,' the injured man said. 'Me and my friend – ' he nodded towards the body under the cloak, ' – we saw them hauling a man in as we escaped over the palisade. He wasn't one of ours.'

Gods be thanked – he's alive.

'Was he conscious?'

'I think so,' he shrugged. 'My friend was wounded so I didn't take much notice.'

Fair enough.

'Besides,' another said, 'their fort is barely begun.'

The Cornovi who had smuggled young Vedica out flicked him a look. 'It's going up fast, like the Gods are helping them.'

I remembered the bridge at the battle of the Meduwaen. The Romans can build both fast and well, I give them that.

Vedica's rescuer turned to me. 'Do you have more warriors on the way? This – ' he gestured at my small band, ' – this is never going to be enough.'

Again I hesitated. How much could I trust them? *Needs must.*

'My wife has raised the alarm with the Silures at the border, more warriors are on their way. But our purpose was rescue alone, today, not to re-take Uricon's fort, so they were just to guard our retreat.'

All of them looked pretty subdued at that, Vedica included, and I felt wretched, but my offer of alliance had been thrown back in my face – more than once. The Gods would not berate me for it, I think.

Young Vedica spoke in a choked voice. 'I know my father is probably dead. But there is still hope for my mother and brother. Will you not try to rescue them too?'

How simple life is at ten summers. Forgive me, Maponos.

'If I can, I will,' I said. 'But it would help if your own warriors help us too. All we need is a distraction.'

Vedica and her rescuer passed each other a glance.

We had a deal.

Not long afterwards my party started up the hill. It was steep so our climb was slow. Nearer the fort the trees thinned out to nothing and, what with the bright snow on the ground, the Roman watch must surely have seen us by now. I made sure we kept formation. The snow had stopped falling and the temperature was dropping every moment.

Each footstep was a crunch as the upper layer iced. When we got within a spear throw of the fort we could smell the scent of damp burnt wood. Half a dozen Roman soldiers standing sentry on the palisade stood out against the starlit sky.

'Halt!' one cried, and we obeyed. 'State your purpose!'

Ambix raised the signum. 'Fourteenth Legio Gemina! We are survivors of an ambush. We have prisoners! Important prisoners!'

Two of the Roman silhouettes bent together in whispering counsel. I felt my heartbeat flying up. *Steady*, I willed myself. *They are right to be cautious.*

'Password!'

Ambix did not hesitate. 'Emperor's triumph!' he yelled back.

The gate was being unbarred. We saw it swing open to reveal the fires within.

Thank the Gods they haven't changed their password. Or was it more than that? Some code for 'We are held against our will' perhaps, or 'Caution, all is not as it seems'? I threw a look at Ambix. With the helmet on and shadow falling from the rim I could not see his eyes and little of his face. Could he turn traitor three times over? No. An eel cannot twist so well, I told myself.

By Cernunnos, let me be right.

Whatever the truth was we were now marching up towards the gateway, right into the wasp nest. The yard was full of soldiers. Dozens of soldiers. They were eating, nursing their scrapes and chatting at camp fires but all to a man looked up as we walked in. I saw a few point at Machan and remark something to their comrades. *It's working.* Machan just looked back at them with calm defiance, worthy of me myself. *Well done, old friend.* All around us the slush was turning to filth and I saw pinkish patches where blood had soaked in.

I felt my arm grabbed and turned to Leonidas.

'Look!' he gasped. As I followed his gaze my stomach tightened like a fist closed round it. Outside the burnt-out shell of the greatest house, Uricon's home where I had shared his food, a cross of wooden beams had been lifted. On it hung a body. He was bruised and cut, and bound to the cross-beam like a crow-scarer. His head was slumped to his chest but from the grey mane of hair I knew it must be Uricon himself. Below him a woman was sobbing on the ground, clawing at the ice-hard mud, and I could see something else in the shadows before her. As we moved further into the yard the figure became clearer. It was a young boy, bound to the base of the cross, also clearly dead. There was no doubt who it must be.

My first thought, I'm ashamed to say, was to thank the Gods it was not Kynbel strung up there, I admit. With the next moment, though, my heart hurt for poor Vedica. If the woman at the base of the cross was her mother then there was still a chance for her, at least – quite how we were to get her out was another matter.

We had stopped dead centre of the fort. There was no sign of Kynbel. Soldiers were drawing nearer, curious to see if their theories about the prisoners were correct, and an officer was coming along the inner walkway of the palisade towards us, called over by one of the guards at the gate. He had the rising-sun helmet I knew to be a centurion's. Behind him another officer, too, looked up from what he was doing and started towards us. This one had a stripe about the base of his tunic skirt which prompted something in my mind. *Tribune*? Yes. Well this isn't good, I thought, but then, as this tribune removed his helmet a moment to scratch his head, I jolted as if punched.

Oh Gods.

Saturninus.

Livia's bed-mate, Adminios's 'friend', Saturninus.

'We must change our plan,' I hissed. 'He knows me. He knows my face.'

Ambix threw me a look you could slice meat with. 'What? You can't change it now!'

'He will know Machan is not me!'

They were in earshot now so I shut up, but it was too late, the damage was done.

Six Into the wasp nest

Saturninus was glaring at Ambix. 'You! What's up with you?'

I could feel the sweat beading on my forehead under the helmet's padding. The Gaul had followed what we planned but now, surrounded by dozens of his erstwhile comrades and pressed by a tribune, he turned to stone.

'Well?'

'Nothing, sir.'

Saturninus turned to me. 'What did he ask of you?'

'We were discussing where we should take the prisoners, sir.'

He raised an eyebrow. 'That wasn't all you said to your superior, though, was it soldier?' he said to the Gaul.

Oh Cernunnos help me now.

'He – he meant no disrespect, sir,' I said, making my voice a touch higher in pitch. 'We just wanted to hurry because our feet are wet.'

Saturninus turned to his centurion comrade and laughed. 'Absolute lions, these Nervii – the great Caesar never did exaggerate.'

The centurion rolled his eyes. 'Well, they did capture prisoners,' he said. 'It's been a good day – the lads were getting stirred up enough with the nephew, now they are saying this is Caratacus himself . . .'

Saturninus flicked another glance at Machan's face. 'It's not him – I know. Besides, I don't think we'll have him in chains as easy as this.'

Thank the Gods for these enormous Roman helmets.

The centurion was looking Machan up and down. 'Prince Adminius spoke of a foster-brother – do you think it could be him?'

Saturninus shrugged. 'You,' he said to Machan, 'Do you understand us? Do you speak Latin?'

Machan looked down at the two of them with marked disdain but no hint of understanding.

'I don't think so,' Saturninus said, but the Gods only know why, since the real Dranis didn't speak Latin either and was just as oblivious, right behind him.

This is taking too long . . . Where are the Cornovi with their diversion? If Saturninus insists I take off this helmet – if he comes inside with us, even – then this is all over. I scanned about the yard again, while the two Romans gloated over the torque they'd taken from Machan – *my* torque. Aside from Uricon's house only two others, near it, were burnt. All the other houses now had legionaries sat around them – all but one. This one, the druid's house by the looks of it, had a soldier stood sentry by the door. The *closed* door.

That's it then.

'You, Nervii.'

The tribune was addressing me. 'Ask him his name.' He jabbed a thumb towards Machan. 'Ask him if he's Silure.'

Oh Gods. Machan and I hadn't planned for this. I couldn't even be sure he'd heard what I'd said to Ambix, about changing the plan, as we came in, we'd been so worried about the Romans hearing. Some of the common soldiers were well within earshot and they could be Gauls, or even British, too – I couldn't risk telling him what he needed to know in our tongue.

'Yes sir,' I said with a nod to Saturninus. I turned to Machan, locking eyes with him, wishing I could put my thoughts into his head. 'Your name, Briton,' I asked. 'Your *real* name.'

He just looked back at me, confused. I could see a trickle of sweat running down towards his eyes. *It's all right. Trust me.*

'We know you are not Caratacos,' I continued, trying to throw him a rope. 'The tribune here has met him. They want to know your name and tribe.'

Machan now threw a look at Saturninus, starting to understand. 'Machan, son of Macanos, warrior of the Catuv-'

A collective yell ripped through the night sky from the west.

At last.

'What was that sir?' I asked. Saturninus pursed his lips and strutted over to the nearest palisade steps. A sentry was already on his way down.

'The Britons are attacking!'

'Here?'

'No sir – the new fort.'

Saturninus swore so loud that the dead might hear him.

'Gemina! Battle ready!' he roared. The soldiers all scrambled for shields and spears. I saw one stumble and knock his cooking pot over. The centurion had drawn his sword and was shouting for his shield. So far the legionary who stood sentry by the druid house door was the only one who hadn't moved. *Now's our chance.*

'Come, we must go.' I herded my party forward like a shepherd's dog.

As we passed her Uricon's wife wailed even louder. She was still at the base of the cross, clinging to her dead son's legs, and perhaps the sight of another British noble brought low was a twist of the knife, I don't know, but for whatever reason she was shrieking again and it caught the tribune's attention, despite everything else.

'Will someone shut her up!'

I saw a soldier beside Saturninus turn with sword drawn.

'We'll lock her with the others sir!' I called back, grasping the woman by the shoulders and hauling her to her feet. 'Come,' I whispered to her in our own tongue. 'Your daughter is alive. Come with us.' She stared back at me as if I had three heads. 'All is not as it appears. Let him go.'

She obeyed, thank the Gods, and I propelled her forward. We all made it to the door and the sentry stepped aside and unlocked it for us without so much as a prompt. He looked young, and scared.

Remember, you are an officer.

'Shut the door, and don't let anyone else in here,' I barked.

'Yes sir.'

Ambix threw me a bemused look at that but it did the trick. I let my eyes adjust a moment to the poor light. The fire in the hearth was out but a couple of rush lights were burning. I could see a man face down, his ankles bound, next to the cauldron. I stepped forward and recognised his fair hair.

'Kynbel?'

I knelt and turned him over, leaning him against my left arm and thigh. 'Kynbel, wake up.' I felt for a pulse under his jaw, and there was one, thank Maponos, but he was still out. He was covered in cuts and bruises too and, as Colleos cut the rope that was binding Kynbel's wrists, his right hand fell. It was bloodied and ragged, as if someone had taken a smith's hammer to it. 'Kynbel!' I urged, tapping his cheek quite hard, and at last I saw his eyelids flicker.

'Uncle?'

'Yes, it's me.'

Leon handed me a cup of water and I moistened Kynbel's lips with it. Despite the bruises it didn't look like he'd been knocked out by a head wound, more like loss of blood – just as bad. I tried to get him to take a little more water. 'Leon, there's a bit of cloth over there by the bed – strap Kynbel's bad hand to his chest for now.'

'Sire,' Hedros said, 'there's someone else here.'

I looked across the house to where Machan and the others were removing their false chains and saw the body-length bundle on the floor. Hedros peeled back a cloak and we saw a bound and gagged woman. He helped her to sit up. Her face was bruised and both eyes swollen but I knew her straight away: my spy Camulora – Livia, by her Roman name.

'Liv – can you see me?'

She nodded.

Hedros took the gag from her mouth and I saw her top lip was cut and massive. Blood was smeared right up to her nose. 'I'm sorry,' she rasped, looking straight at me.

'Don't talk nonsense. Are you able to walk?'

'Yes.'

'Get ready then. Find something to arm her with, Hedros, if you can.'

Uricon's wife seemed to wake up, at that, and took the druid's golden sickle from its hook upon the wall. I could see her hand was shaking as she offered it to me.

'You keep hold of it,' I said. 'Keep it under your cloak.'

Ambix sucked in an impatient breath, almost tutting.

'We must go!' the Gaul hissed. 'We can't take the women – they'll attract attention. Why would we take them?'

I pinned him with a hard look. 'Loyalty. The same thing that stops me from killing you, now you've served your purpose, and taking your clothes to disguise one of them.'

'You wouldn't!'

'No. *I* wouldn't.' I got to my feet, helping Kynbel to his. 'Don't let me down now.'

Ambix dropped his gaze and said nothing further. All the same I couldn't entirely trust him. Dran's eyes and mine met. I could see Dran had found an axe in the firewood basket and he handed it to Livia. 'We need to go, Caradoc,' Dran said.

I nodded. 'Get ready. Colleos, set the fire.'

Machan, Dran and Hedros all picked the chains back up and pretended to be in them again. The women, once encouraged, held onto the chain too. Gods willing no one would notice it was a ruse, and that they were armed. In the heat of an attack, with the blood well up but not necessarily suspicious, I was thinking they would not – that was the plan. Now we needed to have an excuse to flee the lock-up. Colleos took tinder from beside the hearth and lit it in one of the rush lights. He threw it on the bed. The wool blanket would have just sputtered out, likely as not, but he threw the rest of the tinder on as well and a bunch of kindling for good measure. Flames started to lick upwards.

'Right, let's go.' I settled Kynbel into my right side so I could support him if needs be and we all headed for the door. The sentry was still standing there and turned with a start as I wrenched the door open.

'The house is on fire – fetch a bucket of water!' I yelled at him.

'Yes sir!' He snapped and scurried off.

The lad's blind obedience saved him his life. We filed out and headed behind the building. Where now? Soldiers were pouring out of the nearest gate to go and help their comrades but just walking out of the gate with them seemed too high a risk to take. I flicked a look at the Cornovi queen, still taking big breaths and eyes bright with terror, but nevertheless she must have lived here on-and-off since her fifteenth summer and she could be our best hope. 'What's the best way out?' I asked.

She looked back at me at me blank as a cloud then clenched her fists, so hard she must have dug her nails right into her palms. 'My servant hid a rope,' she whispered at last. 'Follow me.'

She led us round the back of the druid's house until we were in the shadowy lane running alongside the western palisade. Soldiers were running along the walkway towards the nearest gate. She let them pass. 'This way,' she said. We were soon going along the back of her own burnt carcase of a house and I saw that she kept her eyes averted from where her husband and son still hung. There was a granary hut ahead of us, not touched by the fire, and this seemed to be where she was making for.

'Uncle?'

I turned to Kynbel. His eyes were more open by then but he still looked dazed. 'Shh Kynbel, quiet. We are getting out.'

I felt him grip my arm a little tighter with his good hand but he said no more. We had come to a halt at the back of the granary and the Cornovi queen took a last look about before ducking down to her knees. She felt underneath the floor, where one of the hut's legs kept it off the ground.

'Is it there?' I asked.

She frowned, still feeling about in the dark, but then I saw a look of relief cross her face. She passed me the rope end. I could see that the rope was knotted every five hand-spans or so. I suppose the idea had been to tie one end to the granary hut leg and throw it over the palisade but I wasn't sure Kynbel was going to be able to do it, not with only one hand in use.

'What's the drop like, there?'

'Not too bad.'

I helped her tie the rope onto the granary hut leg and then waited a moment, to check, before throwing the end over. It didn't look like more legionaries were coming but all the same we'd need to be quick.

'Colleos,' I whispered, 'you go first and help Kynbel as he comes down.' He nodded. 'Kynbel, you'll be next.'

Colleos pulled himself up onto the walkway easily enough but Dran and I had to give Kynbel a leg up. He looked white and I could see the tremble in him. Colleos swung his legs over the fence and disappeared down the rope quick as a rat. Kynbel didn't do it so well. He was clinging on with good hand, knees and and feet tight as ivy on a branch. I was so stilled by dread I didn't even pray as he disappeared down into the gloom.

'He's all right,' I heard Colleos hiss up. 'I caught him.'

'You next,' I said to Livia. She tucked the axe into her belt and didn't hesitate but Dran and I had to help her onto the walkway too. She managed the rope well enough, it seemed. We all heard a simple 'Down' report up from the black. One by one everyone made it to the ground until only Uricon's wife and I were left. I wished I'd got her to go sooner but she'd hung at the back and it was too late now.

'I'll give you a hand up onto the walk way,' I said, but she didn't respond, staring transfixed at something behind me. I whipped round to see the sentry from the lock-up door, complete with his bucket of water, being yelled at in fury by the centurion from earlier. Smoke was billowing out of the house roof by that point, but if I could still see them up near the south-west gate then I knew they could see me.

'Go, quickly now,' I said, heaving the woman up onto the platform like a sack of wheat, but it was too late – the centurion had turned and seen us. He started running down the walkway, sword raised, shouting for help like he had Morriga behind him.

'Down the rope – now!'

The woman had frozen. I sprang up onto the platform, unsheathing the Roman sword as soon as my feet hit the wood. It felt odd, unbalanced in my hand. I could hear Dran and the others calling up from below.

'Halt! Traitors!' the centurion yelled again. 'Soldiers – here!'

His call was answered – I could see more Romans headed for us, some with javelins. The centurion had a shield but I'd left my Roman one in the lock-up. As he stabbed his sword towards me the best I could do was swerve. He missed but I almost lost my footing. I swung my sword at him. 'Go! Now!' I yelled. Still the Cornovi queen hesitated. She was holding onto the rope with one hand, straddling the wooden fence. The centurion plunged the sword at me again and I twisted just in time. The woman snatched the druid sickle from beneath her cloak and slashed the centurion across the throat with it. She watched as he fell, clutching his bloody throat, his eyes like a slaughtered beast, before she went down the rope at last.

I was not far behind her. I heard the javelins smacking into the wood of the palisade just above me.

Seven Fever

Javelins kept coming as we fled the fort. We scattered, sprinting like hares down the snow strewn hillside – how none of us broke an ankle the Gods only know. I saw Kynbel fall.

'Kynbel!'

I leapt from rock to rock towards him. 'I just slipped on the ice!' he shouted so I dragged him back to his feet. We kept running. As we crossed a short patch of snow that was at last free of jagged rocks I risked a glance back. Saturninus was there, up on the palisade, sword in hand but out of spears.

'Caratacus!' he screamed. 'You can't win! You can never win! No one stands against the might of Rome!'

I just turned and carried on.

As we re-entered the tree line we were out of javelin reach from the fort and I took what felt like a first breath in years. All our party were alive. There could be Roman patrols coming for us any moment now but the tree branches blocked out most of the starlight and the reflective snow was patchy in here so they'd struggle to find us. It would also be very easy to lose each other in the dark.

'Head for the meeting point!' I ordered. 'Spread out into three groups then stick together.'

At least the tracks would be confused. *Cernunnos, Lugos*, I prayed, *please make the dawn sun strong, melt the snow*. I knew I should have prayed to Belenos too but that god was no ally of mine. I kept Kynbel with me. Leon and Livia stuck with me too. I saw Dran, Colleos and Ambix head off to the left while Machan, Hedros and the Cornovi queen veered to the right. Both the other groups were faster than us and were out of sight in a few blinks.

I cast a look at my nephew, stumbling along by my side.

'Are you all right Kynbel?'

He did the so-so gesture with his left hand. 'I think I need water – I'm shaking a bit.'

He was, and with the speed we'd left the fort it could not have been from the cold. I heard Livia swear as she walked into a branch. 'We'll stop, just a moment.'

We tucked behind two broad old oaks, their boughs heavy and white. I broke some dark twigs off and got Kynbel to suck the clinging snow from them. We all did the same and it gave me a chance to listen. There was no sound at all, bar Kynbel's breathing, once our crunching footsteps halted.

'It doesn't sound like they're following us,' Livia whispered.

I shook my head. 'I expect they'll wait for the light.'

Even so we didn't tarry long, but at least we continued at a slower, safer pace in the dark. By the time dawn broke we were out in the open again in what was probably cattle pasture during summer. It was colder in the dawn breeze despite the growing light. My fingers felt about ready to fall off.

'How is everyone?' I asked.

Kynbel nodded to reassure me but his face was grim. I could see better now and he was a bad colour, pink as a ripening cherry, and not justified by the speed we'd been going. I felt his forehead – baking-stone hot.

'Fever?' he asked.

'Yes. I need to clean your wound and bandage it properly, and you can rest, when we get to the meeting point. It's not far now, I think.'

Leon had been helping Livia back to her feet as she stumbled and we exchanged glances. It *wasn't* far, if the guidance we'd been given was sound, but I couldn't be sure there'd be much in a disused fort I could use to treat a fever, certainly not in winter, and now it was light the search for us would begin in earnest. We hadn't come far compared to the distance the legion could come, in daylight, and maybe on horses. There was nothing in the vast white emptiness we could hide in, either, now we were out of the woods.

'Let's go faster, now it's light,' I said, and everyone obeyed, though Livia looked almost as bad as Kynbel.

The sun got stronger, the warmest we'd had in days, so at least my prayer had been answered. All our tracks would be turning to slush with every passing moment. The Gods blessing also showed the fort clearly to us when it came. I think a blizzard would have masked it, as this fort was well-ditched and banked but snug to the ground compared with Uricon's seat. No smoke was rising and not a single soul looked out at us from palisade or tower-gate. The only sound was the cawing of crows.

'If we've got here first I'll be stunned,' I said, almost to myself. We stopped and stared, a good two spear-throws away. 'I'll go first, to check it, before the rest of you come in. Stay here.'

Leon looked at me as if I'd run mad. 'No, my king. I will.'

'I'm still in my Roman gear, Leon – if the legions have taken this fort and lie in wait for us like lynxes then they'll think I'm one of them.'

His sharp little face set in a stubborn fix like baked clay. 'The same counts for me, my king.'

He was right, and he looked more Roman than I ever would, even when he was in a striped cloak and checked breeks. I sighed. 'All right.'

I watched him go up to the entrance with an uneasy heart. It was a tall gate flanked by look-out towers, with a second inner-gate behind it, forcing incomers into a tight pass – easy for spear-men or sling-throwers to defend. He seemed very small against the gate. I saw him knock on it twice and wait for an answer. The crows cawed louder but that was all. He seemed to pull a red rag from the first gate and then let himself in.

'Why was this place abandoned?' Livia whispered. With all the bruising it was difficult to gauge her face, but I sensed distaste in her voice.

'Vedica said a sickness spread through the village like fire, three winters ago. Their druid told Uricon to move all the survivors to another place, just for a year, for safety's sake, but none have dared to come back – yet.'

She looked even grimmer at that.

'It was cleaned up. All the dead were given rightful pyres,' I said, in too impatient a tone, I think, and I spied a flash of a smile until her split lip turned it into a grimace.

'It's all right,' she said. 'I'm not going to stay out here with the wolves.'

I turned back to Kynbel, feeling his forehead again. It was even hotter. *Please Gods, don't let me lose him now.* I felt his pulse: running away with itself. *Please Tog, if you are with the Gods, you ask them too.*

Kynbel was watching my face. 'If I pass out,' he said, 'you need to know, I didn't tell them anything.'

'I know.'

The fact that he was still alive when we found him was proof enough that they hadn't got all they wanted. Livia, on the other hand ... I glanced again at her two black eyes.

'I told them as little as I could, the Sparrow is safe,' she said, without any prompt from me. 'She was standing right by me when they dragged me off and I didn't so much as look at her.'

All the same I decided there and then to get my other spy out.

Leon appeared up on the gate-tower, waving to us.

'It's all right! Come in!'

The houses had been locked up for the villagers' eventual return but I soon broke into the best house using Livia's axe. Leonidas got a fire going while I hunted about the house for anything I could use. There was no food left to rot, of course, but I found a needle and fine twine on a high shelf, a cauldron to go over the fire for hot water and – Gods be praised – a small pot with a few scrapes of salt still in it among other pots and cups. I filled the cauldron with the cleanest-looking snow I could find, from a shaded ditch, and got to work boiling it up.

'Livia, Leon, have some of this hot water to drink, before I salt it.' I scooped out four cupfuls. 'Then one of you must keep watch, up on the palisade, for the others.'

I had made a start undoing the makeshift bandage to free Kynbel's hand as I spoke and Liv looked about ready to be sick.

'I'll do it,' she said. 'We can swap once you've done with the open wound.'

'All right.' I took the Roman cloak off over my head. 'Take this – it will be easy to get chilled, now we've stopped moving.'

I let her leave before I peeled the last bit of bloody cloth from Kynbel's hand. It was as bad as I'd feared. Kynbel himself didn't look at it but seemed to be watching the door.

'Is she the spy who used to be your woman?' he asked, and I raised an eye-brow.

'Yes.'

Kynbel sucked in an astonished breath. 'Aunt Nesica will have your head in a bag.'

'Not if there is any justice, Kynbel – I haven't touched her in twelve years.'

'Mathona says a woman can hold a grudge like tree roots hold the soil.'

I almost laughed. 'Let's just get you sorted for now. Try to keep still.'

'I don't want to look at it.'

'You don't need to look, just keep still.' I had a good look at his hand myself as I washed my own hands in a bit of the salt water and passed the needle in and out of the fire. 'I can stitch most of the open area,' I told him, 'once I've cleaned it, but I think one of your hand bones is broken too, so I'll need to splint it, on the palm side.'

Kynbel dared to look down at his hand at last. 'They used one of those small spades they dig ditches with – I'm surprised the bones aren't powder.' I saw him stifle a wince as I started to clean the wound. 'What about the fever?' he asked.

What indeed? I'd found no healing plants in the house or outside, no food that could help his body strengthen itself anew, and he wasn't even likely to get any sleep – not for long enough to do any good.

'Water and rest will see to that,' I said. 'Your body knows what it is doing.'

I wished I believed it myself.

The stitching took longer than I'd like. Kynbel was awake the whole time, trying not to scream as the needle passed in and out, and it was painful enough just to watch. Some of his skin was so ragged there was nothing for me to stitch. I got to the point I could do no more, tied off the twine, and leant him back.

'Rest now,' I said. 'I'll go and get some more water.'

Kynbel nodded, looking back at me with red, sweat-streaked face and gritted teeth. He seemed older. A remembrance of his three-winters self, sat proud and gleeful on my horse, flashed through my mind.

'I'll get the water, sire,' Leon said.

'It's all right. I want to stretch my back any way.'

It was true, but it also felt good to get out of the house. I saw Livia turn as the door banged behind me but she stayed where she was, watching from the look-out post by the gate, and I let her alone. I went up onto the palisade on the western side, sucking in the cold air and stretching my back muscles as I'd said. My stomach rumbled. My movement through the abandoned houses must have disturbed a fox as I saw a red and white flash pass to my left. The fox slowed to a trot as it got out of my reach and I could see it was a vixen, lithe and sleek. She turned her head to look at me.

'I'll not harm you,' I whispered. 'We won't be here much longer.'

She turned back and carried on walking. There was a drain hole at the base of the palisade and I guessed this had been her route in and out, at least since the villagers departed, just as I had once used to escape a fence when I was young and my shoulders were narrower. The vixen pushed herself through the drain hole, a self-set birch sapling flicking buds backwards in a greenish-yellow blur.

Birch.

Another memory floated back to me from more than twenty years before: Gwyfina's voice one sunny afternoon on Ynys Mon, teaching us acolyte boys about wound poisons while I gazed at her in a lovesick haze. 'Birch is useful in winter and early spring,' she had said, 'when our healing stores run low and there's little fresh growth around.'

Thank you Cernunnos.

I got to my knees and pulled as much of the sapling as I could through the drain. I took off most of the leaves and buds, leaving just enough not to kill it.

'Caradoc!'

I turned to see Livia beckoning me.

'I can see Romans in armour!'

I sped up the gate-tower. There *were* two in Roman armour but of the twenty or so people coming most looked British.

'I think it's probably Colleos and Ambix,' I said, 'with Dran and the Cornovi survivors.'

'Could it be a trick?'

'Possibly. I won't let them in until I'm sure.' I handed her the cauldron of snow and all the birch gatherings. 'Take these to Leon and tell him to boil it up for two Cernunnos prayers over.'

'Will he know what that means?'

'Oh yes. He has been my servant a long time.'

She went, and I double-checked the bar was fast on both the gates before returning to the top of the look-out. As they neared I became more certain that the two 'Romans' were Colleos and Ambix, and I thought I could see Dranis too, head and shoulders taller than most. 'Dran!'

He waved back to me.

'Is everyone all right Dran?'

'Yes!'

Thanks be to the Gods. I let them all in and was pleased to see young Vedica with the Cornovi but as I watched the last warrior come through I knew Machan, Hedros and the Cornovi Queen were not among them. I pulled Dran to one side, out of Vedica's earshot.

'Have you seen Machan's group?'

Dran shook his head. 'We saw a group of Romans after us, as soon as the sun was up. They were gaining on us and then they veered to one side.'

'You think they saw the others?'

Dran sighed. 'Maybe.'

The chance to take three as opposed to twenty – and possibly nearer. It made sense.

'How's Kynbel?' Dran asked. 'Can we move him?'

I kept my voice low.

'This is a decent fort, but we have not a grain of food and only twenty-odd to defend it. I don't think we have any choice.'

Eight Old Friends

Kynbel managed a smile as I came back into the house. His face still looked red, and he was gripping hard on the edge of the bed as Leon bathed the stitched wound in the warm, birch-steeped water. I saw strips of Leon's shirt were drying on forked sticks by the fire.

'I boiled them in the rest of the salt-water first, sire,' Leon said.

'Good, well done. Start bandaging in the splint as soon as they are dry enough – we may have to move soon.'

Vedica had crouched by the fire to thaw her hands and looked up to me in surprise.

'Should we not defend ourselves within these walls?'

'Against the initial scouts, possibly, but once the legion with their contraptions turn up it would be no better than defending your father's seat. We'd be trapped like fish in a barrel.'

I saw her lower lip tremble and felt a pang of guilt, but it was true.

'I want to wait for my mother,' she said. 'Your men said she is alive.'

'We *will* wait for her, and the rest of my men, but then we must continue. You go and keep watch for her – you are the youngest of all of us, your eyes are probably the best.'

She went, and I turned back to Kynbel to see an accusing look on his face.

'She's cold, and tired,' he said.

'I know, but it's best to keep her busy, not thinking too much.'

He saw the sense of that. Leon finished dabbing Kynbel's wound dry and started bandaging.

'Do you feel any better?' I asked.

'A bit. No worse at least.'

'Have some more warm water to drink before we get going.' I took another look around the house. 'We'll need to make a stretcher from something – maybe the bed, if I take it apart.'

'I can do that,' Dran said.

Kynbel shrugged. 'I've walked this far.'

Yes. But we haven't actually got very far. 'Your body needs to be fighting the fever, nothing else. When was the last time you ate anything?'

'A cheese bannock while Rhian got my things together for the raid . . . so . . . before dawn yesterday.'

'Exactly.'

I was hungry enough myself but at least the rest of us had been given thin soup and flat bread at the carpenter's camp last night while we planned. I knew we couldn't wait here much longer. *Come on Machan,* I willed, *Gods protect you.*

Dran helped Kynbel off the bed then started hacking one of the side planks off. I saw Livia come back into the house, looking like she had ice for blood, and she had to side-step the plank as Dran swung it round.

'Sit down by the fire, Liv,' I said. 'I'll take a look at your wounds.'

'It's not so bad now. I can feel my lip starting to scab up.'

That was what I'd thought, but I gave her a damp bit of rag to clean the dried blood from her face. The bruises around both eyes were really black by then. She was cautious as she wiped the rag around them.

'Was it Saturninus that did this to you?'

'Yes. Him and his friend.' Her lip curled a bit in disgust as she said it and I saw her wince.

'The centurion?'

'Enjoyed it too. Evil piece of shit.'

'Uricon's wife killed him just as we were leaving the fort.'

'Good.'

I poured another cup of warm water to wrap her hands around. 'Why did they suddenly suspect you, after all these years?'

'I'm not sure.'

'What does your gut tell you?'

She sighed. 'Well I know things are changing – Pomponia said she and Plautius are going back to Rome and a new general is coming, someone called Scapula. So maybe I asked too many questions about him? Or maybe all your successes so far just added up, I don't know, but almost as soon as I'd got my last message out to you I was separated off from Pomponia and dragged up here. I think somehow they knew a message had got out but not *how* it got out.'

It made sense. Not least because it tied with Ambix's tale the day before.

'So that's why they seized you but left the Sparrow alone for now.'

'Yes. I think so.' She looked up to me with a sudden pleading in her sharp green eyes I knew of old and it put me on my guard. 'What am I going to do now?'

'You will come to Siluria and start a new life.'

I realised how flimsy it sounded even as I said it.

'A new life with you? It'll be rather short if your wife has anything to do with it.'

I felt myself nettle like an old dog shifted from the hearth. 'Give my wife one single moment of suspicion and I promise I will put you back where I found you - understand?'

Liv's jaw dropped a moment before she recovered herself, eyes blazing. 'That is *deeply* unfair. I've never done *anything* over all these years to deserve that.'

I had to admit to myself that she was right. I sucked in a troubled breath. 'I did not mean a life with me, I just meant a new start in general.' It still sounded flimsy, even to me. 'You've helped us, many times – you will be welcome.'

She didn't look convinced . . . and I couldn't blame her.

Vedica stuck her head around the door, her face now alight with an unmistakable smile.

'Come look – I think it's mother!'

We all rushed to the palisade. There were indeed three figures edging towards us, and from the outline it did look like one was a woman. 'Let's get ready to move out,' I said to Leon in a low voice, 'in case it is them.' As they grew nearer I became more certain but their slow speed started to niggle me. It looked like Machan was in the middle and the other two were supporting him.

'Colleos – could you - ?'

'I see it, my king.'

Colleos was over to them in a few breaths and I saw him put Machan across his shoulders, whereupon Hedros bent double, holding his knees. We all raced down to the gate as they came in.

'They aren't far behind us!' Hedros gasped, still clutching at his stomach.

'Are you injured Hedros?'

'No – no – it's just a stitch – Father – Father – '

He was spluttering and gasping so I got Colleos to lay Machan down and examined him myself. He was breathing well and I couldn't see a mark on him at all until I lifted a lock of his hair and saw the livid lump on the left side of his forehead. I eased back his closed eyelids one by one and found that his left eye was scarlet with blood.

'You say they aren't far Hedros – how many?'

'Only six – now – but we could see a larger group in the distance.'

I turned to Dran. 'That's that then, we have to get to the border. We'll have to use the stretcher for Machan.' Dran and Leon went to get it. 'What happened?' I asked Hedros softly.

His voice caught in his throat. 'He killed two Romans in one sword swing. He saved her life.' Hedros nodded over to the Cornovi queen, who was now clutching at her daughter as if she might wring the water from her. 'And then one of the others managed to bash a shield up into his head.'

I used the base of my tunic to mop up a trickle of blood as it escaped Machan's eyelid and slid down his cheek.

'Will he live?' Hedros asked of me, and right then I felt useless as a wet wood pile.

'I honestly don't know, Hedros, I'm sorry. We will all pray, and make offerings – but first we have to get to safety.'

'Yes my king.' I gripped his shoulder a moment then got up and turned to everyone else.

'We must go. Make sure you are all armed. For speed all must take a turn at carrying the stretcher – Dran, you and I first.'

We headed west as fast as – well as fast as anyone can when cold, injured and hungry. The bright morn was giving over to dirty-looking clouds, spinning in on a north-east wind, and I knew we would face snow again before too long. We were then passing through bog-ridden ground, the tussocky grass crisped by ice, and the constant lumps and hollows were exhausting us even more. Despite all the ups and downs and changing of turns with the stretcher – every able pair had taken a go and it was back with Dran and me again – Machan still hadn't woken up, not even a flicker, and it was chilling me.

We set Machan's stretcher down, just a heartbeat, to ease the pain in our frozen fingers. Livia had given me the cloak back, without a word, and it helped, but I was still worried about frostbite. I held my hands between my knees a moment and rubbed them to get the blood back in, then checked under Machan's jaw for a pulse.

His son's eyes and mine met. 'All right?' Hedros asked.

'Yes, still strong.' He felt cold though so I pulled the cloak covering him higher up his neck. 'How about you Kynbel?'

Hedros was pretty much holding Kynbel upright so I wasn't comforted by my nephew's response of 'Fine'. The only thing heartening me right then was that our Roman pursuers hadn't caught us up. Given how slow we were it was nothing short of miraculous.

'Ambix, do you think they might have stopped pursuing us?'

The Gaul pursed his lips. 'They might be wary of getting too far from a fort and close to your lines, and with the snow coming . . . possibly. . . but the scouts would have seen that they were outnumbered. I think it's more likely they just waited for the rest of the group.'

I sighed. No doubt he was right. *Bloody Romans.* 'Right, let's crack on then.' I got back to my feet, feeling my knee click as I did so and as I straightened up I saw a change in Dran's face. 'What is it?'

I whipped round. On the horizon, the snow clouds behind them, Roman javelins bristled. Just a dozen or so at first, a couple on horseback, and then the rest swarmed before I'd had a chance to blink. At least forty – twice our number.

'Let's go! Everyone!' I picked up my end of the stretcher and Dran did the same but Ambix continued looking at me, a scowl across his face.

'Go where?' he barked.

'We should have stayed in the the fort!' Vedica pitched in with a plaintive whine.

Maponos forgive me – was she right?

I looked ahead to some higher ground. There were rocks, or something – better than nothing. 'Up there!'

We took off, even my detractors, and as I flicked a look backwards I saw the initial group had been joined by another square of marching Romans. How many now? Eighty? At least quadruple our number then. No, I hadn't been wrong to leave the fort. They'd have starved us out with ease even if they hadn't just over-run us. Not that we were that much better off out here. Dran and I were running with the stretcher as fast as we could but now it was uphill. I could feel my lungs tightening as the incline steepened. When the ground at last flattened out I realised where we were. These were not just rocks – it was an ancestor circle.

'Here! We'll make our stand here!'

I ignored the look Ambix threw at me. We laid the stretcher down next to a boulder that weather had pocked and cracked till it had the look of a giant's face. I took off my Roman cloak and laid it over Machan whilst also unbelting my own sword from his body. 'Kynbel, come here, sit with Machan.' I handed Kynbel my Roman sword and belted the sword of my mother's kin back in its rightful place. Starting with Dran, Hedros and I, everyone fanned out to defend this central point, weapons bared, even Uricon's wife. My eyes and hers met.

'Vedica should keep running,' I said, and she nodded, but that just made her daughter cling to her sleeve.

'Mama no!'

'Yes. Go!'

'No!'

The first flakes of snow drifted in like Samhain souls and I saw one melt upon the tears pouring down the girl's cheek. Her mother ripped her sleeve free and actually pushed her daughter away from the rock. 'Go! Run! Get help!'

Help? Between the white of the snow and the dark of the hills there was nothing out there, but it did the trick, Vedica ran off with a cry into the west.

The Romans were nearing. They had formed up now in two squares. I knew they would go up either side of us once they were near enough to cast their spears. All the Cornovi warriors – bar their queen – had shields, but most of us who had been involved in the plan to get into the fort did not. I looked about me and there was nothing I could use.

Cernunnos, Camulos, Teutates, Epona, help us please.

The Romans were closer. We could hear their gear jangling now.

We are too quiet.

'Yell like banshees! Beat your shields! Wake the ancestors who laid these stones – they are your ancestors Cornovi!' I yelled, slapping the grey lichened stone like an old friend. 'Come on!'

We did as I bade, only Ambix remained quiet. 'But it's hopeless,' he said.

The Roman squares were indeed marching towards us, relentless as the passing of the years.

'It's never hopeless,' I snapped back. 'Have some faith in the Gods.'

'They have faith in you,' Colleos said, his voice low with awe, and I looked up to where he gazed.

A thousand British horsemen crowded the crest of the western hill.

Nine Pain

As the first horsemen galloped past us I spotted Corbennog's shield among the Silure riders just behind them.

'Corbennog!' I yelled. 'They will wall shields – don't let those young hotheads race too far ahead!'

My old friend grinned back at me and raised his spear in war-cry joy as he sped forward. I'm not sure he heard me. The more experienced of them did form up but a few of the fastest were cut down by the Romans javelins from behind the shield wall just as I'd warned – until the sheer weight of numbers did its work. The iron-hard ground was shaking. I saw young Vedica cowering beside a rock until the riders had passed and her mother could make a run out towards her. An elderly Cornovi warrior who had been lagging behind dismounted and threw his cloak around them both. He was not the only Cornovi I could see. Many of the warriors surging forward looked to be Cornovi and, if my eyes did not deceive me, I thought I spied some Ordovici shields mixed in among the throng too. How had my wife managed that?

'Thank the Gods I've found you!'

I turned to see Nes herself, swinging down from her grey mare and running to throw her arms about my neck. I hugged her tight, burying my face into the folds of her cloak. She felt so warm.

'By the Gods, Caradoc, you are *frozen*. Let me rub your hands.'

'Where's Gladsia?' I asked.

'She's with Alwona, they'll meet us at home.' Nesica's broad smile disappeared. 'Is that Machan?'

We both turned to look at him. I checked his heartbeat again, and at least he felt a touch warmer, but there was still no sign of consciousness. 'We have to get him inside, Kynbel too, as soon as we can.'

Nes put her arm about Kynbel. 'There's the fort, the Ordovici fort we just came from – it's near.' She took her cloak off and wrapped it round him, then whistled in the ear-splitting way Nes could. A boy came riding in with my Buanedd trotting parallel and Creegan gambolling beside. The boy smiled and waved at me and I suddenly realised who he was.

'Mocco? Arthewin's boy?' I asked.

My wife nodded. 'And Young Arth too – out there.' She gestured towards the massacre. 'They said they'd help – I think Mocco is a bit sweet on me – but we mustn't tell their father.'

Well this'll end well.

'Arthewin will find out, Nes – and that lad tries his luck with any girl that breathes.'

She threw up her hands. 'Well was I wrong? We are winning aren't we?'

I sighed. 'Fair enough.' Mocco was near us now so I stopped talking about him. He was grinning so wide beneath his huge horned helmet I could not help but smile back. He appeared younger than his seventeen summers, all teeth and skinny legs like a foal, and he had a good nature despite being known by our word for 'runt' by everyone who had ever known him, as far as I could tell. I'd heard his mother died a few days after his birth so I suppose she, at least, was innocent of that. Arthewin was not. I'd been appalled by the way he'd treated both his sons when we'd all met up at Mon last Beltane . . . if not that surprised.

'Greetings King Caradoc.'

'Greetings young prince, you are a most welcome sight. I have wounded – can we rely upon your hospitality?'

Mocco grinned again with a little bow. 'Come to Caer Ffridd, it's not far. Follow me.' He chuckled. 'My brother is enjoying himself.'

I turned back to the battle, worried they would all expect me to join in. I was in no fit state, to be honest, and neither were Colleos, Hedros and the rest, but I couldn't just up and leave. As I got up on Buanedd, though, and took a few first steps towards the fight, I saw the look on my wife's face and was relieved to see that Corbennog was just then riding towards me. I didn't want to have a spat with her right there in front of Livia, Mocco and the rest.

I met Corbennog half way. His tunic was speckled with blood but he seemed fine himself.

'None have got away, sire. The Cornovi want to press on and retake their stronghold – should we go with them?'

I took a deep breath, remembering the steep sides of Uricon's favoured fort. Horses would be no good there, and the ballistas and such like that the legion had used to take it would likely do just as much damage if fired outwards. I couldn't afford to lose hundreds of my men recapturing a rock for a dead king.

'Not to the stronghold, no. The Romans have supplies pouring in from the east. Dran and Leon saw them. Do a snap raid on them and then bring the men home before they get cold and hungry.'

No warmth or food has ever been so welcome to me as that of Caer Ffridd. We made it there before the snow storm reached its heaviest, thank the Gods. Young Mocco, in the absence of his father and elder brother, proved himself a capable host. We were given use of the head man's house and his wife had Kynbel wrapped in blankets and sipping at a great bowl of soup within moments of us getting inside. My nephew's forehead still felt hot, and his hand was on fire with pain, so I made him some dried meadowsweet tea with supplies our hosts gave me and settled him down to sleep. I still feared for him, but not as much as I had.

Machan was another matter. He was given a bed and blankets and we got his temperature back up to normal soon enough but there was still no glimmer of consciousness. If anything he seemed a touch worse. There was fever now. I soaked a rag in snow from outside and laid it over his forehead. The lump showed no sign of going down. Even his breathing sounded shallower than it did before. When I checked my old friend's eyes again the left eye had stopped bleeding but the pupils still didn't look the same. I feared it was just a matter of time.

Nes brought me over a bowl of stew and passed me a bleak look. Hedros was moistening his father's lips with a clean cloth as I'd showed him and didn't see it, but he knew, I think.

'My king, is there nothing else I can do?' he asked.

'You are doing all you can. Just stay with him and talk, he might be able to hear you.'

'Should I go and get mother, tomorrow, when it is light again?'

I sighed. Gods willing Alwona, my daughter, Rhian and the others were all safe and warm back in Siluria by now. By the time Hedros, or anyone, could get there and ride back I expected it would be too late, even if the snowstorm abated. Hedros must have guessed as much by the look on my face.

'His skull is cracked, isn't it?'

'It looks like it, yes.'

He seemed to crumble before my eyes. *Should I say more? Yes, he needs to know.*

'It can't be too big a break or I doubt he'd have survived this long, but I expect there is swelling or blood welling up inside, not able to get out, and that is dangerous.'

'What can we do for that?'

What indeed? I remembered tales, when I was a boy on Mon, of the druids of old drilling holes – carefully – in the skulls of the afflicted to let the swelling expand and retreat, then stitching the scalp over again. The patients had survived, if the tales were true, but, to the best of my knowledge, neither Gwyfina nor Cernos had done this themselves. They'd certainly never taught me. I'm not sure, even if I had stayed to complete my training, that we would ever have got that far. We were told about it, I think, more to show the power of our order over the vastness of time. As I told Machan's son all this, though, it was as if he saw the glimmer through the fog.

'Then there is a chance, at least,' he said.

'Hedros I have never seen this remedy done – I do not even know where to start. If it goes wrong, in even the slightest way, then he will die.'

Hedros looked up at me, tears glistening in the light of the fire. 'You have healed many people, sire – you saved my little brother, when the other druids would not. Is it not worth trying?'

Gods help me.

The warriors began to return at nightfall. I was accepting the gift of some new clothes from Mocco when the word rang out. As I wrapped my new cloak about me and accompanied young Mocco to the gate I was disturbed to see so few, until I realised the only warriors coming back were the Ordovici ones.

'Father said to guard our border, no more. So far we might have avoided his wrath.' The boy shrugged. 'Well, my brother will have – Father needs no reason to berate me.'

'He might come round,' I soothed. 'Any father would be proud to have a son such as you. He probably just hides it well.'

Mocco laughed. 'He hides it very well.'

He was just then perched on the topmost rung of the sheep enclosure down by the south gate, chewing on a strand of hay, looking rather like a peasant about to turn into an owl, but I wasn't being insincere. He was a little awkward, that's all. I hadn't been so very different at his age.

'You know, you are a bit old to be fostered, but you are welcome to stay with Nes and me in Siluria for a while if you like. King Maros wouldn't mind.'

He looked tempted, but then shook his head. 'I might be welcome, but I wouldn't be allowed to go.' He threw his strand of hay down to the sheep. 'Thank you any way.'

I nodded, and we greeted the next group of incoming warriors with good spirits as if all was well. They were happy enough, toting the spoils and few, it appeared, hurt or missing. Arth, Mocco's elder brother, was among the last. Arth slithered off his tall roan straight into the sheep fold, knocking his young brother off the fence in doing so, stuffing a handful of hay down Mocco's neck, but all done in happy affection I think. I remembered Tog and felt a lump in my throat.

'You missed a good battle!' Arth admonished, knuckling his brother's head, then coloured up as he remembered me. 'Not – not you King Caradoc!'

I laughed. 'It's all right cousin, I've seen enough battle this day and night to leave some to you. Is all well?'

Arth grinned just like his brother. 'A victory fit for the harpers' songs,' he gushed. 'Barely a scratch amongst us.'

A victory of a thousand over eighty. It would take a rare harper to win his place by the fire out of that. Besides which I had seen a few horses being led in with their riders slumped over them, and blood aplenty, but I didn't say it and pluck his fine feathers. I was grateful, after all, and I liked this lad and his brother more than I had ever liked their father, kin though we were.

We strode up to the house through the stray snowflakes, the boys telling me more news of their Ordovici home than their father would have wanted, no doubt. As we approached the doorway I saw Hedros hurrying out, his hands across his face.

I could have called out, comforted him, brought him back inside, but to my shame I did not. I didn't know what to say.

Nes and I were made up a guest bed in the head man's house, right in the middle by the fire. I was exhausted yet

I couldn't sleep, my mind swirling and howling like the wind outside, and I resigned myself to an awful night with eyes like burnt holes in a blanket. Everything I'd seen these past days seemed sharper in the dark. Snuggling up to Nes, all warm and soft, was my sole comfort.

'Can't you sleep either?' she whispered.

'No.'

'Is it Machan? Kynbel seems to be getting better.'

It wasn't just that, in truth, but I wasn't about to tell my wife of the sight of Uricon and his son nailed to a beam that kept springing to the fore of my mind once the house fell quiet. 'Yes. I keep thinking about the way to treat him – do you think I should try it?'

Nes swivelled round to face me. 'Do you think you could do it?'

'I don't know. I could make it worse, leave him mutilated, or it could kill him . . . but . . .'

'But he is dying anyway?'

'Yes.'

Nes gripped my arm. 'So you should try, no? The Gods will be with you. And if you don't try you will always have it on your mind.'

She was right. 'Then we'll start at first light,' I said, and kissed her, and Nes smiled, lighting up like a well-built fire.

'I'll help you,' she whispered.

'You do, more than you know.'

We settled into the warm hollow of soon-slumber and my troubled thoughts backed away one by one. Then, as a gull always shits on your new cloak, came: 'That woman you were talking to earlier, was that Camulora?'

'Nes – please – '

'How is that an answer?'

I sucked in a breath. 'She is one of the wounded, I showed no more concern for her than I did Kynbel, Vedica or any of our group.'

A good deal less, in fact, but either way it didn't wash with my wife.

'I never said you did, but something is clearly going on.'

'It is not. I swear – on our daughter's life – it is not.'

Nes held my gaze a heartbeat. 'All right,' she said. 'But what is it then? What *are* you keeping from me?'

So, while everyone else slept, I told her all that had happened at Uricon's seat. Nes kept flicking little looks over to where Vedica and her mother now rested, curled together under the old warrior's cloak like a bitch and her last pup when all the others are homed. I wondered if *they* were managing to sleep, this rotten night.

'What if that is you, one day?' Nes breathed, her eyes huge in the gloom.

'It won't be.'

'Or our little Gladsia . . .' Her voice cracked.

I hugged my wife close, so close I could feel her breathing, and the snowstorm continued to howl.

Ten   May the Gods steady my hands

I was awake early, long before Nes, and used the light from the hearth embers to pick my way over to where Machan lay. Hedros had slunk back at some point in the dead of night and now slept by his father's side. I checked on Machan's breathing – no worse, though he still felt hot – and then crept over to Kynbel. I could hear his breathing, but no more than if he was snoring, so I risked feeling his forehead. Warm, but not hot. His fever had broken, thank the Gods. I tried to pick my way back to Nes without disturbing anyone.

'My king?'

The whisper came from Hedros and made me jump. 'Yes?'

'Is father all right?'

'No worse, Hedros, but no better either.' I hesitated. *Once I tell him I've promised.* 'I – I will try the treatment I told you about at first light.'

Silence, for a heartbeat, which raised a flash of concern in my head, then: 'Thank you sire.'

'All right. Wake me if you rise early.'

'Yes sire.'

When the shake of the shoulder came – probably a gentle tapping in reality, to be fair, but that's not what it felt like – I was in a deep sleep, dreaming, in the odd way we do, of dogs drinking milk from huge buckets that we were all swimming in. I still felt tired as a fat man's horse. Nes insisted I had a bowl of porridge before all else and, as word spread of what I was going to attempt, my people gathered round.

'What do you need?' Nes asked.

'Light, for a start. As much light as we can get.'

'It's brightest outside,' Hedros said. 'The weather has calmed.'

'All right. I'll need somewhere out of the wind though, or my hands will be too cold to work. I'll need a tall bench or table too, something stable.'

'The black smith has one like that,' the head man's wife said, 'I'll go and ask him.'

'I'll go with you,' offered Dran, 'and carry it to a good place.'

The rest of the things I wanted were fetched from about the village with all the swift helpfulness I could hope for: a sharp knife and awl from the leather-worker, fine boiled thread and a slender needle, clean cloths, sheepskins for Machan to rest upon, honey, peeled willow sticks, an array of bowls. The sole down-side of all this was that when I started to work I had drawn quite a crowd.

'Should I try to get everyone to leave, sire?' Leon asked.

Good luck with that, Leon. 'No, no, it'll only annoy them.' We were guests here, after all, and – much as I didn't really want an audience – I didn't want rumours circulating about what I was doing, either. Not bad rumours, anyway. 'Just try to keep them at least four paces back.'

'I can do that,' Dran said. 'You'll need Leon.'

Colleos nodded to Dran. 'I'll help you.'

'Do you need the crowd to be silent, sire?' Leon asked.

'Praying is fine. I'll get them to pray.'

I looked beyond them to where Livia sat, pensive and awkward, on the smith's wood pile. Ambix was near her, without his Roman helmet or mail over-shirt, but still standing out like a grey hair among the dark. To be honest I was surprised he hadn't just slipped away in the night, but then where would he go?

'Liv, could you keep Kynbel company? He's awake, but he still needs looking after.'

'Of course.'

She looked relieved to get away, and Nesica no less that she was going.

Leon had finished lighting the fire that was to warm me at my back and now Nes set a tripod over it, as I'd asked her. She hung a pan of water over to boil. The bench that the smith provided looked big enough, and I checked it was stable. *Nearly there.*

'I need a sharp serrated knife too, like a very small saw – do you have anything like that?' I asked the smith.

He frowned. 'I could make one, but do you want the delay? It would be nearing noon, King Caradoc.'

No, I did not want the delay.

'You'd be better off with a flint for that,' the leather-worker chipped in. 'I'll make one quick as the Gods' own lightning.'

The smith was nodding along so I agreed.

'Right then, let's bring him out,' I said to Hedros, and we carried Machan outside on the stretcher. I'd laid several layers of sheepskin on the bench to pad it so we eased Machan onto these and then put the blankets back on, up to his neck, just leaving his left hand free. 'You stay on this side now, Hedros. Check his heartbeat as I showed you, and his breathing, as we go.'

He looked white as birch bark but, 'Yes sire' was his answer.

I turned back to Nes. 'All set,' she said. 'That's your hand-washing bowl, those are the clean dry cloths and those ones are long enough for bandages.'

'Good. Have you washed your own hands?'

'Yes.'

'Right, you stand here then, by his right shoulder. I'll work from here, from behind the top of his head.'

'What about Creegan?'

Creegan was sat watching us with his big brown eyes, placid and unobtrusive, for now. 'Do you think he will just sit still, when the blood starts? Or should we put him inside?'

'He'll sit still if I tell him to.'

'All right.'

I washed my own hands, keeping an eye on the leather-worker. He had a skin over his knees and was pressing on the edge of a flint with what looked like a piece of antler. Within moments he was coming over to me, a broad grin across his face. 'I made two, King Caradoc,' he said, 'in case it goes blunt. You hold them here – ' He showed me a little smooth patch on each one.

'Thank you. The Gods blessing on you, and all this village.'

He bowed and retreated. I turned back to Machan. 'We need to tie back Machan's hair, away from his face, so it can't drag on the open wound.'

Nes nodded. 'I can do that, you should start the prayers.'

I took a deep breath and looked about the yard. At least forty people were watching me. There were more dogs, which concerned me a bit in case they ran about and knocked into the bench legs, and quite a lot of young children. Dran and Colleos stood a little apart, between me and them, and I could only hope that they would see to that.

'Good people,' I began, 'my warrior is stuck between our world and the Land of Youth. If I do not open his skull and allow the blood that is seeping there to escape, then I do not think he will ever wake up, and, without the ability to eat or drink, he will die a terrible slow death. So I must try something that I've never done before, or seen done before – I need your help. Please pray, to the Gods and to the ancestors, that they guide my hands.'

'Which Gods shall we pray to?' asked an old woman from the back.

All of them, I thought. 'When I was in the same sort of state as Machan it was Cernunnos who helped me, so I will be praying mainly to him. Is there a God who is particularly revered in this place?'

'Amaethonos, King Caradoc, who keeps our sheep and cattle strong,' the leather-worker said.

'Then I will include him in our prayers also.'

'What about offerings?' the man asked. The old woman who had spoken before had now come to the front and was nodding in agreement. I sighed.

'I have already asked so much of you all . . . '

The woman shook her head. 'I'm the birthing woman here, King Caradoc, I always have some supplies in hand.'

I bowed to her, which made her old face crack into a smile.

I turned back to Machan. Hedros was checking his pulse and nodded to me. The water in the pan was boiling, Nes had Machan's hair wrapped up, and the light was still good. There was nothing more to do but start.

Cernunnos, Amaethonos, Camulos, Epona, guide Machan's spirit back to us. Please steady my hands, o Gods.

My outward prayer was more formal as I held my knife in the flames.

First I cut through the flesh of Machan's forehead, just above the lump. It felt just like skinning an animal and the sheer thought of that froze me for a breath. *No. Come on.* Blood started to seep from the edges and then dribble down towards Machan's nose and eyes.

'Cloth, Leon.'

Leon rolled one of the cloths and tucked it beneath Machan's jaw to collect the blood as it completed its stream down his face. I made another two incisions so the skin could be lifted and more blood flowed down to meet Leon's rolled cloths. On the other side of the yard a young man passed out. My eye was drawn to him and a woman, perhaps his mother, flapping above. *No, ignore them.* I used the flat of the knife to see if the skin would loosen and, with a bit of effort, it did – thank the Gods.

'Nes, pick up one of the peeled willow sticks.'

She did so. Her hands were trembling. *Easy, Nes.*

'Right - I'm going to fold over the skin, like we talked about, and you hold it there with the stick. Then keep holding it.'

Nes nodded, pale as milk, but did as I'd asked. The exposed skull was smeary with blood, not all white and gleaming as I'd imagined. Should I risk swabbing it with a cloth? The surface would be less slippery for when I worked with the awl . . . but what of the invisible poisons that cling to everything? *If the awl slips that will be the end*. I decided I had to risk it – the cloths had all been boiled and dried, after all. I chose one from the middle of the pile, bunched it up, and then dabbed at the skull.

'Is his pulse still good, Hedros?'

Hedros didn't seem to hear me, his eyes fixed on his father's blood streaked face.

'Hedros?'

The lad sprang to it. 'The same, sire.'

'Good.'

I picked up the awl with just the tips of my fingers, so I could hold it in the flames for a good few breaths, then let it cool in mid-air for a moment. I nodded to Leon. 'String soon, please.' I placed the sharp end of the awl point down on Machan's exposed skull. Even at this stage the skull felt greasy and slippery, as fresh bone does, and it isn't even flat. *Cernunnos help me*. I held the awl as tight and steady as I could and made my initial twist.

Nothing.

I lifted the awl and there was no visible mark. *Come on, it's fresh living bone – you expected this.* I tried again, this time twisting for a lot longer and even harder. I felt it doing some good, and when I lifted the awl there was a slight depression, no bigger than a blackberry seed, but what I needed. *Thank you Cernunnos.*

'Right, string now Leon.'

I held the awl lightly up in the air while Leon looped the length of string round. I'd chosen an awl with central ridges to help with this part and I was relieved to see that it fell into place. We got the point end of the awl back down into the slight dip and then I held the blunt end of the awl to steady it while Leon pulled on the ends of the string as if starting a fire. 'It's working, I think,' I said, and Leon nodded. Traces of bone dust were building around the edges of the hole.

'Just tell me when to stop, sire.'

Well, that's the question. 'A while yet, I think, the bone is probably thick there.'

It seemed to take forever. As we got deeper into the bone our natural instinct was to slow – perhaps Leon also had thoughts of blood and brain bubbling up through the hole like sticking your thumb through the shell of a raw egg – but we had to get it done. I wished I'd had a chance to practice, or at least to look at some skulls and cut them open. I remembered Siluri's collection she kept for her paintings and was kicking myself, but how by the Gods was I to know?

'Sire?'

Leon had stopped. We lifted the awl and took a cautious look.

'It still just looks like bone,' I said. 'A bit more – steady now.'

We stopped just in the nick of time, as it turns out – the Gods were indeed looking over us. That didn't make the second drill-hole any easier, though. I couldn't be sure the skull was the same thickness all over, so we had to be just as careful.

'Should we swap over, Leon? Are your hands getting tired?'

Leon shook his head. There were beads of sweat on his brow but he had a determined set to his face. 'I think as we have a pattern going, and it is working, it is better we stay as we are, on balance, sire.'

'You're right.' All the same when we got to the third hole our progress had slowed again. I started to think it was the awl going blunt.

'I think we will have to cut between these three holes, like a triangle, not try to do a fourth,' I said, with no great conviction in my voice, but Leon looked relieved. We put the awl and string in a clean bowl, just in case. I picked up the first of the leather-worker's flint blades, ran it through the flames a couple of times over, and risked a look over to the crowd. The young man who'd fainted was now sat up on the palisade, looking out over the snow, his arm about a small child who, I guessed, couldn't bring herself to look either. Everyone else was still rapt.

'Cernunnos, Amaethonos, Camulos, Epona,' I said, loud enough that they could hear, 'please continue to watch over us. Guide my warrior's spirit back.'

The birthing woman had built a small fire on the other side of the yard and I saw her crumbling something into the flames as I spoke. *Thank you Gods,* I thought, *so far so good.*

I began to cut between the holes with the tiny serrated blade, such slow, gentle cuts it was more like scraping.

'Are you all right, Caradoc?'

I stopped moving the blade and looked to my wife.

'You've gone very white.'

I tasted blood in my mouth and realised I'd been biting my lip. 'I'm fine,' I lied. 'Nearly there.'

It took a long time to make the incisions, just as long as the drill-holes. When at last I lifted the piece of skull and placed it in a dish, inner-side-up, I heard someone in the crowd throw up. Yet they couldn't even see what we at Machan's side could see. Somehow I'd imagined the brain would be right there, open to the sky, but it wasn't. There is a skin, a bit like the skin that forms on hot milk if you leave it, but with veins. I could only guess that it is normally a smooth dome, like the head itself – Machan's had a bulge in it the size of a pigeon egg.

'I think the blood has collected under there,' I said. 'But should I cut into this? It must be there to protect the brain.'

I'd directed my question at everyone but only Leon answered.

'I think we have to sire. Perhaps there, where the veins are fewer.'

I could see what he meant, but the downside was that this area was 'off' the bulge. Then again, I wanted the blood to drain off neatly, not spatter us all or erupt up. I remembered my brother's blood-drenched death and stretched and clasped my hands a little to reduce the tremble in them. My gaze met that of Hedros. He nodded.

'Do it,' he said. 'The Gods are with us.'

I changed to the second flint and ran it through the flames, then began. The skin was tougher than I expected – thank the Gods the blade was sharp. To my surprise, and relief, there was no great welling up of blood. Indeed it looked like the blood had clotted.

'Nes, with your other hand pass me one of the peeled sticks to my left hand.' She did so. 'Now pick up another and hold this skin open just like you're doing with the outer skin.'

It was working. *Thank the Gods.* Now I just had to get the clot out without touching the brain.

Eleven **The rumble that shakes the land**

The clot was a deep, gleaming red, the consistency of an over-thickened broth; too solid to just drain out and yet not solid enough.

'If you slip, and the stick hits his brain, what will happen?' Nesica asked, and I took a deep breath.

'I honestly don't know.'

Instant death or nothing much at all? My few years of training at Mon hadn't come near any of this, even when the teaching was about healing and not the stars or the Gods or anything else. The clot pressing on Machan's brain had kept him unconscious for about one whole day by that point so I could *guess* touching the brain would be worse than not touching it at all, but there is a clear difference between a mass pressing on it and a light accidental poke. I sneaked a look at Hedros. He was worried, for sure, but I still felt he had confidence in me. There was nothing to do but try.

I put down the flint and took another of the clean cloths. Using the side of the peeled twig, not its point, I began to ease the jelly-mass towards the edge of the hole and my waiting cloth, slow and deliberate as a child's first steps. Despite my care a part of the clot started to separate off from the rest. I swore under my breath.

'Caradoc?'

I bit back my annoyance, lifted the stick away, and looked to my wife. To be fair I could see why she'd alerted me. Creegan was on his feet, taut as a harp string, looking towards the main gate and sniffing the air. Within a heartbeat all the other dogs were on their feet. Several started to bark, their noise slicing through me. Up on the palisade the young man and his daughter were standing too, looking to the east.

I tried to catch his eye. 'What is it?'

The crowd, patient and quiet for so long, were now shifting about and the chatter level had swollen like an incoming wave. A barking dog started running towards me. I saw Colleos catch it by the scruff of its neck and turn it aside. It snapped at him and he had to pull his hands back.

'What's going on?' I yelled.

Caer Ffridd's head man was on his way up the look-out ladder by the east gate. 'Horse-men!' he shouted back.

'How many?'

'Maybe a hundred!' He peered out again, shielding his eyes from the winter sun. 'It's all right – it's our own princes. Open the gate!'

'No!'

My shout was either too late or it was just so strange to them they ignored it – the gate swung open. Beneath us the ground began to tremble. *Oh Gods*. My eyes met those of Hedros. Hedros, Nes, Leon and I all braced ourselves around the smith's bench as the Ordovici warriors poured in. I hadn't seen Arth or Mocco all morning – hadn't given it a moment's thought, to be honest – but now their absence made sense. The yard was a cauldron of horses and men and there wasn't a thing Dran or Colleos could do about it. Indeed I think the villagers I'd wanted to keep back were now trying to shield Machan themselves, but it was chaos, and chaos always wins. A dog got clipped by a horse's hoof and span off yelping – straight into the bench legs. The little pot containing the piece of skull shot off the bench. Leon *caught* the pot – right side up! – before it hit the ground, a catch worthy of heroes, but as his elbows hit the floor the piece of skull bounced out. Straight into the mud of the yard.

'Shit!'

So loud the dead must have heard me.

'Shit! Shit! Shit!'

Young Arth had his sword raised to the air. He was chanting 'Victory!' and his warriors were repeating it, some of them balanced up on their horses' backs, showing off to the girls. They were whooping and howling worse than the dogs.

Now, everyone turned to me.

'King Caradoc – you have a great victory!'

Arth hadn't seen Machan yet and was beaming at me from beneath his thatch of yellow hair like Maponos on his own feast day.

My voice could have curdled milk. 'And how is that . ?'

Mocco, from the look on his face, was starting to understand the situation. He got off his horse and called a servant over to take it from him. He motioned for calm.

'Your Silures, cousin, have triumphed, we've had word.' Mocco turned to look over his shoulder. 'Tarn, where are you? Come over here.'

Tarn came scrambling forward, the grin on his face disappearing once he saw Machan's open skull before him. Tarn's hands flew up to his face as his stomach retched but he controlled himself, more than young Arth was doing, to be fair. My cousin had gone a pale green like old copper.

'We are trying to save his life,' I explained. 'There is still much to do.'

Tarn nodded. 'I – I can come back sire.'

I sighed. 'Say what you need to say, Tarn. I'm not angry with you.'

'My message is urgent, my king, but – but you don't need to leave straight away.'

Just as well. 'What's happened?'

The boy took a good breath, his grin starting to sneak back as he talked. 'Corbennog sends word that we have won the day! More supplies than you can think of! And the Romans are running east with their tail between their legs. They seem without a leader.'

My mind started working like squirrels in a nut tree. Livia had said Plautius was leaving. Maybe their attack on the Cornovi had been an attempt to impress the new commander, this 'Scapula', and it had slapped back in their face. This was no opportunity to be missed.

'Did Corbennog say he needed more warriors? You said they have plenty of supplies.'

'Yes sire. They are holding a line in the Cornovi hills but there are still some pockets of Romans – they cannot get too stretched.'

I looked to the sky. The sun was moving behind the smith's hut and Machan would be in shadow before too long. I had to get him stitched up before anything else.

'Tarn, go with my cousins and get some food, have a rest and celebrate. I will join you and we'll discuss what we do next, once I've finished with Machan's wound.'

The lad bowed and retreated, and Hedros looked to me with a gentle smile of gratitude. 'How's he doing?' I asked, and his son's smile broadened.

'My king – look!'

Machan was opening his eyes.

It was skirting dusk by the time I joined Tarn and the Ordovici princes by the hearth side. I was cold and in sore need of a drink whereas they were all pretty far gone by then. Machan waking up was a great sign, of course, but it also meant that I'd had to have Hedros and Leon holding him down whilst Nes and I fought to get the last of the clot out and sew up his wounds. He'd been yelling and screaming, not calmed by my reassurances, or those of his son, and I'd ended up getting the blacksmith to lash him to the bench. My shirt was soaked with more blood than a battle. The piece of skull had to be left out, given it had fallen in the filth, so I'd just sewn a few stitches in the brain-skin and then stitched his flesh back over the hole. I'd smeared the stitches over with honey to keep the poisons out, gods willing, and bandaged with multiple layers of clean cloth as a pad. I hoped the sides of the skull hole would grow back, in time, like a broken bone will knit. For now, at least Machan couldn't poke at his wound.

Dran saw me coming through the doorway and handed me a cup of beer. 'How's he doing?'

'The birthing woman and Leon are cleaning him up, and she's given him some meadowsweet tea.' I gulped the beer down fast and regretted it. 'He said Hedros's name, and gripped his hand, as I was leaving – I think he's going to be all right.'

I dared to smile, and Dranis hugged me round my shoulders. I checked no-one was listening to us. 'What do you think of this latest news?'

Dran shrugged. 'It can only be good, no?'

'As long as we don't overstretch ourselves. I am supposed to be at home for Imbolc – Maros has wrangled a meeting with the Deceangli, at last. I can't afford to insult either of them.'

'It's all right – I'll go.'

I sighed. 'Thank you, my brother.'

Dranis waved it away. 'Colleos said he'd go, too, s'long as he's home by Beltane. We can all swap over.'

I understood. Colleos's wife was due about then.

We walked over to where the others were sat and the head man's wife handed me a bowl of stew. 'Your wife has just gone to check on the horses, sire,' she said. 'How is the wounded man now?'

I explained, and the whole circle went quiet while I talked of the risks of his wound running to poison and how long he might take to recover. I paused a moment, before I finished, making sure I looked them all in the eye. 'I cannot thank you all enough,' I said, 'all the Ordovici who have helped us. Although there is kinship between us there is no formal alliance. Your kindness and courage in our struggle have touched my heart.'

Mocco and his elder brother exchanged a look. 'I, for one, would be willing to join you in the fight against Rome,' Mocco said. 'Father might swing round,' he added, 'now they've been so near.'

That's what I thought too – quite apart from anything else it now appeared we might be winning – but young

Arth, though he nodded at his brother's words, was slow to speak.

'I will talk with Father, and Ordovicos, when we get home,' he said, peering into his drink. 'But it's better if you don't say anything at all, brother.'

Mocco shrugged with the ghost of a laugh and a knowing look to me. We were poured more beer so Arth, Mocco and I touched cups in the time-honoured way.

The best I could do, right then, was to leave persuading their father up to them.

It was good to celebrate for once but by midnight everyone was flagging, not least me. When Caer Ffridd's over-tired children were being herded to their beds I excused myself so I could check on Machan and crossed the yard to the birthing woman's house. Her home was small, crowded with so many grown men stuffed into it, but still calm as a pond compared to the larger house. Machan was asleep, a good healing sleep, with young Hedros by his side, and Leonidas was nodding off too by the hearth.

I sat down cross-legged beside Leon. 'There's no sign of fever, sire,' he whispered, 'but he has no sight in his left eye.'

I necked back the tot of elder wine the old woman handed me and felt my head swim. *I've drunk far too much today.* 'For now we must be grateful it's no worse. Has he spoken again?'

'A few words. He thanked you, my king.'

I smiled over at Machan. 'He would do the same for any of us, if he were able.'

The birthing woman pulled on a heavy cloak and left the house to go and relieve herself. Leon waited until the door had closed. 'I heard the news about the Silures,' he said. 'Does this mean we leave tomorrow, sire?'

'I must – this meeting at Imbolc has been a long time brewing. But you, and Hedros, will need to stay here until Machan is well enough to travel. Help the old woman however you can, and try to spread the word – subtly –

about joining together to resist Rome.' Leon nodded. 'I will send gifts, and perhaps our harper, once the snows melt, in thanks for their kindness.'

Leon put another log on the fire. 'I don't think she, or any of the others, did what they did for reward, sire.'

'No, but it's what the surrounding villagers will hear, and see, that matters too – no harm in adding more meat to the feast.'

The woman came back in so I thanked her for the wine, checked Machan's temperature one last time, and left. As I re-crossed the icy yard I saw the breath clouds of someone else, crouched by the wall of the great house.

'Who's there?!'

Ambix shot to his feet, turning to face me with tears dripping down his face. He was holding a cup of wine in one hand and what looked like an oat cake in the other. His sword was still in its scabbard.

'I'm sorry – were you praying?'

He dropped his gaze. 'Yes. For the spirits of the departed . . . my friends.'

'I'm sorry,' I said again. 'I'll leave you in peace.'

I backed away but as I turned he grabbed my arm. 'Listen,' he said. 'We were all told time after time that the barbarians don't care, that their wounded are just left for dead. What you did today . . .' He shook his head. 'I'm amazed. Amazed.'

'I look after my people, Lucius Ambix, I always have.'

He nodded. 'I have seen that.'

'Do you consider me worthy of your loyalty then? Don't be afraid to say no if that's the truth.'

I got my yes, as I wanted.

'Do you think others, among the Gaulish soldiers, might think as you, if they knew?'

'Yes.'

'Then I have work for you, this coming spring.'

Twelve Where the power lies

I woke with a start to find Nes bolt upright and trembling beside me.

'What's wrong?'

'Just a nightmare. Sorry – I didn't mean to wake you.'

'What did you see?'

Her hand in mine was clammy with sweat.

'It was Gladsia, she was crying out for us . . . there was danger, I can't remember exactly.' She shook her head. 'It *is* only a nightmare, isn't it?'

I sat up and held her close. It wasn't dawn yet and the rest of the household were still snoring, even Creegan. I would have liked to get up, dressed and get going right then, just as much as Nes no doubt did, but it wouldn't be decent, or practical.

'Could anything stop us from going home today?' Nes whispered.

'Only a blizzard.'

The day was calm, even warm, thank the Gods. The eaves dripped on me as I left the house. I went to the horse shelter and found Buanedd trying to pull off his blanket with his teeth.

'Easy, boy,' I soothed. 'I'll get it off for you.'

I gave his neck a good scratch and his ears went sideways as he enjoyed it, but then they pricked forward and he – along with all the horses – turned to the doorway as Colleos arrived with a bag of oats. The young Morini was fully dressed, and armed.

'We'll set off soon, sire,' Colleos said, 'and get as far east as we can while this sunshine holds out.'

'I'll raise the alarm as we go south – you should have more warriors on their way in days. And I'll join you myself once this council at Imbolc is over.' Colleos passed me the bag and my Buanedd chomped down on the oats as if I hadn't fed him in years. 'May the Gods be with you, Colleos.'

'Don't worry, sire. We'll be fine.'

I laughed. 'I don't doubt it. You are one of my most capable warriors – your Morini grandfather must be proud, as he watches from the Land of Youth.'

Colleos smiled with a little bow.

I left to go and check on Machan one last time before we left and was pleased, on my way back, to see Vedica out with one of the head man's children, drawing in the last patch of snow with a stick. She was humouring the smaller girl with good heart but, sadly, I think that was all it was.

O Maponos, please take care of this one. All the childhood joy has melted from her.

Vedica and the girl were looking up at me, curious as robins. 'Are you all right, King Caratacos?'

I shook myself from my sad thoughts. 'We leave today, Princess. I just want to wish you well.'

Vedica smiled, with her mouth at least. 'We leave today as well, if the weather holds. North to mother's kin.'

'Among northern Cornovi?'

'No, the northern Brigantes – mother's sister married there.'

It was good to hear they had living kin to turn to, but I didn't envy them the journey. I had never been to Brigantes territory and knew little to nothing of the people. It was a land vast, damp and cold, my former sister-in-law used to say. Her grandfather had fled south like a bird one year to ply his trade among the Trinovantes and never went back.

'The Gods go with you then.'

'You too, King Caratacos. Thank you for saving mother.'

We bowed a little to each other and left it at that.

I came back into the house to find Nes and Livia eating breakfast in ice-bound silence.

'Everything all right?' I asked.

'Yes,' came the reply. United, terse, and unconvincing.

I crossed the house and sat with Kynbel. He was scraping the last of the porridge from his bowl with his left hand and even this simple task looked awkward, for him.

'How's your hand feeling this morning?'

His mouth was full so he pulled back the bandage and showed me. The stitches looked sore, but not inflamed, and his eyes were bright enough.

'Not bad,' I said. 'Are you sure you're up to riding? You'll have to have your right arm in a sling.'

'I'll be fine.' He put down the bowl and pulled on his shoes with his left hand. 'After what I've been through the last few days it'll all be sunshine and honey.'

The weather held, but we were still bone-cold and sore in our seats by the time we reached our overnight camp, even Kynbel, for all his words. I helped him down from his horse and got him inside straight away. Nes lit a fire and unpacked some food to warm up while I went back out to bar the gate behind us and felt the first few spits of sleet. *Thank you Lugos for holding back until now.* I hoped Dran, Colleos and Tarn were safe and warm, somewhere, if they hadn't made it to our lines yet. I asked Ambix to see to the horses while I went back inside to check on my nephew's wound.

'Can I get us some more fire wood?' Livia was asking my wife, as I walked back in.

'Of course,' Nes replied. 'You don't need to ask.'

Such innocent words, but dripping with poison. I sighed.

'Be kind,' I said, quietly, as soon as Liv had left the hut, and my wife's eyes flared.

'*Me?* Am I not being kind?'

'You are, outwardly, but every muscle of your face is saying how much it costs you.'

'How can you say such a thing? I've been your loyal wife all these years – you know how Adminios treated me – '

'I do, and I have done no such thing. You *know* that.'

She bit her lip, tears welling and glinting in the gloom. 'You cannot expect me to like it. Not when she is sharing our house – it's like putting two bears in a cave.'

'I don't expect you to like each other – and she won't be sharing our house once we're home, I can tell you that right now – but she has done good work and she should be treated kindly. That's all I ask.'

'How am *I* the villain in this?'

'You are the one with all the power – you are a born princess of the Iceni, a queen of the Catuvellauni, my beloved wife, mother of my child . . . look at the state of her. Who knows whether her face will ever heal? She hasn't a handful of beans to her name. You have power she'll never have.'

Nes sniffed and dried her eyes upon her sleeve before Livia, and Ambix, came into the house, and we managed to have a civil, if quiet, supper. The next morning, whilst the others busied themselves getting ready for the journey, I took the chance for a private talk with Kynbel.

'Did you hear any of that, yesterday?'

He knew what I meant without further prompting – never a good sign. 'I won't say anything to Livia, or the others, or back in Siluria,' he said.

'Thank you. I'm not expecting this meeting with the Deceangli to be easy and, well, one fight at a time, you know.'

'Wasn't the first man you ever killed a Deceangli?'

'Yes.'

Kynbel snorted a laugh. 'Do they know that?'

'Oh I expect so. But if an alliance *is* made it will be with King Maros, and the Silures, not with me and mine, as such, so they won't lose face.'

'Is Maros really king, whilst you are there?' Kynbel asked, and he kept his tone soft, but I felt the blood rush to my face.

'He is. I am a king in name only – every morsel of food we eat comes from Silures land.'

Kynbel tipped his head to one side. 'That's true, but every warrior looks to you as leader – they have for years. Catuvellaunos said as much when he was with us, last Lughnasa, and Maros was too wine-addled to stan-'

'Enough,' I snapped. 'He is my friend, and we are their guests, we must never forget that.'

'It's hard to forget,' Kynbel scoffed, 'when he can't keep his hands off Rhian.'

I raised my eyebrows. 'Who the wounded party is in that scrap is not entirely clear, I'd say.'

Kynbel shrugged. 'He'd had years to marry her, if he'd wanted.'

'So have you.'

I'd kept it gentle, but my nephew went quiet, fiddling with the edge of his bandage.

'Would you want that?' he said, at last. 'She isn't royal.'

'She is not, and you are my heir, given my daughter isn't even four summers old, but I would support you marrying for love if it *was* love.' I sighed. 'All the spirit has gone from her, like a blown dandelion. I think you should do right by her, Kynbel. If you aren't going to marry her then you need to be honest about it, or you will drive the poor girl mad.'

He just kept quiet, and when the others came back in we set off for home.

Alwona was there to meet us at the gate when we rode up to the Silures eastern stronghold that afternoon. She had been at the top, our own little girl on her hip, smiling and waving as we rode nearer, and the panic must have been rising with our every step closer once she realised her husband and son were missing.

'They're alive, they're both alive,' were my first words. I slipped from Buanedd's back to face her while my wife gathered up our Gladsia. 'Machan is wounded, but recovering, and Hedros is looking after him.' Alwona cried out, covering her face with her hands, her three younger sons all looking up at me like chicks in a nest. I hugged their mother round her shoulders. 'Come, let us sit, I will tell you everything that has happened.'

Most of the women were outside, scrubbing down their household things in the sunshine ready for Imbolc morn, so all eyes were on me in moments. I saw Colleos's wife, and her uncle, our harper, waiting to speak with me next. Eirian and her daughter waved at me from their threshold, reassured by my smile that all was well with Dran. Rhian, too, was hanging back, until she fell upon Kynbel like snow sliding from a roof with a single nod from him. I couldn't see Maros or his mother anywhere.

A fire had been built with logs placed round it for the festival so I sat Alwona and myself down there and accepted that everyone else would gather about us. Alwona and her boys were calm enough once they'd heard all. I put it into the most reassuring words I dared to, without lying.

'If you wish to travel to the Ordovici fort, to be with him, then I'll arrange it,' I said, still gripping Alwona's hand. 'I will be riding to our warriors myself, once the Imbolc parley is over, so I can take you that way.'

Machan's wife nodded, wiping her nose. 'Thank you, sire.'

My young namesake, Caradoc Hare-lip, had been hanging on her skirt but now tugged at the hem of my cloak. 'Can Gla-Gla stay with us?' he asked.

Alwona gave him a light tap. 'You say *King* Caradoc, or sire, when you speak to the king,' she admonished and the boy screwed up his face. He was only a few moons older than my daughter and still chubby like a ripe fruit. The scar where I had stitched his lip stood out white against the pink.

'If only so people do not mistake us for each other,' I said, and it brought a smile to his mother's tear-streaked face.

'Where is King Maros?' I asked Alwona, softly, so the others did not hear.

'Sleeping it off,' she whispered back. 'He had a bad night, my king.'

'And Queen Mathona?'

'She has gone in his stead to meet the Deceangli at the border fort – we thought they might be here, by now, given the weather has improved.'

I looked up at the bright midday sky. 'Well it isn't Imbolc, yet.'

'But wasn't their druid supposed to arrive yesterday, with Siluri? That's what Queen Mathona said, sire, before she dashed off.'

I couldn't imagine Mathona dashing anywhere, at her age, but I could well imagine her panic. A trickle of concern began its slow drip in the back of my own mind.

It was getting dark by the time I got to our own house and could be alone with Nes and our daughter. Gladsia was asleep, curled up on the end of our bed with her chin resting on the cloth fox, so I just kissed her on the forehead without disturbing her. She smelled of wool and soap.

'They definitely aren't turning up tonight, are they, the Deceangli?' Nesica asked. She had a fresh pan of water on to warm and the soap block still out and was already down to nowt but her linen shift.

I shook my head. 'No, we'll have a better feast without them, no doubt.' I started stripping off too.

Nes raised her eyebrows, stifling a laugh. 'No doubt.'

By the time we joined the feast the spit roast sheep was down to its bones. I left Nes to finish getting dressed and returned to the fireside logs to sit. A Siluri servant brought me a cup of beer and a dish of food but there was still no sign of Maros. I wondered if I should go to him, caught between concern and saving him face. I noticed the musicians had set themselves up on the opposite side of the yard to the great house, so the dancing was also away from where he slept, and didn't know if that was as he had ordered or just their good sense.

I wasn't sat on my own for long – within three breaths Dran's wife was on her way over. Eirian beamed, flopped down beside me and slapped me on the leg. Her braid-end dunked in her beer but it just made her laugh.

'I've sorted your problem!' she declared, and I couldn't help but smile.

'Which one is that?'

Eirian leaned closer. '*Camulora.* Nesica said she needed somewhere to live, so she's in with me. That Gaul too – I've got room, while Dran's away.' She narrowed her eyes in mock aggression. 'Away *again.*'

'Not for long.' I smiled. 'Thank you for helping Nes and me.'

She squeezed my hand. We both turned towards the great house as Maros appeared at the doorway like a ghost. I waved to him, trying to force cheer back onto my face, but in truth disappointment and concern soaking within me like a steady fall of rain. All the musicians and dancers started up again as he walked over to me but there had been a brief pause and he must have noticed it. Eirian's eyes met mine.

'I'll go and have a dance then,' she said with a wink and headed towards the music, bowing – briefly – to the Silures prince as she got up.

Maros sat down beside me with a wan smile. He was neat and combed, dressed in his brightest, but nevertheless he seemed diminished, like the sheep on its spit. I stopped myself from sighing just in time. A servant approached him with a cup of beer and I took my chance.

'A crock of cool water and a clean cup too, please,' I asked. 'The salt meat makes me thirst.'

The boy bowed and went, Maros waiting to speak until he was out of earshot. '*You* can get away with drinking water at a feast,' he said, 'but I was never a druid.'

'You are among your friends and kin, Maros, no-one will grudge you water.'

Nor a little self-control, I thought, but did not voice it.

Maros was peering at me, not quite frowning, but concerned. 'You are not wearing your torque,' he said at last, and now I felt embarrassed – it had been his gift to me when I was just shy of sixteen summers old.

'The Romans took it from us, when we rescued Kynbel. I'm sorry, my friend.'

He waved it away, whatever he felt in reality. We both turned to look as the door to my own house opened and Nesica stepped out. She was wearing her best madder-red dress, with a woad-blue cloak over it to set off her copper-coloured hair, and her torque and bracelets glinted in the firelight. I must admit my breath caught in my throat.

'Twelve years married and you still think her beautiful,' Maros said, under his breath. I thought I sensed envy rather than scorn in his voice but I still felt uncomfortable.

'You will be wed yourself before this moon is out, if all goes well with the Deceangli.'

Gods forgive me for swift said promises.

'Yes,' he said, his voice loaded with sadness, 'and maybe this one will outlive me.'

Nes was here so I got up and took her hand. 'Blessed Imbolc-eve,' she wished me, with a kiss, and then wished the same to Maros. He found it within him to smile back.

We all strolled over to the dancers and I was cajoled into joining in, though I have no skill at it. I saw Kynbel was steering clear, given his hand must still hurt like fire, but at least he was tapping his foot. Livia, too, seemed to sway a little as she grasped her cup, but with her bruises and split lip actual dancing would have been unwise. I made sure I did not talk with her, and stayed by my wife's side.

'It's all right,' Nes said to me as the night wore on. 'I feel better now we're home and Gladsia is with us. You don't have to avoid her all night just to stay the right side of me.'

'Didn't you believe me when I said you looked beautiful?'

Nes gave me a look from under her brows.

'You looked even better naked,' I whispered, and she laughed into her cup.

'Enough!' she sniggered.

We resolved to wander over to Livia for a chat but Ambix got to her first, handing her a plate of meat. 'It will help you heal,' we overheard him say to her, and my wife and I exchanged a look.

'Perhaps they are becoming fond of each other?' Nes whispered to me.

'Let's see. I would encourage it, if so, but let's get Maros settled, and the alliance with the Deceangli forged at last, before all else.'

Nesica nodded, squeezing my hand. We went back to the fireside as Nes had been asked to pour the milk libation at midnight, given Mathona's absence and Maros being, as yet, without a queen. She had just poured the first drop when we heard a clatter of horses at the gate.

Mathona rode in, red-faced and sweat-streaked, flanked by guards and two of her wide-eyed daughters.

'They're not coming,' she wheezed. 'The Deceangli – they've refused to come any further.'

Thirteen The Spider of the Deceangli

Mathona slipped from her pony with a visible wince as her swollen ankles met the ground but it didn't stop her speaking. 'I tried and tried to talk them round – I was as nice as I possibly could be to that shrivelled old wreck of a king – but I was getting *nowhere*. I didn't feel safe, Caradoc.' She shook her head, clutching at my cloak and looking up to me. 'I couldn't stay there with them a moment longer – but that journey! I think we heard every wolf howling from here to Eire, and the icy wind on the hills cut through us. Not safe! In my own land! That king is like a spider!'

'Mathona – slow down. Come, sit by the fire.' I put my arm about her shoulders and steered her towards the fireside logs, nodding to a servant as we went. He brought her a cup of wine and she swigged it back in one gulp. 'Come, sit, tell me what has gone wrong.'

Mathona pushed the damp curls back from her forehead and downed another cupful, shaking her head and talking all the while. 'They said you were working with the Ordovici, Caradoc – their sworn enemies. Eburos swore never to feast with an Ordovici nor any friend to an Ordovici, as long as he lives, that's what he said.'

'Well, I have Ordovici kin, that's no secret. He knew that when this council was called.'

Mathona nodded. 'But they've lost so much land to them . . . years and years of battle and strife and now you are seeking *alliance* with them . . .'

I threw up my hands. 'If Arthewin and I were not so cold with each other there would have been alliance long ago, Eburos must know it. It cannot just be that.'

Mathona flicked a glance at her son, the potential groom, still washed-out and bleak of face from too much wine the night before, but did not voice whatever might have been in her mind. Her daughter stepped in. 'It seems they've heard of the death of Uricon too, at Roman hands, and that rattled them – much as they hated each other.'

Nesica frowned. 'What happened with the Cornovi is *more* of a reason to ally with us, not less.'

Mathona's daughter shrugged. 'I know, but Eburos might want to buy himself a peace-pact with the Romans, to save their skins – his grand-daughter said as much, in an unguarded moment.'

A fist closed over my stomach. *No!* A gasp rippled around all of us.

'I cannot allow that,' I said, keeping my voice calm and level. 'If Eburos will not ally with us then I cannot allow his land to be a bridge to us in the north west.'

'But what shall we do?' Nes asked. 'Our warriors are already fighting in the old Cornovi lands.'

Indeed.

'We won't go to war with them, not unless we have to.' I stood up, addressing everyone there, Silures and Catuvellauni. 'We leave for their camp in the morning – if they will not come to us, we will go to them.'

With the main body of my warriors fighting the Roman front line it was an odd procession that left the Silures stronghold that morning. Mathona had taken some convincing but was now dressed in her finest and riding ahead of her son. Maros was straight of back and free of trembling, against all prediction. It was probably thanks to a breakfast of wine so I didn't hold much comfort from it, but still, at least he was on his horse. We were all dressed in as much colour and gold as we could muster and we must have been a merry sight for a morning in early spring, once the dawn mist burned away, for the peasants who came to the path side to bow to us. I made sure we brought the bag of Roman coins we'd captured in the ambush days ago and had Nes and Eirian throw them in handfuls to the cheering children with cries of 'Blessed Imbolc!' whenever we went past a homestead. The biting wind shook the catkins from the coppices, and my own limbs protested at being on horseback again so soon, but I kept up a sunny smile, and I pressed the others to do the same.

I'd sent two riders ahead to spread news of our arrival and Branadain, Maros's twin, met us on the path before the fort. Her dark hair was pulled back into one long braid and what with her sheen-less black druid robes she looked stark as a raven amid the Imbolc-morn buds and sunshine. An acolyte held her colt's bridal for her, under an alder by the riverside, but apart from this girl Brana was alone.

'Greetings, King Caradoc, our guards will be glad to see you,' she said, with a knowing smile. She eased her mother down from her horse and hugged her, then her brother and sisters, before grasping my arm in greeting.

'It's good to see you too. Is Siluri still with our guests?'

Brana laughed, a short bark of a laugh. 'Oh yes, they're still here. Siluri is becoming more impatient by the day. She isn't well, and she wants rid of them.'

Well, I could see her point, and of all the druids of Ynys Mon she was not the one I would have hand-picked for this council, given a choice – but she was still Siluri, while breath was still in her.

Branadain and the acolyte got back on their horses and we rode the rest of the way up the river valley. It took me a while to speak to Brana alone.

'Your brother is sick with too much wine,' I said, and she nodded. 'If his life is to be saved then he must break the cycle.'

She glanced over her shoulder to check he was not near. 'I know – I have an idea.'

'Go on.'

'There is a cave near here, with two mouths. Siluri spent a whole summer here once when the chaos at home got too much – and when you first met her.' I'd heard from Mathona, years ago, that that's what they'd done with Siluri, after Gwyfina and I got away, but I'd never seen the place. 'She said it has an ancient power, and is sacred to the Gods. There is a ritual we could do, to have him reborn, and we could use this cave.'

To be honest I was not convinced. 'Would it work quickly enough, do you think, to save this council with Eburos? We need this alliance.'

'Only you, I think, are going to be able to save it. He loves his grand-daughter, that I don't doubt. That's all you can use.'

Maros must have seen us talking together and was trotting closer, so I asked after Catuvellaunos, once he was in earshot, to change the subject.

'He is well, for such an elder,' Branadain replied with a smile. 'He travels little now, but will gladly see you at Mon if you can visit again. Your nephew, too.'

'How does Tegwyn fare?'

Brana laughed. 'Tegwyn learns so fast the dawn's lessons cannot come soon enough for him. He knows all the stars, all the prayers, as if his mind was a cauldron to be filled.'

I turned to Maros with a smile. 'Tegwyn is a much better acolyte than I was.'

His gaze had wandered elsewhere and he didn't seem to hear me.

There was a great cheer as we turned a bend and the Silures guards on the palisade saw us, and another from the guards and the people as we rode through the gates. The Deceangli warriors scattered among them, however, were quiet. I saw a few furtive glances pass between them.

'Never let any of them get out of sight,' I said to the nearest of my guard. 'Be friendly, but never let them feel alone.'

'Yes sire.'

I had my first sight of the Deceangli king as we rode into the yard. He was standing with a young woman, presumably his grand-daughter, in the doorway of the largest house. She was leaning on him and he on her, like two storm blown trees. I slipped down from Buanedd's back and strode forward, my hand extended in greeting, smiling all the while.

'King Eburos, welcome!'

He still looked wary, peering at me from beneath his tufts of white hair and regal circlet, but he did take my hand and he did force out a smile.

'King Caradoc, son of Cunobelin, greetings.' He looked to the girl by his side. 'This is my grand-daughter, Blodau, daughter of my youngest son.'

We bowed a nod to each other and I smiled but the girl did not respond. She looked to be about seventeen years old, lank and thin like a wet string. She was shivering, weighed down by her heavy silver torques, and closed in on herself like the tree buds. From the scabs around her nose it looked as if she'd suffered a bad head cold in the last days.

'Princess, welcome,' I said. 'Come, let us sit in the warm.'

I threw a quick glance at Maros as we walked inside. He looked bleak.

Serving women were flapping round Mathona and soon we had a fine meal set before us. I made sure, in as subtle a way as I could, that Maros and Blodau were near each other, but not a word passed between them that afternoon, as I remember.

I saw Branadain talking with Siluri at the shadowed edge of the house and took my chance.

'King Eburos,' I said to him, in a low voice, by my side. 'I shall ride to a sacred cave near here this evening, to make an offering to Cernunnos. Might you be willing to come with me, so we can talk alone?'

The old man gave me a long look. 'I'll not leave my grand-daughter without guards.'

'The guards can all stay here. I swear, on all that I love best, I mean you no harm.'

We left while there was still daylight left, but not much. A mist had started to settle on the Gwy and the bony trees were casting long shadows. Branadain rode ahead to show us the route and Eburos and I both brought two guards each, riding just far enough behind us that we couldn't be overheard.

'I am sad that your quarrel with the Ordovici might draw a halt to the hand-fasting,' I said. 'It is I who has kin among the Ordovici, not Maros.'

Eburos raised his eyebrows. 'Aye, well, I know that, but you are king in all but name, and he is sick with drink and has bedded half the women in the west. I'm old but I'm not blind.'

I sighed. 'He is a good man, nonetheless.' *Gods help me – can I say nothing else in defence of a friend?* 'And none of those women were unwilling – which is more than can be said of some men of power. '

The eyebrows retreated even further towards his hairline. 'If your daughter was old enough to wed would you want a husband for her like that?'

I hesitated to answer, I couldn't help it, and he threw up his hands.

'Given the danger we all face I would see her in a safe home, at least, away from threat,' I said at last.

He looked down at his mare's reins. 'You mean the danger from Rome, but I have more to resent my neighbours for. I won't ally with kin of the Ordovici any more than I would have done with Uricon when he was alive.'

'The empire *uses* this division among us. If we all insist on keeping the old hatreds alive then Rome can pick off each people, one by one, just like they did in Gaul.'

'It's easy for you to say, when you have Ordovici blood and not a drop of my people's.'

'My mother was Ordovici, but she died when I was ten summers old. I would ally with Arthewin's sons, if I could, I don't deny it, but there's no love lost between Arthewin and me, not even the kinship a cousin might expect. If your alliance is with the Silures then your people will understand, I think.'

He snorted with derision at that.

'You can't twist it any other way with your silvern words. I'd just as soon she marry a pig – and that's an end to it.'

We'd reached the cave Branadain had told me of. It did indeed have two openings but I must admit the dividing pillar of stone, to me, gave it the look of a nose, a giant stone nose with two nostrils at its base. Brana must have caught the old man's bitter words as she dismounted but we both chose to weather it. She went into the left side 'nostril' and lit a wax-dipped torch with an ember she'd brought in a box. As the flame flared a glow fell on the wooden idol sat inside and I felt a shiver run up my spine.

'Do you have all you need?' Branadain asked me.

'Yes.'

'Then I shall leave you to pray.'

She disappeared off into the trees.

Eburos was looking wary now. I handed him the torch as I knelt and I saw his hand was trembling. The skin on his hands was mottled like a kestrel's back.

'Our guards have resigned themselves to a long wait,' I laughed, seeing them splayed out under an oak, sharing round a huge cheese bannock. 'I won't be long, I promise. It's just I always make an offering to Cernunnos at about this time of year, to give thanks for the life of my daughter.'

'She is sick?'

'No, not sick, thank the Gods, but her elder brother died as a babe and we watch her all the time,' I said, with a sigh. 'She was a long, long time coming to us.'

I smiled up at him and it was the first time I remembered him smiling with any genuine warmth back. 'My Blodau,' he said, 'she is all I have left.'

'You said she is the daughter of your younger son?'

He nodded. 'I had four sons. One was taken by a brain-fever in his seventh winter, the other three all died in battle with those dogs, both east and west. The youngest died of his wounds after fifteen days of screaming and suffering.'

His eyes glistened. 'I cannot ally with them, the spirits won't let me.'

'Then don't ally with them. Ally with me.'

I poured the flask of wine I'd brought with me over the pebbles at the idol's base.

Fourteen On the hunt

Winter returned for a few days, hard and bitter, but when the weather warmed again and Mathona rode south she had a new young woman to shelter beneath her wings. I'd told Mathona to give Blodau plenty of red meat and nettle soup to get some colour in her cheeks and flesh on her skeleton. Only half the dowry of lead and silver came with her, as agreed. More important was that Eburos turned north with the promise not to make a pact of any kind with Rome. To be honest I could have let them keep all the dowry, for the sake of that, but face had to be saved.

Maros himself stayed at the border fort with Siluri and his sister. I didn't envy him days and nights of sweating the wine from his blood with two druids in a cave, and whether the cure would work or not I couldn't know, but I'd sworn to try. I think it's possible Maros hated me by this point, if not earlier. I was sick to the heart but it had to be done. I left the place feeling that I'd both gained a friend and lost one.

The wedding was set for midsummer's day.

I turned north, back to my warriors. They now manned a string of forts in the Cornovi hills, having pushed the Roman forces back to the Corieltavi border, and were pretty pleased with themselves. I stopped a day or two with each group and was met with cheers and tales of victory wherever we went. By the time we rode to the last hill-fort I had been so amply feasted by Corbennog on stores stolen back from the legions I'd even gained a little weight.

It was an impressive fort, long and strong like a boar's back; not as striking as Uricon's seat but larger, to my eye. Rocks clustered off to one side, like the fingers of an up-stretched hand. The morning mist had all burned off by the time my party approached and our warriors must have seen us long before we could pick them out. I could hear young Tarn singing from the palisade as we neared, happy as a blue-tit on a branch.

Our Gladsia had been wrapped up against the early spring cold in a sort of sheepskin chrysalis that Nes had made for her, itching to get out all morning, so now we were near I lifted her free and let her ride ahead of me on Buanedd as we went through the gates.

'I ride Dada's horse!' she squealed in delight.

'Yes. Tarn has changed his song to one of a princess and her horse, do you like it?'

'Yes Dada.' She grinned up at me, sunny with her bright new teeth, and my Nes turned to me with such a look of pride and love on her face I have never forgotten it in all my years. Sometimes, I think, the Gods give us perfect moments to preserve forever.

Dran was walking to the gates, all smiles, as we rode in. I gave him a moment while he embraced his own wife and daughter before I greeted him myself.

'Dranis! You have done well – I think we should name this place Caer Dranis if the Cornovi don't already have a name for it.'

He laughed. 'It's already Caer Caradoc. Too late.' Dran nodded towards two smiths who were melting down captured Roman weapons at a great hearth out in the yard. 'The only Cornovi still here are happy enough.'

'Are there any legionaries left hereabouts?'

Dran shrugged. 'Doesn't look like it. We never found the body of that one you knew, but he must be long gone.'

'Saturninus?'

'If they're still in Uricon's fort then they've kept well quiet. Colleos has it under siege.'

'And there's no smoke? No movement?'

Tarn swung down from the walkway, shaking his head. 'No my king. Colleos has been watching day and night but there's nothing. I took him a message yesterday, sire.'

Dran turned to me again with another shrug and a crooked smile. 'He's right.'

'How many days has Colleos had it under siege?'

Five, it turned out. A drip of suspicion fell in my mind. I think I could keep quiet and still for five days, eat cold food and wait it out, if I had stores enough and dozens of angry Britons waiting like wolves.

We resolved to go and 'relieve' Colleos the next morning.

It wasn't a long way to Uricon's seat from 'Caer Caradoc' so I left Nes and Gladsia to get used to yet another new hut and took just Dran and a few warriors with me. We reached Colleos by early afternoon. He and his men were spread around the fort, watching and waiting.

'So, my king. Back again,' Colleos greeted me. He had a nick across the bridge of his once broken nose that rather gave him the stern look of an eagle. Apart from that he seemed fine.

'Any change?'

Colleos pursed his lips as he looked up at the palisade. 'I thought I saw someone, just before noon – but maybe I imagined it.'

'I doubt that. What did you see?'

'I thought I saw a pair of eyes looking back at me, up there,' he pointed to a rock outcrop up to the left, behind the palisade, 'but they were gone in the next blink. It was probably nothing.' He shook his head. 'I'm sorry, sire – I feel a fool. I've let them get past me.'

I looked to one of the Cornovi warriors who had joined forces with us. 'What's in that area of the fort? Is it another granary?'

'No, sire – it's a rock pool. A sacred well that never runs dry.'

I turned back to Colleos. 'You're no fool – they're still in there. I'd bet on it. They wait for us to give up.'

Dran was staring at the high ramparts and stout fence. 'I could build a ballista, like I did before, if I get enough stuff. Let's see how they like it.'

Colleos snapped round, his eyes gleaming. 'We don't need to wait. We captured one, yesterday.'

It didn't take us that long to get it working. What we lacked were the 'bolts', a sort of spear head, that are its intended missile, but Dran was able to jemmy it to take other things. I must admit we had fun, grown men though we were, but once we'd got tired of loading it up with rocks and horse shit to be fair we'd also got the distance and angle down pat. Still no-one had come to the ramparts. I turned back to the Cornovi warrior who had once lived here.

'Are there any of your people still there, do you think? I saw none apart from your queen when we were in there.'

He shook his head. 'None left alive.'

'Then we shall use fire next.'

The recent snow and sleet meant the thatch roofs were well soaked and we didn't see any immediate flames. A curl of smoke started to drift upwards so we managed to hit something flammable but it didn't come to much. All the same the renewed bombardment did its work – we saw hands raised behind the palisade. Three pairs of hands.

I told Dran to stop the ballista.

'All right. Come on out!'

A Roman helmet appeared above the fence. 'You come in!'

Did they think I had all the wit of a newborn? 'No – we're not coming into arrow range. You come out. Or we start again.'

There was a pause. I supposed they were discussing it, but after a little while with no response I asked Dran and Colleos to start cranking the ballista. It was a loud, brutal thing amongst the gently shivering trees and they must have heard it even if they didn't have a spyhole somewhere.

'All right, all right, we'll come out,' one yelled down at us.

This time the man who spoke stood up so we saw his full head and shoulders – it wasn't Saturninus.

'Show your faces! All of you!'

The three men took off their helmets. They were a way off but even so I was sure none were Saturninus. Two looked quite young.

'Where is the tribune? The one called Saturninus?'

They hesitated, looking to each other, and then the eldest spoke again. 'Dead! Days ago!'

Colleos raised an eyebrow. 'I don't believe them, sire.'

'No. Me neither.' I got some rope from Dran's supplies to tie them up with. 'We'll get them down to the south-west gate, tie them, then have a good look round. Swords and shields, everyone.'

The Romans took their time coming down to the gate.

'Why are they taking so long, sire?' Tarn whispered.

'Fear, maybe. Or they could be setting some sort of trap – stay sharp.'

Once the gate groaned open Dran had all the weapons from them in a few blinks and tied their bonds tight. All the same we passed into the fort wary as deer. Nothing was moving, not so much as a dog. The druid house we burned on our last visit was now a patch of blackened house poles. The other houses were as they had been before, though now strewn with rocks and horse dung. There was nowhere a large force could be lying in wait for us . . . unless they'd started burrowing underground.

'Uricon has gone,' Dran remarked, his tone hushed.

I looked over the yard and saw he was right. The beams were still there but the Cornovi king and his son had been taken down.

'Do you think they buried them, sire?' Tarn asked.

'Maybe. They'd have been scared about disease, especially when the siege started.'

Gods speed them to the Land of Youth.

A piece of firewood falling from a log pile made us all jump, and I thought I spied a smirk flash across the older Roman's face.

'Lash them to the beam while we search the houses,' I ordered. 'Tarn – you keep an eye on them.'

Two of the captives were still scowling back at us as we tied them, trying to tough it out, but one of the younger ones had gone white as birch bark.

Malice is beneath you, I remembered.

'Calm,' I said to him, in Latin. 'You'll be treated as a soldier, not a piece of meat. Not by me.'

We started on the left. Colleos kicked open the door of the first house and we peered into the gloom.

Nothing. Quiet enough for ghosts.

Colleos guarded the door way while Dran and I went in. It took a moment for my eyes to adjust. This one had been used by Romans, recently. There was the smell of something fishy in a pot near the door, and a tunic was drying on hooks near the hearth. I leant down and felt the hearth stones: cold.

Dran had been checking behind a striped drape beside the bed with the flat of his sword.

'There's no-one here,' he said.

'No, let's go to the next.'

This was a smaller hut, dark and cold – colder than outside. I felt a shiver run up my spine. There was a smell of something rotting, thick and heavy like meat left in the sun. I heard a scratching on a shelf full of cups and span round to it, my sword raised.

'Just a mouse,' I said to Dran, embarrassed, but my heart was pounding. I felt a strange softness beneath my feet and shuffled backwards. There was a small cloth doll with woollen braids, eyes looking up, the dirt from my foot now across its face. A little weld-yellow cloak made from cloth scrap was stitched about its shoulders.

Dran's eyes and mine met. He lifted the toy from the floor and put it up on the shelf.

'Let's go to the next,' he said.

I was about to say yes, but the sudden blasting of a carnyx outside the fort cut me off. Tarn was yelling.

'Sire! They are getting away! Sire!'

We shot from the house – and the three Romans were still there, strung up like goods for market.

'Tarn?'

'Not them – the others!'

Fifteen Revenge

'The east side!' a Cornovi warrior was yelling as he scrambled towards us. 'Down the east side!'

We raced to the palisade. There was only one Roman to be seen, curled up and screaming, clutching at his ankle. A dozen Cornovi warriors had fallen on him like crows and put a spear through his chest before I could even think of mercy.

'How many were there?!' I shouted down.

Six came the answer, including this one.

'They will have scattered, just like we did,' I said. 'Dran, you take ten men and aim north-east, Colleos you do the same but veer south-east. I'll go due east.' I turned back to young Tarn and the Cornovi who'd warned us. 'Hold this position and guard the prisoners – mind that the others could double back.'

'Do we take our horses, my king?' Colleos asked.

I looked out upon the rock-strewn landscape and thick woods that lay east. 'No, let's go on foot. Quickly now.'

I glanced at the face of the speared Roman as I sped past him – it wasn't Saturninus.

'Blast a horn each time you've found one!' I ordered, before the others were out of sight. 'Three times for trouble!'

We plunged into the trees. The daylight was on the wane. Everything looked grey.

'Sire, look!' It was Rhyddo, Eirian's son from before her marriage, who called for me. I saw where he pointed. Beside a branch-shaded brook, hidden behind a rock, was a balled-up mail shirt as the Roman soldiers wear.

'And another,' I said, pushing back some hazel branches with my shield. This one was the 'lorica segmentata' type, though. 'They are shedding anything that could catch the light. Careful.'

We padded on through the trees, swift but taut as harp strings. The shadows were growing deeper. As we got further and further from the fort I realised how ill-prepared we were: no food, no water, no dogs . . . weapons and men, enough, but still . . . I'd thought we'd find them sooner than this. *Cernunnos, Camulos, Teutates, Epona, help us find them quickly, o Gods.*

As soon as I completed my prayer we all heard a horn blast to the north. 'Four now,' I whispered. 'Keep sharp.'

Another call of the horn rang out just as night fell, this time from the south. That was the last we heard from our comrades as we continued east. A whole night and day we searched the bleak Cornovi forest. Nothing.

As another day waned it was getting colder and we'd picked up speed, but the failing light slowed us down a little. The ash trees that seemed to have surrounded us forever were thinning out, now, to reveal a swathe of muddy pasture-land.

'They could have arrows, keep your shields ready,' I warned as we entered the open country. I was over-cautious, perhaps, considering there had been no sign of our quarry since the armour early on, but when we came to the sloping bank of a minor river the moonlight showed us footprints in the silt. Studded footprints that a Roman sandal leaves.

'Could it be a trick, my king?' one of my warriors asked.

'It could.' I had used footprints to mislead, myself, in the past. There was nothing about to hide in, though. The nearest cover was a hut or cow byre so distant I couldn't be sure what it was. 'This time, however, I think not. They are fleeing to their comrades as fast as they can.'

We covered the ground between us and the cow byre in a few breaths and checked it for anyone hiding – nothing, only cows. The wind was picking up and clouds were gathering across the face of the moon making it darker by the moment. We had come a long way, and fast, and we were all weary as mules.

'Let's stop here a short while,' I said. 'I'll keep watch.'

Rhyddo and the others collapsed with gratitude into the straw, oblivious to the muck. The cows were lowing at our intrusion so I talked to them in a soft voice until they'd settled again. Outside the night was calm. I could feel the cold air hitting the skin inside my nose and smell the earth. Once the cows quieted I heard the piercing screech of an owl.

Protect us Cernunnos. Help us find the man who tortured my kin.

When it was my turn to rest I must admit I sank to the straw as grateful and blind to the smell as my men had been. The next thing I knew my shoulder was being shaken.

'Sire, sire.' I couldn't see him but it was young Rhyddo's voice. 'Someone approaches.'

We crept to the doorway. The clouds had drifted away on the cold breeze and now, as our eyes adjusted, I could see a human figure by the starlight.

'He looks small,' I whispered.

'Mam says all Romans are small,' Rhyddo whispered back, and I had to stifle a laugh.

I picked up my shield and double-checked my sword was in its place. 'Wake up!' I hissed at my men. 'Quiet, now.'

Despite our stealth the figure had stopped dead about a stone's throw from the byre. He was holding a spear, his head cocked as if sniffing the air.

I could get him, from here. Easy. I looked to my comrades for a spear – then hesitated.

No, don't.

The figure took a step forward towards the byre.

'Hold him!' I shouted.

All eleven of us circled him in a matter of a few strides. As he leapt back the 'spear' fell to the floor and I snatched it up. It was just an ash stake whittled to a point at one end. Rhyddo had the prisoner in a tight grip from behind, his left hand clamped over the mouth. I pulled the captive's cloak hood down and as the starlight revealed his face I thanked whatever God had stayed my hand.

This was no 'he' at all, let alone my old enemy.

'Let her go,' I said to Rhyddo, and he dropped her so fast she stumbled. A girl in man's clothes stood before us, perhaps fifteen or sixteen years old, masking her terror with gritted teeth.

'What are you doing out here all alone?' I demanded. 'We might have killed you!'

'I was only checkin' on me cows!' she shrieked back, and my men couldn't help but smirk at her lack of respect. To be fair she can't have known who I was, at night, without a torque, and no doubt stinking of cow shit.

'Where is your father?' I asked, in a gentler tone, and the scowl slipped.

'Father and grandpa are both dead. In the battle.'

'And mother?'

'Mother only 'ad my baby brother this morning.' She iped her nose on her sleeve and the scowl came back tenfold. 'If you're stealin' our cows then just take 'em then – I can't stop you and we're gonna bloody starve any way.'

I sighed. 'We are not stealing your cows. I am King Caratacos, of the Catuvellauni, and we track two or more Romans who have fled this way. Have you seen anyone, apart from us?'

She shook her head, wide-eyed now. 'I heard feet – jus' before nightfall. Running alongside our pig pen like giant rats.'

'Heading east?'

She nodded.

I exchanged a look with my people. 'The light is better now, we must continue.' Everyone assented, dog-tired as they were. I turned back to the girl. 'How is your mother doing?'

'She doesn't 'ave birth-fever, but she's weak. She lost blood.'

Gods guide me. I wanted to help her but it sounded like we'd lost enough time as it was. My gaze settled on young Rhyddo. He'd turned into a good warrior, with training, but he was a servant and bond-woman's son long before he'd been marriage-kin to royalty. He could herd cows and chop firewood, for sure, and he'd had a baby sister to help take care of not so long ago. 'Rhyddo, go with her and help them, as well as you can. Once mother and child are strong enough bring them all to safety behind our lines.'

'Yes sire.'

We raced on, east, across the flat pasture. The moon and stars showed the way. I would have given my own weight in gold for some clean water. Every muscle burned like a Beltane fire. Even my lungs were hurting. I saw one of my men pull up, clutching at his abdomen.

No! We must not give up!

I ran on.

'Sire! I see them!'

I saw where my warrior pointed. He was right – there were two figures running ahead of us. Their pale tunics glowed like ghosts in the moonlight. I saw one stumble and the other dragged him to his feet.

'Come on – we're gaining on them!'

There was a strip of grey on the horizon. I could smell water on the dawn breeze. I knew this could be the river that marks the border.

'Come on!' I yelled.

We *must not* let them get to the Corieltavi lands – but it wasn't far now. As the light grew stronger I could see buildings, on both sides of the river, and maybe a bridge.

The pale figures had disappeared.

'Keep your shields high,' I whispered, 'and spread out.'

We fanned out behind the wooden shack, silent as foxes, our shields covering us from nose to knee. It didn't look like a soldier's building. I could smell a damp, mud-like scent, coming from everywhere, not just the river. An oven, bigger than a bread oven, sat off to one side. I motioned for one of my men to check it. Nothing. I skirted along the back wall and came to a door. It was swinging ajar in the cool morning breeze.

Do they think I'm a fool?

I gestured to three of my men. 'Stay here,' I whispered. 'Don't let anyone out.'

The rest of us split into two packs. I sent one set to the left, myself and the others went to the right. There were no more doors and soon my feet were in water. I saw that what I had mistaken as a bridge in the grey dawn light was a wooden jetty with a raft tethered to it. Across the water was another raft and jetty then a muddy path led up to a dozen huts and a stockade. The Roman camp, new and bright with fresh wood, stuck up behind it all, stark as a spear through a grave.

If they raise the alarm . . . O Gods.

I slipped on through the water. The front of the building had an awning as if it was a market stall by day. The cloth was thin and pale – if we stood upright by it with the rising sun behind us those within would see us. I motioned for my comrades to keep low. Low, up and under, I gestured. You, stay here. I found a loose edge of the awning and got underneath, my heart pounding. No waiting sword was there to take my head off, thank the Gods. As my eyes adjusted I saw rows of pots and bowls lined up on shelves, a dozen different kinds. The smell of clay was strong. There was no sound but the whistle of the dawn breeze, through the cloth, like the sail of a moored boat. I pulled myself up onto the floor, in silence, keeping my head well down. Ahead was a checked hanging, a back-cloth to the wares.

Round the side, I gestured. My warrior veered to the right, I to the left.

Now I saw him.

Saturninus was crouched down, watching the back door, sword in hand. He whipped round quick as a snake as I stepped out.

'You!'

The other Roman leapt from the side and my warrior took him on. I moved forward, towards Saturninus, but my old foe had too much sense to go out of the door. He lunged towards me, eyes fierce. I had my shield and he did not – his blow glanced off. I slashed out at him but he swerved left, bringing down a board full of pots and throwing one at me. As I ducked he dove forward, trying to get past me to the front. I held my shield up as the pots came flying.

'Coward!' I jeered. 'Will you only fight an unarmed prisoner? Or a woman?'

He just threw another dish. I shielded my eyes as it glanced off and he took the chance to skip back towards the awning. *I can't let him raise the alarm.* I threw myself at him, shield ahead, and we split through the cloth, crashing in the water. I saw his sword stabbing towards me and twisted just in time, swinging my shield into his face, but lost my grip in the force of my swing and it flew off down-river. We swivelled in the water like eels, punching and grasping. I felt his hand grip on my neck – he was trying to push me under.

Help me Tog.

I brought my left fist up, punching him right in the balls.

In his instant of shock I flipped him over and kneed him down to the river level. I held his head beneath the water until the bubbles stopped.

So, Saturninus, does no-one stand against the might of Rome?

Something glinted in the water as I turned him face up and the neck of his tunic flopped open. It was my own torque, now at his throat, along with a blue jewel on a leather thong. I pulled my torque free and put it back where it should be. I was aware now that eyes were upon me: people had emerged from the huts. Half a dozen villagers looked on open-mouthed and meek as sheep as one of my men caught my owl-eyed shield in the river flow and handed it back to me. There was one 'villager' who stood out, black-haired and sharp of feature, wearing nowt but a loin-wrapping and a Roman over-the-head cloak. His gaze was flicking up towards the camp like our tongues seek a sore tooth.

'You – don't even think it.'

My men saw where I was looking and half a dozen spears were levelled at him in an instant. The woman by his side gasped. He looked to her a moment and then raised his hands.

'You will take a message for us, Roman,' I said.

'Thracian,' he said. 'I am Thracian.'

I laughed. 'Then you can take a message to the legions that have enslaved your people as they would do mine.'

His lips thinned. 'All right.'

'Tell them that Caratacos was here. Tell them that any who torture me or mine will be punished. We will not be slaves – not while the Gods are with us.'

I leant down and snapped the thong at Saturninus' neck, the blue jewel coming off into my palm. I threw it as hard as I could into the deepest part of the river. 'To the God Teutates!'

I looked back at these shivering Corieltavi. Beyond their town and lands lay my own lands, to the south, and those of my wife, to the north, the flat wheat-bearing lands of the sun-drenched east. A matter of a day or two's ride. Even the sky felt bigger here. I had not been this near home in more than three years.

Think, I told myself. *You have nine warriors.*

'Let's get out of here before the rest wake up,' I said, in a soft voice, to my own men. 'I have another plan for this moon.'

Sixteen Cracks

I sent Colleos home to Siluria, as the spring warmed, to be with his wife and son for the birth of their youngest. In his place came Leon, and Ambix, and news.

I left Nes to settle Leonidas in with a hot meal while I spoke with Lucius Ambix, first, out by the 'finger' rocks of this Caer Caradoc. He watched me approach with wary eyes.

'Don't worry,' I said, handing over the second cup of hot broth I held. 'I just want as few people as possible to know the task I have for you – for your sake as well as theirs.'

Ambix' dark eyebrows shot up. His red-brown hair had grown out a little in the time that had passed and he looked more Gaul and less Legion, which was just as well. The clothes he wore I knew as old breeks and a tunic of Kynbel's. The cloak, pale purple and yellow check with use of blackberry and weld, looked new.

'My people have been treating you well?'

Ambix smiled. 'Yes. More like a guest than a prisoner.'

I laughed. 'Well that is as it should be for that is what you are. Who gave you the cloak?'

He went a little sheepish. 'The woman who was a spy, Livia – though they all call her Camulora now.'

It crossed my mind to wonder how Liv had got it, given I'd never known her to weave or sew in her life. 'Did she tell you how she used to work for us?'

'Yes.'

'Well, that is what I have in mind for you, if you are still willing.'

'I thought it might be.' We sat upon the nearest decent rock and he looked out upon the setting sun. 'I haven't changed my mind, King Caradoc. Where do you want me to go?'

I took a sip of broth. 'To the Corieltavi lands, first, then on to the Iceni and my own old lands in the east. I need you to talk with the auxiliaries you meet and spread dissent, if you can. If you can also get word from my kin I left behind, and my brothers-in-law in the Iceni, then I would be grateful.'

Ambix looked pretty bleak. 'How am I to pass through all these places without losing my head?'

'You need to be someone who is *expected* to move about, so nobody thinks twice. I was wondering . . . perhaps a storyteller? Can you sing?'

Ambix laughed. 'No. By the Gods no.'

'Fair enough.'

He looked to his feet. 'My grandfather made shoes, back in Gaul – it's been a while, but I think I can still do it. Soldiers' shoes need repairs, often, and I can talk with them while they wait.'

'All right. Come inside now and get some sleep – don't tell anyone the plan. Then in the morning Leon will take you to Uricon's seat to get together all that you need. Leave, alone, from there.' I clapped him on the shoulder. 'Gods protect you, Lucius Ambix. There are none braver than those who spy, I have always thought it.'

He smiled. 'But you think there are spies among the people here, too?'

'I doubt it, but there could be. You'll keep your head longer if you use it.'

We sauntered into the house as if chatting about nothing much and Ambix went straight to bed, pleading an early start. He got a bit of a ribbing from the men for turning in at the same time of night as my infant daughter but it was gentle enough. I sat down beside my wife, at our hearth, opposite Leon.

'You said you have lots to tell me, Leonidas,' I began. 'Is it good news?'

'A mixture of good and bad, my king. First of all – Machan lives.'

'Thank the Gods.'

Leon threw a scrap of bread onto the fire as he nodded. 'He had a slight fever, after you left, but he survived it. He can walk and talk, at least.' Leon's black eyes looked up to mine plaintive as any dog's and I felt my stomach freeze.

'His sight has not come back, on the left, has it?'

Leon shook his head. 'More than just that, sire. After we brought him home he had a fit, like an over-hot child sometimes gets, right in front of his wife and children. He recovered, but – but – '

'Go on.'

'Well . . . he's had another one, since. I don't think he will be able to fight again.'

I sighed, dropping my gaze to the hearth, and Nes took hold of my hand. 'He wouldn't be alive at all, if not for you,' she said.

I smiled back at her, but my heart was heavy. 'What of Kynbel?' I asked, to change the subject, and Leon's scarred, gap-toothed face lifted a little.

'Much better, sire. He is able to grip now, and the stitches are out.'

'Good. Has he got bored?'

Leonidas smiled. 'A bit, sire. But he has befriended Camulora and they are doing their best to get word to the Sparrow, to get her out, so that has occupied him a little.'

'Has there been any news from her?'

'Nothing sire, either good or bad.'

Gods help her.

'Does Kynbel plan to come here, soon?'

Leon's plaintive look returned, quick as a cloud crosses the sun once you've shed your shirt. 'He asked me to ask you if you could instead come home, sire. A storm is building there.'

Nes and I exchanged glances. 'Is it Maros?' I asked.

Leon nodded. 'It concerns him, my king. King Maros is still with the druids but his betrothed will be stolen from under him if does not take care.'

Blodau? I recalled the skinny scab-ridden girl I had met. 'Who is trying to steal *her*?' I said, and then I felt rude, as even I could hear the astonishment in my voice. 'I doubt any of my people has the poor sense to steal a king's bride,' I added.

'I phrased it badly my king – she herself strays. The man is our own Hedros and he, I believe, is innocent.'

'Hedros?' Again I was astonished. 'He has been home what – ten days?'

Nes laughed. 'Time enough. You remember what it's like to be young?'

My wife was right. I, of all people, was unfit to judge in this.

Leon spread out his hands. 'You did not see him as she sees him, sire. He arrived helping his father like Aeneas fleeing from Troy with his old parent at his back. He is young and handsome, quiet and sober; he shows nothing but respect and care for his kin . . . For a moth like the princess young Hedros is the flame.'

'Well, he has sense enough to let it blow over.'

'Not yet, sire, and now Alwona and Mathona are at each other's throats, like any mother wolves fighting for their cubs.'

I think I rolled my eyes. *Oh by the Gods.* This was bad but surely it didn't need *me* to cure it. Not with our lines here to hold and Rome sure to make a move before the spring was out.

That was my cut-and-dried thought before I went to bed, but I spent a restless night, disturbing my poor wife, and as we stood yawning in the dawn drizzle to see Leon and Ambix off she turned to me with resolute gaze.

'We must go home,' she said. 'If we lose the alliance with Eburos that's bad enough, but to lose our refuge among the Silures . . . that's disaster.'

I threw my cloak around her and we snuggled under the eaves. 'I agree. I kept turning it all over in my mind last night and I agree. I shall have to send Hedros here, to keep him away from Blodau, to restore peace among them all.'

'But you feel sorry for her, don't you?'

'I do.'

Nes smiled, and hugged me tighter.

Ambix and Leon had almost disappeared from sight in the grey morn light.

'Do you think we'll ever see him again?' Nes asked.

'Ambix? I don't know. If he decides to rejoin his old side then there is little harm he can do, to be honest – there is nothing much he could tell them that Adminios won't have already said.'

'Did you ask him to get news of my brothers?'

'Yes. And Tog's wife and daughters, if he can.'

Nes took in a good breath. 'Then we can only hope he does remain loyal.' The drizzle was turning to real rain and Nes pulled her cloak closer. 'Let's go inside and wake up Gladsia. We can have some breakfast before we leave.'

I looked out over the wet hills, still cold and bleak in the first true moon of spring. 'You don't need to traipse all the way back with me, love. I'll sort it out as well as I can and be back here in days.'

My wife's face froze. 'Of course we're coming with you.'

'There's no need – stay here, in the warm. It will be better for Gla-Gla.'

Tears were springing to her eyes. What had I done?

'Don't use Gladsia as an excuse,' she rasped. 'I'm coming back with you even if I break my legs.'

I couldn't speak for a moment. I felt my own eyes sting as the reason she didn't want me to return alone dawned on me.

'All right, come with me then – and if she catches a chill because you couldn't control your jealousy then you'll only have yourself to blame.'

Nes gasped. 'Don't tempt the Gods!'

I held up my hands. 'I don't. I don't. I just want you to see sense.'

That just raised a snort and she looked back out over the landscape so I could not see her eyes. 'Look, they're coming back,' she said. 'They must have forgotten something.'

I wasn't pleased, but I was glad to focus on something else. As soon as I looked, though, I knew something was wrong. 'That's not them, there are too many. And they had a packhorse but no cart.' I sighed so hard it was almost a tut. 'It's probably just a peasant come to sell something. Let's go inside and pack.'

It wasn't just a peasant. It was young Rhyddo with the cow-girl, her mother, the baby, cows and all. I came to greet them with a bowl of porridge still in hand and ashamed of my hasty words. They looked well enough, if a little thin. I held back while young Rhyddo was embraced by Eirian, Dran and Eithinen, his little sister, then greeted him myself.

'Sorry I took so long, King Caradoc,' he said. 'The baby went yellow, for a time.'

'Not at all, you followed my orders. Is he all right now?'

Rhyddo nodded. 'Yes sire. And also – we have word on the Legion. They're moving.'

'Well, Scapula was bound to get my message sooner or later. Did you see them?'

'No sire. A Corieltavi cow-herd told us they are on the move – they were going *east*.'

'The whole legion?'

'He thinks so.'

I passed Dran a look. 'Not what we expected.'

'You're sure he said east?' Dran asked and Rhyddo nodded. The girl shrugged.

'Tha's what he said, he wasn't lyin'.'

'I had no way to check,' Rhyddo continued. 'It seems mad.'

'Something must be happening in the occupied lands – perhaps among the Catuvellauni we left behind . . . ' *Protect them Gods, please.* I had not seen my two nieces in more than three years but their faces flashed across my mind right then. Had Verla stirred up unrest? She was no weakling, that's for sure – Tog's daughter in more than just her hair. The distance between me and my wider kin never felt greater than now. 'We should send scouts to confirm what we've heard. You've done well, Rhyddo, have a rest.'

Dran put an arm around his step-son. 'Are you still going?' Dran asked me.

'I think I must . . . the alliances cannot be allowed to break, whatever else is happening.' I looked to the sky for help. 'I think I must send out the scouts first, find out for definite, *then* go on to Siluria. We could run more raids into the western reach of their occupied land to draw some heat away from whatever they're doing in the east.'

My foster-brother looked back at me in disbelief. 'We can deal with it. We've been preparing for them to attack us for over a moon – it'll be good to be doing something.'

Again I felt ashamed. 'I'm sorry, Dran. You're right. Let me know, once we hear anything else.'

It took us three days to get back south to the Silures seat, but it felt longer. A dark fog was wrapping me. We couldn't ride as fast as Epona, not with Gladsia with us, and, with the 'spring' weather bad as any winter, I could mask the true reasons for my gloom. On the third day we reached the western banks of the Hafren river, studded with yellow gorse and tough sheep, and I felt relieved that we were almost there, at least.

We stopped, at noon, to rest our horses and shelter from yet another bout of strong winds and cold drizzle. I flopped myself down in the lee of a gorse bush with my daughter and Creegan, sheltering Gladsia beneath my cloak, while Nes took care of the horses.

'Are you all right?' Nes asked me.

'Yes.'

Nes carried on cleaning Buanedd's hoof and I couldn't see her face.

'Are you still angry with me?' she said, at last.

'No. I wasn't angry with you to start with.'

Nes turned to look at me, bafflement and more than a little impatience on her face. 'Well what is it then? You've barely said a word all morning.'

I took in a good breath. 'Well I'm worried about what's happening – east *and* west. I'm sure I'll be able to sort out the mess over here, but who knows what's happening in our lands? What if Verla is killed?'

Nes frowned. 'Well it might not be anything to do with Verla – and even if the Romans *are* attacking her and the people that isn't your fault.'

'Of course it's my fault. I killed one of their tribunes only a moon ago, I've been opposing them for years.'

My wife crouched down beside me and took my hand. 'We all have. And everyone made their choice when they pricked their thumbs above the cauldron that day. Verla understood – she'd be with us now if she hadn't been injured. You told me so yourself.'

I nodded along, given I knew she was right, but I couldn't force myself to smile. Nes got up again and got our bronze cups down from the baggage. 'I'll get us some water and then we'll have our packed meal. That'll make us feel better.'

I smiled then but mainly to please her. Nesica weaved her way down through the bushes, Creegan at her heel, her copper-coloured hair bright even in the rain.

Thank you Gods, for her, at least.

'Dada?'

'Yes darling?'

'Fox is getting wet.'

I looked where Gladsia was looking and saw that her toy had been exposed when Nes got the cups out.

'All right, let's bring him under the cloak with us. We'll just make sure we don't forget him when we ride on.'

I stood up to get the toy for her and spied something floating down river from the corner of my eye. Something large and pale. I would have thought nothing of it except right then Nes started shouting.

'Caradoc! Caradoc! Someone is drowning!'

122

'Stay here! Don't move!' I ordered Gladsia.

I shot through the gorse to Nes. She was running ahead, down river. She was right. The upturned boat raced away as the current swept it down and in the shallows up ahead a body flailed. It looked like a woman, and she was struggling to grasp at the edge. We waded into the river, feeling the suck and swirl of the mighty Hafren on our calves, and both of us hauled on the woman's clothes to pull her up onto the bank. Her dark hair was plastered to her face.

'There are two more!' she gasped. 'Two with me!'

I sat her up and pulled the hair away. I knew her in an instant.

Melistia, of the Dobunni, handmaiden to the Dobunni princess. The same young woman who had once led us to safety in our flight to the west.

My spy; the Sparrow.

Seventeen The Iceni spring

I shed my cloak and wrapped it round Melistia. She was starting to shudder.

'Get her to Gladsia and the horses,' I said to Nes. 'There's a Silures watch-point a short ride south of here – get down there and warm her up. I'll look for the others.'

Melistia was nodding even as she coughed. 'A woman and a boy,' she rasped.

I started my search a little upstream of where we'd found the Sparrow, just in case, but found nothing, so I turned downstream. To be honest I was expecting to find bodies, if anything at all. The river is wide and fierce, this far south, subject to the Noadu surge, and I could see the steep peaks and troughs. No wonder they'd lost control of that small boat. I scanned the brown water for any flash of colour that could be cloth, an arm, a hand, anything.

Nothing.

I found the upturned boat banging into a rock at the side so grabbed its edge and flipped it over. Nothing. They would have been thrown out but I'd had to check. My eyes searched the shallows, dreading the sight of dead faces looking up at me.

Please, Gods, if they are alive let me find them. Teutates, I beg you.

A low-flying gull screamed above me and I ducked as it came near my head. As I looked up again I saw a flash of brown ahead among the bright yellow gorse. I thought it was a sheep but in the next blink I got a clearer glimpse – a woman in a brown dress.

'Hey! Stop!'

I ran forward but so did the figure. She was taking big steps, swaying from one side to another as if drunk. It looked like she had a child strapped to her.

'Stop! I'm not going to hurt you.'

I caught up with her and grasped her right hand. She span around, raising her left hand to protect her head, and I saw she had a bad gash above her left eye, blood streaming down her face, mixing with the rain water. Her eyes stared back at me wild as a snared beast.

'Shhh, shhh, sit down, I will help you. I'm a friend. Shh shh.'

I eased her to the grass, trying to get a look at the child's face. He had been tied to her torso with a length of rough cloth and had his back outwards. I was sure he was alive, as I could hear his breathing and see his small shoulders heaving, but I was concerned being tied up was making his panic worse. The woman resisted him being untied, punching out with what strength she had left.

'It's all right, it's all right. I'm not going to hurt him. I just want to make sure he isn't wounded.'

She stopped hitting me and seemed to come to her senses, or calm down a little, at least. I finished untying the length of sackcloth and freed the child. He still gripped on to her, taking big gasps of breath, but I could check the rest of his head at last. He seemed fine – the woman had succeeded in protecting him with her own body.

'Well done, he's all right. Let me take a look at that wound now,' I said, and the woman nodded. She was quite young, as far as I could tell, with light blond curls now stuck to her scalp with water and blood. I could see a pale line around her neck as if she had worn a torque every day through last summer – which seemed unlikely. Her dress was made from the coarsest wool I'd ever seen. It was thin, too. She was shivering, her teeth starting to chatter. I checked the pupils of her eyes – fine. The gash was long, but not too deep. 'The cut looks worse than it is, it will stop bleeding soon,' I said, in my calmest voice. 'I'll clean it for you when we get to camp, but I'm not sure you'll even need stitches. Did you hit a rock?'

She nodded. 'Yes. Under the water.'

It was our language, not much accent.

'We need to get you both into the warm. My wife has taken the woman who was with you down to the watch-point already, she is all right. Come with me.' She still looked a little wary, and I realised I hadn't even told her who I was. 'I am Caradoc, King Caratacos, of the Catuvellauni. You don't need to fear me.'

'I know, King Caratacos. I'm Airdinna – we've met before.'

I must have been open-mouthed as a fish. She rubbed her face, removing some of the blood smears, and I could see it now, though I'd had no thought of even guessing. The one time I'd ever met her was almost four years before, at the Beltane war-meet when Cunobelin died. I remembered how happy she had been in the arms of my nephew, the evening sunlight catching the gold thread of her cloak as he'd swung her round. She had been a Princess of the mighty Durotriges then, fresh and gleaming like a bright new morn.

'I need to get you into the warm, first of all,' I said. 'I can carry your boy on my left side and help you along on my right.'

Airdinna shook her head. 'He won't let you carry him, not until he knows you,' she insisted, and so I went along with it, though it was madness. She was still unsteady on her feet and the child, who looked to be about three, was a dragging weight on her own spare frame. We walked south at the pace of porridge dripping from a spoon, our teeth chattering. I was relieved beyond measure when I saw a horseman up ahead. It was an old Silure warrior with my Buanedd in tow.

'Your wife sent me looking for you, sire,' he said, handing me the reins and one of the blankets he had flung over his mare's withers.

Thank the Gods.

Nesica and the old warriors on the watch-point had a good fire going in their hut and we all thawed out soon enough. With food and warmth came a torrent of talk, like a dam bursting, from Melistia at least, while Airdinna stayed quiet as she tried to rock the young boy to sleep. He looked much of an age with our Gladsia but when my daughter tried to talk to him, and stretched out a bold hand to touch his curly hair – now springy and pale as fresh wood shavings – the boy shrank back into his mother's chest. He still hadn't said a word.

'He's been like that all along,' Melistia commented, between mouthfuls of stew, as she saw me looking at him. 'Three days on the run and not a squeak – but at least he didn't give us away when we were hiding from the soldiers. I paid a smith to remove her neck ring – ' she nodded towards Airdinna, ' – and the rat did it, took my money, then snitched on us to the nearest centurion. We had to hide in the roof of a boat-builder's shed a whole morning and he was quiet as a little mouse.'

I looked again to Airdinna. 'You were a slave?'

Melistia nodded, answering for her. 'That's how I found her. Prince Aesu asked me to buy a wet-nurse for his daughter and I found Airdinna in the same hut. I remembered Prince Kynbel talking about her once when I was in Siluria, telling me all about her, so the pieces fit. I thought you'd want her out, if I cou– '

'Aesu has a daughter?' Nes interrupted.

'Yes.' Melistia sucked in a breath, her big brown eyes turning to my wife. 'Your brother has been bereaved and blessed in the same day, as so many others. My lady did not survive the birth but their daughter is alive, so he needed the wet-nurse for her.'

'Where is Aesu now?' Nes asked, panic rising in her voice.

Riding north to his Iceni homeland, it turned out. Melistia told us everything. Princess Coriona, may her spirit find peace in the Land of Youth, had not died of birth-fever alone. Aesu had called in the tribe's druid, Dobunnos, for help when she started to slip away, but her own father, king of the Dobunni, refused him entry to the palace – such is the Dobunni king's pathetic love for his Roman overlords.

Aesu's years of restraint snapped at last and he drew a sword on his father-in-law, but even then he couldn't bring himself to actually kill an old fat idiot cowering in a corner. So he rode north, instead, all his Iceni warriors following like a pack of wolves. The Roman guards on the gate just waved them off – if the Sparrow's hand gestures as she talked were to be believed – and got a flogging for their negligence in the morning.

Nesica had hold of my hand so tight by this point she was hurting me. 'Well that explains it then,' she said. 'The Legion aren't marching on your family, they're marching on mine.'

She was right, I could feel it in my bones, and Melistia's emphatic nodding hammered the point home. 'Prince Aesu went off swearing a curse on all Romans. The King blabbed the whole lot to the tribune next morning. They'd see it as a threat of war, I should think,' she said, and Nesica's gaze dropped to the embers. I put my arms about her.

'What of our young niece?' I asked. 'Did Aesu take the baby with him?'

'No, no. She was not strong enough yet for such a journey. He told the wet-nurse to take her into hiding.'

'Olla is tough,'Airdinna chipped in. 'I knew her from before.'

The Sparrow nodded. 'And Dobunnos is helping her. She'll be all right.'

'Dobunnos is allowed to live freely there?' I asked, surprised.

'Not really. He keeps his head down, living in the woods, but the people love him so that the king hasn't the nerve to let the Romans hurt him.'

Nes and I exchanged a look. 'They will head for Ynys Mon then, as soon as they can. Catuvellaunos will send us word,' I reassured her, and my wife smiled up at me.

I turned back to Melistia. She was flagging now, lulled by the warmth and safety, with bags under her drooping eyes.

'Just a few more questions,' I assured her. 'Camulora told me Plautius was leaving. Has he left?'

Melistia nodded. 'Yes sire. He and his wife have gone, so Aesu said I couldn't do much good as a spy any more, and I was to tell you everything I know, then stay in Siluria.'

'Have you met the new general?'

'Scapula? No, but Aesu and my lady did, briefly, when he arrived. He is a bit of a dry stick, by all accounts, cold and cautious, then full of flames once lit.'

The worst possible kind of enemy.

'Any family with him?'

'A grown-up son. A soldier.' She looked up to me with her weary eyes. 'I could try to meet him . . ?'

'We'll see. For now, you must rest. You have done very well.'

Later, while Melistia and Gladsia slept, and even Nes had let herself doze off, I managed to have a word with Airdinna alone. She looked younger now, dried out, her fair curls frizzy and the cut above her eye cleaned up, but she had still lost the shine of youth. Her eyes sought mine with a cautious frown gathering her brows.

'Don't be mistaken,' she whispered, her gaze falling on the dark-haired girl as she slept, tucked into the wattle of the wall. 'She is all cocky and proud that she spied for a king, and got away with it, but I know she cried and cried, like a little child, at the death of her lady, when she thought I didn't see. Please don't send her back.'

'I won't.' My gaze turned to the yellow-haired boy now slumped and snoring like a puppy at her chest. 'He is your son?'

She nodded. 'And Kynbel's. He was born at a time when I had been with no other.'

Her face clouded at my sharp intake of breath, and my heart sank, but I couldn't help it.

'To be a slave is to be like no other, it is worse than being a dog,' she snapped. 'I was a part of the household and a guest would not be stopped from using me – no more than the towels.'

I rubbed my hands over my face. 'Gods forgive me, Airdinna. It is just that is a fate I would wish on no woman, least of all the betrothed of my kin.'

'You don't have to call me that,' she said. 'It's not as if I will hold him to it.'

'Almost four years have passed, neither of you is held to anything, but my nephew has a right to meet his son, and to know you are alive, at least,' I said, with some force, and she nodded, casting her eyes to the floor. 'His heart was broken and ground to powder when we heard of the fall of Mai Dun.'

'Didn't Kynbel marry someone else, if he thought me dead?'

'He has a woman he has lived with, for over a year, but he hasn't married, no. She is as much an innocent in this as you are.'

Tears were falling from her chin, and I felt guilty. 'What is the boy's name?' I asked, to change the subject.

'Temlyr.' She sniffed. 'After my father. I thought it would help Father to love him, in time. It didn't work.'

'Does he never speak?'

She shook her head. 'He did then, even though he was terrified of his grand-father he was starting to say a few words – and then he saw the massacre.'

'Did you see it too?'

'Yes, the last of it, at least.'

'How did you survive?'

She drew in a shaky breath. 'We survived because of Father's servant, Sel. He was an old sailor, who'd washed up on our shores one day and stayed, with skin brown as a beech-nut, like no other, and he was the only person who could get father's right shoulder back in when it popped, so Father loved him. Sel hid us under a cow hide and defended the door for as long as he could.' She reddened, pulling at a loose thread in her dress. 'I wish I'd fought by his side, but I was scared, and Temlyr was screaming for me . . . You should hear the noise of the bolts when they come – even the bravest were scared.'

'You are no coward,' I said, patting her shoulder. 'I doubt your boy would have survived, even as a slave, if you were not alive to protect him.'

Airdinna nodded. 'I *am* a coward, but you're right. I'm the only of my kin left alive. The Legion let us bury all my brothers before they sold us off, so I saw their faces one last time. Gods forgive me but I was pleased I was not lying dead there among them.'

I looked towards my own wife and daughter, asleep on the other side of the hearth, with Creegan snoring and twitching as he dreamt by their side. Thank the Gods Nes had not heard all of this.

Airdinna looked over to where I was looking. 'You really love them, don't you?'

'Of course.'

'Then it must have crossed your mind that you might protect them better by a peace-pact – I know my father thought so, when all was lost, even after all his roar and bluster.'

I sighed. 'Well , the thought *has* crossed my mind, but we haven't lost, we could still win, don't forget that. If your Durotriges had joined us instead of fighting alone we would be a step closer to winning. And I have been to Gaul, and seen what an occupied land is like after a generation or two. Look what happened to you.'

She blushed, remaining silent.

'And look at what is happening with the Iceni – they did make a peace-pact with Rome, for all the good it will do them.'

Airdinna shook her head, tears still rolling from her chin. 'If it's even half as bad as what they did to us then may the Gods help them.'

Eighteen **The perils of love**

The morning was cool and windy, but dry at least, so Nesica gave Airdinna her madder-red cloak and gold brooch, for the ride into the Silures' seat, so she looked less a slave. Nes plaited the girl's hair too, leaving just a few curls free at the front to mask the livid gash above her eye. A wash and a straighter back had already done wonders.

'Kynbel will love her, still, I think,' my wife whispered, to me, as we rode up ahead. 'It wasn't her fault, what happened while she was captive.'

I turned to Nes in shock. 'You were awake?'

'Yes . . . more or less. I heard everything.'

'Oh Nes . . .'

She bit her lip. 'I'll be all right. I will pray for my kin – that's all I can do, from here.'

The north gate of the Silures homestead was in sight, and we found Tyllan, my old harper of Calleva, sat in the lee of the big ash by the path side, harp in hand. His great-nephew, young Coll, was swinging on a branch, making the young leaves shake, and both stood to bow and beam their welcome to us.

'My niece is close to giving birth, sire,' Tyllan explained, 'so I thought I would get us both out of her way, but I'm not getting much further with my song.'

He laughed, his grey old face now bright as a new coin, and I slapped him on the back.

'And Colleos, how is he?'

'Gathering nettle tops for Dag – she craves buttered nettles, so we oblige.'

'Has the row calmed, over young Blodau?'

Tyllan's brows gathered. 'No, my king. My song for Beltane is an intended balm, on the perils of love, but I'm getting nowhere with it.'

I smiled. 'We'll let you get on then.'

I glanced towards Airdinna and saw my wife do the same. Here was a reunion about to happen that was worthy of a bard's song, but I didn't want to voice it and 'tempt the Fates' as Leon would say.

Up ahead the gate was open. I could see dozens of people pottering about, doing their morning chores, including young Rhian, who was feeding the pigs. She had her shift tucked up into her belt a bit to save the hem from the muck, and a cloth bound round her hair. For a moment I felt a pang of guilt that we'd beautified Airdinna as much as we had. *Gods help me. . . this poor girl.* Rhian, like everyone, had raised her head and looked to the gate as we approached. She'd never met Airdinna in her life but she was staring at her now, stiff and straight as a fence post, as if she knew, with that innate sense women say they have.

'Greetings sire.'

I looked down. A stroke of luck, perhaps – Hedros was the guard on the gate. I dismounted from Buanedd and greeted my old friend's son. He was thinner than when I'd seen him last. He looked tired.

'Hedros, do you know where Kynbel is?' I whispered.

'Yes sire. He's exercising his horse – in the south meadow, last I saw.'

'I need you to go and fetch him. Ask him to come to my house, straight away. This is Airdinna, and her son.'

Hedros's big eyes turned to Airdinna as if she was a ghost in our midst.

'I need to speak with you, and your parents, Hedros – I'll come to the house after the midday meal, but first I must deal with this. You understand?'

'Yes sire.'

Hedros hurried off to the south meadow while a stable-lad bowed and took our horses. The rest of us progressed into the yard. Nesica had lifted Gladsia down and our daughter scampered towards our house with skips and hops, Creegan following, his ears flapping and tail well high. Nes and I smiled to each other.

'You settle our guests in,' I said, quietly, to my wife. 'I'd better speak with Rhian.'

Nes squeezed my hand and led the others to our house. I steeled myself and turned to Rhian. Rhian had put the pig-meal down and was now standing with her hands wringing each other and more than a note of a scowl.

'Is that Airdinna?'

'Yes. She was a captive and she has been freed – we never knew for definite she was dead, Rhian.'

Tears had welled up with my first word. I reached out to hug her about her shoulders but she took a step back.

'That's it then – I will be thrown out like the scraps. He always loved her.'

'You will be treated honourably, Rhian, I promise it.' I said. 'This isn't your fault any more than it is hers.'

Rhian snorted. 'Well I know that.'

Gods help me . . . 'Where's Mathona?' I asked. 'She can comfort you better than I can.'

I was surprised, to be honest, that Mathona hadn't appeared on the threshold of the great house at the sound of my voice.

'Mam's with Dag. The pains have started.'

Of course. I looked around the yard in desperation, wishing Branadain, Catuvellaunos or even Siluri were here. My gaze settled on Camulora, who was watching from Eirian's doorway, pretending, I think, to wring out a cloth. She caught my eye and crossed over, now, gathering the young girl into her arms. Camulora was not shaken off.

'I'll look after her,' Camulora said. 'Not all problems are in your gift to solve.'

They walked towards the house and I was grateful to see them go, I must admit.

My own house was much calmer, thank the Gods. Gladsia was showing Melistia all her things, gabbling away, while Nes found a better dress for Airdinna from our stores. Young Temlyr was still silent as a stone, hiding in the folds of his mother's clothes while Creegan tried to sniff at him.

'Here, Creegan.' I settled the dog down with me beside the hearth, eased my shoes off, and started lighting a fire for hot water. 'I need a blackcurrant leaf tea. Anyone else?'

Melistia smiled. 'Where are all your servants?'

I laughed. 'Fighting the Romans.'

I'd just poured us all a cup when Kynbel burst in through the door, his face sweat-streaked and his mouth hanging open. 'Airdinna?!' The two of them looked at each other a heartbeat, like startled deer in a glade, then fell together. He clasped her so hard he might have broken her ribs. 'Thank the Gods, thank the Gods,' he kept saying. I felt my own throat tighten and Nes had tears streaming down her face. *Do you see this, Tog?*

'Where have you been? Why didn't you find me sooner?' Kynbel gasped through his sobs.

I turned to Nes and Melistia. 'Come, let us take our drinks outside,' I whispered, 'they have much to talk about.'

We withdrew, sipping our tea in the morning sun and chatting with the people who came to welcome us back.

'Where's Maros?' Melistia asked. 'I haven't seen him yet.'

'Do you know each other?'

Melistia smiled. 'Yes. Very well.'

Oh by the Gods.

'He is with Siluri, and Branadain, being treated for his sickness,' I looked to her eyes and was sure she knew what I meant, 'the last I heard.' I glanced over my shoulder to make sure none of the villagers were in earshot. 'Remember to refer to him as *King* Maros, please, even with me. Our residence here is on a knife edge.'

Melistia blushed red as Nesica's cloak.

'Of course. Sorry, my king.'

'It's all right, now you know. Also, you should know that King Maros is betrothed, to Princess Blodau of the Deceangli. She is a guest here too.'

Melistia bit her lip, at the start, then dismissed it with a shrug and a burst of laughter.

'I never had a hope of marrying him any way. Good luck to them, sire.'

Our Gladsia grabbed Mel's hand again and started showing her all our plants, the bee skeps and whatnot, which Melistia tolerated with good heart, may the Gods bless her.

Nes leant in to talk to me. 'When will you go to see Machan?'

I sighed. 'I said I would after the midday meal – I should go to Mathona first, really, but she is busy with Colleos's wife.' Nes raised her eyebrows. 'The birth pains have started.'

'Ah.'

'I never meant to insult the Silures in my whole life but whatever I do . . . '

'I'll pop to Dag's house, take them some food or something, and explain to Mathona that you are back and mean to discuss the Blodau mess with her. *I* can go in there.'

'Thank you, my love. Maybe avoid describing it as the "Blodau mess", though.'

Nesica smiled and I hugged her. At that moment Blodau herself came out of the great house and crossed the yard. I assumed she was coming to greet us, but she turned to the north gate, talking for a moment with the guard there.

'She's checking where Hedros is, she must have noticed him missing,' Nes whispered, and I nodded. 'She looks a good deal better. That pale-woad dress suits her colouring.'

It was true. Gone were the lank hair and scabs. She looked a little rounder, and even from this distance seemed to have a touch of colour in her cheeks. The dress Nes admired did indeed look good against her fair hair, now clean and well-combed. I thought I could see blossoms behind her ears.

'I suppose all of us look rotten with a head-cold,' I conceded. 'Maybe Maros will warm to her after all.'

'I doubt it. People used to say that about Addy and me, but the damage has been done. She loves another.'

Blodau must have noticed us watching her and did come over, then, though reluctant as a dog to a wash.

'Greetings King Caradoc, Queen Nesica,' she said, in such a soft voice I could hardly hear her. She was blushing up like a ripe fruit yet we hadn't said a word of admonishment.

'Good morning, Princess. You have settled in well to your new home?'

She nodded. 'Everyone has been very kind, but I miss grandfather.'

That I could believe.

'Perhaps we shall travel to Ynys Mon for Lughnasa, if the war is going well, then we can visit him on the way.'

A genuine smile played about her lips, then, broadening to a true grin. I followed her gaze and saw that Hedros had appeared at his threshold, with his little brother Caradoc, keen to see his playmate, our Gladsia, no doubt. Hedros saw that Blodau was with us and looked horrified but it was too late for him to duck back in as young Caradoc was already on his way over. Blodau did not even try to mask her delight.

Nes and I exchanged glances. We had our work on, here.

When we all retired to bed that night it was well past the usual time. Kynbel and Airdinna had sat side by side through dinner, hands clasped whenever they were not eating, and whatever misgivings I might have had about how he'd take her history had to be put aside – unless, that is, she just hadn't told him. Once that occurred to me I watched them giggling sleeve-to-sleeve and comparing scars with a rising sense of disquiet. It wasn't dispelled when Kynbel reached out to embrace his new-found son and the child shrank back like a snake.

'Give him time,' I said. 'You are a stranger still.'

Kynbel nodded, but with the hurt clear in his eyes.

'I should settle him down to sleep,' Airdinna said, patting my nephew's hand. 'Where are we to sleep?'

I looked to Kynbel with raised eyebrows. The whole afternoon and evening he had never mentioned Rhian, and it was I who'd had to suggest he go to speak with her. She wasn't in the house they'd shared, as far as I knew, but all her things must be.

'I must . . . there is someone I must talk with,' Kynbel muttered, red to his ears – as well he might be.

'She's at Eirian's house, with Camulora,' I said. 'In the meantime we will make up beds for you all in here. I won't have her thrown out of her house with her belongings like a thief.'

'No, Uncle.'

They both hung their heads, and I felt mean, but it had to be said.

'Two beds?' Nes whispered to me as we encouraged our daughter to her own.

'Yes. They can get in with each other if they want but at least they don't have to if they don't want – it might be too soon. And I don't want Rhian's face rubbed in it.'

Nes nodded, pulling blankets out of the pile. 'How did it go with Machan?'

I let out an exhausted breath, leaning into the shelves. 'He was so pleased to see me, love – I felt so bad.'

'You have been his friend all these years, of course he was.'

'I know, but with the patch over his left eye, and he's lost weight, I could see it . . . he's heartbroken that he cannot fight any longer, I'm sure of it.'

'Perhaps he can train others? The young ones? With so many at the front line you need a warrior to do that.'

'That's a good idea. I'll see if he is up to it.'

'And Alwona? How is she?'

I sighed again. 'They're both more worried about Hedros's fate than anything else. I said I'd get him away from the girl – that's the best I can do for now.'

Sleep was welcome, that night as always, with all the worry and doubt knocking about in my head. Even then I was harassed in my dreams. I saw a wren, caught in a tangle of ivy, shrieking its little heart out. I reached out to help it but the ivy tightened upon the creature as if it was a nest of snakes.

'Caradoc!'

I turned at the shout and could see nothing but fog, at first.

'Caradoc! Help her!'

The voice seemed familiar, but I couldn't place it. A woman's voice, not unlike Mathona, yet not her.

'Caradoc! Wake up!'

A hand shot out of the fog and slapped me, hard, on the right of my face.

'Wake up!'

The voice was now a scream. I reached out into the mist and grabbed at the hand as it slapped again – and as I pulled her forward I saw a face I had not seen in twenty-seven long years: my mother, glaring at me like an enemy. In life she had never hit me.

'Mother?'

'*Look*,' she seethed.

I awoke, drenched in sweat, breathing like I'd just stormed a fort.

'What is it, love?' Nes asked me in a sleepy drawl.

'I must get some air. I'll be back.'

I grabbed my shirt and plunged out into the night, Creegan following. All was calm. The moon showed the village was still and everything was where it should be. I mopped my face with the shirt before putting it on, feeling a fool – then I noticed the north gate was ajar.

Creegan started to whine, his tail held low.

Oh Gods, what is it Gods?

I wished I'd picked up my sword but something was telling me there was no time. I ran though the gate, my heart racing. Creegan barked and as a cloud skipped across the moon a shaft of moonlight fell upon the old path-side ash.

I saw a girl's body, suspended like a chrysalis, twitching and jolting as she hanged.

Nineteen The longest night

I sprinted towards her, grabbing her knees and lifting as soon as I got there. I felt the cord go slack, thank the Gods, but even a young lass as light as Rhian was still dragging towards the ground like a boulder.

'Rhian! Rhian! Can you hear me?'

Nothing, but I didn't feel that she was dead – not yet. *If I can just keep the rope slack.* I kept one arm grasped about her thighs so I did not let her slip so much as a finger-span, and got my shoulder under her pelvis so I had a better chance. I gripped her then with my right arm around her pelvis while my left hand stretched for her throat. I could feel the cord, feel a bit of 'give' in it, thank the Gods, but it was not so loose I could just put it over her head, far from it, and not from this angle. *O for a knife.* I cursed myself. If I'd strapped on my sword as I should have done then I could have had her down in a heartbeat.

Heartbeat, heartbeat. My left hand felt under her jaw for a pulse and I couldn't find one.

'Rhian!'

I felt her weight dragging and had to return my left arm to holding her up. *Help me, Gods, for I am so alone.* All around me the moonlit pasture, still and silent, the ash leaves above grey in the poor light. There were a hundred people asleep just three or four spear-throws away. *Help me, please, help me Cernunnos.*

I was *not* alone. Creegan was cowering low, yelping in dozens of little whimpers. I had never seen him so terrified.

'Creegan – bark! Bark!'

Nowt but another cascade of whimpers.

Nes had taught him many things, but not this. *Think.*

'Creegan – go to Gladsia.'

He looked back at me as if I had run mad, but at least he was now paying attention.

'Go to Gla-Gla.'

Creegan obeyed, shooting off towards the gate like he had Morriga behind him.

I changed position as careful as a bird with its egg. I could feel my muscles straining, the burn spreading as time wore on. *Come on Nes . . . come on.* At last she appeared, running through the gate with my sword and shield in her hands and Creegan striding ahead of her.

'Nes! Cut the rope!'

My wife gasped at the sight, but she did as I asked, sawing away at the rope with my sword in both hands.

'It's taking too long, swing at it!'

'I could hit you!'

'No – I trust you. Do it!'

She swung, missing us by a good arm's length. As soon as I felt the rope go I laid Rhian down on the earth beneath the tree. Again I felt for a pulse, from a better angle this time, and there was one, thank the Gods, but she was unconscious. I could hear her breathing now but it was a strange, whiny breath like wind down a crevice. I freed her from the rope and turned her on her side in case there was vomit to come out, or blood, as I had been taught by Gwyfina. There were black blotches on her face. I thought it was dirt at first but it didn't come off when I touched it.

'Come on Rhian . . . come on lass.'

Rhian's skin felt clammy so I rubbed her arms and her back. I needed a blanket or a cloak and I had none. I couldn't see Nes but I could hear her throwing up behind the tree. She was only wearing a linen shift. 'Nes, I need you.'

'Is she alive?'

'Yes, but she's not safe yet.'

Nes came back around, wiping her face on her shift. I could see her shivering. 'What do you need? Is it water?'

'I'm not sure about water, not yet. Her food-pipe could be crushed, I don't know. Get a blanket, though, and cloaks.'

'If Kynbel wakes up . . ?'

'Just tell him I've been called to someone sick.'

Nes nodded and hurried back to our house. As soon as she returned we wrapped the blanket and cloaks around Rhian. Her breath still had the whiny sound, but it hadn't got any worse, so I talked to her in a low voice, as you would a wounded animal. Nes knelt by my side and held Rhian's hand.

'As miserable as I was when I was married to Addy, as lonely and wretched . . . I could never have done this,' she said, in a choked voice, and I could see her tears falling. 'She's not going to make it, is she?'

At that moment I saw Rhian's eyelids tremble. 'Come on Rhian! Come back.' I flicked her cheek with my fingernail, which must have seemed cruel, but it did the trick. Now her eyes were open. They didn't look right, as if they were blotched too, but I was sure she could see me. Her lips moved as if she was trying to speak but nothing came out.

'Shh, shh, don't try to speak, not yet, it will hurt.'

Rhian was trying to push herself up from the floor so I helped her to sit up then wrapped the blanket back around. She rubbed her eyes and then passed her hand before her.

'Can you see?' I asked. 'Just nod or shake your head.'

She nodded.

'Can you see as well as usual?'

This time a shake of the head. 'Lights,' she hissed.

'Cernunnos sent you back, as he did me,' I said. 'It's probably to bring you back towards us.'

Maybe. I hoped I sounded reassuring.

We waited a while longer before helping Rhian to her house. It was still dark, and the village remained undisturbed, but even so it was a relief to get inside and close the door. We had settled Rhian down on her bed and revived the fire in the hearth before Nes turned to me and asked 'Why was there no guard on the gate?'

I looked to her, mouth agape, and realised she was right. There *hadn't* been a guard, not at our entry just now or my exit some time before. I left Nes to make us some tea while

I placed myself by the door, leaving it ajar, so I could watch the north entrance. It wasn't long before the guard appeared, from outside the palisade, holding his knees as if he'd run. He closed the gate and bolted it behind him, casting a wary eye about the settlement in case anyone could see. I ducked back into shadow, but not before I'd seen the man's face.

Hedros.

My blood ran cold. *Oh Gods if Hedros has turned traitor then what hope is there?* I watched a moment longer as Hedros settled back into his post, straightening his tunic and taking big breaths. *Should I confront him now?* I flicked a glance back at Rhian. She was breathing, but leaning against the house wall with her eyes closed, pale as death. The black spots on her face, in the light of the hearth, turned out to be red, as if blood was caught under her skin. I couldn't leave her to Nes's care alone, it wouldn't be fair. I eased the door closed.

Nesica looked to me.

'Hedros,' I whispered. 'I'll have to speak with him – once we're sure Rhian is all right.'

Nes raised her eyebrows.'Is he in much trouble? He wasn't away for that long.'

'Well it's what he was doing while he was away that worries me.'

My wife blushed. 'Well what do you think he was doing? A young man with a fair princess madly in love with him on the quiet?'

Oh. Now it was my turn to blush.

'But Hedros doesn't return her love. He has too much sense.'

'Or there's another who already has his heart . . . '

'If you're right then he's still in trouble, he shouldn't have left the gate unguarded – and to be honest I pray that that's all it was.' I gulped at the tea a little too hot and regretted it. 'My first thought was treachery – there could have been a messenger waiting somewhere.'

Nes rolled her eyes a bit, pushing my arm in jest. 'Well if we're surrounded by Romans at dawn then I'll admit you're right.' She glanced at Rhian, still leaning on the wall with her eyes scrunched up in pain, but breathing without noise by this point. 'Should we give her something to drink, now?'

We decided we should, but given the decision was based on pure guesswork I gave her tepid water, and in small sips. There was just the one bed, Kynbel and Rhian having shared this small house alone, so I encouraged Rhian to lay upon it and sleep while Nes and I sat at the stools by the hearth and listened, for the slightest change in her breathing, through the long night.

'Does it remind you of when Gladsia had lung-fever, that second winter?' I whispered, just before dawn. 'It does me.'

Nes looked back at me with heavy eyes and a sad smile. 'It does. Sometimes I wonder if the Gods did not give us more children because we end up looking after so many others.'

We clasped hands, staring into the fire.

'When will you talk to Mathona?' Nes whispered.

Indeed. I wasn't looking forward to that conversation.

I rubbed my eyes. 'Soon. I heard a baby crying, a while ago, did you?' Nes nodded. 'Then I'll wait for her to come out of Colleos's house and ask her to come over.'

'And . . . if it goes badly with Mathona . . . do you think we'll have to leave?'

I hesitated, focussing on a broken string of glass beads thrown into the hearth's edge – a gift from Kynbel, last summer, as I recalled. 'I don't know, I hope not. I – I'm not sure the warriors would stand for that, to be honest, whatever Mathona, or even Maros, says.'

I glanced over at the bed, to make sure Rhian was still asleep, and Nes gave me a long look, with fear in her eyes. I felt the blood rush to my cheeks. 'You cannot want it to fall that way,' she breathed.

I spread out my hands. 'No, by the Gods and all I love dear, no.'

We heard a door bang, across the yard, and my wife and I looked to each other, bleak as winter skies. I ran to the door. It *was* Mathona, drifting across the dawn-lit earth with her servant. They both had their heads hung low but I think it was just from fatigue as Mathona looked up and smiled when she saw me.

'Another healthy boy, all is well,' she said, then frowned. 'Why are you at Rhian's?'

I beckoned her over, and explained all.

Mathona stood over her foster-daughter's bed with hands clasped tight over her mouth and eyes wide. She started to rock back and forth so I put my arms about her to steady her. I was surprised, to be honest, that she did not push me away.

'Will she live?' Mathona gasped, at me, her eyes still wild.

'I think so.'

I couldn't be more definite than that. Mathona let out a great strangled sob and now she did free herself from my arms.

'Caradoc, how could you let this happen?!'

Well when the Gods saw fit for me to be born they made me king of my own people as well as a foster king to yours, a father to more than I would ever be blood-father to and scourge of the Empire besides. What would you have me do? Exile my nephew to a lonely isle so he can never break a maiden's heart?

Thank the Gods I stayed my tongue.

'I'm sorry, I should have been sterner with Kynbel, and steered him right. I see it now . . . but when one is thrown into the parenthood of the child of much-missed kin . . . my instinct was to indulge.'

Mathona's expression softened. 'I know, I know,' she said. She sat on the edge of the bed and pulled the cover higher towards Rhian's chin, hiding the mark the cord had burned. 'I blame myself as much as anyone,' Mathona continued, in a voice strangled with grief. 'She was used by my son, before Kynbel even met her. I – I should have stopped it.'

That was true, but I felt guilty enough to want to comfort her away from too much self-blame. We sat side by side, watching Rhian sleep, while Nes prepared some breakfast and popped over to our house to check on Gladsia.

'Maros returns at Beltane,' Mathona said, just after Nes went. 'Branadain sent word. That's tomorrow.'

My heart sank, but I didn't show it, I hope. 'He is cured?' I asked, in a bright voice that might have rung hollow if she wasn't so tired.

She shrugged. 'I suppose so. Branadain said there was news from Ynys Mon, too, so it might be more because of that.'

Great.

Mathona looked at me with red eyes burning. 'Better Maros knows nothing of this.'

I couldn't help but agree.

It was a relief, I admit, to be out of Rhian's house and into the morning light, but despite my eyes like burned holes in a blanket there was something I had to do, king as I was, before I could retire to my own bed. I found young Hedros rubbing his own eyes and yawning as wide as a dog does as he came off watch, plodding towards his house at last.

'Hedros, a word.'

The young man looked to me with terror in his eyes and I felt a pang of guilt, not for the first time that day.

'Is it Father?'

'No, no. Come, sit in the sun here a while, I just need to talk with you.'

We sat, on the grassy bank east of the gate, Hedros pulling at the wolf-fur arm-band at his wrist and I not knowing where to start.

'I know you left your post a while last night, Hedros,' I plunged at last. 'I saw you absent and I saw you come back.'

Hedros looked at me aghast.

'Where did you go?'

He drew in a shaky breath. 'I – I'm sorry my king. It isn't my secret to keep. I don't want to get the other person into trouble.'

I looked to the sky. 'It's you who are being questioned by your king, Hedros, think of yourself.'

He pulled another tuft of fur from the band and cocked his head. 'With all due respect, sire, under the same circumstances . . . you would not.'

I laughed, though there was no joy in it. 'All right, I will guess. You resent me for not restoring your father to full health and have now thrown your lot in with the Romans. You got a message out to a waiting horseman, last night.'

'No!'

'What then?'

He pursed his lips, staring straight ahead.

'So, another guess. My wife thinks you are able to resist Princess Blodau's attention not thanks to love for your people, and respect for me, but because you have another girl on the go, and it was her you were meeting with last night.'

His eyebrows lifted in the ghost of a smile. 'No, not that either.'

'Well what then, Hedros? Because I cannot unsee what I have seen and old friend and son of my friend or not you are facing a flogging for this . . . or worse, if it *is* treachery.'

He shook his head. 'I promise, sire, it is not.' He wrenched a clump of plantains from the ground and threw them beyond his feet. 'If I tell you, sire, then please don't upset her. I think she is heartbroken as it is.'

I turned to him in surprise. 'Do you mean Rhian?'

'. . .Yes.'

'Go on.'

'She lied. She lied to me – she said Blodau had run away, because of *me*, and I had to fetch her back or else there'd be trouble. I went all the way to the river.' He rubbed his hands over his face. '*She* was running away, that's what was happening, I can see that now, but I was so tired . . .'

Ah.

'I'm sorry, my king. I shouldn't have believed her.'

Something else was occurring to me. 'You had been on watch in the morning, when we came home – why were you on guard again so soon?'

He shrugged. 'I've missed so much, I often have to swap with people because of looking after Father, so I'm made to feel that I should take on more, whenever anyone says . . . And now the Silures hate me because of Blodau . . . ' His voice cracked.

I put my right arm round his shoulders. 'Rhian hasn't run away, but she's sick. I've been taking care of her,' I told him. 'It's not your fault, and you're not in any trouble now you've told me the truth. I'll be leaving here in a few days, all being well, and you can come too, to get you away from Blodau. Machan will be well cared for, I'll make sure of it.'

'Thank you sire.'

I smiled. 'And by the time you come back Blodau will be married. She'll leave you alone in good time, I expect, so the Silures will have nothing to reproach you for.'

Hedros turned to me with big hazel eyes plaintive as any dog's. 'Perhaps you're right, sire. But you are thinking that she bothers me, and that I don't return her love, and in that, well, in that sire you're wrong.'

Twenty **Bargaining**

I remembered how I'd felt, watching Gwyfina process off for her hand-fasting with Cernos, twenty-two years ago, almost to the day, and was returned to that moment as if it were the day before. *Maponos protect you, Hedros.* There hadn't been a damn thing I could do about it then and it still hurt, even now. And I had been a lad of not yet sixteen, a druid acolyte, not a proven Catuvellauni warrior of twenty summers who could expect to marry a girl like Blodau at first admiring glance if she hadn't been born a princess. My heart hurt for him, but I was at a loss for what to do.

'I'm sorry,' I said. We stared out over the points of the house roofs. 'Even a king is tied. The alliance rests on this marriage and, well, even if neither bride nor groom wants it, it might be too late to stop it now.'

Hedros nodded. 'I know. I shall avoid her, as you advise, sire.'

He still looked low as a beaten dog and I felt wretched. *Bide your time,* I wanted to say to him, *patience might hand you what you want,* but I was wary of giving him too much hope. 'Go and get some sleep,' I said at last. 'I can put a stop to your mistreatment from the guards at least. Have faith in the Gods, Hedros. Sometimes our troubles lift like mist and sometimes they don't. We'll see.'

I was good to my word and had a talk with the captain of the guards, ensuring a fairer split of the duties without, I hope, implicating Hedros in any of it. By the time I returned to Rhian's house to check on her she was sat up, sipping tepid soup Mathona had made her, and I feared for her no longer, in body at least. Nes, Mathona and I resolved to never let her be alone, dividing the coming days between us and keeping the situation to ourselves. By Beltane eve Rhian was no doubt sick of the sight of us.

'It's all right,' Rhian whispered, her voice still raw, as I came to the end of my latest stint. 'I'm not going to do it again.'

We'd had the same exchange several times already so I wasn't budging. 'You know I can't leave.'

'You are a king, you must have better things to do.'

'Any king who thinks that isn't worthy of the name.'

The truth was I did have other things to do, and I could hear the Beltane celebrations gathering outside so I knew I'd soon have to show my face. 'Everyone has been told you are ill, so it's no surprise for me to be here,' I said, to reassure myself as much as her.

She relented, and we settled into another game of stack-twig while the noise levels outside built. Nes knocked once and stuck her head around the door.

'Maros and Branadain have just arrived,' my wife said, with as unconcerned a face as she could muster. 'I'll just get Gla-Gla over to Airdinna and then I'll take over.'

'Right you are then love.' I got up to swing on my cloak and Rhian peered up at me with her blood-speckled eyes. I knew something had been gnawing at her all afternoon and now it came.

'Have you told *Kynbel* the truth?' she blurted.

'Yes.'

And yet he hasn't darkened your threshold . . . not yet. Come on, Kynbel.

'I can't stay here.'

No, I tended to agree. 'Do you have kin anywhere else?'

She wrenched a loose thread from her dress and threw it in the fire. 'I have a step-brother, twelve years older than me. He is a spear-man at the seat of King Arthewin. He is my kin . . . but he could have taken me in when I was an orphan child and he did not.' She dropped her gaze. 'I suppose he was very young.'

'Have you seen him at all in the years past?'

Rhian nodded, picking at the beads in the hearth. 'Yes, at Beltane last year when we all visited. He asked after my health.' *That's all?* My face must have fallen. 'But Prince Mocco said I was welcome any time I wished.'

'Did he now?'

Her face lifted in a lop-sided smirk. 'It's all right – I know what he is like. At least he's friendly.'

True.

'I'll arrange it, if Mathona agrees.' I pinned my cloak in place and took a swig of blackcurrant tea. 'I'm glad you are still with us, Rhian.'

She nodded, but still hanging her head. 'It was a moment . . . it's passed. I won't do it again.'

All the same I didn't leave the house until Nesica was there.

Beltane should be a joyous feast, but I cannot think of one in my entire life I have truly enjoyed and this one was no different. I was king, though, and tried not to make it plain. I admired Colleos's newborn son along with everyone else and, despite everything, I couldn't help but smile to see Kynbel and Airdinna sat hand in hand, listening to the songs. Their child still hadn't said a word but he had lost his fear of Gladsia at least and the two were poking rowan sprigs into the wattle around the doorways, copying the older children. I took a sprig from my beaming daughter and smiled at our young kinsman. He didn't smile back, but he held my gaze and did not duck behind the nearest object, so I felt some pleasure in that.

'You look like you need some sleep.'

I turned to find Branadain behind me with a cup of wine in her extended hand.

'Thanks. You look pretty blanched and wilted yourself.'

She laughed. It was true. Brana was pale and drawn as ever in her habitual druid black and the spray of hawthorn some well-meaning child had stuck behind one ear didn't change the overall look. We slumped upon the nearest log seat and accepted the dishes of food well-wishers brought to us. I noticed she had a new tattoo, a crescent moon, on her right wrist.

'We all have one,' she said, once we were alone again. 'Maros, Siluri and I. All of us who were at the cave. It was part of the ritual.'

'Is he cured?' Again I tried to keep my voice bright but Branadain pursed her lips and returned my no-doubt sceptical look.

'He'll never be fully cured. You know that, I think. But he can hold it at bay – now – as a good shepherd can outwit the wolves.'

'Cernunnos be praised. I am pleased for Maros, truly.'

Brana squeezed my hand. 'I know.'

'Does he want to talk with me?'

She paused, just a blink, but nevertheless I felt another straw of my friendship stack with Maros drift away on a cold breeze.

'Yes. But he would rather wait until the feast has waned and talk with you alone.'

That was fine with me. 'Agreed.' I looked out over the people as they gathered, putting their left-over winter stores and their most threadbare clothes onto the left hand fire. 'I haven't seen Siluri? Did she go back to Mon?'

'Yes, she went back with the messenger. She may never leave Mon again, ill as she is.' Brana took a sip of her wine, seeming to choke back a tear, which was also a bit uncomfortable for me, much as Siluri and I had managed to live in respect these past years. 'I can do the festival rituals, and the hand-fasting to come.'

For a moment I thought she meant Kynbel and Airdinna but then I saw her gaze was resting on young Blodau. Blodau was circle-dancing with young Coll and one of Mathona's grand-daughters, happy for once, and I warmed to her a little more.

'Has your mother told you what has gone on, there?'

'Oh yes. That's one of the things Maros will want to talk with you about.' One of her raven-black brows shot up. 'I'm so glad I am a druid. You and I nearly went through all this, you know.'

'Yes.' I smiled. 'I'm not sure who is more grateful for the way things turned out, you or my wife.'

'Your wife I think. I'd have muddled through.'

We laughed and touched our drinking cups in the time-honoured way. I could see Tyllan coming across the yard with his harp, to sit at a stool between the fires, and knew we'd all be quiet soon. 'What was the message from Ynys Mon about?' I asked. 'Was it news from Icenos?'

'Icenos? No, it was a message from Catuvellaunos. He says he has someone who wants to meet you and he thinks you should.' I must have looked intrigued and I saw a smile play about Brana's lips. 'A Brigantes noble, no less,' she revealed, 'the consort, Venutios.'

'Have they had their fill of licking Roman arses?'

She shrugged. 'I expect so. You'll find out if you take up the offer.'

'Of course.'

Across from us the great carved chair was being carried out from the King's house so that Maros could listen to the music among his people. I sensed everyone was a little tight in their breathing as we waited for Maros to emerge, not just me, and there was a collective sigh of relief when Maros looked straight-backed and sober as he walked out. There wasn't even a cup in his hand until a servant brought one.

'I should sit with my brother now,' Branadain said.

'You should. And I need to greet him, for all to see.'

'He needs to greet *you*,' she corrected.

Quite right.

Maros and I managed to grasp each other's hands in greeting and touch our cups. He sat back upon the dragon chair and I spared a moment to choose where to sit. I saw Melistia and Camulora perched on a log near the fires, having a good talk, and passed on by with just a nod and a smile. I *wanted* to sit with Machan, but given Blodau's glances at Hedros were turning into damn-near a fixed gaze I decided, with regret, I could not. Kynbel, too, though my kin until the end of days, had a cloud above him for now with Rhian's spurning, and I felt I should not sit by his side either.

'Dada – come see the baby.'

Gladsia had hold of my hand and was pulling me towards Colleos and his family, all smiles. *Thank you Maponos*. In truth I had already congratulated them but now they had thrown me a rope. I sat with them, Gladsia on my lap, and listened to the song with all the front of placid, easy grace I could weave. Tyllan's song, despite his concern, was a triumph. He sang of love lost, love spurned, and the healing of time, and I felt many hearts around the circle were touched, not least mine. As he finished and we applauded I noticed Nes standing in the shadows of Rhian's doorway and I blew her a kiss, which raised a fresh cheer, from Silures and Catuvellauni alike, and I saw Maros's expression freeze, just an instant, like a leveret with a hawk above. I pretended not to notice and went to speak with Tyllan as he stood.

'As beautiful as ever, Tyllan. Thank you.' The old harper bowed as I gave him the gift of an enamelled arm-ring I had saved for the occasion. 'Might I come and speak with you in the morning? There is something I need you to do.'

'Of course, my king.'

The Beltane fires died down and the people drifted to their beds. Mathona took over from Nes so I could hand my sleepy daughter back to my wife. Almost as soon as I did so a Silures guard came to fetch me to the great house.

'King Maros asks for you, sire.'

'Right with you Brynn.' I straightened my tunic and tipped out the dregs of my cup. 'How is your father?'

The lad smiled. 'Very well, sire. He often talks of how you helped him and my great-grandsire with the sheep.'

I was pleased. Nevertheless my mouth was dry as Lughnasa wheat as I ducked under the porch. Maros was sat up in bed but dressed, even down to his torque, as I walked in. He held a cup. I couldn't tell what was in it. His hair was a little longer in the time that had passed and seemed to have more curl. I thought I spied the first few grey hairs within the dark. I smiled as I greeted him but Maros simply looked back at me, grey eyes glittering, and it put me still more upon my guard.

'I see you have your torque back,' he said.

'I killed the man who took it from me.'

Maros looked down into his drink, a smirk fleeting across his face. 'Yes. For a druid you turned into a mighty warrior.'

'I wouldn't say that. I do what I can.'

That raised a snort. 'And you succeed. The men love you for it.'

I smarted. 'Not that alone, I think.'

'No indeed. You have a way with words, you always have. You managed to weave a betrothal where neither me, the bride, nor the bride's father wanted it. Outstanding! The Gods must surely love you.'

'I needed to stop Eburos allying with Rome – you are a king too, surely you see that?'

'The Silures will ally with them, if that's what it takes. But I don't want to wed with her and *she* as sure as milk will sour doesn't want to wed with me. If your cow-eyed young follower wants her then he can trek up north to Eburos and ask for her hand for all I care. I don't give a shit.'

My heart leapt. 'The betrothal need not go ahead – not if the alliance can hold. I see that now – '

'*And* you see why I am displeased?'

I swallowed, choking back my words. A flash came into my mind of the two of us kicking about a cnapan on an enormous south Silures beach, wearing nowt but rolled up breeks, just two summers ago, while Nes steered our Gladsia through her first steps in the ocean surf. We seemed such a very long way from then.

'I should not have sent you to the cave,' I sighed. 'But I had to stop your drinking – I thought you would kill yourself.'

Maros bit his lip, turning down his eyes. 'It's not that.'

He toyed with the tattoo on his wrist, as if he too was biting back his next words, and so I plunged, as we sometimes cannot help but rip off a scab. 'Then what is it, Maros? Do you want the torque back?'

Again his eyes glittered but now I think it was because they were rimmed with tears.

'No, oh no,' he said. 'You are my friend, and you will always be my friend, and not just because of this.' He touched the old scar upon his throat. 'I love you like a brother, I do. But, from now on, you must be living elsewhere.'

Twenty one **Exile**

I left for Caer Caradoc two days later. I had much to do, before I left.

I met with Tyllan at breakfast as I'd planned. We sat in the morning sun and shared some of Nesica's fresh made bread as if what I was about to ask him was nothing much. I was aware that all eyes would be upon us but I was careful none could hear.

'You remember we talked of you visiting a fort in the Ordovici lands, to play for them as my gift in thanks for their help, some moons ago?' I started.

'Yes my king. I am happy to do so.'

'Now Dag's babe is born and all is well I am keen you should start out soon. The days are warm, it's a good time for a journey.'

'Yes sire.'

I could tell from the curious look in his eye that he knew that wasn't all so I dove straight in. 'And I want you to take young Rhian with you. What she ails from is not catching, but she needs looking after, and you have a wise head on your shoulders. I remembered the two of you singing together at the Winter Solstice as I listened last night and I thought you'd get on well.'

The old harper went red as a ripened fruit. 'My king – you honour me. She – she is a very pretty girl, and a fine singer, yes, but –' He looked back at me with pleading in his eyes, 'but I cannot marry her, or any woman. The Gods did not make me that way.'

'Oh no – I didn't mean for you to marry her.' I felt my own face colouring. 'I just mean for you to accompany her on the journey. I cannot let her journey to her northern kin alone, and I know I can trust you.'

'Oh!' He rubbed a hand over his face. 'Of course sire.'

I cut another slice and passed him the butter. 'Start tomorrow, if you can. I talked it over with Queen Mathona during the night and she agrees. But take your time with the journey – give a chance for her face to heal. The lesions already fade.'

Again there was curiosity in his eyes. 'May I ask what ails her, sire? I thought it was a broken heart.'

I checked no-one had wandered into ear-shot, and told him all.

The two of them set out at first light, the next day, before the rest of us. I saw them exchange a gentle smile, the first real smile I had seen on Rhian in many moons, as Tyllan held her horse for her, and was reassured. It was a cool morning, despite the prospect of a fine day, so the hooded cloak Rhian wore did not attract that much attention. Many came to wish her well, Mathona and her daughters chief among them, while Maros claimed urgent matters to attend to and did not show his face.

I saw Kynbel himself hanging back, awkward as a crow-scarer at a feast, while everyone else lined up for tearful hugs, and my heart felt heavy.

Come on Kynbel, be a man.

He saw me looking at him and when Mathona had wiped her eyes and retreated to the great house and Rhian mounted up on her grey mare, Kynbel did approach at last. Rhian watched him come towards her from under her eyelashes and did not smile.

'I'm sorry. I never meant to hurt you,' Kynbel said. 'I couldn't have got through the last few years without you.'

She nodded, eyes downcast. Just then a gust of wind sent down her hood and the blood-spots were revealed for all to see. I saw Kynbel's face contort in pain. He turned away, into the horse's neck. I stepped forward to comfort him but Rhian herself extended her left hand. She touched his wheat-gold head. 'I'll be all right,' she whispered, her voice still hoarse. 'May the Gods keep you, Kynbel.'

Tyllan mounted up too and they rode out of the north gate, Kynbel watching until they were out of sight. I put my arm around his shoulders and walked him back into the house.

Our own departure, later in the morning, was as unremarkable as we could make it. It's not as if I hadn't left with my family and warriors on campaign dozens of times before, and a new line of our territory in the Cornovi hills needed to be maintained. Everyone knew that, but all the same the rift was clear to see. Dag and her newborn were coming with us, for a start. Nesica had never stripped our house so bare she had to load two pack-horses before. She wept like snow-melt when she said farewell to our bees. And not once, in twenty-two years of friendship, had Mathona failed to hug me as she saw us off. Neither Maros nor Branadain were anywhere to be seen.

We'd got as far as the Hafren when I saw a black figure in the distance. She was down on one knee by the river's edge, casting an offering into the water, and none were too surprised when I said I would canter ahead and join her.

'I should give an offering myself, to ask Teutates for a safe journey,' I said as I drew near.

'I've done it for you,' Brana replied, with a smile. She stood up and stroked Buanedd's nose as I slid down from his back.

'I am glad we are still friends . . . whatever else has happened,' I said.

She looked back at me with a lop-sided smile, her eyes screwed up against the morning sun. 'We are still friends, and I am still my brother's twin, despite his ire to me last night.'

I was shocked and must have shown it. 'You too?'

'Oh yes. He was always going to punish us for revealing his weakness, you know. Give him time.'

'If the warriors were to turn against me there would be no time, for any of us.'

'The warriors are loyal to you,' she snapped. 'Maros is more than aware of that.'

I sighed. 'And I am loyal to you and all your family, that hasn't changed.'

Her face softened. 'We also. Every cloud passes.'

'But your mother . . . '

Brana laughed, her short bark of a laugh more like a crow's caw. 'Mother's ill-mood is aimed at Blodau more than you. When Maros released her from the betrothal yesterday she was so sob-soaked with gratitude she clasped his knees – I'm quite relieved she is not to be my sister-in-law.'

I flicked a glance over my shoulder to where young Blodau rode with Machan's family, chatting with Alwona, merry as a songbird in the spring. 'She's not so bad – just young.'

Branadain raised an eyebrow. 'I wish you all joy of her.'

'Do you stay here, now?'

She shook her head. 'I'll go back to Mon, to be with Siluri for her last days.'

'You can get word to Venutios that I wish to meet him?'

'I will. Look out for him as the Solstice nears.'

I swung myself back up onto Buanedd and rejoined our long line of people and horses. Branadain watched us pass by, a sorrier figure than usual with her bagged eyes and muddy knees, but I saw her give a little wave back when our Gladsia called out to her. I felt something in my heart ease, like a tight belt loosened.

We settled into our new homes at Caer Caradoc well enough. New houses were built so there was room for all. I explored every hand-span of the place with Dran until I knew it down to each rock, cave and stand of clover. We strengthened the fortifications where we felt we needed to. The raids on the Romans' western border were going well and we lacked for neither food nor treasure.

The Solstice neared . . . and passed. There was no sign of this Venutios.

Another visitor appeared, though, as we made preparations the eve of Kynbel and Airdinna's hand-fasting. I had agreed, somewhat against my better judgement, to do the ceremony myself, given we were without our Catuvellaunos or even Branadain, and I was out on my own, up by the 'fingers' rocks, practising the words, when I saw Leonidas approaching, his face a little more worried than usual, if such a thing were possible.

'What's up, Leon?'

'Lucius Ambix has returned, sire. The Queen has him sat in the great house and he is blurting everything to everyone.'

'Well that isn't so important now that he's returned – alive, no less. Nes isn't daft.'

Leon shook his head. 'I know sire, but it concerns her kin. She is not herself.'

We ran down to the settlement and I could understand Leon's concern full well when I entered the house. Ambix was sat right in the middle and a good dozen people were there: Nes, Gladsia, Dran's wife and daughter, Airdinna, Dag and her children, Alwona, Blodau, young Tarn's mother, even Camulora though she scarce set foot in here. Every woman and child looked stunned as a just-caught fish. Nesica's face was wet with tears. Not a warrior was there.

'Caradoc – come in, you must hear this,' Nesica exclaimed.

Yes, *I* should, I thought. I wasn't so sure about every last person most inclined to panic. I held my tongue and sat down opposite Ambix in the gap they all shuffled aside for me. Ambix was bruised, his left cheekbone puffy and bleeding in just the one place as if he'd been hit by someone wearing a ring.

'It's good to see you alive, my friend,' I said.

'Yes, sire, but only just.' He grinned, with his mouth at least. His eyes were grim as a bear's.

'Start from the beginning again, if you will.'

Ambix nodded, and took a big breath. We heard of how he'd picked his way through the Corieltavi lands unimpeded, making shoes and spreading dissent, as agreed.

'I did the same when I reached the Iceni lands,' he said, 'but I had wandered into a quagmire, there was no need for me to spread the word against Rome there.'

'They were trying to disarm the people – they had Saenu imprisoned!' Nes cut in, looking at me.

Ambix nodded. 'I arrived the same day as your wife's other brother,' he said. 'It was then that the gates of Tartarus were flung wide.'

Aesu had found the Romans melting the swords taken from his kinsmen and my other brother-in-law already under arrest, as Ambix told it. Aesu and his warriors broke Saenu and his men free and they all went on the rampage, 'mad as dogs'.

'That must have been when we heard the Legion was recalled,' Nes said, in a choked voice. 'It was a massacre.'

I reached out to hold her hand and she squeezed mine tight. 'Are Aesu and Saenu dead?' I asked, as gently as I could.

Nes nodded, wiping her face on her sleeve. 'Yes, and Saenu's sons, even the youngest. Saenu's daughters have been sold into slavery and taken away – Ambix saw it all.'

Everyone around the circle murmured their displeasure at this and I shot a look at Ambix. *Why didn't you wait for me? What are you up to?*

'Prasutagus is safe, and his wife and daughters. The local commander has put him in charge, to calm things down,' Ambix added, though this was little comfort to me, or my wife.

'What were *you* doing, while all this was going on?' I asked.

He didn't hesitate a blink. 'I was still keeping up my pretence of mending shoes. I was at the barracks the day the Legion marched out to fight them and still there when they came back . . . well, most of them.'

'When did they start to suspect you?'

'They didn't. I packed up my work and left the next day – that's when I saw all the bodies. I moved south, towards the Catuvellauni lands, as we'd planned. It was at the border I got stopped and harassed – and even then I don't think they'd guessed the truth, they just said they didn't want anyone moving south from Venta Icenorum, not for now.'

'So why this?' I gestured at his bruises.

'The Romans didn't do this – after they'd taken my money and tools I was starving and I stole some bread. It was a market-stall holder who did this.'

'A rich one?'

He shrugged. 'I don't know.'

I gestured again at the cut on his face. 'He was wearing a finger-ring.'

I thought he tensed. I might have imagined it. 'Oh this? He hit me with a bread-peel.'

Well I don't believe you.

'It looks like it will heal on its own well enough,' I said, calm and even as a crock of cool water. 'What you need more than anything is some food and a wash, I dare say. Leon? Can you take him over to your house and sort him out?' I smiled at Ambix with all the sincerity I could gather. 'Too many women in here.'

Camulora passed me a look you could slice meat with. 'I can do that. I've got plenty of food, and clothes ready for him too.'

'But don't forget we are preparing for a wedding at sundown – you'd said you were doing Airdinna's hair.'

It was a lie. Cam knew it was a lie, so did Nes, even Airdinna knew it was a lie, but none gave me away, may the Gods bless them. I watched from a crack in the door and let Leonidas lead Ambix right across the yard before I turned to face them all.

'Caradoc, what's going on?'

It was Nes who asked, grief sharpening her voice. I took a deep breath.

'I think he's lying.'

'You mean my brothers could be alive?'

I realised my mistake and kicked myself. 'No, sadly I think all that is true. I just don't believe how he got beaten up, it doesn't smell right. And if he is lying about that then what else is he up to?'

Camulora frowned. 'He made it back here to deliver his words, as a good spy does – at great risk. If he isn't loyal to you then why return at all?'

I raised my hands. 'Look, I'm not accusing him of anything yet, I'm not going to hurt him. I just have doubts and that, well, it justifies some digging.' I looked around at the circle of women. 'Surely I am not the only one who doubts that story?'

Tarn's mother was looking at me. I saw her open her mouth to speak then think better of it it. 'Go on,' I urged.

'My king, when Leon said he was going to fetch you, I saw fear on his face. It was just a moment in passing but . . . but I think it was there.'

Alwona nodded. 'I saw that too.'

Something, but not much. 'Anything else? Did anything about his story change in the re-telling?'

'Yes,' Airdinna said. 'As he'd been so close I asked him if there was any word from Camulodunon, about Kynbel's mother and sisters, and he just said he hadn't heard anything. He didn't say a thing about being stopped at the border or having his tools and money taken.'

Eirian nodded. 'That's right, he didn't even say he'd been to the border.'

'None of us asked, though. He just gave more information the second time,' Cam added.

She was right. It was not enough to incriminate him, but it didn't make me any less suspicious.

'Why do you feel he is lying about the wound?' Nes asked, so I explained.

'He was a soldier for many years,' I added. 'I don't believe he's going to get beaten up by a baker.'

'Maybe he was hit by a girl. He'd lie about that,' Eirian laughed.

'This is madness,' Camulora protested. 'Why would he even come back and tell you the news if he didn't have to?'

She had her hands on her hips and was stood a good stride away from all the others at the edge of the house. I met her gaze.

'Cam, I know you have grown fond of him, but I ask you this, if, when you were a spy, you had all the news he had, would you blab it all to everyone most likely to be upset by it?'

She dropped her head. 'No,' she said. 'I would have waited for you.'

Nesica was looking from me to Cam with her eyes still glistening with tears. 'If you think he is deliberately trying to shake us then maybe what he says about my brothers *is* untrue.'

Gods help me. I raised my hands again. 'Look, I don't know. I just think something is up. And if I were the Roman commander and I had managed to turn him back to his old loyalties then what better assassin is there than the one who is welcomed back like kin?'

Nes bit her lip and Eirian put an arm around her. Everyone was quiet.

I sighed. 'I want to believe him, I do, and maybe it is just that all these years of battle and strife have frayed my nerves like an old cloak. I don't know. I just know I need to be sure.'

Twenty two Jumping at shadows

Airdinna was looking pale. 'Do we go ahead with the hand-fasting?' she said at last.

I didn't hesitate. 'Yes. You two have waited long enough. Plus no-one should be alone tonight. The hand-fasting will keep us all visible to each other.'

'You will be the target, if anyone is,' Cam said, to me.

I shrugged. 'Maybe. But it could just as well be Nesica or one of the children – if Adminios is still with them then they know exactly how best to wound me.' I looked to Alwona. 'Look at the risk we all took to save Kynbel and how we have paid for it.'

Alwona agreed, and all the women, I think, held their children a little closer. Nesica was frowning as she clung onto Gladsia.

'I don't think he would hurt a child,' she said. 'Remember what he said when we first met him.'

I raised an eyebrow. 'I don't want to take that chance. Do you?'

Cam had a slight frown twixt her brows too. 'Leon is alone with him at the moment. Should I go over there?'

'No, I will. You all need to stay here and get Airdinna ready or he'll get wind of our suspicion. I can get changed there.'

'You shouldn't go alone,' Nes said, then blushed. 'I know you have been in many battles but. . .'

'This is different. I know.' I looked to Tarn's mother. 'Pel, you have clothes and things at Leon's, don't you?'

Her jaw dropped. 'My king . . . you know . . . about that?'

I smiled. 'We all know, Pel, ever since we moved here. It's quite all right.'

She looked about the circle, realised the truth of it, and went as red as Nesica's dress. 'I – I shall come with you sire.'

Alwona, smiling, nudged her with an elbow. 'Wait till your lad hears you were bodyguard to the king.'

I rubbed my hands together. 'Right, let's go then. You all get your finery on. Nes, we have some daggers in here don't we? Maybe conceal a few amongst yourselves, under clothing, just in case.'

Eirian let out a snorting chuckle, her arm still round my sombre wife. 'Well it sounds like it's gonna be about as cheerful as my wedding was.'

Nesica wiped her eyes. 'Our own tying of the knot was witnessed by two peasants in a mudflat, and we are happy enough,' she said.

We all laughed. We couldn't help it, but then we got to work.

It was as glorious a summer's eve as we ever saw on that hilltop, the golden light stretching as far as the eye can see, like an old soul's first sight of the Land of Youth when worn out with years. Much as I had my sword belt on and ready, and a knife hidden beneath my tunic besides, I allowed my heart to swell with pride as I saw my nephew being carried out through the south gate by the warriors, shoulder-high.

His bride walked from our house to the rocks on a path of campion blooms that Rhyddo's 'cow-girl', Retta, and other Cornovi survivors had gathered from the field edges for her. Airdinna was radiant – there was nowt of the slave about her now. The dress Nes had made for her was a tawny pink with alder bark dye Nes had gathered specially, and it was a triumph, set off with silver ornaments young Blodau had loaned. I saw Nes straightening out the folds as the bride drew to a halt, still sombre-faced with all that must be on her mind, so I dared a wink once I'd caught her eye, and managed to raise a smile.

Ambix himself had done nothing else to raise a hair of suspicion and I was starting to doubt myself. With my back to the rocks and surrounded by my people I felt safe, as safe as I ever could be, but nevertheless I kept a close eye on his movements. He was over to the east side now, with Leon, having watched Kynbel being carried out, and was just sipping at his beer and chatting. I thought I saw him take a step back when the warriors lined up with swords and spears to form a guard either side of the path, but that was natural enough. I lost sight of him for a few moments as the crowd moved forward and felt my heartbeat rise.

Concentrate on the task at hand, I told myself. You are becoming skittish as a deer.

Now both the bride and groom were in front of me a carnyx was blown for the start of the hand-fasting and the people fell quiet. I raised my arms to the Gods.

'We join this couple in the presence of the Gods, witnessed by their kin and their ancestors. Are there any who hold that they should not be joined?'

Silence. Silence, thank the Gods. Then, down at Airdinna's right knee, their boy Temlyr sneezed, louder than any sound he'd ever made in his life, and it made everyone laugh.

I repeated the question and this time there was not a squeak.

Eirian, to my left, passed Airdinna a cup of ale.

'Airdinna,' I asked, 'do you pledge to be wife to this man?'

Airdinna gave her cup to Kynbel. 'I pledge.'

Kynbel took a sip then handed it back.

Dran had hold of Kynbel's sword, back from the smith all bright as if new, and now passed it to our nephew.

'Kynbel, do you pledge to be husband to this woman?'

Kynbel laid the sword at her feet. 'I pledge.'

Eirian took back the cup and Nesica now handed the three cords to me. Kynbel and Airdinnna crossed hands, right to right and left to left. There was a moment's pause in all the crowd, not least me, to see what young Temlyr would do, and a collective sigh of relief when he raised his chubby little right hand to hold onto that of his parents'. We'd held off the hand-fasting until he'd lost his fear of Kynbel but given he had yet to say a word it was still a bit of a gamble. I did not delay. I laid on the golden-yellow cord and looped it round.

'Gold for the Catuvellauni wheat,' I said, and the crowd cheered.

Next the blue cord. 'Blue for the Durotriges sea.'

There was only one true Durotrige there and that was the bride, but a good cheer was raised nonetheless, may the Gods bless them all.

'Green for the Cornovi hills,' I said, as I looped around the last cord, which raised the loudest cheer of all.

Kynbel and Airdinna smiled to each other, tears in both their eyes.

'Now say the words we learnt together,' I whispered.

'I pledge I shall be a shield for your back, an ear for your words and a pillow for your head, for as long as love shall last.'

I placed my right hand on my nephew's head, my left on Airdinna's.

'This couple have been joined in the presence of the Gods, witnessed by their kin and their ancestors. Let no one come between them.'

Bride, groom and son all turned to face the people, still tied at the hand, the carnyx blew three times and there was one last burst of applause, and that was it, the ceremony was over. I pulled at the brooch at my throat, loosening my cloak that had ridden up when I raised my arms aloft.

'You all right?' Nes whispered.

I grinned. 'Since I fled from the druid life I never thought I would do a hand-fasting. I'm glad nothing went wrong.'

She sidled up beside me and patted me on the behind. 'Well I for one am glad you did not stay a druid.'

I laughed and hugged her. 'Are *you* all right?' I asked.

Nesica's gaze had settled on our Gladsia, who was throwing around the campion blooms with young Eithinen and Caradoc Hare-Lip, the three of them all squealing in delight. 'It's a pity she will never meet her uncles,' Nes said. 'But I always knew they would die in battle. It was as inevitable as the sun rising.'

I sighed and held her closer. 'We will do what we can for Aesu's daughter.'

'Is there any word from Catuvellaunos?'

'No, not yet. We can go to Mon for Lughnasa, if our line here in the west still holds.'

She glanced over at Ambix, chatting with Cam down by the roasting hog. 'He hasn't done anything else, has he?'

'No. I'm starting to think I was jumping at shadows.'

Little Temlyr had joined the other youngsters and Gladsia now skipped up to us. 'Tem'yr says he's thirsty,' she said. 'Can we have some beer?'

We both burst out laughing. 'He said no such thing,' Nes admonished, but with a laugh still in her eye. 'He's never said a word. I have elderflower-and-honey water for all of you, come along.'

Nes went off back to the house, all the little ones trailing her like ducklings, while I headed over to the hog for some food. Machan was there, a patch still over his bad eye, but smiling and happy, with an arm around his wife, and I thanked the Gods, that moment, that I had pressed ahead with the treatment, despite my doubts. We touched our cups and watched the dancers together, his son Hedros dancing with Blodau just behind the bride and groom.

'They are still keen then?' I joked.

Machan and Alwona smiled. 'Yes sire, very,' Machan said. 'But they remain chaste – our younger boys have been teasing them mercilessly.'

We ambled down to the buckets for some more beer. 'I'll go to see the Deceangli on my way to Mon at Lughnasa,' I promised. 'I'll speak up for Hedros. To be honest if Eburos sees how happy his grand-daughter is he may need no persuading.'

'Thank you my king.'

Alwona thanked me too, but she was smiling and tapping her foot, so I apologised, in jest, for keeping them both from the dancing. Machan shook his head.

'No sire. I can often tell when I am about to . . . fall, but only a few heartbeats before – I don't want to be the thing everyone remembers about Prince Kynbel's wedding.'

I hung my head. I could understand, but I still felt wretched. He'd had two fits in the time we'd lived here, one worse than the other, and had turned down my offer of training the young warriors because of it. Machan reached out and gripped my arm.

'My king, don't feel bad. I'm not in any pain, and if the Gods intend it then I will live to see my grandchildren – not many can say the same.'

I had a brief dance with Alwona, with Machan's blessing, so she did not miss out, but I felt uncomfortable and handed her over to her next-eldest son at the first opportunity. The sun had set and Kynbel and Airdinna were running to their new house, laughing, as well-wishers threw grain at them. I looked for Nes in the crowd but she wasn't there. Gladsia was with Eirian and young Eithinen, both little girls sipping at their sweet drinks, and young Temlyr and Caradoc Hare-Lip were drinking too, but Nes wasn't with them. I stepped over to our house and poked my head around the door, expecting to see my wife still inside, but she wasn't. I turned back to Eirian.

'Where's Nes?'

'Went for a piss,' Eirian said, loud as a thunder-clap, then blushed.

I laughed and headed back towards the beer buckets, intending to replenish my cup . . . but stopped dead in the middle of the dance ground. It was as if some helpful God put the doubt back in my mind. I scanned the host for Ambix – for the first time in . . . how long? The edges of the settlement were disappearing into shadow. Most people were still in the middle, eating, drinking and dancing.

Ambix was nowhere to be seen.

My eyes sought Camulora next and found her fast enough. She was still by the hog.

'Cam – where's Ambix?'

'Had to go for a pee,' she mouthed.

Oh Gods.

I ran through the houses towards the midden-hut *still* telling myself I was skittish at nothing but as soon as I got to it my shout rang out for my warriors. Creegan was slumped in the doorway next to the ash bucket. His grey furry side was rising and falling, too fast, with a whistling wheeze. Blood streamed from his throat.

'Leon! Leon!'

He was at my side in an instant. 'Look after him.' I yanked off my cloak and laid it over Creegan's side. 'Everyone else, spread out – search for Nes.'

'Sire!'

Colleos's yell came from near the entrance. I raced that way, the others behind me, but we all pulled up when we could see what Colleos could see. Ambix had a knife held to Nesica's neck, his other arm gripping her round the chest. Both the guards at the gate had their hands held high and looked to me with absolute terror. Ambix himself tightened his hold once he saw me.

'Let us out or I'll do it! I swear!' he yelled.

My voice was tense as a harp string. 'If you shed one drop of her blood you'll be dead before you hit the ground.'

It was true. There must have been two-dozen spears levelled at him. Nes was the only reason he was still alive. She was pale as milk and shaking; I could see it from here, but she wasn't bleeding yet.

'Nes, love – keep calm. I'll think of something.'

Nesica's eyes flew from me to our screaming daughter, being held back by Eirian.

'I'll be all right, I'll be all right. Keep her back!'

'Let us out!' Ambix ordered again.

I raised my own hands. 'Colleos, Hedros, the gate.'

Both men flicked me a look. *Don't try anything . . . please*, I willed. *Not yet.*

Ambix watched them looking to me. 'They can put their swords down first,' he growled.

They obeyed, and the two entrance guards stepped backwards too as the gate swung open onto the black night.

'How far do you think you're going to get, traitor?' I goaded.

'Well I've got this far.'

Despite the brash words I could see his hands were shaking too. The cut on his face had opened up and a trickle of blood mixed with the sweat pouring down. They edged backwards towards the causeway. He risked a quick look over his shoulder then dragged poor Nes back some more. We all took a cautious step forward.

'Not a step closer!' Ambix warned.

The knife touched Nesica's flesh and I saw her flinch but he didn't draw blood. I gestured a halt to everyone behind me and our hesitant shuffling ceased.

I beg you Gods - what must I do?

I knew he could have a horse tethered somewhere out of sight - if the whole tale earlier *was* a lie - and I also knew, in the dark of my heart, that as soon as he felt away and free Nes wouldn't survive a moment longer. My eyes met my wife's. She knew it too, I was sure of it.

'Caradoc, think of Gladsia - don't risk yourself,' she begged.

'Stay strong, ' I willed her. 'We'll come for you.'

Just then something moved in the darkness behind the causeway: two figures, it looked like, moving fast across the old ancestor barrow. Ambix must have seen us all look behind him and he swivelled to check, loosening his hold on Nes for just a heartbeat. *Now!* Nes elbowed him in the belly, ducking out from under his arm in the merest blink that he recoiled. Ambix caught hold of a handful of her hair and wrenched her back but Nes snatched the dagger from beneath her dress and she lashed out, slashing him across his right arm.

'Now!' I yelled.

Hedros grabbed a spear from one of the gate guards and threw, the throw of his life, skewering Ambix through the

173

right of his chest. The Gaul slumped to the ground. Colleos kicked the knife into the long grass and pushed him right down, pinning him to the earth, Hedros on the other side. Nesica flew to me.

'You're all right, you're all right,' I soothed, stroking her hair, but now the fight instinct was passing the sobs of shock began. Eirian released our daughter and Gladsia ran to us, clutching onto her mother's legs.

The two men we'd seen sprinting over the barrow raced in, swords in hand. One was Corbennog, my old Silure friend, clasping his knees and gasping for breath.

'I'm sorry, I'm so sorry sire. I got here as soon as I could.'

The other man I did not know. He was a striking sight, almost as tall as Dran but broad with it, with bronze-coloured hair arranged in three-dozen braids or more, twisted off into a coil at the nape of his neck. He wore a huge thistle-purple cloak with gold thread at the hem, a heavy electrum torque, Roman-style shoes and, I noticed, a large gold ring on the middle finger of his right hand.

'It's my fault,' the man said. It was a deep voice and a drawling accent unfamiliar to me. 'I knew about the assassin and came to warn you, but I went to Uricon's old seat first, by mistake.'

I looked to Corbennog and he nodded the truth of it.

'Thank you, all the same,' I said. 'I am Caratacos, King of the Catuvellauni of the west. Welcome.'

The man grinned, a big toothy grin like a happy dog. 'I know who you are,' he said. 'I am Venutios.'

Twenty three The Prince of thistle and heather

A blood-curdled gasp from the ground snapped my attention back to Ambix. Hedros had pulled the spear from the traitor's chest and his blood was now seeping out, in regular bursts, onto the grass of the causeway. There was a spray of blood around his mouth from where he had tried to speak. His eyes met mine.

'I . . . had . . . no . . . choice.'

'There's always a choice!'

I said it in such anger I saw my own spit leave my mouth. My own wife and daughter flinched. I took in a good healing breath. 'There is *always* a choice,' I said again.

His eyes went still and Colleos closed them. 'Should I leave the body out here sire?' Colleos asked.

May my ancestors forgive me but I was tempted.

'No . . . no. Let Camulora clean him up if she wants to. We'll build a pyre in the morning.' I looked back to Corbennog and Venutios. 'How did you know he was planning to betray us? Can we expect an attack tonight? Or tomorrow?'

Corbennog shook his head. 'No sire, he was alone.'

'I knew he was an assassin 'cause he outright told me,' Venutios said, bronze eyebrows climbing upwards. 'I was on my way here, to you, but I didn't tell him that, so he just assumed I was loyal to Rome. He shared my camp-fire one night and poured out the whole tale like I held him to the flames – I think his mind was troubled.'

Nesica nodded. 'I think so too. He told me men in his cohort would be stoned to death if he betrayed them again.'

By the Gods.

Nes lifted Gladsia up to settle her on her hip as she used to when Gla-Gla was smaller. 'Is Creegan alive?' she asked, her eyes searching my face, and my heart sank.

'He was when we found him . . . but he doesn't look good.'

Nesica's expression hardened and she planted a swift kick in Ambix's ribs.

'Come away,' I said, steering her from the body. 'Let's get Gladsia inside.'

Colleos stayed to clean up, the rest of us went back to the village. Nes and Gladsia were still clinging close to me and Venutios, Prince Consort of the Brigantes, followed on behind. Everyone stared, a bit, but not just at him. Every dog in the village was barking its head off. I saw Kynbel standing at his doorway. His sword wasn't belted on but he had it in his hand.

'What's going on?' he called.

'Don't worry, it's all over,' I called back. 'I'll tell you in the morning.'

I ushered Venutios and Corbennog into our house and closed the door. Leon was there already, unfurling clean bandages from our household stash. He'd carried poor Creegan in and laid him on a pile of sheepskins by the hearth. The dog was still breathing, thank the Gods, and thumped his tail a bit at the sight of Nes, though he made no sound. Nes sank down beside him.

'Do not touch his neck, my lady, please,' Leon warned and my wife nodded. 'I haven't cleaned or stitched yet.'

'I can hold him while you work,' she said.

Leon, from behind her back, passed me a cautious look. 'Are you all right yourself my lady?'

'I'll be fine. Better to be busy.'

I could see the sense in that. I also knew that I would have to concentrate on my duty as a host, since my wife was – Gods help her – in no fit state. Once I was certain Leon had everything he needed I led Corbennog and the Brigantean prince back out of the house, taking my daughter with me, so that Nes and Leon could treat Creegan in peace.

'We can eat by the central fire,' I said, a little embarrassed. 'There is food and drink aplenty from the wedding feast earlier. Sorry, but, well, it's a dry night, and warm.'

Venutios held up his hands. 'Don't mind me. I am the easiest of men to please, and after what you have gone through the Gods only know I would not expect any ceremony.'

It was true, to be fair to him. Despite his regal appearance he turned out to be more than easy to please. Venutios wolfed down a dish of roast hog, buttered greens and barley bread, and a big cup of beer, as if he hadn't eaten in years.

'That is *good* food,' he said, the strange accent warmed still more by a tinge of nostalgic awe. 'I haven't had the like in over a year.'

'Are things bad in the north?' I sympathised. 'My sister-in-law told me the land is bleak, even in summer. Is the harvest ruined?'

Venutios looked back at me for a moment in stunned silence then tipped his head back and guffawed. 'Said like a true southerner!' he exclaimed, and I wished the Gods would open up the earth and take me. 'I didn't mean anything like that,' he laughed, shaking his head. 'My wife just insists on every morsel of Roman muck she can find.'

'I – I'm so sorry.'

He waved it away, still bubbling over with laughter. 'Where's the furthest north you've ever been?'

'Three years on Ynys Mon, as a boy. The odd visit since,' I said, with a wry smile. 'Never further than that. I can only ask that you pardon my ignorance.'

'Aw, no matter. I am just as ignorant of the south. You know me as a Brigantes prince, but that is by my marriage. I was born even further up, among the Carvetii, and bleak is not what I would call it. The lands are purple with heather, lively with deer. It's cold but it's clean – we have no mire-fever there. You should see it for yourself.'

I raised my eyebrows. 'I think if I rode over your border your wife might see it as an act of war. I know she was one of the nobles lining up to kiss Claudius's arse.'

He looked into the fire. 'That's fair,' he said. 'But I don't agree with her. Neither does our chief druid. Nor a lot of the people, either.'

'Does she even know you are here?'

'No. I am just on my way to Mon to pray as far as anyone at home is concerned.'

Really? Either he is naïve or they are stupid.

'You seem to have travelled completely alone – was that wise?'

Venutios laughed. 'Maybe not. I had my shield-bearer with me to begin with but then he got sick in his stomach and I had to send him home. Even my horse went lame. The next person I fell in with was this traitor of yours.' He rubbed his chin. 'We landed a few punches on each other before I got to my sword and he ran off like a hare.'

Corbennog was listening, I'm sure, but also making shadow shapes with his hands to amuse my daughter and looked to me with a knowing smile as I turned to her.

'Thank the Gods you both arrived when you did,' I said. 'Or my daughter and I might have been mourning my wife on that pyre in the morning.'

Venutios nodded. 'She was the target all along – you, if he could, then her if not. He told me. Scapula wants to draw you out, out to a battle in open country. Something they can win.'

Gladsia ran over to me and I cuddled her.

'When Ambix arrived earlier he told us that my wife's kin among the Iceni are dead and the revolt has been crushed. Is all that true?' I asked.

'Yes. I'm sorry to say it but yes.' He held out his hands, palms up. 'That is why I am here, to throw in my lot with you if you'll have me. My own people have been meek as babes with the Romans just like the Iceni were and what good did it do them? Why should we watch the swords of our ancestors being melted before our eyes?'

My hand went instinctively to the hilt of my own sword, the sword of my mother's kin, forged in the Ordovici mountains in my great grand-sire's day. One day, Gods willing, it would be Gladsia's, and she could gift it to her son or daughter when the time came. I would hurl it in the nearest river for Teutates before I'd see it melted.

'I will not be drawn out, by Scapula or anyone else they send, until it is a battle I'm sure *I* can win. I won't be sacrificing my men any more than I would my wife and daughter. I'd advise you to do the same.'

Venutios nodded. 'That's why I'm here. I know what happened to Temlyr and Uricon when they tried to stand alone – Vedica and her mother are guests in my household, have been since the spring. I've heard it all. *Together* we could drive the legions into the sea. Britannios, your own Catuvellaunos as was, said that if all the peoples of the Isle had fought together the Romans would never have even got off their ships.'

It was everything I could have wanted to hear but one snag remained to gnaw at me and it wasn't something that would go away lightly. 'Your words are very welcome and you yourself are welcome, Venutios,' I said, with a sigh. 'But while you and your wife are at different ends of the log and she is the one who rules, how many Brigantes can you truly command? I'm sorry, I do not wish to be rude, but it is true is it not? Can you change her heart?'

He raised an eyebrow. 'Naw. I doubt it. Never have done yet. There's more love between stoats and weasels than between us.'

'Why did you marry her?'

Venutios laughed but this time there was no mirth in it. 'My parents said she was pretty. They didn't lie, in fairness. And given our lands are smaller than hers and I have half a dozen brothers I didn't get much choice.' He eased the torque from his throat and gave his neck a bit of a rub. 'Listen, Cartimandua is one thing – maybe she will go off Rome, maybe she won't – but the people are quite another. There is already whispering. The treatment Uricon and his son received is going down like bad milk. Now the Iceni, too – people aren't stupid. I think we can help you fight them.'

'I'm sure you can.'

'So what do I do now?'

Gladsia, by this point, was slumped and dozing against my chest, and I shifted her a little to get the blood back into my left arm and – in all honesty – to give me a moment to choose my words. Venutios, co-ruler and prince, just a few years younger than me by the looks of it, was looking back at me with his brown eyes as trusting as young Hedros or Tarn would be and it threw me a moment.

'I think you will need to muster the support you have talked about and be ready to rise up against them,' I said at last. 'But choose the time to revolt as carefully as a farmer chooses when to gather his wheat. We have held them back this long but sooner or later they will *have to* attack us. Perhaps the Legio Augusta who are raping and slaving their way towards Dumnonia will turn north. Or the Hispania will turn west to shore up the Gemina. Either way it would help us like a gift from the Gods if the Brigantes chose to revolt just then. They've had three years of their so-called peace - now the oppressed must erupt around them like a swarm of bees.'

Venutios nodded. 'I can do that. There are many thousands of us who want the Empire out.'

'And can you hold your warriors in check until the time is right? Preferably without your wife having you executed?'

He laughed again. 'Aw she wouldn't do that. She knows she can only pull on the Carvetii's rope so far.'

Well, I hope you're right.

I saw Leon coming towards us. He looked exhausted but I was relieved to see a smile playing about his lips.

'I think the dog might survive, my king,' Leon said, with a quick bow to the two of us. 'The arteries were untouched, and I think the air-pipe too, so as long as I can keep the swelling down he will be able to continue breathing.'

'What have you used for the swelling?'

He rubbed his eyes. 'A barley poultice, sire. The Queen is holding it in place. I've tried to get him to drink willow bark water for the pain – I've used almost all of it.'

'That's all right, that's what it's there for. He's breathing well now?'

'Yes sire.'

I was pleased, if surprised. 'It looked worse than that when we found him.'

Leon nodded. 'His voice-organ was a mess, that is what bled so much. The Queen's dress is soaked in blood.'

Gods help us. 'I'll go to her now, try to get her to sleep. Well done, Leon – you go home now. Tell Pel everything, make sure the news is spreading beyond the village in the morn that my wife survived and the traitor is dead.'

He bowed again. 'Yes sire. The guest beds are made up, the healing herbs are away out of reach.'

'Thank you my friend.'

He walked to his hut and Venutios waited until the door had closed before speaking. 'Is your servant *Roman*?'

'No, he's from a place called Piraeus, in the old Greek lands. Listen to some of his stories while you are staying with us, if you get the chance.'

Corbennog nodded, smiling. 'Have him tell you the tale of the king he is named after, and the Hot Gates. My kids loved that, last winter.'

I smiled too, at the memory, looking over to Leon's house. 'Yes. Rome made slaves of them long ago, but they never lost their stories.'

Venutios's happy face fell, like a sling-shot bird from the sky. 'Pray Gods it does not come to that,' he said.

Twenty four The Deceangli

Nes and I, in fear of nightmares, let Gla-Gla sleep in our bed that night, the first time out of her own little bed in a few moons. *She* slumbered well, returning to her usual chatty self at breakfast. It was Nesica who had a rough night, what with getting up to check on Creegan every second breath and worrying that one, or both, of our guests could also be assassins, despite all the comfort I could give her. We emerged from the house the next morn like shipwrecked souls at Samhain. Eirian, Gods bless her, took one look at us and brought over honeyed porridge with raspberries in.

I took this opportunity to introduce Venutios to Dran, and when Dranis offered to take our guest down to the paddock to choose a gift horse to be honest I welcomed the rest. I sat outside our house, letting the morning sun soothe my exhausted flesh, while Gladsia gadded about our garden patch watering the plants.

Camulora came over as soon as she could see I was more or less alone.

'Ambix has had his pyre,' she said, voice flat and shoulders well down. I'd seen the smoke billowing to the east so I'd guessed as much but I thanked her for telling me.

'Are you all right?' I asked. She shrugged.

'You did what you had to. A traitor is a traitor.'

'I know, but . . . well, I know you were growing fond of him.'

She just shrugged again and for a moment I was at a loss.

'I think he only did it because of dire threat from Scapula,' I continued at last. 'I will say the druid prayers for his soul when we bury his ash.'

I saw tears spring to her eyes then and she looked away. 'Thank you,' she whispered. She toyed with her belt-end, still avoiding my eyes. 'I – I think I should go back to Siluria. Melistia would house me.'

'If you wish.' The last I'd heard Melistia was back sharing Maros's bed, so in all honesty it wasn't what I wanted, but I was reluctant to refuse, either. 'I'm giving Corbennog two moons away from our lines to see his kin, so you could ride back with him. But your home is here, and remains so.'

She thanked me again, the tears rolling down her face, then wiped them away on her sleeves. 'When does he leave?'

'Tomorrow. Colleos will be taking his place at Uricon's old seat, and Dran will be in charge here while I go to Mon.'

'You go tomorrow as well?'

I nodded. 'With this news from Venutios I'm inclined to travel earlier, by his side, so I can get to know him better.'

She raised an eyebrow. 'You realise, if I was planning to betray you too, you've just told me everything.'

I put my hands over my eyes in mock despair. 'No, no – not you too!' She snorted a grim laugh. 'Seriously, I can't live like that, Cam, not any more. I feel like I've spent this whole year on a knife edge.'

She looked over her shoulder to where Prince Venutios and Dran were coming back in from the paddock, leading Caboledd, a five year old dark-bay stallion, one of Buanedd's sons. He'd been Tegwyn's horse, when he was younger, and before Tegwyn went to be a druid acolyte.

'Can you trust this prince?'

I got to my feet, putting on my torque and straightening out my cloak.

'I trust that his heart is in the right place. Whether he can really do any good . . . well, that remains to be seen.'

We stopped talking as they grew nearer and she withdrew. I waited for Dran and Venutios to stop by the smith's, for a repair to Caboledd's bridle, before we three men wandered down to the weapons practice ground, Gladsia riding on my shoulders. All my household warriors were there, bar Kynbel of course, given the day off. At the moment we arrived they were sat in a half-moon around Colleos and Corbennog, who were showing them a defence with shield and spear against the Romans' stabbing *gladius*. I let Gladsia down from my shoulders and allowed them to finish before I addressed them.

'Warriors, yesterday we faced another shameless attempt by Rome to break us. My wife would be on her pyre *if* their plan had come to pass. I thank you all.' I bowed a little, to them, and they all laughed and cheered. 'Everyone played their part but there is one I would like to thank before you all. Where is the warrior who threw the killing spear?' I scanned the crowd, knowing full well where Hedros was, sat near the back, shy as a maiden, beside his father, as ever. The host all turned to him. 'Come forward, Hedros!' They cheered and jostled him to the front, as I had wanted. He stood before me, bird-cherry red. 'That spear throw was worthy of Lugos himself!' I clapped him on the back and everyone whooped and howled, happy as a pack of wolves. Young Hedros bowed, still flushed to his ears, but smiling in pride despite himself. 'Tomorrow,' I said, in a quiet voice, only to him, 'I leave for Ynys Mon. I will go via the northern route and visit King Eburos on the way. You and Princess Blodau will be coming with me. I'll ask his consent for you to marry her, as proudly as if you were my own son.'

The lad's hazel eyes widened. 'Thank you my king,' he breathed.

'Go on back to the others now and complete your morning's work. You can tell the Princess at the midday meal. Be ready to leave at first light.'

'Yes sire!'

Hedros, and Blodau, were ready at first light all right, probably long before. The rest of us had to scramble a bit to keep up. I said farewell to Nes, Gladsia and Creegan at the threshold of our house with a bannock still in hand and pulling my shirt on.

'Sorry I'm not coming after all,' Nes said, kissing me and getting half bannock. 'I don't want to risk his stitches.'

I smoothed poor Creegan's head, avoiding the edge of the bandage. 'Don't worry, I'll be back before you know it. I'll be sure to get word of Aesu's child.'

Nesica nodded. 'Take care. Give my love to Tegwyn.'

We had another, better, attempt at a kiss and then I swung myself up on Buanedd. I could see Kynbel taking leave of his own wife and child, deep in a long hug, at their door way.

'You two are so *lucky*,' Venutios remarked, voice dripping with such blatant envy I couldn't help but laugh. Thank the Gods he laughed with me. It was true. What with Hedros and Blodau all loved-up like a pair from a bard's tale it must have been an uncomfortable journey for him.

'Back for Lughnasa!' I called, with a wave to Nes and Gladsia as I turned at the gate.

Gods forgive me for swift said promises.

The first hint we had that something was wrong was late on the second day. It was getting towards evening when we reached the Deceangli border. We'd been hosted by my own warriors at a northern Cornovi fort the night before, and all appeared well, so to be honest we cantered up towards the riverside guard-post without a moment's thought for our defence. No spears did come, thank the Gods, but no-one appeared on the stockade to welcome us, either. The gate was closed.

Kynbel looked to me. 'Maybe we've caught them sleeping?'

Maybe.

Nevertheless we retreated out of spear range before I yelled a greeting. Nowt was disturbed except a flight of jackdaws.

We tethered our horses and waited a short while but irritation won out over caution in the end: I tried the gate. It was unlocked. All was quiet inside the stockade, an eerie quiet. There was no blood, no bodies, but something was niggling me. By the doorway of the hut a whetstone had been left on a log seat, just where the morning sun would settle. The door was shut.

'Check it,' I whispered. 'Careful.'

Kynbel and Hedros drew swords and stood either side of the door, turning to kick it open in one quick burst.

'Come on in,' Kynbel called. 'There's no-one, dead or alive.'

We allowed our eyes a moment to adjust to the dim light. Venutios was looking about the walls. 'All the weapons have gone,' he said.

I knelt to check the hearth and found it cold, but a bowl of blackberries was balanced on the baking stone. They hadn't lost their shine.

Blodau was shaking her head. 'Grand-father won't be pleased about this.'

'How many warriors does he usually have at each post?'

'At least two,' she said.

Two?! No wonder they'd run for their lives . . . but from what?

We opened the back gate, the one that faced the Deva, flowing fast and dark even in high summer. There was a rope and post but the boat had gone. Another hut lay across the other side and the boat was there.

'They must have gone over for supplies or something,' Blodau reasoned. She stood on the lower rung of the fence and waved. 'Hey! Bring the boat across!'

Hedros grabbed her round the midriff and yanked her down.

'What?!' she said, play-punching him with a laugh. 'They wouldn't hurt me – this is my land.'

'You've never seen what Roman arrows can do,' Hedros replied, and poor Blodau went white as if all her blood had been drained at the ankle.

'No!'

I gripped her shoulder. 'We don't *know* why they've gone, but he's right to be cautious.'

She nodded, biting her lip, and her hands were shaking as Hedros helped her back onto her mare. We rode upstream and crossed at a shallow stretch, just as undefended, before re-finding the path. All around us the fields were empty. We saw a homestead in the distance but not a wisp of smoke rose up from the roofs. I was reminded of the village raided by slavers Gwyfina and I had sheltered in all those years before.

'Should I ride ahead a while?' Kynbel said, in a low voice, sidling up to me. 'To check?'

'No. Let's stay together.' I could see Blodau had reached the rise of a hillock. 'Keep with us, Blodau.'

She looked back towards us, face stricken. 'I can see a body.'

It *was* a body, and in the poor light it could have been a person, but as we rode closer we realised it was a heifer. I slipped down from Buanedd to check. The heifer had an infected sore on her foreleg, livid and stinking, but it was a slash across her throat that had killed her.

'Someone has given her a swift death,' I said. 'Peasants wouldn't leave this much meat and leather out for the wolves unless they were in fear for their lives.'

Venutios nodded. 'The call must have gone out to retreat to their fort.'

'Crow Hill, where we're going,' Blodau said. She looked about her, eyes wide. 'We're never going to reach it by nightfall.'

Blodau was right, it was dark by the time we were riding up the steep side of Crow Hill. By then we were not alone. Dozens of fleeing peasants surrounded us for the last stretch of the ride, happy to see their princess, and me, once they found out who I was. They called out tales of soldiers moving along the river in boats, or marching in squares through their lands. The numbers varied from hundreds, which I believed, to thousands. I prayed *that* was exaggeration.

The head man of Crow Hill met us at the gate with the briefest of bows. He was of middle years, tall and thin, with bags under his eyes the like of which I'd never seen. 'The king isn't here,' were his first words.

'We didn't expect him to be,' I snapped back.

The man coloured up, a bit. 'Mitios,' he said. 'People call me Miti. Welcome, King Caratacos.'

He didn't actually ask 'What are you doing here?' but it was so blatant on his face I took pity on him and set his mind at rest. He ushered us into the yard and called over a lad to take our horses. The place was crowded, every house spilling over with people, all talking so fast in their shock and distress that they were setting off the dogs and babies. The sheep pen was over full, the animals pressed up to the sides and protesting, their bleats a constant moan. A woman heavy with child was trying to squeeze herself through with a bucket to top-up the water trough for them.

'Let someone else do it!' Mitios shouted at her.

She looked back at him, confused, shielding her belly from another panicking ewe. 'Guests! We have guests!'

I sighed. 'Calm down, we'll help you. Hedros, please.'

Hedros hopped the fence and helped the woman back through the hurdle without being butted. He took the bucket from her. I turned back to Mitios.

'How many soldiers are there? We've heard talk of thousands.'

Mitios nodded. 'Yes, it's no scouting party – I reckon a whole legion.'

'You're sure?'

He ran a hand through his greying hair. 'Fairly sure. I counted five hundred myself, west of here, and there's talk of more.'

'When?'

'Noon today.'

'They didn't attack?'

'Nope. They just passed straight on by.'

'Didn't *you* attack?'

Mitios looked back at me with a curl to his lip. 'I have sixty warriors.'

By the Gods.

'Has a rider been sent to Eburos? Does he know they're coming?'

Another curt nod. 'My eldest daughter, just after noon. But she won't reach him until nightfall tomorrow, at best.'

'If she reaches him at all!'

Hatred flared in his eyes. 'She's our fastest rider – and we could spare no other. They'd have to catch her to do anything to her and she's devious as a cuckoo.'

Well I hope you're right. A stranger praise of a daughter I'd never heard. *Cernunnos watch over her.*

Mitios led us into the largest house. The pregnant woman clapped her hands to remove two brindle bitches from the long seats by the hearth and bade us sit down. Other women were rushing about, making up beds in every last hand-span of space. A huge cauldron of soup hung over the hearth and its smell hitting my nostrils made my stomach rumble. I hadn't realised how hungry I was. I sat down, elbow to elbow with Kynbel on one side and Venutios on the other, my mind working like squirrels in a nut tree all the while.

'How did a whole legion get here without passing though my lines?' I asked, frowning. 'We'd not heard a word. Do you know?'

The Deceangli didn't hesitate. 'They came in from Brigantes territory then straight down the Deva,' he said.

Venutios's jaw dropped. 'What? No!'

Mitios scowled. 'How else do you explain it then? We know they didn't come in west – did the birds drop them?'

Venutios took off his torque and threw it in the hearth. 'That stupid cow!'

Everyone under that roof stopped what they were doing and stared.

'Your wife might have been forced to do it,' I said, in a cack-handed effort to comfort him, but Venutios shook his head.

'Oh, she knew what she was doing. I always thought she'd whore-out her land for a shipload of wine.' He turned to me with pleading eyes. 'I need to get home.'

I sighed. I tended to agree with him but it was night, we'd been riding all day, and he needed food and rest as much as the rest of us. 'Hold off leaving until morn. It's still summer, the light comes early.' He assented. 'I'll be heading on then myself.'

Mitios looked at me askance. 'You're *still* going on?'

Blodau, who'd been quiet, on the seat opposite all this while, now raised her head. '*Of course* we are,' she said. 'Grandfather will need help.'

The Deceangli snorted. 'And just what help will you be princess? Like a feather on the wind?'

'You forget who you speak to!'

She was bright red by that point and Hedros was on his feet beside her, so Mitios flew to his.

'I forget nothing! Your father and all your uncles are dead!' Mitios yelled. 'Half our warriors are dead – our lands are open for the taking. Wake up!'

'Sit down!' I bellowed. 'All of you.'

I was obeyed – somewhat to my surprise, I admit.

I cast a stern look about the circle. 'We're all tired and hungry, worried beyond our minds' girth, but let us not forget who we are at war with. We must plan what we do next. There must be a reason they marched straight past this fort.'

'It's a tall fort, never taken – not in all our years of strife,' Mitios dismissed.

Kynbel shook his head. 'My wife's home fort makes this fine hill look like a pimple but the Legio Augusta were still able to break it in a day.'

'They are heading straight for grandfather,' Blodau said, her voice catching.

I sighed. 'Maybe, but it still doesn't make sense to leave warriors loose behind you – even a small number.' I nodded to Kynbel. 'It's not what they did when they conquered the Durotriges.'

Venutios frowned. 'They were in a hurry – they must have wanted to get through before you or any ally got wind of it.'

Perhaps. I still thought there was more to it.

Kynbel was giving Mitios a hard look. 'Did you pay them off?' he asked.

'What? No!' Mitios boiled up in fury once again and even I could have kicked my beloved nephew then. 'We don't even keep much silver or bullion here,' Mitios countered. 'We're too close to the Cornovi border. Don't accuse me when you don't know anything.'

Silver.

Of course. Blodau's dowry came to my mind. All her jewels that weighed her down. There was one thing the Deceangli were rich in: bleak hills full of skinny sheep and barely a crop of wheat to their name but they had all the metal you could ever want. Silver, copper and lead. I knew it, Venutios's wife Cartimandua must know it too, everyone did.

And now the Romans wanted it.

Twenty five **The Empire's spite**

Venutios left at the first gleam of dawn. I held Caboledd's bridle while he swung himself up then passed him his torque.

'Mitios's wife fished it out of the ashes and cleaned it for you,' I said. 'There is enough war in this world without war with your wife.'

He laughed. 'I agree with you, but she's the one who's forever poisoning the well, not me.' We shook hands. 'I'll help if I can – if nothing happens to the good then just assume I'm dead and all my loyal household with me.'

'We can do better than that. Send word that you are safe.' I snapped a loose blue thread from the base of my cloak. 'Here, wrap it three times around whatever token you might send with the message and I will know it is truly from you.'

'I will. May the Gods go with you.'

He rode out, a large, purple dot well into the distance, a target a child could strike, and I prayed for him under my breath.

I turned back to our host's house intending a quick breakfast but then I saw Mitios himself, leaving, at speed, and to be honest my mind leapt to suspicion before all else. He didn't appear to see me, he just ran off, his hands over his face. I followed, at a good distance, and saw him pull himself up onto the western palisade. The guard on that side spotted him too but it looked like he just wished him a good morning.

I approached, in the open now, and climbed the ladder to sit beside Mitios.

'What do you want?' he asked.

I laughed. 'You know, you are the best of hosts. You remind the rest of us how good we are.'

He went as red as his tunic at that but said nothing.

'I saw you on your own and thought I'd better see where you were going, in case there was trouble,' I explained, which was honest as far as it went.

Mitios lifted an eyebrow. 'Well there's trouble enough. I've had a night full of nightmares – I just wanted some cold air. I don't want my wife any more rattled than she already is.'

I believed him. We both looked out upon the surrounding hills, warming in the pink light, as the crows that gave the place its name wheeled and swooped. All appeared quiet.

'You must fear for your daughter,' I said. 'I know I would, under the same circumstances.'

He nodded. 'Aye, and my son too – the son of my first hand-fasting. He's a spear-man with the King's guard.'

I warmed to him a little more, though I did not feel I could put an arm about his shoulders in comfort as I might have done one of my own men. I whispered the short version of the Maponos prayer. 'Maponos protect him,' I finished. 'And your daughter.'

He dropped his gaze. 'Thank you.' The breeze was cold, up this high, even in the wheat-ripening moon, and I saw him pull his cloak higher up his skinny neck. 'Do you still want to speak to all the warriors once breakfast is done with?'

'Yes. Everyone, if possible, not just the warriors.'

'I'll see to it. Use the platform above the north gate to get high enough to speak to all of them, that's what I do.'

I could see what he meant. There was a wide patch of clear ground in front of this gate-tower, the mud pounded flat, where these gatherings must have been held many a time. It was also away from the noisy sheep and cattle pens, thank the Gods. I sat and waited, Kynbel by my side, as every man, woman and child drifted out from the huts. The old people, and Mitios's pregnant wife, were given the few benches and the rest stood. The warriors, armed with every weapon they could bear, crowded together off to the left, sharing jokes and banter. All the others looked as sombre as they would beside a pyre.

When Mitios emerged from his house, holding his spear and well-battered shield, I assumed all had gathered, then realised Blodau and Hedros were missing.

'Have our two young companions given up on their chastity?' I whispered.

Kynbel shook his head. 'Not that I'm aware of. You could've put a chariot between them last night.'

The door opened again and now the two of them did come out, Blodau leading. She was wearing Hedros's change of clothes, the belt tied tight, with her fair hair braided and tucked up on her head. The two of them turned left and went to the group of warriors. The warriors, for their part, had been silent with shock for a breath, but now there was a cheer.

Kynbel and I passed each other a look. 'Verla would have done the same, to be fair,' he said, 'if her ankle hadn't been broken.'

'And imagine the horror in Camulodunon if the Romans had killed her.'

'What will you do then?'

'I'm not sure yet. . . She may do some good.'

I stood up and waited a moment for the murmur of talk and coughing to settle. 'Thank you for coming out to listen to me,' I began. 'I am King Caradoc, of the western Catuvellauni. I have been fighting the menace you face now for these three years past. As I speak the Legion are stripping your lands of their wealth. In all likelihood many of your people are already dead, and they will take slaves. If I send word to my own army they will arrive too late to stop it, and the Romans outnumber your own forces by far, so we need to use our heads.' I took in a deep breath. 'Where, among the mines to the north, or the route between them, is the best place for an ambush?'

I looked about them all. Over to the right the smith of the place passed a glance to his father, a one armed man with hair white as blackthorn blossom. The older man got to his feet.

'I know a place, King Caradoc. My son can guide you there.'

'Good. Is there enough cover for sixty warriors?'

He shook his head. 'Not all in one place, no. But half there, half a bit further down.'

The warriors started talking amongst themselves again, discussing how they would divide themselves, but a warrior towards the back of the pack, silent, with his arms folded, caught my eye. He was glaring at me like I'd just spat in his breakfast.

If there's a blight in this crop here it is. Best get it out in the open straight-away. I motioned for him to speak.

'Where will you be?' he asked, bold as a boar, 'While we are getting massacred?'

'I'll be right there with you,' I shot back. 'And you'd better hope they do kill me because then my loyal warriors will reduce this legion to dog-meat.' Everyone's heads dropped at that, not least my nephew, so I added 'My wife alone will slaughter a cohort,' to make it seem a jest.

There was a ripple of laughter and the murmur of talk started again. I raised a hand to call for silence. 'Seriously, we *can* do it if we plan the attack well. We've ambushed Romans many times – their blind obedience can be used against them. Do we have sling-throwers?'

About fifteen men raised their hands. Blodau, looking round at them, raised her hand too. 'I can use a sling,' she said. 'Grandfather taught me when I was little.'

Hedros nodded. 'She's good, sire.'

'All right.'

Mitios was scowling. 'We can't take *all* the warriors with us. Some must stay here, to guard.'

I sighed. 'If the Legion come back this way and decide to attack then it doesn't matter if there is one warrior here or sixty, this fort will fall. That's why I asked everyone out here – the people who can't fight need to get out of the fort and hide, somewhere.'

Shock ran through the villagers. There were voices of dissent, albeit under their breath, and then a stout woman in a weld-yellow dress spoke out: 'He's right!' They all stopped muttering and turned to her. 'He's right,' she repeated. 'My cousin lived at King Uricon's seat once she wed and that fort is easily as steep and strong as this one. Now she's dead, and her children with her.'

Mitios's wife started to cry. The stout woman went forward and squeezed her shoulder. 'I know good places to hide – caves and hollows by the river. We'll be ready. We'll be all right.'

I nodded. 'Good. Are any of you trained with a weapon, as your princess is?'

Several women raised their hands. One woman, of middle-years, shivering beneath a thin cloak, looked embarrassed and raised her hand just a little.

'Speak,' I said.

'I'm skilled with a bow, King Caradoc. I know it's shameful and cowardly . . . but my family were starving, when I was girl, before I wed, so . . .'

'So you learned it to hunt with?'

She nodded, her thin face colouring up pink. 'Yes. . . I suppose an arrow can bring down a man just as well as a deer.'

'Absolutely.'

The danger we all faced was brought home that afternoon, when we reached the nearest of the mines. We rode up to the place under heavy grey clouds, the silence pressing down on us, before we saw what we feared. It was clear the Legion had been there before us. Each body we found was stiff as wood. Most had been killed by a simple sword thrust to the torso or neck but one, the smallest child, appeared to have just died from cold or hunger overnight with the death of his mother.

Kynbel had been the one who turned the boy over. He looked up to me with tears in his eyes. 'I thought they took slaves?' he asked, his voice hoarse. 'Why didn't they take them as slaves?'

Mitios, beside me, let out a bitter snort. 'Their hands were already full. Look.' He jabbed a thumb towards a shed with its door wrenched off. 'There was an ingot cache in there knee high. I was here to count up the King's portion for this moon, and I saw it, not five days ago.'

Now there was just a slight depression in the floor to say it had been there at all. Every hut was the same: anything of any value was gone. All the weapons too.

Mitios shook his head as we looked around the biggest of the huts, stripped bare as a wintry tree. 'They even stole the baskets to haul it all away in. The woman who is dead out there, she made good ones.'

Blodau's head sank. 'We need to build a pyre, before we move on. We can't just leave them for the crows.' She looked to me, tears glistening her eyes too. 'We have time, don't we?'

I cast a glance at Mitios and the smith.

'We'll be cutting across the land, they won't be able to, even if they know where they're going,' Mitios dismissed.

'We can't be sure of that. Traitors could be guiding them.'

He shrugged. 'Well, maybe, but I saw them marching past – mule carts, trumpets, standards, the Gods only know what else, and now the loot too, they'll be slow as you like.'

On the strength of his words we *made* time, but we couldn't risk the smoke plumes of pyres in case the Legion were still nearby. There was little wood to be had anyway in this hard, grey place, so we carried the bodies to a fissure in the rock, then blocked the entrance with stones and thorny gorse. I sang a Cernunnos prayer at the entrance, once we were done, my own voice cracking.

Not a single enemy body, not one. It must have been over in moments.

I saw a tiny linnet land among the gorse above the fissure, as I sang the last note of the prayer, its russet chest glowing ember-red among the golden flowers. He sang back at me, his song much sweeter than mine, and I felt my heart ease, just a touch.

'Come, let's get going,' I urged, my voice still rough. 'If we don't get ahead then there will be more villages like this.' I placed the last rock. 'Cernunnos will look after them.'

We arrived at the planned ambush site, without having been spotted, as far as we could tell, and before the first heavy drops of summer rain began to soak us. I'd already told everyone to put their hoods up, if they had them, to blur their shape, but the rain meant I didn't have to ask twice. I settled Buanedd into the hiding place we'd chosen then strode back alongside young Hedros so that I could have a word with him alone.

'It's brave of Blodau, to join her warriors, but do you truly want this?' I asked him, and the lad's stride faltered.

'I'm proud of her, of course . . . but I am worried, sire.'

'Did you try to talk her out of it?'

He looked at me as if I had run mad. 'She is a princess ...'

'Well, yes, but she must respect your opinion, at least a morsel, or she wouldn't be hankering to marry you.'

'Even if I could have persuaded her to stay behind it's too late now . . . and she *is* good with a sling, sire.'

I sighed. 'I don't doubt it – but you must have heard what happened to my first love, from before you were born?'

'Yes sire.'

'I don't want that to happen to you.'

'No sire.'

I checked behind us to make sure none of the others had wandered into earshot. 'Have another word with her while we ready ourselves. And if she insists on this course then never let her out of your sight.'

I let Hedros head to the sling-bearers and made my way to Mitios and the main body of our warriors. Kynbel handed me my shield and a bundle of spears. 'Everything set?' I asked and both men nodded.

'Much as we'll ever be,' Mitios muttered.

'The smith has gone up ahead to signal when they're near,' Kynbel added.

'What's the signal?'

Mitios gestured to the left. 'The trickle of that brook there, it will stop. He just has to drop a boulder.' I must have looked sceptical. 'It's balanced on an edge, a mere flick of a stick will do it,' he explained, with the insolent shrug I'd come to expect.

'All right. And you're all sure they'll come this way?'

Another shrug. 'If they are going to the next cluster of mines then yes, it's the only way to go without crossing swamps or scaling mountains.'

I wasn't sure either was beyond the Legion, to be honest, but we relied upon their desire for speed. We spread ourselves out among the reddish rocks and boulders either side of the vale and waited. It was still high summer, the days were long, but even so the daylight was on the wane and the rain clouds weren't helping. The water trickled on.

'It's no good, I'm going to have to go for a piss,' Kynbel whispered, and I thought he was joking, but he did back away for a spell without going into the open. When he came back he was frowning.

'Can you hear horses?'

'Our horses? They're too far away.'

'No I mean hoof-beats – a galloping horse.'

Another young warrior just across from us nodded. 'I can.'

'From the south?'

I cast another look at the water but it was still dribbling away – I could hear it, but my eyes hadn't trusted my ears.

Kynbel shook his head. 'From the north.'

Oh great. As the light began to fade I'd already started to think we'd missed them, despite our so-called 'quicker' route, and now what? 'If it's just one horse, that could be anyone, a messenger, maybe. Let's stick here for now and – '

I stopped. I could hear it now too. There *was* just the one horse, yes, but some other noise behind it. I risked standing a moment to see better and I saw Hedros and Blodau, higher than we, were also on their feet. Hedros saw me looking and gestured north with both hands.

Kynbel tugged my cloak. 'Uncle – look.'

The smith was out of his eagle-high perch, leaping down through the rocks like a goat, yelling at us and waving his arms. 'Hundreds! Hundreds coming! From the north!'

As soon as he was in reach I whisked him down behind the rocks with us. 'A whole legion, it must be,' he wheezed. 'One rider up ahead and then Romans – as far as the eye can see.'

Kynbel's eyes met mine. 'They don't usually send one scout ahead alone . . .' he said.

No, indeed, and this was no Roman scout. As soon as the girl sped into the vale on her foaming black mare I heard Mitios gasp and I knew who she must be. The horse had two arrows embedded in its rump and another two thudded into the poor beast as she raced past our sling-bearers. Three Roman archers appeared over the crest behind her. They were felled by sling stones before they knew what hit them, but they were just the first drops of the flood. Dozens of archers surged in behind them. The black mare collapsed dead into the brook at the heart of the vale, her rider thrown forward, arrows missing the girl by the Gods' own will.

'Dillyn!' Mitios cried.

He ran to her, using his shield to protect them both, hunkering down into the grass. As soon as he broke cover every other Deceangli followed, spears and sling-stones raining down on the first wave of auxiliaries. It was like hunting deer in a pit, for a blink, but the main body of the Legion were well warned now. I could hear the commander yelling, see the shield wall going up.

Shit.

I grabbed Kynbel's arm. 'This is never going to work, not now. Let's get Mitios and his daughter.'

We both scrambled down to Mitios, shields high.

'Let's get out of here!' I shouted at him as soon as we were in reach. 'Order the retreat!'

Our warriors were still slaughtering the first wave of auxiliary archers but he could see what I meant – the shield wall was advancing. We'd be in javelin range in moments.

'Into the bog land, it's our only chance,' Mitios said. He got to his feet, back to back with me so we had shields fore and back, while Kynbel shielded the girl. 'To Lal Moor!' Mitios yelled. 'Everyone! Into Lal Moor!'

'What about our horses?' Kynbel asked.

'Don't worry. We're going that way,' Mitios said, helping his daughter to her feet. She was nursing her left arm, close to her chest, as if her wrist was broken.

We took off, scrambling up through the rocks towards the high moorland. I looked back and checked on Hedros and Blodau – they weren't far behind us. To be honest it looked like most of our people were alive, thank the Gods, but given only a few of us had arrived on horses to start with there would never be enough mounts for all.

'Dillyn, you share with me,' Mitios ordered as we reached the sheltered spot where we'd left the horses.

'No, with me – we two together are lighter,' Blodau countered, and she was right, but I ran over to the two of them before they galloped off.

'Careful! Her arm is broken.' I ripped a strip off the bottom of my cloak and strapped Dillyn's arm to her chest. It would have to do for now. At least her fingers were still pink. She herself was white-faced but gritting her teeth. 'Keep it as still as you can,' I warned, 'or you'll be in agony as the fight instinct passes.'

I helped her up onto Blodau's mare, with the princess behind to support her, then threw myself up on Buanedd. All around us our men were running for the moorland, swift as deer. The Legion were still advancing on us in their square, relentless as a tide, but only the slowest met with javelins.

We disappeared into the dark.

Twenty six Shells

We didn't stay on the horses for long. It wasn't safe. Mitios insisted he knew the moor like his own house but night had fallen and I didn't trust his confidence. Between heather and tussocks were patches where the ground quivered like skin on cooling porridge as we passed it. Late into the night I turned my ankle on a clump of grass and when I righted myself my foot was a mere finger-span away from a pool of this sucking, crusted, porridge. I felt a sick shiver run up my spine.

'You all right?' Kynbel asked.

I straightened my clothes and gave Buanedd a reassuring pat.

'Yes. Looked worse than it felt.'

'Further to the left! Follow me closer!' Mitios ordered.

We all obeyed.

We didn't stop until we'd reached an outcrop of rock on the highest ground. The rain dried up and the clouds cleared, so there was more light than there had been for our flight, but we were all tired, and it was as good a patch as any to group up and rest in. I'd been looking at my feet in nervous thrall for what felt like forever so it was a gift to sit upon a rock and look up. I don't think I ever saw so many stars, or stars so bright. The great milk streak towered above us like a plume of smoke, bright and awesome as the eyes of a god.

'My king? You're shivering.'

Hedros stood over me, concern filling his face.

'Am I?'

He undid the strap from Buanedd's saddle cloth and wrapped it round me. 'You need it more than him,' he protested as I tried to wave it away.

'I hope I'm not sickening for something.'

He shook his head. 'Blodau is the same, sire, I think it's just the shock and worry. She'd never killed anyone before.'

I looked to him in surprise.

Hedros nodded. 'She saved my life. I'd speared one archer and turned to fight the next but another had his arrow trained on me – she got him *right* between the eyes, as deft as she hunts a duck.' He chuckled. 'We have to get wed now – it will be a good tale for our grandchildren.'

'I don't think there's any doubt now that Eburos will give his consent.' I lowered my voice still further. 'Do we even know he's alive?'

Hedros shook his head. 'I heard Blodau and the Deceangli girl talking,' he whispered back. 'Dillyn never made it to Eburos, sire. She said the force we've just fought are only half the total – they were told to plunder what they could while the rest sped on to the sea. Blodau said that if that's so then they must have met with the king's forces, at his seat or near it, yesterday or today.'

I cast a glance to where the two girls sat, beneath the one cloak, heads bowed, Dillyn still cradling her broken arm. Blodau's face was wet with tears.

If I'd known all this was to happen . . . I would have brought an army, not four of us.

Having none of our spies still in place has cost us dearly.

I took in a deep breath. Hindsight is easy, but it achieves nothing.

I turned back to Hedros. 'You've done well, Hedros. Your parents are rightly proud of you.'

He seemed to colour up, even in the starlight. 'Thank you, sire.'

I got up. 'I should splint Dillyn's wrist if no-one else has.'

No-one else had, and it took me a while to find any stick worth the name to splint it with from amongst the scrappy heather, rocks and moss. Most twigs I found were soaking wet and weak to the point of spreadable. I wound up using one end of a spear shaft. I talked to the lass as I worked. She confirmed everything Hedros had told me. Dillyn was thin and dark, like her father, but with a healthier face. I gave her one of the better sticks I'd found to bite down on whilst I realigned the bones and she bore it like a warrior.

'There, done,' I said, and she let the stick drop from her mouth. 'Your father sang your praises when I first met him, and he was right. You did well.'

'Not well enough.' There was a bitter twist to her mouth like sucking a sloe. 'I should have got to the king! I *almost* snuck past them.'

'How close did you get?'

'I could've spat at them. They wouldn't have seen me at all if one hadn't slunk off for a shit.'

I put the splint in place and bandaged it with plenty of strips of my ever-shorter cloak to pad the broken end of the spear-pole. *Sorry my Nes ... another cloak ruined.* 'I'd get you something for the pain, if I could,' I said. 'But there's nothing out here.'

She shrugged it off. 'I'll be all right. Better than my poor horse.'

Her father had been sat on a flat rock with his head in his hands but he came over and hugged her at that. 'We should get moving soon,' he warned. 'In case they're coming after us.'

Kynbel had been balancing atop the the highest rock and shook his head as he jumped down. 'No, I could see torches in the distance – they're going south-east.'

Mitios and I looked to each other. 'If they *are* coming after us they'd have more sense than to use torches. Maybe they've split their forces again,' I said.

Mitios nodded. 'We should get going, to be sure.'

By the time the sun was coming up and warming our poor flesh the earth was getting harder, with more heather and less moss, and we were dropping down to lower ground. I felt more at ease. We were also heading north and west again, towards Eburos ... or most of us were. Some of the Deceangli men had drifted away in the night, fearing for their wives and children with the Legion marching south towards the Deva again. I couldn't blame them, to be honest, given what Kynbel had seen. I was just thankful we'd got everyone out of Crow Hill.

'Why do you think the Legion's going back?' Kynbel asked me. 'Because they've stolen their fill and everyone's dead?'

I flicked a look at Blodau, stretching out up ahead, her horse at arm's length behind her. She didn't appear to have heard.

'I don't know. Maybe the defence of the king's seat was stronger than we fear.'

Kynbel's eyebrows lifted but he said nothing. He'd seen where my gaze turned.

We both knew my words were more about hope than belief.

It was near evening again when we approached the king's seat. We were filthy and weary by then, hungry as wolves, but no hospitality awaited us. Every peasant we'd found alive was weeping for their burned home, wailing for their stolen sheep, and I felt bad even asking them for water. No-one had news of Eburos.

As we reached the seat and saw the cold blue ocean in the distance for the first time, all hope had gone. We'd run out of living people to ask anything of: here were only corpses. I watched Blodau running from body to body, picking the white haired ones first as a bee moves from flower to flower, and felt an actual pain in my heart.

Curse you Rome. Is half the world not already enough?

Blodau moved behind one of the grey defensive walls and dropped, disappearing from my sight.

Oh no.

I ran to her, finding her on her knees with her hands clasped over her mouth, but the body before her was not Eburos. It was a woman, her flesh as naked as a newborn apart from a copper ring around one ankle, as people sometimes wear for aches. There were smears of blood on her thighs between her legs and blood all down her neck. Falling from her left hand was a sharp piece of flint.

'She stabbed herself,' Blodau whispered through her hands. 'She stabbed herself in the neck.'

The girl began to shake and I reached out to put an arm around her shoulder but she flinched. Within moments she vomited. I took off what was left of my cloak and covered the woman up before anyone else came over.

I gave Blodau a moment then handed her my water pouch to swirl out her mouth.

'You knew her?' I asked, and I kept my voice soft, but it still sounded too loud.

The slightest of all nods. 'She . . . she was my wet nurse, when I was a baby. I – I saw her not six moons ago. I used to play stack-twig with her children.'

Hedros had run over and he tried to hug her but again she flinched and he let her go.

'I must find Grandfather,' she begged, her voice choked.

We renewed our search of the village. Houses skirted the more sheltered lee of the hill, only about a dozen, clustered behind the walls that had not saved them. We found none alive. There were dead guards in and around the great house, and suspicious gaps upon the walls and shelves where the king's greatest treasures had been taken, but Eburos was not among his warriors. I watched Blodau searching every last corner of the house for clues with a heavy heart. I was relieved when even she gave up and left the house. A low wall just outside seemed to bother her.

'The heads have gone,' she said.

I thought she meant Eburos kept the heads of slain enemies there, but she told us that carved stone heads, depicting her father and his three brothers, had stood there for years.

'He must have taken them with him,' she exclaimed, eyes gleaming. 'He must have got away.'

'Blodau – stop. You are torturing yourself.'

'We haven't found Decanglos either! They *must* have got away.'

'I don't think your grandfather would have abandoned his people . . .'

Her eyes refilled with tears. 'Neither would Decanglos . . .'

'It's different – if there was any hope for even the life of a newborn peasant then Decan-'

I broke off as we both heard Kynbel's shout. He was perched at an angle on a rock in the ankle-breaker field to the south-east of the village defences.

At his feet lay a man, two arrows sticking up from his back, his white hair moving in the wind.

'No!' Blodau cried.

She set off and I followed her, picking our way through the rocks as fast as we could. Kynbel snapped the arrows off and gently turned the man over.

I knew it was Eburos, Blodau's cry had been sign enough, but now I saw his face. His torque was missing. Even the mottled flesh of a man of his age had a tan at this time of the year and from the paler band on his right forearm it looked like an arm-ring was missing too. His cloak was coming loose where the brooch had been ripped off, only the arrows held it on.

Blodau dropped to her knees. 'Have they *no* shame?' she asked.

My voice came out a bitter growl. 'No. I don't think they have.'

We had no real choice but to stay at this village of ghosts that night. Food had been left in the houses and once we and the horses were fed and watered there was firewood enough to grant decent pyres for all the people we'd found, three or four to a pyre. We were dog-tired but it was done, and when at last we could do no more none of us could bring ourselves to sleep in the beds so we built another fire, out in the yard, and we all slept out there, wrapped in blankets, as shepherds do. Exhaustion lulled us deep, ghosts or not.

As the day dawned we gathered the ashes and buried them, in a new mound we built up, bucket by bucket, to the south of the one Blodau's father and uncles rest in. I watched young Blodau, tears sliding down her face, as I led us in another mournful prayer and was relieved when she let Hedros clasp her hand.

'You are queen now,' Dillyn said to Blodau as we left the mound. 'What do you want us to do?'

I saw a flash of panic in the girl's eyes but she steeled herself. 'This place is no longer a home . . . I think we should leave it. You should all go to your own homes and check on your families.'

Mitios's eyebrows twitched. 'Are you sure, Princess?'

She nodded. 'You have not found your son . . . he could be there, looking for you.'

'What will you do yourself, Princess?' another Deceangli warrior asked.

Blodau took in a deep breath, flicking the briefest of glances to me. 'I – I think I should continue to Ynys Mon with King Caradoc, to seek the counsel of the druids. Our own Decanglos could be there.'

I nodded. It was the wisest thing she could do, in the circumstances. 'I agree.' I straightened my back and looked around to them all. 'It looks like the Legion have left, for now, but we need to strengthen the border lines – to give us an earlier warning in case they come back. With all the hills we should have beacons, regular look-out posts – and more warriors based near the boundaries.'

Mitios agreed. 'I can start that. I'll get on with it.'

'I will visit Ynys Mon and consult with the druids as I always planned but as soon as I am back at my seat I'll send spies into the Roman held lands. I won't be caught napping again, by the Gods.'

Kynbel had turned away. 'Someone's coming,' he said.

We all tensed like deer at a wolf's howl but the men coming in from the north-west didn't look a threat. Two were walking out in front with a gaggle of warriors behind them. As they neared I thought I could see Ordovici shields, and by the time they were a couple of spear throws from us I was certain the man on the right was young Mocco. He was smiling as usual despite a great storm-cloud of a bruise all about his left eye.

'It's one of the Ordovici princes,' I said and saw an immediate look of horror cross Blodau's face before it settled into a frown. 'It's all right, I know him.'

'Decanglos is with him,' she said.

I waved to Mocco and he waved back. The man next to him was indeed a druid, dressed all in black but muddy to the knee. I could see it wasn't Ordovicos, but it was not the Decanglos I had a vague memory of from my boyhood at Ynys Mon either. That one had been built like a bear. This was a skinny pole of a man with a three-legged wolf on a lead.

'We are relieved to see you safe,' I said and he returned a shy smile, nodding to both Blodau and me as if he knew me too. He looked quite young for a chief druid, thirty-five summers at most.

'Thanks to the prince here, Arthewin's son.' He passed his left hand through his thin rusty hair. 'I was out teaching the good berries and the poisonous ones to the older children when the attack came – I was bringing us all home for supper when the Ordovici war party stopped us, thank Maponos.'

Mocco nodded. 'The Legion came a mite too close to our border, so Father sent us out to stop them crossing it.'

He looked to me as if he wanted to say more.

'Go on.'

'They got within sight of the crossing to Mon,' he said, shock clear in his eyes. 'And then they turned back – I'd love to think it was the sight of hundreds of our warriors on the border but I doubt it.'

Blodau's frown hadn't gone away. 'Couldn't you have *crossed* the border, to help us?' she snapped.

'We did help you,' he barked back, in kind, his face flushing red. 'We've saved your druid and twenty of your children, and captured four of the enemy. Not bad for people you've always regarded as worse than rats.'

I raised my hands, stepping between the pair of them. 'Where are the children and these prisoners now?' I asked.

Decanglos tipped his head back towards the coast. 'We're all camped on the beach.'

'My men are looking after them,' Mocco added.

'What are you going to do with the prisoners?' Kynbel asked. 'Why did you capture them alive?'

Mocco shrugged. 'Well I was going to give them to Ordovicos to take to Mon, for a sacrifice at Lughnasa if he wants, but it's *her* land . . .' He looked to Blodau with contempt. 'What do *you* want done with them?'

Blodau didn't hesitate a breath. 'I want to execute them.'

I felt my stomach turn. The little girl I'd met at Imbolc had long gone. 'Wait . . . malice is poison. Don't rush to something that will play on your mind.'

Blodau glared. 'You've seen all that I have seen these days – how can you deny me vengeance?'

'Vengeance isn't justice.'

'I don't care.'

I drew in a sharp breath. I looked to the others around me for support. 'We could get useful information from them.'

Kynbel raised his eyebrows. He nodded back towards the mound. 'Think how you would feel if it was Aunt Nesica and your Gladsia in there.'

Gods help me.

I saw the truth of it on everyone's faces.

'All right,' I said at last. 'At least let me question them first.'

Twenty seven Prisoners

We took food and other useful things from the village, with Blodau's blessing, before setting off for the coast. I went to the druid's house with Decanglos and helped him strip it of all the dried healing herbs we could carry.

'Did the Romans steal anything of yours?' I asked and he pointed to a hook above the door.

'My sickle, from up there. And a cauldron I'd just had made.' He shrugged. 'Thank the Gods Brith was with me.'

For a moment I didn't know what he meant then realised he referred to the wolf. Quite what the legions would want with a wolf at all, let alone a three-legged one, I didn't know, but I humoured him.

He handed me a black cloak from a basket by the bed. 'Here. It will be cold by the sea, even in this moon. The wind blows straight from Eire.'

'Thank you.'

He smiled. 'You don't remember me at all do you?'

My heart jolted. 'Remember? . . . I'm sorry.'

Decanglos laughed and the wolf wagged her tail just like a dog does. 'It's no matter – you're two years above me so we didn't share many classes – but I remember you. When you stood up to Britannios – the old one – ha! I was pleased. I was called Modwyc then.'

Modwyc . . . Modwyc . . . Gods help me.

A weasel-thin red-head boy came to mind, trembling before the ire of the old Britannios.

There.

'You freed the raven! You were the one who freed the sacrifice raven for Samhain that last year! I remember Britannios hauling you out in front of everyone and shouting at you.'

He giggled a nervous laugh. 'Yes, I remember that too. Quite well.'

'You were brave.'

Another laugh. 'Me? No. I just don't like to see anything suffer.'

I slumped myself down on a stool by the cold hearth. 'If that's so . . . how do you feel about sacrificing these prisoners?'

Decanglos pursed his lips. 'They are the Queen's prisoners.'

'The Queen is a green-shoot of a girl who has seen enough horror these days to break anyone. She needs our counsel.'

'That she does.'

'So will you talk to her, with me, then?'

He sat down upon the edge of his bed. The wolf laid her head on his thigh and he fondled her ears. 'We can't stop this . . . and we shouldn't. It's not just the Queen, it's the people. Justice must be done.'

On such a sunny afternoon in the wheat-ripening moon the children should have been larking about in the sand and surf. Instead we found them huddled together by the cliffs like sheep in a storm. Blodau ran to them and was engulfed in hugs, their high-pitched questions drowning her.

The Deceangli survivors and their Ordovici hosts were camped on a patch of beach near where a fresh water stream spilled to the sea. The prisoners were out of sight, in a birch thicket a bit higher up, where a giant slab of a mountain loomed over us all. Prince Mocco took me to them.

It was quiet in the thicket, the trees dulling the sound of the waves. Three of the Romans were tied to birch trunks, watched, at a distance, by wary, scowling guards. All were silent. The fourth Roman lay prone, a red cloak over him up to the neck, and as soon as I was within a few paces I could tell he was dead. I knelt and closed his eyes.

'What happened to him?' I asked, in Latin, and the oldest of the three jolted as if prodded.

'In the fight for the fort, yesterday, his rib was broken. His lung crushed together like an empty wine-sack.'

'So you stayed with him?'

He nodded. He was about my age, with a few grey hairs spotted among the dark, and a sallow skin like Leon.

'Yes. I am *tessarius* for this troop . . . and I have some skill with wounds.'

Tessarius? I was unsure. Watch-captain, or something like that. Maybe 'night-watch commander'.

'These are his friends,' he added.

I looked the man in the eyes. *By the Gods . . . it could be me.*

'I will see he is given a decent pyre,' I said.

He sighed. 'He was a follower of Christo – could you ask that he is buried?'

'All right.'

The man peered at me, his mind turning over like earth to the ard. 'Are you Caratacus of the Catuvellauni?'

'I am.'

All three of them blanched.

'What is to be done with us?' the lad on the left asked.

My breath caught in my throat. 'You are to be executed.'

They crumbled before my eyes like dried flower-heads in a fist.

'I've heard many tales of you,' the *tessarius* said at last. 'None of cruelty.'

I kept my voice even, whatever was in my heart. 'It's true. I behave myself in open conflict as befits a man – my father and my uncle taught me well. *This*,' I gestured back towards the village we had come from, 'the rape of servant women. Letting babes die of cold. *This* is not it.'

All three hung their heads. 'We – we had nothing to do with that,' the youngest said.

I raised my eyebrows. 'That could be true, but I have no proof either way. Make your peace with your gods, if you can, for I cannot save you.'

The lower lip of the youngest one began to tremble and I looked away.

'The Legion will come back for us,' the man on the right insisted, and I saw the *tessarius* roll his eyes. He saw that I saw.

'Why did the Legion withdraw?' I asked.

'Scapula received word,' he muttered. 'There's a revolt among the Brigantes.'

What?! Venutios can't have even made it home yet.

The man on the right looked about ready to gnash his teeth. 'We shouldn't tell him that!' he seethed.

'What bloody difference can it make!' the older man yelled back.

I stayed quiet a moment and let them calm themselves. 'Have you any knowledge of my kin? My brother's wife and my two nieces, in Camulodunon?'

I didn't expect an answer, to be honest, but it was worth a try. The *tessarius* shook his head.

'I don't know for sure. There was talk they were all dead, but now the word is that was a ruse.'

I looked back at him in shock. He shrugged.

'It's one way to get out of a wedding.'

Gods be praised.

'Thank you.' I got to my feet. 'I'll make sure it's quick.'

I walked out of the thicket, catching Mocco's eye as I went. 'Tie them to posts on the beach,' I said. 'And give each able-bodied Deceangli a spear.'

I carried on walking.

'Aren't you going to give the order?' he asked.

'No.'

I walked to the surf, stripped off all my clothes, and bathed in the cold sea.

Later, as the sun set, Mocco wandered to my side. The four Romans were, by then, buried in the loose earth at the base of the cliffs and the posts had been taken down. We built a fire, away from the spot, and set a tripod over it to cook a stew. Some of the children were still as awake as owls, gabbling away to Decanglos, but several now dozed, using their princess, and Hedros, for a pillow. Kynbel was sound asleep too, on the sand, snoring like a pig – he being one of those lucky souls who could sleep on a knife's edge if he needed.

Mocco handed me a bowl of the stew and slumped down by my side. 'I spoke with Decanglos, earlier,' he said. 'He told me he'd rather not take the children to Mon. There's an old fort up on that hill that he thinks they could bring back into use.'

'Fair enough.' I took a sip of the stew but it was too hot. 'I'll still make a quick visit to Mon, then I want to get back to my wife and daughter. What about you?'

He gazed out at the setting sun. 'I'd better get back to Father. We can escort you to the crossing but then I should get back – we were only supposed to guard the border.'

I gestured to his black eye. 'That didn't happen to you in the fight yesterday, did it?'

He shook his head. 'No. Days ago – I made the mistake of paying Father's latest girl a compliment.'

'*She* hit you?'

Mocco snorted. 'No no, he did. I could have taken it from her – the girl's a lamb.'

'Was he drunk?'

'No. Never is, really. It's not so bad – Arth dragged him off me before he could do any worse.'

'Do you think he blames you for the death of your mother? I know it's madness to blame the babe but it has been known. The mind plays tricks on us all.'

'That's how it started, maybe. I don't know. But it doesn't explain the rest.' He shivered. 'He can have someone flogged for no reason at all, sometimes. There'll be ten days of it, dozens bleeding and pitiful, and then he calms down and the people ease their breath.'

'Doesn't Ordovicos stop it?'

'He tries, when he's there, but he's on Mon a lot. And Father only has to harp on about some slight the poor wretch is guilty of and Ordovicos flows with it anyway.'

I set down my bowl and put my right arm about his shoulders. 'My offer still stands, you can come and live with us if you want. You could be a great help in the fight to defend our people.' I sighed. 'But it sounds like you need to defend your own people, from within, and I can't in all consciousness take you away and leave Arth to do that alone.'

I saw Dillyn hanging about near the fire, she seemed to be trying to catch my eye.

He brushed some sand from his striped breeks. 'No, I wouldn't do that to him. My brother is the favourite, I've always known it. He's the bright star, the best crop of wheat the farmer ever grew . . . but even the stars need the darkness, and the wheat needs the dirt.'

I smiled. 'Keep talking like that and your father will wish he'd packed you off to Mon.'

He laughed. 'I wish that sometimes. But Ordovicos never said I had a mind for it. Brain like an over-boiled bean.'

'*That* is not true.' I hugged him a bit tighter. 'Listen, you are my kin and you are always welcome. Don't wait for him to blow up like a lidded pot on the hearth – not again. Come to me for help, even if it's only for a few days away.'

His chin was well down to his chest but I saw him nod.

'I think I've got sand in my stew,' I continued. 'I'll get some more. Do you want some?'

'Yes please.'

I rose and went over to the fire. Dillyn greeted me with a smile, or at least an attempt at one. Her eyes were clouded.

I spooned myself out some stew. 'Can I help you, Dillyn?'

'Yes. I think so.'

'Has Decanglos given you some willow bark tea?'

'Oh yes. It's not that.' She flexed her fingers as if to show off how well she was faring. 'It's just . . . earlier . . . you talked of spies? Going into the Roman lands to alert us?'

'Yes. I did.'

Another attempt at a smile. 'Well I think I could do that. I want to.'

I looked over to where her father dozed on the sand. 'What does Mitios say about it?'

'He agrees. He thinks I'll be good at it.'

'I don't doubt that, but isn't he terrified of what could befall you?'

She swung her good hand around. 'What choice do we all have?' She raised one of her crow black brows. 'And I have spoken with him. He thinks as I think.'

I took in a good breath. *Maponos bless this Dillyn.* 'All right. Once your wrist has healed you will go to work. That gives us the time for you to learn the tricks to keep yourself alive. Do you speak any Latin?'

'None.'

'We'll start with that then. I can teach you some whilst we travel and when we're back at my seat I have people who can teach you to write it too – it can be useful. That and many things.'

'To fight?'

'Yes, that too.' I looked back to Mocco, sitting quiet and alone while he waited for his stew. 'Are you betrothed to anyone?'

She laughed. 'No. No-one ever asked.'

'Can you take this stew to that lad over there and have a chat with him, then? No-one can point the finger at you for it.'

Dillyn frowned. 'He's Ordovici.'

I shrugged. 'So am I, in a honeysuckle winding way. We who fight the Empire must see each other as kin or all will fall.'

She bit her lip. ' . . . I don't have to do anything else with him, though?'

'You don't *have to* do anything. It was just a suggestion.'

The bowl was taken from me. 'All right then. Is his name really Mocco?'

'Everyone calls him that. If his mother intended to call him a better one she died before the druid could name him.'

'I'll stick with "my prince" for now. And you – if I work with you should I start calling you "sire"?'

'My people do. But Blodau remains your queen.'

We both looked over to where the girl now slumbered among the remnants of her people. 'Is she really queen?' Dillyn asked. 'With everything that has happened – even if the Legion doesn't come back – this land is open for the taking. . . '

Her piercing eyes looked up to mine. I knew straight-away what she implied. I remembered the girl's grandfather sitting with me in friendship at the Silure cave all those moons before.

'Blodau remains queen,' I said. 'I have other battles to fight.'

Twenty eight Kin

Ynys Mon was beset with summer downpours as my party stepped onto the shore and it was still grey and drizzling when we approached the druid encampment. Even so it appeared a far happier place than the one I'd escaped from all those years before. I could hear young acolytes singing an Epona prayer in a round, off in a glade to the north, while other young druids built a shelter from green branches for the noon meal. The smell of fresh-baked bread filled the air. I noticed with a smile that some youngster was drying their under-breeks on the warm dome of the oven – *that* would never have been allowed.

Our own Catuvellaunos was sat under a wide oak, teaching a group of initiates, but he broke it off and walked towards us as soon as he saw me, bringing the group with him.

'Lughnasa will be all the better now! Thank the Gods you are safe,' he exclaimed, a broad smile across his face. He was older than ever, thin as a rope, but none the worse for it, it seemed. 'I'll send word to Tegwyn that you're here – he has been watching the sea for days, sure you were going to arrive any moment, and now he finally gives up you appear.'

'He is well? He thrives here?'

'Yes. Very.'

'Don't worry about sending word, just tell me where he went and Kynbel and I can go to him. I have news about his mother and sisters.'

Catuvellaunos lowered his voice. 'I hoped to have word on that front myself by now. My . . . informer . . . has not sent word as they promised.'

I sank my head. 'May the Gods protect them. But if what I heard yesterday is true perhaps I have good news.'

'We'll talk more later. Tegwyn is by the pool.'

I left Hedros, Blodau and Dillyn in the care of the druids while Kynbel and I set off to the pool on foot. Tegwyn was sat alone, when we found him, skimming stones. He turned when he heard us and his eyes were bright but it wasn't just at the sight of his kin.

'Did you see that?' he exclaimed. '*Six* bounces.'

'I did.' I ruffled his hair and he grinned even as he squirmed. 'Surely that isn't what Britannios sent you here to do?'

'No. I am to gather watercress for the meal, but I have enough.'

A pile of the plant rested on one of the flatter rocks, not so much to destroy the stand by the water's edge, but enough.

The lad turned to his elder brother, bracing himself for the inevitable hug, but Kynbel lifted him clean off the ground. 'You are getting big!' Kynbel puffed.

'Fourteen winters now,' Tegwyn agreed, serious of face. 'I know all the prayers and all the stars, every plant and every beast. Catuvellaunos says I might be made Initiate by my sixteenth Samhain.'

I glanced at the pool, clear and beautiful, now, but scene of far more sinister memories for me. 'But are you sure you're happy here, Tegwyn?' I sat down on the flattest rock and gestured for him to sit by me. 'You know you can come home to your kin any time you want.'

My nephew considered it a moment, head cocked to one side. 'No. I belong here,' he said.

'All right. You will be a better druid than I ever was, I think.' I looked again to the pond, taking the time to choose my words with care. 'I have heard a rumour – I cannot say it is more than that – that your mother and Verla and Lalga have pretended they are dead, in order to get away from Camulodunon. So if you hear somehow that they are dead keep those words in mind, as it may not be true.'

Tegwyn looked back at me steady as a wall. 'They are not dead,' he said. 'Mother said she would send word to me if she was dying and she has not.'

There could be any number of reasons why Briga would not be able to fulfil such a promise and a clever child such as Tegwyn must know it, but I allowed him his conviction. We skimmed stones with him a little while and then he took us on a short-cut through the woods, back to the others.

'Do you know if Dobunnos is here? With a bond-woman and a small baby?' I asked him, when we were almost back.

'Oh yes. The baby is Aunt Nesica's niece.'

'Yes. And mine, by marriage.'

'They have been given a hut away from everyone else because of the baby crying.'

'Could you take me to see them, after the midday meal?'

'Yes but then I must get to herb practice. I mustn't be late.'

I smiled. *Gwyfina watch over this one.* 'That's fine.'

The stone-bottomed and thatch-topped hut, ringed by coppiced hazels, was only about a hundred paces away from the camp but I could see why the arrangement was better for all concerned. The baby had colic and was screaming the roof near off as I arrived.

'She is well, apart from that?' I asked. Plump-cheeked Olla, her nurse and bodyguard, responded with the broadest of grins.

'Strong as a bull,' she said.

I looked to Dobunnos, thinking this over-confident, but he agreed. He was a man of about fifty summers with a grey beard and eyes green as grass. He looked slight but strong with it, like a cat.

I handed them the clothes and gold my Nesica had packed for them. 'What name has the child been given?'

'Aesa, after her father,' Dobunnos said, smiling. 'Princess Coriona was never keen on her name.'

'You knew her, as a child?'

'Yes, and her mother before that. They both did more good in a single moon than Eisrig Boduocos has his entire life.'

I could believe it. I'd only met the Dobunni king the once but he'd not impressed me.

'I am sorry the Dobunni lands have been lost. Do you think, if my forces pushed forward to retake them, there would be enough resistance among the Dobunni people to aid us?'

He chewed it over. 'Not enough,' he said, after a while. 'Not now Coriona and her husband are dead. Prince Aesu took a lot of the best warriors with him when he rode out of the realm in ire.'

'And you know what happened in the Iceni land?'

'Yes – they took a good few Romans west with them I hear but it was a slaughter in the end. And sadly there would be too many Silure warriors among your army, I think. The loyal Dobunni would be torn as to who was friend and who foe.' His face took on a bitter twist. 'Besides, those who live for treasure are doing very well out of the Legion's presence, Eisrig makes sure of it.'

Olla handed him the baby so that she could serve us a mint tea and the old druid winded and comforted the babe adept as a mother of ten. Olla smiled at him with clear pride.

'This is not the life you imagined for yourself, I think,' I commented.

He laughed. 'I am happy. The child is safe and now the loyal Dobunni will not die protecting me – it was getting close to that.' Dobunnos handed the baby over to me for a cuddle. 'It could be worse,' he said. 'It could always be worse.'

Night had fallen before Catuvellaunos and I could talk alone. He sat me down on a simple stool in his own larger, private tent while he brought us over a hot drink from the communal hearth. His latest dog, a leggy tan hound, sidled up to me for a pat.

'What became of your dog who trotted all the way from Camulodunon with us?' I asked and my old friend smiled.

'He made it to last winter, grey-muzzled as he was. Twelve years is good for a dog, but I was sad to see him go – he was my last knot to Camulodunon, it feels.'

'I know what you mean. Sometimes I can see it so clearly it's as if I am standing right there, and sometimes I struggle to remember whether the coin smith's hut was next to the blacksmith's or the carver's.'

He stared up to the roof. 'The carver's,' he said after a bit. 'The blacksmith was opposite.'

We laughed, though it was hollow as a blown egg. 'It's all changed now, anyway,' he lamented. 'Prasto's wife came here last Imbolc – to pray for her younger daughter, who had a cough, she said – but she told me a lot. She was like a dam bursting. The Legion are settling their old soldiers there, more by every moon. The buildings have all changed. It was she who told me Adminios and his Roman masters were planning to marry Verla off.'

'Is Prasto's wife in agreement with our cause, then?'

Catuvellaunos raised his eyebrows. 'More than you might think. On the quiet, at least, but as such I fear for her. She said she would send a servant with more news by Beltane or the solstice at the latest and no-one came.'

I bowed my head and took a sip of the blackcurrant tea. 'The Iceni have been crushed, from what we heard. It might be better for her if she kept her head down. Did she say Tog's family seem well, apart from Addy's scheming?'

Catuvellaunos nodded. 'Yes, fairly. They have no power to speak of. Not really. But Verla is betrothed, of her own will, to a warrior of yours, a Louernos?'

He looked to me and I nodded, smiling. 'Yes, I remember him, it's a good pairing – Lern the boat-builder's son.'

'Ah! Yes, I know who you mean. That makes sense then – Bouda said they had some plan to build a boat and sail off somewhere.' He flopped himself down onto the edge of his simple bed roll. 'Sympathetic as Prasto's wife is I don't think it was wise for them to tell her that.'

'Maybe it's a feint, like the shrouded pig carcases on the pyre – or however it was they did it. Verla has her Father's courage and Briga has seen enough life to build wisdom . . . They'll be all right.'

Catuvellaunos went silent, praying, I think, and for a moment all I could hear was the breathing of the hound.

'Do you think there is *any* hope of us regaining Camulodunon?' he asked, in a hushed tone, when he spoke at last.

I kept my own voice low. 'Earlier this year, when we pushed them back from the Cornovi hills, I thought there might be. Everything that has happened since . . . I don't know. And now this rampage through the Deceangli. I did not foresee it.'

The old druid's eyebrows again shot up. 'You and your warriors are like the rock in the river flow, they must go round you. And you know Eburos had flirted with the idea of a peace-pact with them?'

'Yes.'

'Well then, they were always going to lash out at him for throwing his lot in with you. My guess is they'll try pushing across the southern Hafren next. They've already felled the Durotriges, the Dobunni are pliant as soft clay,' he let out a worried breath and plonked a hand on his patient dog's head, 'and it's been a good six moons since I heard from Dumnonios.'

'And no doubt Scapula has heard about my rift with Maros . . . Are Branadain and Siluri here? I haven't seen them.'

Catuvellaunos shook his head. 'Siluri is, but she keeps a hut on the coast for her lung-sickness. Branadain stayed a while but was called home – all is not well there.'

'I can imagine.'

'Given the warriors are still cleaving to you I think it would be worthwhile trying to darn that tear, Caradoc. Branadain said as much before she went.'

'You should have heard what he said to me . . . and it's only been three moons.'

'Even the cosmos can shift in three moons.' He downed the last of his tea. 'There can't be two kings in one land, I understand that – but look what the legions did to the Deceangli when they scented weakness. My counsel is either to make peace with him, or to take over, for once and for all.'

I hung my head. *Peace it will have to be, then.* 'The Ordovicis are a weak plank in the bridge, no? This latest attack got within sight of Mon and Arthewin barely let his sons fight it.'

'You're changing the subject.'

'Yes.'

He laughed. 'Have you a mind to take over the Ordovici kingdom instead?'

'Might be wise. If only to hold it in my care until Arthewin's boys come of age. I am their kinsman.'

Another bitter laugh. 'Well I'm sure that's how Arthewin would see it, no? To be fair Ordovicos shows precious little loyalty to his tribal king every time he worships here.'

'Nor to me, though.'

'Oh I don't know. At least he doesn't describe *you* as a madman.'

Well, that's a start.

Catuvellaunos got up with a creak of his knees and went out to refill our cups. 'I've been thinking,' he said as he came back in, 'of suggesting Ordovicos to the Order as my successor when the time comes.'

'Really?' My voice had no disguise and I saw my old friend's eyebrows twitch.

'You know of good reason why he shouldn't be?'

I hesitated. Not *really* . . . just how I felt. 'What about Dobunnos?' I asked. 'He seems good.'

'Well he is, but he's also chief druid to a conquered people and a lost land. The same goes for Decanglos, now, more or less, and also he seems very young. Not that youth should matter if the choice is good.'

'Branadain, then.'

'Even if Siluri wasn't still living Branadain would be out of the question. She holds on to her family ties too much.'

'Well she would be my choice.'

'I don't doubt that, but it isn't your choice to make.'

I threw up my hands. 'What about Brigantos, what do you know of him?'

'Briganti, it's a woman,' he corrected. 'And I know practically nothing of her, she never darkens this threshold. I've seen more of Venutios.'

'Ordovicos can be cruel, vindictive, and I have reason to doubt his courage.'

'Everyone has their faults. Many said I was too tied to my Catuvellauni root to be a suitable Britannios but I've made do.'

'It's not the same. I'm talking about defects of character – blight in the wheat, not just over-proving one dough.'

'It could have been *you*,' Catuvellaunos interrupted, fixing me with a stern look. 'Remember, Caradoc, it could have been you.'

I said no more.

Ordovicos was due to arrive for the Lughnasa festival but to be honest I was glad when he did not. We stayed to celebrate with the rest of the Order and I got up before dawn to bless the lay-folks' fields with the druids. It was the first time I'd done so in more than twenty years and it was a good feeling, if chilling to see how few druids there now were. Each Elder and Initiate had to bless a good dozen fields a piece, so I decided to assist Dobunnos, given he was looking the most tired and drawn.

'Do none of the druids from Eire come to festivals anymore?' I asked Dobunnos as we got to the corner of our last field.

'None this time. Two are coming for Samhain, apparently.'

Two? I remembered dozens in my youth.

'Since the Durotriges were massacred there's too much chance of a trireme or two in the water to risk it often,' he reasoned.

Gods help us. 'We could do with our own triremes . . . '

Dobunnos took the pot of beer from me and dribbled the last of it on the field corner with a short Belenos prayer. 'Dumnonios said much the same, last time I saw him,' he said when he'd finished. 'Gods preserve him.'

Gods preserve him indeed. 'When the druids from Eire come for Samhain could you suggest it to them, perhaps? Or ask them to come visit me. I was always told they made good boats in Eire.'

Dobunnos smiled. 'I will. Don't hold out too much hope though – I'm sure they feel very safe in their storm beaten island.'

'So did we,' I said. 'When we used to take in druids fleeing from Gaul.'

In the evening, as the great fire was lit, Hedros and Blodau had their hand-fasting. Catuvellaunos told me that she'd asked him for the ceremony pretty much as soon as he'd swallowed his last spoonful of breakfast porridge and, given she had no living kin in the whole Isle to object, he'd agreed. I was relieved I was not going to have to do it, in truth. I could understand that a hand-fasting at Lughnasa on holy Mon would be auspicious indeed, anyone would want that, but I felt disquiet. 'Are you sure you want this, Hedros?' I wanted to say, 'She is much changed,' but I could see the way he looked at her as they tied their hands and I could imagine the answer: 'Not to me, sire. Not to me.'

We packed up and left the next morning, even Blodau and Hedros. They were still knotted as bindweed with each other but, to my mind at least, they did not look as happy as they should have been. *Cernunnos, Teutates, Maponos, Epona,* I prayed, *watch over them. Something is wrong here.*

'Uncle?'

Kynbel broke me from my reverie as I was watching the two of them pack their horses in silence.

'Yes?'

'A man has come in on the ferry, asking for you by name. He says he has news of people you have an interest in – those were his words.'

'Oh by the Gods – not a raid on our home?'

Kynbel shook his head. 'No, nothing terrible like that, but he seems keen to speak to you.'

We wandered down to the jetty and I saw the man Kynbel meant straight away. He was dressed well, in so far as a peasant can be, strong and healthy looking, yet slight. His brown curly hair was cut quite short but curled a bit around his ears. At a guess I would say he was around thirty years old, or thereabouts. The man was beaming at me like I'd just granted him a crock of gold.

'Yes? Can I assist you?' I asked, smiling back at him.

'Perhaps I can assist *you*, King Caradoc. Do you remember me? I'm Tynos.'

Twenty nine A dangerous game

'What?!' I laughed with more joy than I'd felt in a long while and embraced him like a long lost brother. 'You were just seven years old the last time I saw you! It is good to see you alive.'

'And you too! Tyllan said you might be here for Lughnasa.'

'My bard is well?'

'Yes, but we have much to discuss, sire.'

I turned back to Kynbel. 'Nip over and ask the ferryman to wait for us, please.'

Tynos shook his head. 'No need. I can come back across the water with you – I only came to Mon in the hope you were still here.'

As it was I sent Blodau and Hedros ahead with the horses while the rest of us waited for the next crossing, so I had time to sit in the sun and unwind-the-wool with my old friend.

'I have heard much about you, over the years,' Tynos said.

'And I nothing of you. How is your mother, Tarena? I remember her well.'

Tynos smiled but gave a little shake of his head. 'She was fine until this last winter, then she slipped on the ice and broke her hip.' He sighed. 'That was the end.'

'The Land of Youth be good to her. She was a fine woman.'

'She lived to see her grandchildren, which is more than most. She was happy, sire.'

'You are married?'

He laughed. 'Me? No. My little sister – you remember her? She is married to a shepherd down on the peninsula. They have fifty goats and thirty sheep and three babes already. Two sons and a daughter.'

'Gods bless her. It doesn't seem so very long ago she was riding my shoulders.'

'Tyllan said you have a daughter yourself? Princess Gladsia? I am happy for you, sire. I wept to hear of Gwyfina's fate.'

We both stared out across the straits a moment until I broke the silence.

'Is Tyllan coming home soon, do you know?'

Tynos hesitated. 'He . . . he might. He wants to, but I am to ask you what you advise. He's reluctant to leave Rhian as things are – he is concerned for her.'

Kynbel had been sat with Dillyn on the end of the jetty, talking about food, as far as I could tell, and happy enough, but now it was as if his ears pricked up like a dog's.

'Kynbel,' I called. 'Come over here. It might be best you hear this.'

I cast a glance back at Tynos and it was clear Tynos had recognised Kynbel's name. I was glad he chose his next words with care.

'Rhian is well. She has recovered from her. . . accident. But her presence at the seat of Arthewin has turned over already stormy water. You know how the king treats his sons, especially the youngest?'

I nodded.

'King Arthewin is not a man to be disturbed – not any more than he is, and to begin with Tyllan thought Rhian entertained him as a way to avoid his bed. But her voice is no longer good for singing and *now* she foretells the future. Tyllan does not think it wise.'

'How does she do that? She never showed any knowledge of such things while she lived with us.' I looked to Kynbel and he shook his head, as surprised as I was.

Tynos leant forward. 'Since her escape from death she says she can see lights, and dreams that are more like visions. She said Cernunnos sent her back and now she dreams of him, and Belenos and Morriga too. She says she can speak with spirits of people long gone. Tyllan asked Ordovicos to help but the druid encourages her.'

I took in a good breath. 'I think it could be true,' I said. 'I have experienced similar dreams myself, especially after the wound that nearly killed me.' I touched my right shoulder and Tynos's big eyes went still rounder.

'No? Gods be thanked.'

'I often do. Does Arthewin try to drag more visions out of her, then?'

'No sire, but Tyllan believes that Rhian, knowing her power, sometimes comes up with visions that are *lies*. Lies to help Prince Mocco or Prince Arth or someone they favour – this, well this is a dangerous game.'

I cast a knowing look to Kynbel and we both sighed. 'She has a sweet nature,' my nephew said. 'It would be just like her to try to comfort the prince.'

Isn't that just the truth? Gods help her. I remembered what Mocco had said only days ago about his Father's latest woman being a sweet lamb, or something like that, and started piecing it together.

'What about her step-brother?' I asked. 'Doesn't he steer Rhian away from all this?'

Tynos hesitated. 'He is skilled, as a spear man, but a weak and shy *man*, in truth. As soon as King Arthewin showed any taste for her he backed away.'

A druid acolyte brought us over cups and a crock of cool water and it gave me a chance to think.

'Do you . . . do you get on well with Tyllan, Tynos?'

He nodded. 'Yes sire.'

'And he's not in any danger from Arthewin himself, you think?'

'No, he is barely noticed. The household appreciate the music, as have all the villages he's stopped at, but King Arthewin himself is about as musical as a gale through a cracked door.'

I laughed. 'Poor Tyllan.'

'It's not so bad. He can keep an eye on Rhian without too much attention.'

'Good.' I took a sip from my cup and leaned forward a bit myself. 'Listen, I want you to return to Tyllan and assist him, if you can, but ask him to stay where he is, for now, and keep watch. If any danger rears its head get yourselves and Rhian out, but for now keep an eye on Arthewin, and look out for the welfare of the young princes. You can come and go as you please?'

Tynos shrugged. 'Yes. I'm no-one important.'

'Excellent.' We both laughed. 'Come to Caer Caradoc and report to me then, every other full moon if you can, but vary the routes and excuses a bit.' He nodded. 'Tynos Protector, does anyone else know of your previous story with me, apart from ourselves?'

'People know you saved an Ordovici village from slavers, when you were young, but not about me . . . I suppose only my sister, and Tyllan now. Not even Rhian as far as I know.'

'Good. Keep it that way.'

'Yes sire.'

'And be wary of Ordovicos – sometimes he is a friend and sometimes he is not.'

'I know.'

'If I have to be away from the Caer at all I'll make sure my nephew is there to meet you in my stead.' I nodded to Kynbel and the two of them shook hands.

I lowered my voice still further. 'I'm likely to face a Roman attack, either this autumn or early spring, maybe in the south, or possibly even straight at our strongest lines. It would help me a great deal if the Ordovicis joined with us to fight. Do you sense any call for this amongst the people? Against Arthewin's wishes?'

'*Yes,*' Tynos whispered back. 'Even Ordovicos has said so in his festival addresses. The people are frustrated – and scared, that the Legion has got so near. It's like watching the flood water lap closer to your house and not so much as rolling a towel.'

Well put. 'May the Gods go with you then, my friend.' I hugged him about his shoulders. 'And remember, the first sign of danger, get yourselves out.'

The four of us who had set out, ages ago it seemed, arrived back home on a perfect late-summer day with bellies full of blackberries and a hawk-sharp Deceangli girl with her arm in a sling. I intended to introduce her to Leonidas as soon as I could but to tell as few people as possible what her true purpose was. Dillyn's training had already begun, but now it gathered speed. Given what she was about to do I regretted not trying harder, before I left, in my attempt to get Camulora to stay.

I was flabbergasted, therefore, to ride up to the Caer and find Cam sleeve-to-sleeve with my wife, of all people, up on the palisade and waving me back in.

'We had a talk and she decided to stay,' was all Nes would say, at the gate, as she hugged me near tight enough to crack my ribs.

'Anything else unexpected? You're not leaving me for Leon I hope?'

She cuffed me round the head light as a bat's wing and laughed. 'No! There's something a bit unexpected though – Dran and Eirian are due another baby, Imbolc or near enough.'

'Good!' I looked over to their house and Eirian was sat outside, hulling beans, but she waved and started to head over once she'd seen me. I hadn't thought about it at all but it occurred to me then that she seemed a bit long in the tooth for another one. Rhyddo, her eldest, would be wed himself before too long.

'Where's Dran?' I asked.

'Riding the northern reach with Colleos – we were all worried sick when we found out about the Deceangli.'

'It would have been still worse if the Brigantes hadn't rebelled just then. Have you heard anything about the Brigantes, or Venutios himself?'

Nes shook her head. 'Not a word.'

We wandered arm in arm into the centre of the lower yard so that I could greet everyone and I was pleased to see Kynbel back in the embrace of Airdinna, their boy clinging to her skirt as ever.

'Is all well there?' I whispered, to Nes, and she looked where I was looking and nodded.

'Temlyr has even said a few words. Just to Gladsia and Eithinen and little Caradoc Hare-Lip, but it's a start.'

'Where *is* Gladsia?'

Nes laughed. 'Don't worry, she's healthy as a spring morn, she and Creegan both, but she has something to show you. I'll take you there soon, once you've greeted everyone and got some clean clothes on.'

'Oh go on, tell me. I could be out here a while.'

'All right then.' Nes grinned and her freckled nose wrinkled just how I loved it so. 'I've got her a horse and she is proud as Epona! You should see her. Young Coll had outgrown his pony so I bought him from Dag last time she visited.'

I felt like I could feel my own face whiten. 'Isn't she a bit young yet?'

'She's already a year older than I was when I learnt to ride,' Nes countered. 'And I watch her while she learns. She's off at the paddock now giving him some oats with Rhyddo and his lass – not galloping across the hills.'

'Sorry, love. You're right.'

My wife patted me on the behind. 'It's all right. Mathona said all early babes get coddled and we're no different. Come, everyone will want to see you.'

Indeed. Time to be a king. I realised Dillyn was standing alone, now that Hedros and Blodau were being welcomed by his parents at their threshold, so I tethered Dillyn's horse and introduced her to Nes. We all sauntered over to Leon's hut.

'You can tell Leon what your duty is, and Pel his woman, and anyone else I send to you to teach you something,' I advised Dillyn as we walked, 'but keep it at that, if at all possible. Even if people aren't going to turn traitor in a thousand years the less that people know, the less reason there is to torture them – that's a good thing to keep in mind.'

She nodded and I flicked her a little look.

'Yes, sire,' she corrected and I smiled.

'Anything that makes you stand out less is good. For now, with a broken wrist, it's natural you would stay in Leon's house. He is the best healer, after me, and my trusted servant.'

'I'll get you some clothes,' Nes said. 'Pel doesn't have that much, in a household of men.'

Pel herself had appeared at the doorway, pink as blossom and flustered. 'My king! Leon is so sorry he was not at the gate to meet you – he was all stripped off having a wash and naked – '

I burst out laughing and held up my hands. 'It's all right! Really, Pel, it's all right.'

We sat admiring their garden gooseberry bushes and gave them a moment.

I called a gathering for the next day but I left it until mid-morning to give everyone, not least me, the chance of a lie-in with their wives. When we were gathered together in the lower-yard I told them the tale of all that we'd seen in the Deceangli lands, calling on Blodau and Dillyn for more when I needed to. I felt a little cruel, telling my people all this, but it would have been still crueller to leave them ignorant. Towards the end, when I spoke of the rebellion among the Brigantes, I saw a Cornovi warrior of middle-years start as if stung. Once I'd come to an end I invited him to speak.

'My younger sister married a man of the southern Brigantes, King Caradoc,' he said. 'She lives there still, and I'm worried for her.'

In my younger days I would have offered to let him travel north to visit his sister. I might have even offered to go myself, but to my shame the seed of doubt was now rooted in my head. Did he plan to desert? To inform Cartimandua, and thereby Scapula, on our strength, our plans?

'I hope to receive word from the Brigantes soon,' was all I said. 'We shall ask after your sister's village.'

He bowed and seemed grateful but I still felt wretched.

The rest of the morning we planned and divided tasks between us, and I sent young Rhyddo riding off to Colleos to keep him informed. Rhyddo returned, next morning, with Dran, and better news than I could have hoped for, for the Cornovi warrior at least: the Brigantes messenger.

The man was brought before me whilst I ate breakfast outside our house and I might have guessed he was a friend to Venutios before he said as much. He made me look as drab as a sparrow, what with a rainbow of colours in his clothes, his clanking bracelets and his red-gold hair the women would envy. This hair was braided, but only along the centre line of his head, which rather gave him the look of a horse. I guessed he was about twenty years old.

No sooner had Rhyddo introduced him than he dropped to his knees.

'Get up, friend, get up,' I pleaded. 'Here, have a stool.'

Nes had brought a spare one from inside the house and now placed it behind him with a reassuring pat on his shoulder. 'Porridge?' she asked and I thought he might burst into tears.

'Let's start from the beginning – what is your name?' I asked.

He appeared to pull himself together but the words still came out in a tumble. 'Brigparios son of Prince Brigparios, I am nephew to Prince-Consort Venutios.' It was the same strange, rumbling accent as the latter. 'You can call me Brig, if you wish, great king.'

'Brig it is. Did Venutios give you anything to prove yourself friend?'

He drew something from his belt. It was a plaited leather and wool wrist-band with tiny silver salmon studded through it, each with an eye of coral – a sort of marriage of Roman taste with that of our own. Quite beautiful, in its own way, and clever, for if he had been caught then the blue wool wound three times, neat as a rose-bud, round the strap end just looked part of the pattern and no code at all.

I took it from him and then turned to Rhyddo, who had been hanging back, poised as a heron, hand on sword-hilt, this whole while. 'Thank you Rhyddo, it's all right. Go and have some breakfast with your parents.'

'Yes sire.'

He disappeared and this young Brig offered up a sad smile. 'We can't be too careful,' I said, with an apologetic shrug.

'No, no. Of course, great king. To be honest, given what I've just come from, I expected to find you ringed by warriors.'

My bodyguard right then amounted to Nesica, ladling porridge, and our Gladsia picking the low-hanging beans in our garden patch, so I could see what he meant. *Gods help us, let it not come to that, though.*

'Is Venutios alive and well, therefore?' I asked. 'If so then my prayers have been answered.'

'Yes, great king. All Gods be praised. He arrived back after the uprising had swelled and been quelled so, as far as the vermin are concerned, he is as innocent as the Queen.'

'He is safe, then?'

'As long as he keeps his mouth shut and does as the queen says.'

'Not safe at all, I fear.'

'No . . . and there have been losses.'

Nes had come out with porridge for him and her eyes and mine met.'I know where that warrior lives,' she said. 'I'll fetch him.'

'One of our people with kin among the Brigantes,' I explained.

Brig nodded. 'The fight started well but many warriors have died, and several of our leaders. Do you know the man's name?'

'This is a woman, his sister, in a south-lying village.'

'She is probably all right then. The only woman I know to be dead is Briganti herself. They said she was one of the 'ring-leaders', and my father too – they held their executions until the end. Their heads . . . their heads are hanging from the south gate.'

His great ard-blade of a jaw began to tremble so I reached out and held his shoulder. 'We will pray for them together,' I murmured. 'Their spirits live on whatever is done to their bodies.'

'Thank you, great king.'

'Call me Caradoc, please – you are a prince too.'

'Not any more. Can I stay, King Caradoc? My uncle sent me here with his message 'cause I'm a dead man if I stay at home – my father's rebellion is my own. '

'Of course you can stay, and welcome.'

'I'm a good fighter.'

'I don't doubt it.'

Brig was as good as his word, joining my warriors for training from that very morning. A Cornovi widow housed him and the two of them were wed before the autumn was out. He was the first of many, too, as quite a few of the northern rebels distrusted their 'pardon' and drifted to our lines. I made them all welcome but kept my old precaution – once they were in, they stayed.

The Brigantes who made it to our lines all said the same thing: the Legio Gemina were licking their wounds, reluctant to turn their backs on the north, but everyone agreed it was just a matter of time before they would attack again. Some of these Brigantes had seen Scapula himself, when he was with the Gemina. They said he was a plain, ordinary-looking man, quiet, but with a sharp tongue on occasion. 'Like me, then?' I felt like saying. Perhaps the Gods give us the enemy who suits us best.

The Brigantes were a good source of information but I had others. Tynos kept to his first moon-meet and fed me the news from Arthewin's court as I asked. He said the household had calmed, for now, but unease was spreading through the people as rumours about the fate of the Deceangli went from from village to village. Enemies for generations they might have been, but it still put a shiver up.

Dillyn, too, was ready to start her work by the time of the first frosts. I called her to my house one evening along with all those I'd asked to teach her.

'Latin as good as Claudius, sire,' Leon said, smiling, proud as a father.

'Good!' I turned to Dillyn, and to Latin. 'What's your favourite colour?'

'*Rosea, mi rex*,' she shot back.

'Good. Be careful who you reveal your knowledge to – don't let them see that you understand.'

She bowed.

I turned next to Dranis, sat cross-legged by the hearth. 'How have the fighting lessons gone?'

My brother did the so-so gesture with his hand. 'Good with a dagger, not so much with a spear.'

'Right, that's just as well. Two daggers then, Dillyn, one worn openly so they don't touch you and one under your clothes in case they do.'

'Yes sire.'

'Do you feel ready?'

'Yes sire.'

'Then the next thing we need is an excuse for you to be there.' I looked from Dillyn to Camulora. 'Any ideas?'

Cam nodded. 'Always best to stick close to truth,' she said, with a thin smile. 'So . . . her brother is still missing. We thought she could be looking for him, and believe he might have deserted to join the Legion.'

'Good. She might even find some sympathy for that.'

Cam shrugged. 'Well maybe, but we need more if she's not to starve. If she's not going to sleep with them then she needs *something*. She does have a talent but I don't know . . .'

I raised an eyebrow. 'What is it?' I asked Dillyn. 'Can you sing? Tell stories?'

Dillyn shook her head. 'I'm a good mimic, though, sire. I make people laugh.'

'Really?' Up to then she had shown all the humour of a stone in your shoe.

Dillyn drew herself up a little straighter, tipped her head back a bit and to the left. She turned to Nes. 'Thanks for the tea love. Can I have some porridge? I feel hollow as a blown egg.'

There was stunned silence for a heartbeat and then we roared with laughter, me most of all.

'Careful with that, though,' Nesica warned, with a smile. 'Not everyone is such a gentle pup as him.'

That made everyone laugh again.

'I've made you a cloak,' Nes continued. 'Double-thick with a hood and inside pockets. You can wrap up and sleep in it under the stars if you need to.'

'Thank you, my queen.'

'And you are comfortable with writing too?' I asked. Dillyn answered yes and both Leon and Cam agreed. 'Good, then. You can head off tomorrow. If anyone outside this circle asks after you we'll say you have gone west, back home to your father, now that your arm has healed.'

'Yes sire,' she said. 'Thank you, for giving me the chance.'

'Thank *you*. You are showing great courage, and will be plenty of use. Gods go with you.'

She bowed again. 'I'll set out just before dawn.'

Thirty **The best of intentions**

The autumn deepened and I started to think we would not see an attack before spring. Dillyn disappeared into the dark as she'd said and we could do little but wait. We carried on raiding the edges of the Roman-held territories, stealing – or stealing back, I should say – whatever we could. Machan had become so adept at predicting his falls that he agreed to take up my request to train the youngsters after all, which gladdened my heart. The morning air crisped, the days grew shorter. I watched my daughter learn to ride her pony, my wife spinning and weaving with the diligence of a spider and my sister-in-law swelling up with every passing moon.

'Eirian looks tired,' I said to Dran one cool morning as we walked down to the weapons practice ground. 'Does she drink the nettle tea? I know it's vile.'

'Yes, but she's . . . she's not herself.'

He went quiet and I felt bad but I knew of old I would have to prompt him. 'You're scared for her, aren't you?'

The slightest of nods.

'She – she said it's not *sitting* right, not like with Rhyddo and Eithinen. It might even be two.'

I held his arm. 'I could send for a healer from Mon, someone with experience – just in case.'

'Queen Mathona?'

He said it without thinking, I knew it, but then coloured up red. 'I – I'm sorry.'

I sighed. 'No. You're right. Only, I think it might be too much for Mathona to ride this far in winter, as bad as for Eirian herself.'

I looked out over the surrounding hills. The leaves were dry and crackling, the local peasants were thinning out their herds of sheep, but it wasn't full winter yet.

'I've been meaning to darn the tear with Maros, if I can. I'll go soon. I'll ask.'

I set off south, the morning after Samhain, with Rhyddo in tow, while Kynbel led a raid on one of the supply columns heading for Glevum.

I was cheered back in by the guards at the Silures border and by the people of every homestead I rode past, Gods love them. It was only at the seat of Maros Mathanrheg itself that my welcome cooled.

Rhyddo and I were ushered straight to the great house without so much as a cup of water. Maros sat in the dragon chair, as was his right, but now another, carved to be almost as ornate, stood beside it, and this was where Melistia sat, leaning in towards him. *She* managed a wan smile. He just watched me, wary as a deer. They were both dressed all in clothes of madder red as if someone had told Maros that red makes you look healthier. There was a distinct tone of yellow in his face and hands, yellow as butter, and I stifled my sharp intake of breath just in time. Rhyddo, though, was open-mouthed and wide-eyed.

'Why do you bring a bodyguard to my home?' Maros barked, at me. 'You've no need for a shield-bearer here.'

'It's not wise for anyone to travel alone,' I countered. 'And Rhyddo is here because I've come on his behalf, or rather his mother's.'

That brought curiosity to Maros's eyes, and he heard me out, to be fair. As I finished he rubbed his hand over his face.

'I can understand why you're worried,' he said. 'But my mother is in no state to ride to the Hafren, let alone your seat.'

'I'm sorry to hear that. I'll visit her, while I'm here, if I may.'

'Of course.'

'Can I help, at all?'

Maros waved it away. 'I don't know that much more can be done – Brana's in with her now.'

We all heard the door open and I turned to find Branadain herself slipping through the doorway, wiping her hands on a cloth. She nodded to me. 'What's going on?' she asked, and after going through it all Brana was resolute. 'I'll come with you, to help with Eirian,' she said. 'Mother can't.'

Maros frowned. 'What about Mother?'

Branadain tipped her head and puffed out a breath. 'Well, there's not much I can do that you and our sisters can't. I'll leave plenty of herbs.'

'And Siluri?' he asked. 'Aren't you supposed to be going back to her?'

Brana shrugged. 'I will. I'll go on, in the spring like I said I would, once Eirian is delivered.'

Her brother's frown deepened. 'You were going to lead our hand-fasting,' he said, with a nod to Melistia by his side.

'I can do that tonight, before I pack,' Brana shot back. 'Doesn't take two blinks.'

Her twin's face clouded still further, and Melistia's head dropped, taking a sudden concern in a speck on her skirt.

By the Gods.

I tried to keep my face impassive.

The feeling was better at dinner. Mathona was there, puffy-faced, pale, but smiling. She seemed to have forgiven me, regarding Rhian, at least enough to be as warm as she used to be. I told her that Rhian had been welcomed at Arthewin's seat and that my harper was still looking after her, which was all true enough, but said nothing of the visions and dreams.

Maros and I sat side by side as we ate, as we ever did, and he bade me eat more and asked after my family. He was drinking again, both wine and ale, but he did not get drunk that night and we remained civil. It was the next morning, when Branadain had left with us, that things took a turn for the worse.

Branadain waited until we'd stopped for a mid-morning stretch of the legs and Rhyddo had gone off to relieve himself before she spoke.

'Is the thing about Eirian actually true?' she asked.

I looked back at her in astonishment. 'Of course it's true.'

She'd been building a small fire to make tea and she continued pottering about, avoiding my eyes. 'I thought you might just want to get me away, to plan.'

I felt my heart jump as if my whole body was now on alert. 'I would not lie to your brother, Brana. Whatever else you might think of me I have not done that.'

She pursed her lips. 'Well *he* has lied often enough. He swore he'd stop, at the cave, and now he's back to veins and guts full of wine. You must have seen how yellow he was?'

'Yes.'

'Well, then.'

'Well what?'

She straightened up and glared. 'Are you going to challenge him for the kingdom?'

'No!'

Brana sank down upon the nearest log and put her head in her hands. 'I don't know how much longer we can go on. It's as if he and mother are racing to see who can die first.'

I checked over my shoulder to make sure Rhyddo was not on his way back. He wasn't, but I still kept my voice low. 'I'm sorry to take you from them. You're clearly needed at home.'

She blurted one of her crow-like laughs. 'Oh I spend my life surrounded by sick people. Add another to the throng – I dare you.'

Gods help me. I crossed to the log and sat beside her. I almost took her hand but now I could hear the rustle of leaves and I knew Rhyddo was coming back. 'We who are strong are always stretched like yarn to the loom,' I whispered. 'The Gods see that we are strong and add more weights.'

She sniffed. 'I don't think I believe in the Gods. Not anymore.'

It hit me like a tree falling.

Forgive her for such words, Gods, I beg you.

Rhyddo came back into the clearing and to be honest I was glad for I knew not what to say.

'Thank you, for coming to help my mother,' the lad said, giving her a little bow, and she smiled back at him, but he must have seen the tears still in her eyes. He threw me a panicky look.

'We will all do what we can,' I said to him. 'Your mother is strong and healthy, she always has been.'

'Yes sire.'

'Come, let's have this tea and get going.'

We'd almost got to the Hafren shore when Corbennog and Tarn found us. I heard Tarn's shout and the blast of his horn before I recognised either of them. They rode up at a gallop.

'News sire!' Corbennog called. 'Leon read it and sent us to find you at once.'

Tarn took a piece of leather from his pack and handed it straight to me. It looked like the material of another bag, unstitched and returned to flat. The words had been cut into the inside of the leather with the point of a sharp knife.

GEMINA MARCH SOUTH

VALERIA MARCH WEST

COMING FOR SILURES

ARRIVE

V   8 DAYS AFTER SAMHAIN

G   10

I looked back to my two men. 'Who brought this?'

'A stable-lad of the Brigantes, sire,' Corbennog said. 'He said "the cuckoo" asked him.'

Dillyn. Good.

'And what has happened so far? Leon did not just send you for me I hope.'

Corbennog shook his head. 'Prince Dranis has raised the call – over a thousand of our men are heading east to meet the Valeria. More warriors are pouring towards them every moment, and a good three hundred have been left to defend the caer in case it is a trick.'

'Good!' *Now we must prepare for the arrival of the Gemina.* I turned to bring Branadain in. 'If a whole legion wants to cross the Hafren badly enough then they will do it – I've seen it at the Meduwaen. We need to stop them before they even gather at the eastern shore. I need you two –' I nodded to Corbennog as well, ' – to raise the call at home.' I held up the piece of leather. 'Tell the Silures what is in this.'

'Yes sire,' Corbennog said.

Branadain nodded too but she was frowning. 'So many of our men are already with you – it may take longer to gather warriors from the hills than we've got.'

She was right, in a way. The eight and ten days in Dillyn's message were from the moment she'd written it, and it must have taken a good three or four for the stable-lad to get down to my seat, plus more for my two men to get to me.

'Light the beacons. That's what we set them up for.' I held up the message again. 'And tell *everyone*. This, this is serious. If any Silures have been slow to follow me from loyalty to their born king I do not hold it against them, but we need to fight together now, as one. Remember what I told you of the Deceangli.'

Brana held her horse's neck and swung herself up. 'I'll do everything I can.' She passed young Rhyddo a weak, guilty smile. 'There's time yet. I won't forget.'

I stayed that night at a look-out post on the western side of the great river and by morning I had gathered warriors, as might be expected, but also dozens of boats. I was careful to cluster neither boats nor men too much together, though, and I removed my torque and turned my cloak dull-side-out every time I was on the shore-line. There were often people over on the Dobunni shore. They looked like peasants, digging for bait worms or the like, but I couldn't be certain they were as innocent as they appeared.

By nightfall next we were ready to go. There was a Noado surge, but a minor one, so we let it pass then slipped the boats into the water. I'd ordered dark clothes and silence. An otter could not have faulted us. It helped that the moon was a mere crescent that night. The gloom helped us to get across the river unseen – if there was anyone watching, and I couldn't be sure there wasn't – but it did slow our progress through the land. Slow was good, in the sense that our gear did not jangle nor our feet crack too many sticks. 'As quiet but steady as clouds,' I'd ordered, during the day, and I was obeyed.

At dawn we were still in sight of the Hafren but we'd got to the point where it narrowed to river instead of estuary. In the distance I could see the points of house roofs.

'Head to the trees,' I whispered to the warriors nearest me.

We carried on, north, now using the woodland as cover. My *plan* was to arrive with my group, south of Glevum, so we could meet the Legio Valeria as Dranis and the rest of my warriors met them from the north. They would be expecting a defence from my men, but not, I imagined, coming from the south, not through the Dobunni lands they held beneath their heel. We could snap at them from two sides, neat as a swift snaps a fly twixt its beak. That was my thinking, but it all depended on us getting to the Legio Valeria without any Dobunni first raising the alarm – easier said than done. The trees were thinning out, more than I remembered.

'Slow down,' I whispered to the men behind me. 'I think I can hear someone.'

We continued to creep forward, but I was right. There was a clearing ahead, with a hut at its heart, surrounded by dormant bee skeps and sheltered timbers in different stages of being seasoned. A man of middle-years was digging a ditch, to better drain their pig-pen, by the looks of it, while his wife was spreading out laundered clothes on the hazel bushes to dry in the strong morning breeze. The man had his back to me but he was less than a spear's throw away.

Oh Gods.

If they see us, and run for help . . . we would have to kill them.

I raised my hand for halt but as slowly as a flower opens. 'Back away, slow,' I mouthed to the men either side.

I put my left foot behind, feeling for sticks before I put any pressure down, then dared another step back.

No noise, please Cernunnos, no noise.

One of the men behind me sneezed.

Oh no.

I saw the Dobunni man look up.

Oh no.

Don't turn around. Please don't turn around.

A mistle thrush shot from a rowan by my left cheek and sped forward, going towards the man and settling on a fence post right beside him. She sang out, loud as a carnyx.

Cernunnos – what have you done? How have I offended you?

My heart was beating so loud I thought they'd hear it.

'Look love, she's back,' the man called to his wife. 'Did you save the bits from breakfast?'

They both scampered into the hut, happy as children.

Thank you Cernunnos.

We managed to skirt around two more settlements before noon but all the same it was a shock when we stumbled upon the road. It stood out like a scar. The trees either side had been hacked down, the smell of their naked stumps sharp in my nose. The road continued about thirty paces further south-west from where we were before coming to an abrupt stop. We padded down to the end and found piles of rubble, bags of sand and broken tiles.

'There's blood, sire,' Rhyddo whispered, pointing to the side of a sack.

Tarn, crouched beside beside a heap of rubble, looked up. 'More here sire.'

I nodded. 'But no bodies, and no tools or weapons. Someone has come and either rescued the wounded or cleared the bodies.' The blood the lads pointed out to me was dry and dark but even so . . . 'Let's get off the road,' I said.

'Yes y'should,' came a voice from the trees.

We all spun round, spears and swords bristling, but the old woman coming towards us with hands raised looked about as much threat as a feather. She carried a large bundle of twigs and sticks on her back, making her look even shorter than she was, and her feet appeared too small for her.

'Easy, easy,' she breathed. She had more eyes than teeth in her head from what I could see and the words came out a whistling lisp. 'I'm loyal t'Dobunnos an' no threat t'you.'

I motioned to all my men to lower their spears. 'Did you see what happened here?'

The woman nodded. 'The Romans was attacked firs' thing 'is mornin'.'

'By Dobunni warriors?'

She shook her head and gestured to my shield. 'Naw. Like you.'

Like us?

Realisation hit me like a bucket of water. 'Did one have two white horses on his shield?'

She nodded.

Kynbel. Of course.

I sighed like it was my last breath.

So much for stealth.

Thirty one Hunters and prey

'Do you know where the other warriors are?' I asked. I saw the old woman hesitate just a blink. 'You're going to have to come with us, whether you know or not. You won't be harmed – I just can't risk you blabbing to the Romans.'

She chuckled a gappy laugh and shrugged. 'I unnerstan'. Jus' as well I knows.'

The woman shed her bundle and we set off, a little slower now. Before long we were out of the woods and into open meadowland. The old peasant woman led us down a stream gully and started heading north-west. 'Keep us heads dow',' she lisped, and I soon saw why. An enormous hill-fort, the same one we'd skirted north of on our flight to the Silures, years before, loomed ahead.

'Is King Eisrig there? At the moment?' I whispered.

'Aye.'

She spat on the ground.

Heads down indeed.

Once out of sight of the hill-fort's palisades she scuttled over another meadow and into the shade of a smaller wood, thick with coppiced hazel and berry-stripped hawthorn. The old woman ducked and swerved through the branches with surprising ease, being so small, while we, loaded with shields and spears, struggled behind her. At the edge of the copse she raised one bony finger to her lips and pointed. A wet meadow lay ahead, with grass still lush for this moon, and dozens of our horses grazed there. The warriors were beyond, clear to see – a festival of colour and movement. One of them was even standing on his stallion's back, circling at a canter, while other men called out cheers of encouragement from atop an old ancestor barrow at the far end. I saw Kynbel among them and sighed.

Rhyddo, to my left, looked to me, confused. 'Isn't that Prince Kynbel's group, sire?'

'Yes, and if we were a troop of Roman archers instead of their blood kin half of them would be dead before they even knew we were here,' I muttered, then regretted saying it out loud. 'Never throw away your life, Rhyddo – the Gods don't reward carelessness.'

'Yes sire.'

We made ourselves known, lest we be reduced to dog meat in their surprise. As it was my nephew's jaw still hung slack at the sight of me.

'Uncle!'

'It is I who should be shocked, given you were supposed to raid that column and then go home.'

Kynbel coloured up red, his companions dropping their heads, and again I felt a twinge of guilt at berating him in front of others.

'Everyone, leave us please. Tarn, make sure our guide gets food and water. Rhyddo, post a look out south.'

They all snapped to it and I climbed the slope of the barrow to sit by my nephew's side.

'Are you angry with me?' he blurted.

I took in another good breath. 'I am worried. It's not the same thing. And I shall have to change my plans, so that could have a cost. What happened? Why are you still this side of the Hafren?'

He frowned, scratching the scar on the back of his right hand. 'We *did* lay in wait for the column – but it was huge! There must have been five hundred men, and the fort at Glevum isn't even what it was. They've built another, twice as big, upwind of it. The place was swarmy as a nest . . .' He looked to his warriors. 'I didn't feel I could bring them home empty-handed.'

'So, you attacked the road builders.'

He looked surprised that I knew, but nodded. 'Yes, and a hunting party east of the fort. We've been moving too fast for them to catch us – we weren't going to be here much longer.'

I raised an eyebrow. 'Well I was brought here by an old Dobunni woman who was out collecting firewood – be grateful she's no traitor. Do you know the Romans have been out to the road and recovered their dead?'

He shook his head, reddening again.

'There are two legions heading this way. That's why the fort has been made bigger. Your Uncle Dranis is leading our men out to meet the first one from the north – my plan was to surprise them with my party from the south, just before they reach the fort. They weren't supposed to know we are here.'

Kynbel looked up at me, his fair hair catching the strong breeze. 'We still can,' he said. 'They know *we* are here – but they still don't know about you.'

We left as soon as our plans were set, having tarried here quite long enough. Kynbel's men galloped off north, straight towards Glevum, while we headed north-east, still on foot. The meadows sank to wetland at about the same time the bright, breezy morning turned to a typical dank, dark afternoon. We were making pretty good time, though, and I was hopeful of finding somewhere in sight of the fort's eastern road to bed down in before darkness fell. When Tarn came running up front, puffed out and red as a bird-cherry, my heart sank.

'She's gone, sire – the old woman. I'm so sorry – I've lost her.'

'You've *lost* her?' He shrank before me. 'Tarn she is as old as the soil!'

'I – I'm so sorry sire. She – she said she needed a piss. I couldn't follow her.'

I pulled at my hair. *By the Gods.* I remembered that I had said she was no traitor.

Well, I hope I'm right.

I looked about me. The route we were following, shored up in places with duck-boards and log bridges, was the *only* practical route, at least for dozens of men with no boats.

The soggy ground was breaking up into great pools of open water, where heavy rain in the moon before had swollen every brook and stream and beaver dams split the flows. The old woman had said we would face this, to be fair, and I'd thought it would be a good spot for an ambush – but that could work two ways.

'We'll stick with this route, for now,' I said. 'Stay alert everyone.'

We continued, in silence, until I heard a splash behind me. I turned to find Tarn hauling himself out of the mire. 'I slipped, sire,' he said, looking up at me from under his eyelashes and, not for the first time that day, I regretted my outburst of temper.

I went back and helped him back on to the board. 'Are you all right? Did you turn your ankle?'

He shook his head and I gave him a quick hug. 'All right then, let's get on. I'm not angry with you, Tarn. The old lass probably just wanted to get home.'

A curlew's call rang out and I jumped like it was a banshee's cry.

Everyone froze, and looked to me. A curlew was common enough in this landscape . . . but there was something hollow about it, not as piercing as usual.

Another call burst out among the reeds. This time from the left.

'Prepare for attack,' I said. 'Shields off your backs.'

In an instant my men formed up to defend each other, shields outwards, as best they could on the firmest ground, and as soon as we all did so we saw the piece of cloth atop a spear out to the left, waving side-to-side.

'Hey hey hey! Easy!' The man stood up among the reeds, reeds sprouting from his clothes and shield. 'We aren't here to attack you – we want to join you.'

Another thirty or more stood up behind him, and twenty or so at our right. All were disguised with leaves and reeds that put our own attempts at discretion to shame. One man, about twenty paces away, was grinning at us and only given away by his eyes and teeth. Every man had a spear and rough shield. I saw no swords among them.

'Then welcome, Dobunni,' I said, but a wary note must have crept into my voice. The first reed-man to speak tipped his head with a lop-sided smile.

'We *are* Dobunni,' he said. 'But you needn't fret. Mam told us where you'd be and what you're doing. Rome is no friend to us – the last bloody thing we need is another thousand soldiers eating our crops and our sheep.'

'You are loyal to Dobunnos?'

'Aye.'

Cernunnos watch over us if they are lying.

We reached the land east of the fort just before sundown, as I'd hoped, with the Dobunni's help. Further to the east were hills, disappearing into shadow, whilst the last of the day's light cast reflections of clouds and birds into the water to the west. We could just about see the smoke of cooking fires rising from the fort, and hear the distant sound of one or more hammers driving in nails. Kynbel was right – it was bigger than the old Glevum fort. All was tranquil, for now.

'How will we know when Father and the others are approaching?' Rhyddo asked me, as we ate a cold supper of food we'd brought with us, washed down with the cleanest water I could find.

'We won't, I think.' I smiled. 'Unless the legion are running for their lives.'

That raised a bit of cheer. It was true, though. We posted a pair of swift runners up on the nearest hill so we'd get a good warning of the approaching legion – and so both lads could get a decent rest – but in terms of my own men the only group I could be certain of was Kynbel's. Assuming everything had gone to plan and he was still all right, that was . . . *Maponos watch over my nephew*, I prayed, then remembered if he was getting a bit old for Maponos, given he had a child of his own. *Cernunnos and Teutates too.*

'We're not likely to see the Legion today, are we?' the first Dobunni asked. He was packing out his shoes with fresh strips of sheepskin he'd pulled from an otter-pelt bag erstwhile hidden beneath all the reeds. 'They'll never camp out in the open like we're doin'.'

'No, so they could stop at a fort well east of here, or build one of their night-camps, or they might press on to try to make it here before nightfall.'

The Dobunni grinned, casting a glance up to the pink and orange clouds. 'They're running late, then.'

I shrugged. 'We'll see.' I handed him half of my cold cheese bannock and he nodded his thanks.

I was right, as it turned out. The men chosen for second-watch had only just bedded down to attempt sleep when the warning came. We heard the Legion long before we saw the two runners on their way down the hill. It wasn't just the trudge of a thousand pairs of feet. There were horns blowing, shouts, something that sounded like a whip cracking. Mules brayed like tortured souls.

My gaze met Rhyddo's and we smiled. 'Here we go then,' I said. 'Get them all up.'

We were armed and in position when the Legion came hurtling into view. Most of them were foot soldiers, as I'd expected, but there were cavalry too, some riding up the sides and shouting to gee the rest on.

'Sling throwers,' I whispered.

'Yes sire,' came the low hiss back.

'Aim for the mounted warriors first. Wait for my word.'

I let the Legion charge closer – but not too close. The Romans in the fort must have seen them too by now. They would be preparing to support their comrades. *Are you there Kynbel? Now would be a good time.*

It had been a long while since I'd used a sling myself, to be honest, but nevertheless I judged the distance to a hair. 'Now!' I yelled. Dozens of sling shots sang through the air. A good twenty of the mounted soldiers were thrown in an instant, their horses rearing and neighing. The scene erupted into chaos. I remember the face of the nearest scout, eyes wide and mouth open, as my forces surged out of the reeds.

I raised my shield and the sword of my mother's kin and got to work.

Surprise had done its job, and in the distance to the east we could hear more screams and yells where Dran's forces must have caught the column rear. Those of the fore-column who were still alive were haring towards the fort walls and meeting the spears of Kynbel's swift riders. A group had attempted to leave the fort to help their comrades but Kynbel's men had put an end to that. Thus far Kynbel had kept his warriors from getting too close to the fort and he appeared to have lost few, but we couldn't lose that room to move and my own group couldn't edge too close to the fort, either. My other concern was the fat middle of the column, who were solidifying now. Rome's warriors are no chaff to be scattered to the breeze. I am the first to grant them that. I could hear an officer yelling and see the shield wall getting wider and wider.

Time to move.

'Everyone all right?' I called.

I got a 'Yes sire!' from all around, except the Dobunni leader, who was knelt beside one of his own. He looked up to me and gave a little shake of his head.

'If he is wounded we can carry him, if we go now,' I said.

Another little shake of the head. 'Dead.'

'Gods guide him to the Land of Youth,' I prayed, out loud, and *Forgive me for ever doubting them* inside.

'Are y'going back the way you came?'

'No – the northern crossing, if we can. We can't sneak past Eisrig now.'

He nodded. 'I can lead you there.'

I raised my shield to catch everyone's eye. 'Give the signal, Tarn.'

With three blasts of the bronze horn we took off, north, through the dark marshland with the Dobunni man at our head. I asked Tarn to blow the horn again once we were well clear of the road. Kynbel's group heard and galloped through to join us. To the east we could still hear the carnage at the rear but all was black in the sky now. There was no way to tell who was winning.

Camulos, Cernunnos, Teutates, Epona, please look after my brother Dran.

'We need to stop on some higher ground!' I called out to the Dobunni.

He skirted right and took us up into the eastern hills but it didn't do us much good. The moon was covered with clouds, the evenstar had long-since disappeared behind them. I still couldn't see the rear of the column or Dran and his men.

'Give the signal again, Tarn,' I said, and Kynbel looked at me askance from up on his horse.

'That will show the Legion where we are.'

'They know fine well where we are – they're not coming after us.' I gestured down to the 'fat middle' who were still visible . . . and visibly moving east. 'Look. They've turned back to help their rear comrades.'

Kynbel swore. Rhyddo did too but I saw the stricken look on the lad's face.

'Try again, Tarn,' I said but as the three blasts rang out I realised my mistake. *The Romans have horns blowing too . . . and our men don't even know we are here.* 'Stay here, keep trying as long as it's safe to,' I said. 'Kynbel, your men keep our line of retreat open – the rest of you, come with me.'

We scrambled down through the hills back towards the road in the darkness. I could hear the sound of the bronze horn growing more distant behind us but then Tarn did something clever. Instead of just the three simple blasts for 'retreat' he blew the pattern for 'mount your horses', 'rally to the king', even 'dinner'. It could *only* be us. At last

I heard hooves coming our way and caught snatches of our own tongue.

Well done, Tarn.

'Careful,' I warned my companions. 'Don't spook the horses.'

We cleared a path and greeted our warriors as they came through. All of them to a man were astonished to see me. Most were spattered in blood but unwounded, thank the Gods. I saw a few riders had wounded men slung over the withers. None were my brother, as far as I could see.

'Where's Prince Dranis?' I yelled to the nearest warrior.

He shook his head. 'I don't know, my king – we lost sight of him.'

The others agreed. They all looked shocked and worried but no-one actually knew anything. 'He was with us, he was yelling for us to get out, then he just disappeared,' one pleaded. 'I'm sorry, sire.'

'All right – get to Kynbel, all of you. Follow Tarn's music. My group, still with me.'

I put my hood up for better cover and we plunged on, down through the darkness. The noise was abating but I could hear snippets of Latin now. The groans and shouts of the main group on the road, helping their wounded and squaring back together, were separate from another group, off to my left. They sounded excited. I heard '*Euge!*', their word for 'well done', and a few swear words.

I gestured behind me for the main group of my men to halt then crept forward with just Rhyddo and a few others, on our bellies like snakes, to the crest of a low rise.

There!

A circle of legionaries stood beneath us, no more than fifteen, with one older, helmeted, man on a high horse, grinning like a child given a present. His horse scuttled backwards, just a heartbeat, and I caught a flash of a dead horse in the centre, a javelin through its side. Dran's horse.

My brother was there. On his knees.

Thirty two Every man, woman and child

Rhyddo's breath caught and I clamped my hand over his mouth just in time.

Quiet, I told him, with my eyes alone.

I loosened my sword in its scabbard then turned back to the others. *Come up now, low, quiet*, I gestured. *If we do this badly Dran will die too.* Though my heart was pounding in my chest I forced myself to stay calm, but then I heard the sentence from the old Roman that broke even me.

'Take the torque off of him before his head, fool.'

'Now!' I screamed.

Our spears hurled forth and it was the Gods will alone that none hit my brother. My own spear, in my fury, did not meet its mark. It glanced the shoulder-top of the old Roman and span off, useless, into the turf. The man reared and wheeled his horse, out of the circle for the blink of an eye.

'Dran! Run! Run!'

Dran was on his feet and running towards me. One of the Romans who was still alive tried to grab him but I slashed out my sword and cut off his hands.

'Run!'

I smashed my shield into the face of another soldier who reared up to my left. Dran snatched up a spear from the ground and finished him off.

'Father!'

Dran's saw his step-son at the crest. 'Go!' he yelled.

'Get to Kynbel! Follow the horn sound!'

We raced back the way we'd come. It was the Gods own blessing that none of us broke an ankle in the darkness. I could hear the old Roman I'd missed calling for help from the forces on the road.

If they give chase on horses it could be the death of all of us on foot. I urged everyone on faster.

'To the Hafren!' I yelled as soon as we'd made it back to Tarn and Kynbel's group. They all greeted Dran but Kynbel had a worried look on his face.

'Here, take my horse,' he said, to me. 'They could be coming after us, even in the dark.'

'No. You lead us from the front, I'll shepherd from the back.'

'But you are king!'

'*Because* I am king.' I smiled. 'Besides, you stand out like a beacon, I'm dark as a pot bottom.'

He grinned and took off on his bright white horse, shield raised high and calling out 'To the Hafren!' as loud as I. The other riders all set off with him, the rest of us running behind.

For all my words my lungs were hurting by the time the river was in sight. The clouds were spinning away on a high breeze and I caught a glimpse of the crescent moon reflected in the water. I spied the glint of torches too, on the other side – the Silures were waiting for us.

'Nearly there,' I wheezed at my brother. He was helping one of the wounded and looked tired himself. 'Here, I'll take him.'

'I'm all right. You carry on.'

Rhyddo was looking behind us into the gloom, his head to one side.

'I can hear hoof beats,' he said, and Tarn nodded.

All our own riders were well on their way towards the river. Rhyddo and Tarn were in the first bloom of youth but my hearing wasn't *that* bad, so if I can't hear them …

'All right, keep moving. Those with wounded just keep on, fast as you can. The rest of us behind them, spears and swords ready.'

I heard splashing and cheers as our first warriors made it to the river. *How far north are we?* There were places I'd crossed the Hafren on horseback many a time but never on foot.

Teutates guide us.

'They'll need to come back with horses,' Dran commented, as if he read my mind.

'Or we'll need to skirt further north, and I don't think we've got time.'

We ran on, closer and closer to the river, but I could hear the hooves too now. *Twenty horses? No. More.*

The Silures were calling out to us. There seemed hundreds of them, thousands even, their shouts booming across the water like a thousand war horns. I could see Kynbel and the other riders who'd made it across were turned back and ready to defend us.

'Come on! Not far!' I urged, and it was true, but no sooner had the words left my mouth than I heard Tarn's shout. I looked back to see the Roman horsemen, hot behind now, maybe three or four spear throws away. Rhyddo fell, tripping on a tuft, and I hauled him up by his hood. We sprinted on, Tarn just behind us. I risked a look over my shoulder. One of the cavalrymen was pushing further forward, closing in on Tarn fast, javelin in hand.

Oh Gods – I have no spear. I saw Dran still had his, on the other side from the wounded man.

'Dran! Spear!'

He tossed it to me and I took aim. This time I did not miss – I got the Roman straight through the arm pit, knocking him off the horse. The others all roared at that and kicked their horses on but it was too late, my feet were in water. Kynbel and the other riders were plunging back through the river to haul us out. I saw Dran pass the wounded man onto the horse of a Silures rider – was that *Branadain*?!

'Get back!' I screamed.

A thousand Silures voices answered, their spears and swords bristling the far shore like hairs on a boar's back. Some of them were singing. The taunts and insults flowed free.

The Romans had pulled up now.

The old Roman was still on his fine horse but he was struggling to get it under control. His helmet had come off.

I could see his face, flat-haired, sweat-streaked and contorted into a grimace. He looked like his heart was about ready to burst.

'Death! Death for all of you!' he screeched. 'I won't stop! Not until every last Silure has been struck from the face of Mother Earth!' He raised his fist and shook it, like a starving farmer at the crows. 'Death! Death! Every man, woman and child!'

'Not if we kill you first!' was the best retort I could muster, then.

Kynbel scooped me up onto the back of his horse and we plunged across the water.

It was a good moon before I was on my way home to Nes and Gladsia. Our line still held, thank the Gods, but we couldn't drop our guard a moment, and there were wounded who needed care so neither myself nor Branadain could be spared. Not that I was a great deal of use to anyone for the first ten days or so, to be honest, thanks to the worst bout of campaign-belly I'd ever known, and I wasn't the only one.

I felt light as dandelion seed when I sat down for one last talk with Maros before my departure, but I still looked healthier than him. We sat either side of the hearth, he sipping his wine and me nibbling on dry bread, and it felt like the ill-feeling between us had slipped away like smoke on the breeze.

'That man – the more I think about it, the more I think he must have been Scapula,' he said, and I had to agree. 'Do you think he *meant* what he said?'

'Everything I know about Rome points to it being Gods-sworn truth, unfortunately.' I sighed. 'Don't worry, I'll do all I can to draw him away from your people . . . I have an idea.'

'The Ordovicis,' he said, eyebrows raised. 'Well, be careful. Arthewin must know you are a threat to him.'

'Oh I know – not to mention he's mad as a sick dog.'

Maros laughed, and it was good to see, despite his bloodshot eyes and hollow, yellowed cheeks.

'I'm glad we are friends again,' he said, the smile still on his lips. I felt a lump come to my throat.

'We never stopped. But I'm glad too.'

We touched cups, his wine to my water, and talked of my journey to come.

I wondered if I would ever see him in this life again.

My men, and Branadain, arrived back at the Caer two days before the winter weather hit us, thank the Gods. Not that I should fault the gales and sleet. Colleos and his men had held our line against the Gemina like the heroes they were but it was winter that offered us real respite. The Legion retired to their forts to lick their wounds and we to ours. Nes had the chance to feed me up, and Branadain had time to plan with Eirian.

One night, in the cold moon before Imbolc, we were all sat around the hearth listening to one of Leon's tales of Odysseus, my sister-in-law guffawing her head loose as ever, when Eirian's waters broke.

All was calm, at first. Brana had the birth house ready, and Eirian was no scared first-time mother, but when day dawned, and noon followed, then dusk after that, and there was still no baby, disquiet began to rise in the village as weeds unchecked will fill a field.

Nes was pale when she came back to our house that evening. 'Still no sign?' I asked, as she threw her wet cloak onto the fire-dogs to dry, and she shook her head, biting on her lower lip.

'She's still trying to push but she grows weaker by the moment – she can't walk about now, and Brana said it wasn't doing any good.' Nes slumped upon the nearest seat and pulled our Gladsia to her for a cuddle. Creegan had already gone to her side. 'They're asking for you.'

'Me? My training on Mon never ran to this . . . I didn't stay long enough.'

'Well yes – but you'd never opened anyone's head, either, and look at Machan.'

Indeed. Blind in one eye and fitting at least once a moon. I didn't say it but my wife knew the looks on my face well enough.

'He's alive,' she countered.

We took Gladsia over to Airdinna's then went to Eirian's house with heavy hearts. All was quiet as we crossed the threshold – too quiet. Eirian's children – and Dran – had been banished earlier on, when Brana felt the presence of a crowd was distracting her charge, and they now languished at Machan's house, biting their fingernails to the quick. It was hot, too, inside. A pan of camomile tea, for calm, simmered away above a fire of birch wood, to symbolise birth, but we'd moved beyond any of that, I feared. My sister-in-law was delirious, her eye-lids flickering but never open. Brana had a wet cloth to her head.

'Fever?' I whispered and Branadain dropped her gaze.

'I'm not sure. It could just be exhaustion.'

I'd seen her walking Eirian about all day, stepping up and down on the log seats by the hearth, and she'd been pushing and pushing besides, but it seemed more like fever in someone as strong as Eirian.

'What else have you tried?' I asked, and Brana's voice trembled as she answered me. She'd given her dried raspberry tea to strengthen the pushes, massaged her belly with plantain oil, sung every birth prayer and Epona prayer right through . . . all to no avail.

Nes knelt down beside Eirian and held her hand. 'Is the baby still moving?'

Brana frowned. 'Yes, but not so much, and only from up here.' She pointed to the upper part of Eirian's belly. 'There were kicks from down further too, to begin with.'

'You think there are two babies?' I asked.

She nodded. 'Yes – I always thought there might be, and now I'm more certain. And neither is coming down as it should.'

I sucked in a breath. *Gods help us.*

I remembered Eirian helping me when I was close to death – she had barely known me, then.

'Is there *anything* else we can do?'

Branadain's voice was getting higher. 'I've already tried to turn the baby – mother showed me how, years ago – but it *won't* turn. And if the cord is around his neck then turning isn't going to do any good.'

'And you think the lower baby is blocking the path of the upper one?'

She shrugged, wiping the sweat from her brow and throwing her hands back down. 'I can't be *sure* of anything – but it makes sense.'

We were silent a moment, listening to the sound of the rain pounding the roof. Branadain calmed herself and went back to cooling Eirian's head. I steeled myself to speak a few times then backed out. When I did speak the words came out choked.

'I think it's time to get Dran and her children back in, before she goes.'

Again we were silent. There was no sound but the rain and the crackle of the fire. Brana sat back against the nearest house pole and buried her head in her arms.

'There's one more thing we *could* do,' she said, without looking up.

'What?'

Now she did look at me, but it was with eyes of pure terror. 'I've heard of babies being cut out – I've never seen it, but I've heard. Mother said her own grandmother was cut open and the baby survived.'

I felt my stomach turn and Nes looked much the same.

'Your Leon has heard of it too,' Branadain added, her voice getting still higher. 'We talked about it, at Solstice. I feared it might come to this.'

I took in a good breath. *Epona, if you watch us now, give us the strength to do what is right for Eirian and her children.*

'Do you think you could bring yourself to do it?' I said, to Branadain, and saw her blanch.

'I – I thought you might. You have treated more wounds than me, when it comes down to it.' Brana held her open palm to Eirian's belly again. 'There is *still* movement – they have a chance. And our only other choice is letting three people go to the pyre.'

Nes was looking to me too, her hare-bell eyes rimmed with tears. 'If it was me, I would want you to try to save the babies,' she said.

'All right,' I said at last.

Thirty three   The last path to take

I took in another good breath. 'We – we should have one last try at pushing, I think. Try to get her to sit up and get some water or honey-and-water into her before she loses consciousness completely.' Branadain looked at me incredulous but she obeyed. 'Nes, you go over to Dran and ask him to come back – I'm not going to do anything to her without his say-so. And fetch Leon. Ask him to bring the full wound-kit.'

Nes pulled her cloak back on. 'What about Rhyddo and Retta?'

'Yes, them too, and Eithinen. They should say what they need to say before there is any blood.'

She left, and Brana did try to get Eirian's strength back, but it didn't work. Eirian was too weak to speak let alone push. We laid her back down and let her rest. Her eyelids were not moving at all, now.

I discarded the tea and set a cauldron of water boiling. Hot as it was inside the house I built the fire up to boil the water and for the extra light and lit every bit of tallow I could find with a wick. I found some old blankets in a basket, some already chopped up to make cleaning rags, and rolled up the best of them, laying a good few rolls either side of Eirian.

'I think there is going to be a lot of blood,' I explained, in answer to Brana's questioning gaze. 'Still moving?'

She put her palm to Eirian's belly again. 'Not much. You should sing a prayer – the strength-giver, perhaps. The birth prayers did no good.'

'You should do it. You are the druid.'

'My prayers are wheat falling on stones – you know what I said.'

'It is your faith in your *self* that has foundered, I think.'

I meant it to come out gentle, but I failed.

'Easy for you to say,' she snorted. 'You've never lost your faith in the Gods.'

'You don't think I've come close? I *saw* them, when I was close to death – poor Eirian might be seeing them now. Come on, we must do all that we can.'

We were singing the strength-giver prayer together, in low voices, when Nes came back with the others. They let us finish then approached Eirian one by one.

Retta, her new daughter-in-law, was the first to bend low and kiss her on the forehead. 'Thank you for making me welcome,' she said. 'I promise I'll look after them.'

Dran had hold of little Eithinen by the hand but he let her go so that she could whisper in her mother's ear. She would have stayed clinging onto her mother but Rhyddo gently drew her away, and kept hugging onto her as he said his own choked words. Dran was last, stroking Eirian's wet hair back from her head. He had no words at all, but I saw tears rolling down his cheeks and falling upon his wife and I felt the lump coming back to my own throat.

'Should we stay?' he asked, looking to me.

I flicked a look at Nes. She nodded. 'I told them.'

I turned to young Eithinen, no older than my own daughter. 'I – I think you should, Dran, but . . .'

Retta followed my gaze. She knew, well enough. 'We'll take her back to Alwona's then I'll come back. C'mon Rhyddo.'

Leon arrived as they were leaving and I got all the wound kit lined up near the bed. I saw Dran pale as I put the knife end into the flames.

'It's just to clean it,' I reassured him. 'The blade will have cooled by the time it touches her.'

Brana had rolled the covers back again to expose Eirian's bare abdomen and Dran was biting on his lip as he looked at his wife. '*How* will you cut her? Straight down?'

I felt my heartbeat rising. *Please Gods let me still have a loving brother after this.*

'Across, down here.' I pointed to my own lower abdomen. 'As far away from the moving baby as I can, and so the wound will bend and move with her. The stitches are less likely to tear, then.'

His blue eyes flared and I regretted my words. 'You think she might survive this?'

'I – I don't think so. I think it will bleed like a war wound, and with the fever . . . but I'll give her every chance I can, I promise you, brother.'

He held my shoulder. 'I trust you.'

Gods help me.

I managed a few quiet words with Leon as we washed our hands. It was as Brana had said – he had heard of babies saved in this way but he'd never seen it, either.

'Can I really be much use, sire?' he whispered. 'It feels wrong . . . with someone else's wife . . .'

I had seen his uneasy look about the crowded house as he'd come in with the kit, and it was worse now that Eirian was so bare. 'I know what you mean, but you and Nes have seen Machan's wound and got through it with me. Dran is in no state to help,' I lowered my voice still further, 'and Branadain is not herself.'

His worried face looked no less worried at that.

'Everyone trusts you with wounds just as well as me, my friend. You are here for me as much as for anyone else.'

'Yes sire.'

I rolled up my sleeves and turned back to the room. 'Nes, Brana, you two stay on her right side, with blankets ready for the babies. Dran, you stay sat there near Eirian's head, keep speaking to her. Leon, stay behind me and pass me what I ask for.'

I knelt beside my sister-in-law. 'Eirian,' I said, in a soft voice, 'you have been my friend and kin all these years and you know I would never hurt you. I am going to try to get the babies out of you so they have a chance to live. As the Gods observe me I only do this to save life. Please forgive me, Eirian.'

Leon passed me the knife and I began the cut. I saw Dran close his eyes and turn away and to be honest my own stomach faltered. The blade was sharp and I felt it go through the skin, fat and muscle with relative ease. I'd made the cut about the width of my palm. *Is that enough?* It would be enough for a baby's head and thence all of it I imagined if the baby was straight but we knew it was *not* straight. I went a bit further. *Easier to stitch a clean cut . . .* There was bright red blood seeping out now but it was not as bad as I'd feared.

'Cloth, Leon.'

I wiped away the blood as best I could and eased back the sides of the cut. I suppose I'd had some vain hope the child would just fall out, or at least be visible, but all I could see were the raw bloody edges of the wound and the gorse-yellow globules of the fat layer. I had sliced into the muscle, but not gone far enough.

Please Gods don't let me cut the baby . . .

'You all right?' Nes asked, in a wary tone.

'Yes. Half way,' I answered, as if it was intentional. I checked Eirian's pulse at her left wrist. It was weak, but it was still there. 'Clean blade, Leon. The shortest one.'

I cut into the cut, in the same direction, and now it did bleed, by the Gods. The wall of the womb when I saw it was as deep and dark as a liver and just as soaked with blood. My rolled blankets were a help but not enough. I felt the warm wetness reach my knees. *Oh Gods . . . Eirian.*

'Reach in,' Brana urged. 'While you've got the chance.'

I felt sick, but I did it, and wet and slippery as it was I felt what appeared to be a baby's arm and shoulder beneath my left hand.

'Brana, ready,' I warned.

I gripped on and pulled. With the space now free he came out in a blink but my heart sank at the sight of him. Blue, limp, lifeless. Branadain got near enough to take him from me and with the cord still attached she put him head downwards along her left forearm, tapping him on the back and flicking his feet with her fingernail. The taps turned to slaps and we waited for the cry, but it didn't come.

I looked to Dranis and felt my own eyes well.

No. Be strong. There is another one yet.

'Nes, get ready for the next one.'

I reached in again and eased out the afterbirth. As soon as I had done this I saw the next baby's head. It was smeary with blood but still looked a better colour than the other. 'Out you come, little one.' I reached in further with my left hand and hooked him under one arm with my first two fingers, easing him back towards my waiting right hand.

He was moving. *Thank the Gods.* He was moving.

All of us gasped. Retta had come back in earlier and was crouched down near the door. I heard her cry of joy.

He wasn't crying, but he was moving. 'Tap him on the back and feet, as I was doing,' Branadain urged and I obeyed. The lad opened his mouth and made a choked, gulpy noise. I tried again and within a heartbeat there was a full on cry.

Thank you Gods.

'Eirian, you have a healthy boy.' I smiled at Dran. 'Go on, speak to her.'

'We have a son, love,' he said, through his tears. 'He's all right, he's all right.'

'I'll put him next to you. One moment.'

There was a second afterbirth to deliver but as soon as it was out I tied off and cut the cord and handed the boy to Nes to wrap up warm.

'Put him near her head so she can hear him crying.'

Now to Eirian. If we are to save her then there's not much time.

'Leon, line and thread – quickly now.'

I rinsed the blood from my hands and took the line and thread from Leon. *Where do I start?* The womb wall itself would need stitches. I could hardly see the edges in the blood.

Guide me, Gwyfina.

'Caradoc.'

I looked up to Dran.

'Caradoc, stop. She's not breathing.'

I looked back to him in horror.

Branadain put the first baby down and felt under Eirian's jaw for a pulse. 'It's true,' she said.

I threw down the needle.

'Are you *sure*?' I demanded and she pressed her lips together, her chin sinking to her chest.

'Yes.'

Even so I had to check for myself.

It was true.

'I'm so sorry, Eirian.'

I could see my hands shaking. Nes came around and gripped my shoulder. 'She will know,' she soothed. 'She will know all of it. Now we must do what we can for her son.'

Her son. Dran, and I, both looked down at the child at an absolute loss. He was crying, still wriggling down by his mother's shoulder, and it felt the cries were getting louder. Nes wrapped the cloth back round him and lifted him up for a cuddle but the cries continued to fill the house, running through us like knives.

Brana had picked up the first baby to lay him on Eirian's chest but now she turned to the living one. 'He will need milk. We will need to find a wet nurse.'

Now we think of this? *By the Gods.*

'Dag,' Nes said, to me. 'She's still nursing little Tyllan. He's only eight moons old. She'd do it, I'm sure.'

'I'm sure she would, but she's over at Uricon's seat with Colleos, and it's nearing midnight and chucking with sleet.'

'I'll ride over, I'm not afraid,' she retorted.

'And the wolves? What if your horse goes lame? No. *I'll* go.'

'*I'll* go,' Brana insisted. 'You are all kin, you should stay here.'

Leon nodded at that. 'I could go, sire.'

272

'Wait till morning,' Dran said, voice flat as a pond. 'He's strong. He'll be all right.'

I glanced at the wriggling child bawling out his lungs. *I'm not so sure of that.*

Retta was on her feet now and looking round to us all as if we were mad. 'Mam. Me mam. She's still nursin' m'little brother – she's only a few houses away. I'll go get her.'

Dran sat quiet and unmoving as the house poles but the rest of us couldn't hide our relief.

It was late by the time Nes and I were back in our own house – too late, really, to wake Gladsia and bring her back from Kynbel and Airdinna's but as it was what we both wanted, however mad, it happened without argument. She was too sleepy to ply us with questions, right then, which was a blessing.

We got clean and retired to our own bed but neither of us could sleep. We ended up making love but there was sadness in it and we still couldn't sleep. I resigned myself to just laying there the rest of the night, holding onto each other and listening to the rain on the roof.

'You know, I would have loved more children,' she whispered to me. 'When I was teased for having none, back in Camulodunon, and Calleva, I would sometimes joke that at least I had more teeth in my head than most women my age – if I wasn't just too heartbroken to speak at all. But sometimes I wonder if it saved my life.' Her voice was wobbling and I hugged her tighter. 'Poor Coriona, my auntie that Gladsia's named after . . . now Eirian.'

'And Epaticos's first wife. You never knew her – neither did I, but I know it broke his heart.'

'The baby died too, didn't he?'

'Yes.' I took a deep breath. 'That's how come I exist, I think. My mother comforted him, perhaps a bit more than she intended, and they had a short time together, maybe when Cunobelin was at war.'

'You never told me this!'

'I've never told anyone. I mean, Atrebati knew – she was the one who told me, and I think Adminios guessed, or at least suspected. But no-one else can know. Not even Dran and Kynbel.'

Nes swivelled round to look at me, confused.

'How long would I be king, if everyone knew?'

She sucked in a breath. 'You would still be king if you were reborn an ant,' she said.

I laughed. 'The gold always shines in the gravel, eh?'

'Well . . . yes.'

'I didn't feel like that today.'

She kissed me. 'No-one can win all the time. With everything.'

I think at least half the time is expected, though.

We grew silent again, listening to the rain drip from the eaves and Creegan's soft snores down by the hearth. In the distance the cows in the south-side shelter were lowing.

'We should try to sleep,' Nes whispered.

I sighed. 'It's probably near dawn. We might as well get up, have some breakfast.'

'Just a little sleep. If we wake Gla-Gla this early she'll be waspy all afternoon.'

From across the house our 'sleeping' daughter turned and pulled back her blankets, her cloth fox falling out and missing the night-pee pot by a hair. 'Why are you awake so *early*?' she whined.

Nes smiled, raising her eyebrows. 'Breakfast then?'

'Breakfast it is.'

We left the funeral until the afternoon of the next day, to allow time for word to spread, and for Nes and the other women to prepare a fitting feast. I was torn between honouring my sister-in-law with the ceremony a princess of the Catuvellauni deserved, and taking too much from the hard-pressed Cornovi peasants in this cold and hungry moon. As it was I need not have worried – Eirian had been well loved, the mourners came in from homesteads all around and there was more than enough food.

Branadain led the prayers about the pyre, as she should, and I said my own words of praise, but there was no comfort to be had, in truth. The surviving baby, fed, cleaned and cosseted though he was, screamed and keened like a flock of gulls throughout the rite and the grim grey skies were mirrored in all our faces.

Branadain moved us away from the pyre for the boy's naming ceremony, up to the 'finger' rocks, and, bitter though the wind was, I think she did the right thing. The boy carried on whimpering in her arms as she crumbled the handful of bread over his head and presented him to the crowd.

'There's no whale in the wide ocean as lonely as a twin without their twin,' she said. 'May the Gods keep you and guide you, Albucos. Know that as your mother and your grandsire watch you from the Land of Youth, so do your family watch over you here.'

'Why Albucos?' Nes whispered to me.

'Eirian's father's name. She must have told Dran – none of us knew him.'

Branadain raised the child up, we cheered his name three times, then headed back down to get out of the wind, Nes and I hand in hand.

'She did all right, didn't she?' Nesica said, in a low tone, looking to Brana.

'Yes it all went as well as I could hope.' I sighed. 'Though I'm surprised Blodau didn't show her face. Is she sick?'

Nes shook her head. 'No, nothing like that, but she has a terror of childbirth so these last days have shaken her badly. She's at home, in bed. Alwona told me earlier.'

'Is she with child? I'd heard nothing.'

'No – nor likely to be, from what Alwona told me.'

We both glanced back at Machan's family, before we could stop ourselves, and saw the embarrassment clear on all their faces, not least poor Hedros.

'By the Gods – I thought she'd just been avoiding Brana whilst she's here with us. . . I'll try to have a quiet word with Hedros tomorrow.'

Nes raised her eyebrows. 'I'm not sure there's anything you can do about a problem like this, king or no.'

'No, you're right.'

I saw our Gladsia take Eithinen by the hand and lead her over to where young Coll and some of the other children were. It brought the first smile to my face that day.

As night fell we drew the feast to a close and retired to our houses to thaw out. Nes and I had Colleos and his family in our house as guests, as well as Branadain, so it was pretty crowded, but I managed a quiet word with Colleos alone as our wives cajoled the children to their beds and Brana went to say a last sunset prayer by the embers of the pyre. Colleos looked tired, and grateful for the short respite from his duties I think, despite the sadness of the occasion.

'Do you think we will hold back the legions, once spring is upon us?' I asked him. 'You can answer frankly, Colleos – I trust your judgement, and value our people's lives over my pride, when all's said and done.'

I saw his mouth turn up into a smile, if a sad smile, as he looked into his cup of beer. 'My king, the truth is I don't think we will.'

'Go on.'

'The legions took the Cornovi lands once and they will do it again – they must, for *their* pride's sake. We cannot allow them to surround the forts . . . and we cannot allow them to goad us into a big battle on the flat, sire.' He looked up, brown eyes steady as a horse. 'We just don't have the men for it.'

'We could do with a few more like Brig, no?'

He laughed, though it was bitter. 'Another ten thousand more, sire.'

'Then we are of one mind.' I put another log on the fire. 'I've been told that many in the Ordovici territory would

276

join us, given the chance – I think the time has come for *us* to join *them*.'

Colleos nodded. 'I agree, sire, but King Arthewin must have loyal warriors. Has my wife's uncle given you an idea of how many? We're bound to have a fight on our hands.'

I opened my mouth to answer him but a bang on the door stalled me.

Alwona came in, milk-white. She bowed.

'Speak, Alwona – what's going on?'

'I'm sorry, my king, but we need your help. Blodau is missing. We think she's run away.'

Thirty four One odd fish

Nes put her arm about Alwona's shoulders and tried to draw her into the house but Alwona was too tense to be led, or even to sit down. Behind her we could see the sky was black. A chill wind blew through the open doorway and it was starting to pelt with rain yet again. 'We can't leave her out all night in this, sire,' Alwona implored me. 'She won't survive.'

Well, I wonder . . . she's tougher than she looks. 'Did she take anything with her? Her horse?'

Alwona shook her head. 'Not her horse, but her thickest cloak, a knife, yes. Some bread I think.'

I passed a look to Nes. *At least we don't have another Rhian on our hands.* 'Has Hedros gone out looking already?'

'Yes, and my Machan – but now it's completely dark, and the wind could slice you in half. I'm worried, my king – for all of them.'

I got to my feet and gathered her into a big hug. 'We'll find her,' I soothed. 'She's probably seen her mistake and started on her way back.'

Nes nodded at that, patting her on the arm. 'She'll see sense. Those of us who stay here can light torches and put them about the outer palisade, so that she can see her way home.'

I threw my cloak about my shoulders and strapped on my sword. Colleos was putting on his. 'We won't be long,' I said, to my wife, though that could have been a bald-faced lie for all I knew. 'Ask Tarn to blow the war-horn at intervals through the night, so we can place ourselves in the dark. Just two blasts for "no change", four short bursts in a row for "she's back", and long continuous blasts for any trouble.'

Nes nodded. 'You think this could be some sort of trick?' she asked, in a low voice, as she pinned my cloak closed.

'I doubt it, but I don't feel I know Blodau well enough to be sure. Perhaps none of us do.'

'Take Creegan. He'll have a better chance of finding her at night than any man.'

Colleos and I left, Creegan at our heels, and hurried down to the west gate. I saw Dran at his doorway as we passed, little Albucos in the crook of his left arm.

'What's going on?' he shouted.

'Stay here, with your children,' I called back. 'We'll find her soon – Nes will tell you all.'

Rhyddo joined us for the search, though, and Kynbel. As we were leaving I could see Branadain was on her way back in, her arms about young Hedros.

'Sprained ankle,' she called out to me. 'He'll be all right.'

No doubt, but the pain was clear on his face.

'Do you think she went west?'

Hedros nodded, speaking through gritted teeth. 'Yes sire. I found footprints, while I still had a lit torch – little feet, like hers.'

It wasn't much, but it gave us somewhere to start. Creegan ran off into the gloom without any bidding from me, excited to be out in the dark with so many men. He charged about in the gorse, barking as well as he could with his raspy voice. I felt it might do some good. We found Machan soon enough, or he found us.

'Do you know how long she's been gone?' I asked.

Machan shook his head. 'We can't be sure, sire – it could be since the start of the funeral.'

While it was still light then. She could be halfway to Mon now for all we knew.

'Go home, Machan, get some clothing of hers, or a scrap of her blanket, and ask everyone with dogs to come out looking.'

He came back with men, dogs and lit torches. It was still like searching the ocean for one odd fish. We shared out the scraps of cloth between us and split up, heading north, south, east and west, but most of us west. The rain got

279

heavier and heavier, starting to soak even through my own good hood and seeping down the back of my neck. We couldn't see much beyond our own feet. The dogs scampered off in every direction, barking away. I listened for any change, any howl.

'At least it will keep the wolves away,' Kynbel muttered.

'Did your Airdinna get any wind of this? They get on all right, don't they?'

He shrugged. 'Not that she's said.'

We continued, mad as it was. The rain was starting to sting my bare hands as it turned to sleet. I clenched and unclenched them to keep the blood flowing.

Cernunnos, Maponos, Lugos, Epona, look after this girl. Whatever is in her head no-one deserves to freeze to death.

Over to my left I heard Machan swear.

'Are you all right, Machan?'

'I just stumbled, sire. I'm back on my feet.'

I wasn't surprised. It was as black a night as I'd ever seen and he had half the sight of the rest of us. *What if he has one of his fits out here?* 'Go back to the fort, while we can still hear the war-horn,' I ordered. 'You are her kin now, you should be there if she doubles back.'

It was a weak excuse, given Alwona, Hedros and his young brothers were all there, but he did as I asked. The rest of us carried on.

We found nothing.

No more footprints, not a shred of her cloak, a spent torch, a broken stick. Nothing. Meanwhile we were getting soaked.

'I think we have to turn back, for now, and come back out when it's light,' I said, to Colleos, as we took a breather by some rocks. 'I can't risk losing any men out here, whatever she might be up to.'

'You think she might have turned traitor?'

I couldn't see him clearly, our last torch having long since sputtered out, but I could hear the surprise in his voice.

'I don't see what she has to gain, but I'm not ruling it out.'

Kynbel had joined us and climbed up onto the rock, Creegan at his heels. 'She's just an odd stick,' he said. 'Useless as a holly stuffed bed. Hedros is well shot of her if she has gone.'

I raised my eyebrows, remembering the broken look on Hedros's face as he limped back in. Not all that pain had been down to his ankle.

'Has Blodau done something to you, Kynbel?'

'Me? Gods no – but Hedros deserves better. '

Creegan came back down to me, thumping his tail against my leg, which served to emphasise how soaked my breeks were. I could hear Coll's teeth starting to chatter. I offered the scrap of Blodau's shift we had to the dog to sniff again. 'Go on, *find*,' I urged, and Creegan ran off into the murk once more. He was away a while but when he returned, dejected and confused, I'd had enough.

We started back, as fast as we dared in the darkness, relieved when we could hear the war-horn once more. It was still just the two blasts at a time. We were back near one of the springs on the west side when Creegan scampered up onto a crest, sniffing the air.

First he whimpered, then one of his low, raspy growls.

I shushed everyone quiet.

There.

'I hear it,' Colleos called.

On the wind, like a distant banshee, a woman's voice was calling for help.

We ran back, more or less the way we'd come, as far as we could tell in the blackness. When I could make out the moving shape ahead of me it looked too big to be one slight woman.

'Blodau? Is that you?'

'Yes!'

We ran up to them and I realised it was two people. She was supporting a man, his right arm across her thin shoulders, and from the way he hung limp I guessed he was near unconsciousness. 'He's wounded!' she shouted, above the wind. I reached under his jaw to check his pulse and in doing so raised his head.

Tyllan. My old bard of Calleva.

Oh Gods no.

'Colleos! It's Tyllan!'

I put the old man across my shoulders and carried him for home.

We got him back to the fort as fast as we could. As we burst through the door I saw Hedros gasp but he said nothing, burying his pained face down to his chest. Branadain continued strapping up his ankle and Blodau retreated to the shadowy edges of the house like a spider.

They can wait till later.

'Blankets!' I ordered. 'And hot tea – something with lots of honey in it.'

Nes and Dag snapped to it. In the light of the hearth it became clear Tyllan was bruised and grazed but not bleeding. His main danger was that he was ice-cold. He was mumbling away as I checked him for broken bones but not making a lot of sense.

'Easy, old friend, just let us get the warmth back into you.'

He gripped my sleeve, looking up into my eyes, and in all the babble I hooked upon one word: 'Tynos'.

Oh no.

'Was there anyone else out there, Blodau? Did you just help Tyllan because he was the only one alive?'

'No, he was alone.' She didn't come forward. Her small voice just sang out from the darkness. 'I found him on the bank of a swollen stream. . . I couldn't leave him.'

Colleos was removing Tyllan's soaked, ragged shoes but I now saw a look pass between him and his wife. Dag dipped a slight bow to Blodau.

'Thank you, Princess. Thank you for bringing him back to us.'

Blodau waved it away and crouched back further under the eaves. As soon as Nes had handed Tyllan his hot drink and closed his hands around it she turned to the young woman herself.

'Alwona went home with Machan to get dry clothes but I should pop over there and let them know you're all right. All your kin were worried sick about you.'

Blodau's face fixed into a sullen slouch. 'I just went for a walk. I got lost.'

We'd seen the sling tucked into her belt as she came in, the knife, the little pouch of food. That lie convinced no-one. I saw Hedros raise his head though, and look at her for the first time. I thought I saw some colour come to her cheeks.

You're trying to save his face, aren't you?

I nodded to my wife. 'Go and reassure them. I'll help Hedros home once he's had something for the pain. Blodau can stay here for tonight.'

That brought a flash of concern to both Hedros and Blodau's faces. *Yes. I will speak to you both alone until I get to the bottom of this. So get used to it.*

Nes left and I turned back to Tyllan, wrapped up like a new leaf in his blankets and still clutching his cup of tea. His colour had returned to near normal, between the bruises.

'Are you feeling better, my friend?'

He nodded. 'Yes my king.'

'You were trying to tell us what happened, earlier, but the cold had got to you. Is Tynos also lost out there? Do we need to go looking for him?'

Anguish creased his face. 'No sire, he's a prisoner.' His lower lip began to tremble. 'King Arthewin is going to have him executed.'

'When?'

'Imbolc eve.'

Alive then – for now. Thank the Gods.

'Is it because he spied for me? Does Arthewin know?'

He shook his head. 'I don't think so – but he suspects everyone, all the time, so who knows? Poor Tynos was in the king's house with Prince Mocco when the king attacked him. He tried to protect the prince.'

'You mean Arthewin attacked Tynos or Mocco?'

'Prince Mocco, sire. I did not see it but the servants told me after – the king went wild. He had the boy on the floor with his knee on his throat – if Tynos hadn't wrenched him away then the prince would have died, but Tynos pulled a knife on the king, when he was cornered, so . . .'

'So that is treason, wherever you go, mad king or not.'

Tyllan nodded. 'Yes sire. Even so Ordovicos helped Tynos, I think. The king would have just run him through but Ordovicos was able to calm him and delay the execution to a sacrifice at Imbolc.'

'I'm not sure that is really help. . . '

'Oh I know sire – he is the sort who likes his bread buttered both sides. But he did help me, and I think the delay was so that I could get to you.'

I gestured to his bruises. 'Who did this? Was it Arthewin?'

'Yes. He smashed my harp right in front of me and beat me with the pieces.' He raised his eyebrows. 'I knew nothing I said could help Tynos but I protested Mocco's innocence.'

'Innocence from what?'

'He is accused of killing his brother, sire. Prince Arth is dead.'

Nesica was coming back in the door just then and I threw her a look. *Oh no.*

'It was an *accident*, sire. *I* witnessed it and so did Rhian and half a dozen others! Mocco is accused of pushing – he was twenty paces from him! But the king will listen to no-one. Young Arth was larking about on the palisade, showing off to the girls, and he fell. That's all there was to it. Maybe there was ice, but he fell.' He shook his head. 'It was tragic. I'm sorry for the boy, but no-one is to *blame* for it. Of course the king does not see it like that. Once he'd beaten me senseless he had me tied to a post in the yard and it was the druid who loosened my bonds under cover of night and told me which side was least guarded.'

'Where are Mocco and Rhian now?'

'I don't know, sire. The young prince was imprisoned before I was. Perhaps Ordovicos helped him to escape too?'

I wonder . . . my old friend had already shown more backbone than I would have credited him with.

I looked to Colleos, and Nes. 'Well, this makes up my mind. We will ride to my cousin's aid. We must travel to the Ordovicis.'

Thirty five Land of my mother's kin

No-one disputed my words but as I looked around the house floor all I could see was fatigue right then. It must have been past midnight. The children were wide awake, sat up in their little beds, watching all, but with bags under their eyes.

'There's nothing more that can be done tonight,' I added. 'Let's get you home, Hedros.'

I got on his bad side and helped him to his feet. Nes held the door open for us and he passed out of the house without a word to his wife, still crouched under the eaves. We were half way across the yard before he'd said a word to me.

'I'm so sorry, my king.'

'Sorry for what? What have you done?'

'I – I mean for causing trouble . . . me and Blodau. You have enough trouble, sire.'

Well when the Gods saw fit to make me King they decided I was strong enough for all the weights.

'It's no great bother – but ask for help, from me or someone. Don't just let things fester.'

We reached his parents' house and I handed him over to their welcoming arms. I was tired myself by that point but I told them the core of all that had happened with Tyllan.

'We'll be ready to move, as soon as you say the word,' Machan said to me, with a nod.

Gods be thanked for my people.

I awoke the next morning half expecting to find Blodau gone, to be honest, but she was still asleep down by the hearth, wrapped in her cloak and a blanket Nes had given her. I noticed she hadn't taken her shoes off, though.

'Should I pack today?' Nes asked, in a whisper.

'Yes . . .' I nodded over to the sleeping girl. 'But there are things to sort out. I need to get this settled before we leave.'

I looked over to Tyllan too, deep in a good healing sleep. 'I don't want to disturb him, though.'

'Take her over to Camulora's, to talk to her,' Nes suggested.

I frowned. 'Why Camulora?'

'She has room in her hut. Blodau can stay with her a while if necessary.' She got out of bed and pulled on her shift and over-dress before she had a chance to shiver. 'Besides, she might be able to help – more than Alwona can.'

'I'm not sure how. Alwona has only ever been kind to the girl.'

'Yes, and I like Alwona as much as you do, but maybe a woman who's borne six sons, joyfully wed to the same man since she was fifteen, isn't what the lass needs right now.' She handed me my shirt with a little shrug. 'Let alone that she's Hedros's mother.'

I woke Blodau and took my wife's advice. Cam received us both with good grace, considering the time of day. She didn't even appear that surprised.

I sat down by the hearth, on the opposite side to the girl. *No time to dally about.* 'So, why did you run away? What are you up to?'

'Nothing.' Again her face slumped into sullen torpor. 'I just wanted to get away for a bit. Not forever.'

'Were you planning to meet someone?'

She frowned. 'No.'

'Has someone done something to you?'

This time it was a shake of her head.

I sighed. 'We have rules and justice – don't be afraid to say if it's so. Even if it's Hedros.'

'No. Hedros has done nothing wrong.'

I kept silent a moment, hoping she would say more. I could see her hands trembling.

I tried to make my tone more gentle. 'If you don't love him any more it would be kinder to sever the knot with him than to just run off into the night,' I said, but she shook her head again.

'No, I do love him.' Her cheeks went redder than I'd ever seen, in her. 'It's just . . . I don't want . . .' She looked up to Cam in desperation.

Cam had been pottering about, making tea, but now her eyes met mine. 'Leave her with me, I'll talk to her. You have things to do.' She handed the girl a cup. 'Don't worry, there's no treachery at work here, I think.'

I left her to it, I admit with some relief, and strode back through the village. All was quiet, but I saw other fresh footprints in the mud and spotted Brana, out by the embers of the pyre with a pot, collecting up poor Eirian's ash. She looked sombre in her druid black, and broken, like a lightning struck tree.

I went over and hugged her. 'Thank you, for all you did,' I said. 'No-one could have given her a better chance, at life, or a finer start to her journey west.'

Branadain wiped her face with her loose sleeve. 'The Land of Youth will be all the merrier with her there. Everyone liked her – even at home, when things got tense.'

I smiled. It was true. 'What are you going to do now?'

She tipped her head to one side with just a twitch of her eyebrows. 'I promised to go back to Mon, to nurse Siluri. If you're going that way, to Arthewin's seat, then perhaps I should ride with you?'

Gods guide me. I only say what I say now for the greater good. 'May I give you my advice?'

She looked wary, but she said yes.

I took in a good breath. 'Don't go back to Siluri. The hold she has over you isn't good for you – it never has been. Go back to your brother. He needs you more, I think. And – and I don't think he has long, either.'

She sank down upon one of the log seats. 'No, I think you're right.'

I sat down beside her. 'And I think you should be the Silures' Queen, when the time comes. I don't think your mother would stand in your way, even if she was well, and I don't think any of your elder sisters would either.'

Brana looked back at me in shock, for a heartbeat, then nodded. 'I think you might be right about that too.' We both looked out a moment upon the swathe of mud and fish-flesh clouds speeding across the sky. 'What of Melistia?'

I sighed. 'You would know more than me. Tell me, is it her who kept putting off the hand-fasting or him? I got the impression it was her.'

'Yes, definitely her.'

'Then she doesn't want to be queen – not a widowed queen within a few moons, constantly watching her back, and I don't blame her. If they had a child in the mean time it would be even worse. The ruler of the Silures needs to be strong, with thousands of Romans at our door, not a babe in arms.'

'And is that truly me? I've been a druid all these years.'

'You were packed off to Mon because you were the youngest, and canny. Much the same reasons as me. It doesn't mean we can't rule. You might be bloody good at it – I've been all right.' She barked one of her crow-like laughs and I put my arm back about her shoulders. 'There, that's my old Branadain. Come on in and have some porridge before we freeze.'

I rode west, with a good thousand of my warriors, the next morning. Much as I feared for Tynos and Mocco I could not risk withdrawing the whole army at once. I left enough of a presence behind, for now, to trick the legions into thinking we hadn't left at all. If they had spies among my people who were worth their pay then the ruse would only hold for a few days, at best, but I felt a few days might be enough. I sensed I would either take Arthewin's seat fast, or not at all.

I left the old Cornovi lands without too heavy a heart. It had never really been home. One winter atop this 'Caer Caradoc' had proved quite enough, with icy winds to steal your breath and streak the snot right up the children's faces. I expected Nes to shed some tears as she stripped out the house but I saw none. The day was busy for me too, planning, packing and giving orders. I found a few moments, once the sun had risen, to walk Gladsia up to the little cave – she realised she'd left one of her toys up there – and as we came back down and crossed the yard, crowded with my people packing their horses, I feared I would see some resentment, even annoyance, unmasked on the faces. Some of the faces, at least. What I got were smiles and greetings. Perhaps it gets easier, every time one leaves one's home, after the first. We packed up everything that was ours, took nothing that the local peasants could hate us for, and left the fort much as we found it. We resolved to take Eirian's ash with us.

I allowed five days for a journey that would take three in summer. Every river and brook was a swollen torrent and mud-slipped tracks slowed us half a dozen times a day, and that was before we'd even reached the Ordovici border. 'How much of a resistance do you think we'll face?' Colleos asked me, as we rode out, and my honest answer had to be that I didn't know. I sent Rhyddo and Tarn ahead, in plain dull clothes, to test the water, but for one whole day inside the Ordovici lands we saw no-one at all. Not a single soul.

'They must *know* we are here,' Nes whispered, her eyes searching the surrounding hills, as we rested in a mountain pass for the swiftest of midday meals.

'I'm sure they do.'

I cast another look about the slopes – for the hundredth time that morn no doubt. They were dark in winter shadow, even at high noon. Each rock and gorse could hide a warrior. I didn't sense it, but I couldn't take any chances, either.

'Let's keep moving.'

Before mid-afternoon we had to stop for another 'rest', this time because a mudslide had cast rocks and boulders into our path.

Is this the work of winter or an ambush in the making?

'We must check it,' I said, to Nes, as I lifted our daughter down. 'Stay on the lee side of the horse.'

'I need to check the hooves of Gladsia's pony – can't I do that?'

I threw another look about the gloomy slopes. The day's light was starting to fail.

'All right, but stay sharp. You have your sword?'

She patted her side with a patient smile. 'I do. Don't worry, I'm just as cautious as you are.'

Just then a shout from above made us start. The sound of wa rriors unsheathing their swords echoed all around – but that was coming from us.

Kynbel was up on one of the boulders that was blocking the path and turned round with a grin. 'Don't fret – it's Tarn!'

Tarn was indeed scampering back down to us, his arms raised, but not until I had seen the broad smile upon his own face did I let my heart ease.

'My king! Come see! You won't believe your eyes.'

We entered the Ordovici village like lost family returned. Hundreds of warriors lined the path on either side, their spears dipped in honour as I passed, like a breeze through barley. Their wives and children were banked behind them, cheering their voices hoarse, waving coloured cloths. Still more people cheered from the palisade of the enormous hulk of a fort we were headed towards. Some sat on the roofs blasting out horns, dozens more were spilling out of the open gate. I think if they'd had any flowers, in this coldest of moons, they would have thrown them at our horses' feet.

I am told the generals of Rome have a servant stand behind them, as they ride their chariots in glory, whispering all the while 'Remember you are but a man'. That is wise, I suppose. My saddle sore arse served as well for me. . ! But I was pleased, in truth. How could one not be?

Rhyddo met us at the north gate, beaming with joy, and when we all saw who was behind him our own smiles grew wider still.

'Catuvellaunos!'

In my pleasure I forgot to call him Britannios but he didn't care. He was wearing the full ceremonial white though, filthy to the knee, and with the hood of his cloak up against the biting wind. He looked in pain, and was leaning on a stout alder stick, but no age or aches could diminish his joy at the sight of us. I slipped from Buanedd's back to embrace him and with his free arm he hugged me back.

'I received word from Ordovicos, I knew you would be riding out.' He tapped his left leg with the stick. 'Even my own knees couldn't stop me.'

'Thank you, my friend.' I laughed. 'If every village is as welcoming as this one then I have more hope.'

He nodded, but his eye was caught by an Ordovici woman wrapping furs about my wife and daughter.

'Let's get everyone inside before the light goes.' He squeezed my shoulder. 'We have much planning to do.'

We walked up the track to the huts arm in arm.

It was a large fort with a hundred huts or so but all the same it was a squeeze to get everyone housed and all our horses fed and sheltered before nightfall. The villagers could not have been kinder. By dusk, when the first flakes of snow fell, we were all sat about the welcome hearths of these good people.

Catuvellaunos and I held a council about the head man's hearth once everyone was settled, but we allowed the fort's head man to speak first, out of courtesy, and because he knew the state of matters better than we. He was called Elidoros, Elid for short, and we worked out that he had a tendril of kinship with Ordovicos, and me, by way of a great-aunt on my mother's side. We'd had a good laugh at our matching noses over dinner. I liked him immediately.

'The tide turned still more towards you in the last ten days,' he said, nodding to me, 'but the direction has been clear for a few years. Now, with the druids favouring you, there are fewer Ordovicis who are loyal to Arthewin by the day.'

'Are the prisoners still alive?'

He nodded. 'Last I heard, yes. Ordovicos has reserved them for Imbolc sacrifice so Arthewin is too scared to kill them sooner – though even Ordovicos has felt the back of his hand by now, so I'm told.'

I cast a look at Colleos. 'Arthewin might have found out that the druid freed Tyllan.' I turned back to Elid. 'I have never been to Arthewin's seat myself but my harper told me it's perched high, like a crow's nest. I'm concerned about how we take the fort. I mean, we could build ballistas like the Romans do and storm it, but we don't have time – and I don't want to shed a drop of Ordovici blood if I can help it.'

Elid looked to the hearth. 'It's good to hear you say so, but I don't know that we can avoid it. The seat has never been taken, not since the Gods were young.'

Kynbel was straining to speak so I bade he do so. 'I was thinking – could we sneak into the fort, to open it from inside, like Leon's tale of the horse of Troy? There's a woman at the seat we know, Rhian, who could let down a rope or something, if we could get word to her.'

He reddened, as if the ill wisdom of asking Rhian of all people to let down a rope suddenly dawned on him, but the *idea* was sound.

'My younger daughter knows Rhian, she works there too,' Elid said. 'I'm sure I could get word to her . . . but for the people I think the victory over Arthewin needs to be public . . . and honourable.'

Catuvellaunos nodded. 'I agree. For a change in power like this to "take" it has to be symbolic as well as decisive.' He looked to Kynbel. 'But some of our people on the inside wouldn't hurt.' He sat back, easing the knee of his left leg with a stretch. 'I had in mind a ceremony . . . Caradoc do you have your half of Cunobelin's great torque with you?'

'Yes. It's safely wrapped up among our things, as ever.' I sighed. 'I admit I haven't looked at it in over a year.'

Catuvellaunos met my gaze with a sad smile. 'The time has come to set down roots elsewhere, so that you may grow anew. Casting the torque half to the Gods, in the land of your mother – no symbol could be better to the Ordovicis that you mean to stay.'

We all agreed, even those of us who were Catuvellauni born.

'What of the *most* loyal core?' I asked. 'What can I do to turn them from Arthewin for once and for all?'

Elidoros looked me in the eyes. 'Single combat, you against Arthewin. It has to be.'

Thirty six   **Single Combat**

There was snow on the ground and brightening the mountains when we left the next morn, yet we reached the great lake with ease thanks to our Ordovici hosts. Our numbers grew with every farm and homestead we passed. By the time I stood on the shore they were chanting my name.

The lake sparkled in the morning light. Even the gnarled old trees on the southern shore glowed. Those who reached the lake first gathered along the shingle and in the gaps between the trees, crowding every hand-span of space, but they parted to let the chief druid, Nesica and me through. Nes and I dismounted as we reached the edge.

'Ready?' she whispered.

I smiled. 'Arthewin could be a real bear and I would have no fear, with this crowd.'

I don't think anyone but the nearest of our people could have heard our words but she smiled back at me and even such a small gesture as this raised a cheer.

I helped the chief druid from his own horse and up onto one of the oldest oak stumps. Catuvellaunos raised his stick to call for silence. It took a few moments for word to drift through to the back rows but silence fell. An acolyte took the stick from him.

'Ordovicis!' he bellowed. 'Your born king has lost his mind and angered the Gods. Let me show you now a worthy king.'

I stood before them all then turned to the druid. He put both his hands upon my head, saying the words of the greatest blessing prayer.

'A bad king is no king,' he concluded. 'Let this prince, your kinsman, restore strength to these lands. The Gods will it.'

There was a ground-trembling cheer. Those with shields beat them. I turned back towards the crowd and the chanting began again. Nesica unwrapped the torque half and passed it to me, taking my owl-eye shield from my hands. I held the torque above me for the gold to glint in the morning sun.

'Ordovicis! This torque is precious to my people. When we left our born home we cleaved it, in two, as our own hearts were breaking. It has passed down to me from my Father's kin. I cast my portion now to the Gods, in the most sacred land of my Mother's ancestors!'

I felt the weight of the gold torque in my hand one last time. Halved as it was it was still heavy.

Whatever you do, don't drop it.

I settled the torque into my left hand, holding it lightly, and swung my whole upper body. As I let go the torque spun out over the water, arcing far and high before dropping into the lake, with a satisfying splash, a good fifty paces out.

Now the cheering went wild.

I drew the sword of my mother's kin from its scabbard and held it aloft in my right hand.

'I pledge, to the Gods, to my ancestors, and to you, that I will be your loyal king, for as long as there is breath in my body.'

And how long is that going to be?

It would depend on what happened the next day, Imbolc Eve.

There was no hiding thousands of warriors marching on Arthewin's seat. What only a handful of us knew was that a small group had left before us, in the dark, to spirit themselves into the fort. Despite it being Kynbel's idea we remembered that he and Arthewin had met, at Mon, a year or two ago, so Colleos volunteered to lead the party in his stead. Five men went, three of mine and two native Ordovici, but from outlying villages, all in plain dull clothes and with their weapons hidden. I told them to make themselves known to Ordovicos only if they needed to. Rhian and Elid's daughter were to get them in and after that their orders were simple: keep the prisoners alive, by any means necessary.

I said a prayer with the group just before they left and that was all I could do. I wouldn't know, until I reached the seat, whether they prevailed or not. I wished, in truth, that I was going with them.

As we rode along the valley that approaches Arthewin's hill-top seat Kynbel trotted up beside me in a brief spell when I was alone.

'You all right?' he asked.

A simple question . . .

'To be honest I'm not as scared in my bones as I was the day I challenged your Uncle Adminios . . . that, in itself, is worrying me.'

He laughed. 'Well, he's the sort of man who gets bit by a horse fly and screams like you've chopped his arm off. That sort's always a tricksy piece of shit – at least Arthewin's got the mind of a warrior.'

'Yes, and he's been at weapon practice more or less every day since he was eight summers old. That's more than I have, when all's said and done.'

Kynbel snorted. 'And what's he been doing for the last few years? Sitting on his arse? You've been in actual wars.' He scratched his mare between the ears. 'Besides, isn't he really old?'

Now I laughed. 'He's eight years older than me, which makes him forty-seven summers. Neither of us are ancient as the land itself just yet.'

'The years will still favour you – wear him out. The rest of us will watch your back.'

I smiled, remembering the little lad I'd once been able to lift with one hand. 'You know, you have never been more like your father than you are today.'

He smiled too, dropping his gaze to his mare's mane. 'He is with us, I think. Sometimes I see him in Temlyr's eyes.'

I reached across the space between our horses and held his shoulder a moment.

We'd entered a woodland, dark with yew and holly, and started ascending. Icicles hung from the branches. I could hear a stream babbling through rocks. As we rode higher I could see the stream was pooling into an ice-rimmed basin at the foot of moss-kissed boulders, forming a true waterfall. Beautiful, in its own way, but cold.

I saw young Brig was coming back down towards us, inching his horse with care down the steep path. 'We've reached the gates, sire,' he said. 'No-one is defending them, and there's a lot o' noise coming from inside.'

I hurried up to the front, Kynbel by my side, and found Elid, still on his horse, just over a spear's throw away from the main gate. He was conversing, in shouts, with what looked to be a young boy, peering out from the tower – all we could see were big eyes and a thatch of dark hair.

'Da said not t'open the gate until everythin's *calm*,' came the cry.

Elid feigned fury but I think in truth he was trying not to laugh. 'And *I* say to open the gate!'

The thatch of hair shook. 'Naw. It's not calm yet.'

'Well, *I* am calm,' Elid returned. 'It's calm as a pond out here.'

'In here I mean! Some foreigner has the king cornered – 'e's threatened to horse-whip him!'

That will be my Colleos.

Elid saw me from the corner of his eye and stifled another smile. 'Boy! Tell your king that King Caratacos and the Chief Druid of all the Isle are here, with a war host of thousands, so a whipping is just his first headache of the day!'

The boy raised his head further above the palisade and saw the truth for himself.

'I'll get my Da.'

The gate swung open at last, the boy's father bowing to us as we entered. He had a bandage around his left palm and a cut on his chin. 'Please stop this, before any more blood is shed,' he pleaded.

'The prisoners? Are we too late?'

His head dropped. 'For the young Prince . . . I think so.'
Please Gods no.

I sprang from Buanedd's back and ran up the steep track towards the houses, Kynbel and the others right behind me. No one stopped me as I ran. I could hear shouts and cries but the mass of people at the edge of the yard meant I could see nothing. I unsheathed the sword of my mother's kin.

'Let me through!'

The people gasped and parted. I saw Mocco on the ground, bleeding from a chest wound, Ordovicos kneeling by his side with a blood soaked rag in his hand. Behind them was firewood, like a pyre, but piled around a hitching pole. *Had he planned to burn them?* Behind all that, at the far side of the narrow yard, Arthewin stood, sword in hand, trying to swing at Tynos and Rhian, both up against a cattle pen. Tynos was holding his ribs. I could see Rhian was breathing but she was out cold. Colleos was protecting them but just with a whip as the boy had said. The rest of the men I'd sent were being held at bay by Ordovici warriors, twitchy as hares. Coll's sword was out of his reach, half buried in a heap of fodder the other side of the cow-pen.

Arthewin lunged at Colleos again but Coll dodged to the side and snapped the whip. Arthewin fell back with a yelp, clutching at his eyes.

'Colleos, leave him to me.'

Everyone turned. I saw Ordovicos scramble to his feet. He raised his arms aloft. 'No-one interfere! The two kings must decide this for themselves. Back away, all of you!'

I stepped out into the heart of the yard as all the bystanders obeyed their druid. Arthewin was still holding his face but he growled, facing me. He could see me all right. He held his sword hilt in a white-knuckle grip in his right hand but had no shield.

'Someone give my cousin his shield,' I ordered. One of the guardsmen broke away from the pack holding my men and scooped up a shield from near the stockade fence, handing it to his king. All the while the man's wary eyes were on me. Wary . . . but curious.

'Cousin! Shall we finish what we've started?'

He spat into the mud, those cornflower eyes fish-stare empty as ever. 'You! I can kill my own son if I want! None can stop me! Not even you, you smug self-loving sack of shit.'

I flicked a look to Ordovicos. 'The boy lives, for now,' he said.

Arthewin lunged again but this time at me. I dodged right and missed his sword swing but my own swipe just smacked into his shield. *Not too much of that. Remember what Kynbel said.* I swooped my blade low, towards his ankles. He was agile enough to leap backwards but I bashed into his face with the edge of my shield while he was still moving and I saw him totter. The crowd gasped.

'Not as easy as beating up old men, is it?' I taunted.

Arthewin's eyes narrowed. He scuttled back further then lowered his shield down his left side, as if inviting an attack.

'Careful,' Tynos wheezed. 'He has a dagger on his left, beneath his tunic.'

Arthewin roared in fury and plunged left towards Tynos. Colleos cracked the whip again and this stopped him – or the ripple of jeers from his people.

'Fight *me*,' I jeered.

He ran at me then, fast as a she-bear. I had to use my shield to protect my head but I was quick too and his next swipe missed. My own parry almost caught his right shoulder and there was another shocked gasp from the circle as the people saw the rip in his tunic. He dashed to the side, getting too near his prone son for comfort.

'Gorfan! Get the boy away!'

Arthewin could see I'd dropped my concentration a blink and charged at me again. I used my shield and felt the wood thump as his blows rained down. I pushed backwards, slashing out with my own sword and soon had him in retreat, edging towards the firewood pile. *Keep going. I'll have him pinned in a moment*, I thought, but he knew every finger-span of his own yard and rallied in time. Our swords clashed, steel on steel, sword on shield, again and again, but neither of us could wound the other. I was the younger, yes, and stronger, but in skill we were about matched and his sheer mad fury gave him power. He knew he only had to veer into stabbing range of his son for my blood to ice.

'For the Gods sake get the prince away!' I screamed and at last Ordovicos and a few other men dashed out and carried Mocco from sight.

'What do you care? He's not yours,' Arthewin sneered, breathing hard.

'No worthy king would say such of *any* of his people,' I returned and that raised a cheer from the circle, not just the people who'd come with me. Arthewin ran at me again, forcing me to parry. We were edging across the yard, back towards the stockade.

Please Gods, if I am worthy then let me win this.

At that moment, as my sword struck his shield, I heard a crack.

Praise Gods!

His shield had split down the middle, to the boss and past it. Only the leather cover held it together now, so the two pieces hung from his left hand like a loose scab. Arthewin swore and cast the shield aside but as I swung my sword for his unguarded left he snatched the dagger I'd been warned of and lashed out at me. He caught the back of my right hand, loosening my grip on my sword just a blink – it was enough. It flew from my hand and into the enclosure with the cattle. *Oh Gods.* I punched out with my shield boss, smashing him in the nose. Blood ran down into his moustache. I kept my shield well up and advanced, punching again. He staggered backwards but he stayed on his feet. He still had hold of the dagger.

I heard the whip snap. 'My king! To your right!'

Coll's sword was there, in the pile of winter feed. I snatched it up and thrust out. Straight through Arthewin's heart.

There was a shocked intake of breath from all around. Silence hung over us for a heartbeat.

Now is my moment.

As Arthewin slumped to the mud I put down my shield. Blood was running from the back of my right hand but I felt no pain. I crouched beside my cousin and used my left hand to close his eyes.

Colleos fished my own sword from the pen and as I stood we swapped back.

'This sword belonged to my mother's grand-sire,' I said, to the watching people. 'He was king here, as was his son. I don't think it would let me shed the blood of a kinsman, but now the Gods have shown their will.' I snapped the sword back into its scabbard. 'I am your loyal king, if you will have me.'

There was another pause but one by one the surrounding people dropped to their knees. Ordovicos ran out from his house, I suppose to support me, but realised he didn't have to say a word.

'Does Mocco live?' I asked.

He nodded. 'He's lost a lot of blood but if I stitch now -'

'Fine, go. This is just a scratch.'

My wife ran over with a scrap of cloth and bandaged up my hand. I could see Colleos and Rhian, now conscious, helping Tynos out of the yard.

I need to help with the wounded.

I took one last look about the circle of Ordovicis. The men who had been holding my advance party at spear-point looked crest-fallen, but they'd put their spears down. No-one had gone to my cousin's body, not even a crying woman.

'Is there anyone, *anyone*, who seeks vengeance for Arthewin? Speak now, and let us settle this. Do not let it fester.'

Not a word.
I nodded back to them all and walked to the Druid house.

Thirty seven Who breaks first

That first night in our new home, lying in what had been Arthewin's bed, I don't think I slept more than ten blinks. I had Nes with me, and our Gladsia got in with us too, but with the wind and the wolves howling around us it was a long night of staring at the door. We felt better, the next day, with our own things unpacked to cheer the house and Arthewin safely on his pyre.

I gave Arthewin a rightful pyre and had his ash buried beside his eldest son. It was this, I felt, that eased the minds of the last few doubting Ordovicis. I didn't blame them for their doubt, to be honest. Thanks to the recent moons of madness and chaos there was much neglected work to be done, enough to weary a hero, so I rolled up my sleeves and got on with it from the first morning. There was fear – justified fear – over food supplies. I ensured all the people had enough and showed my usual restraint in my own household. When the rest of our people arrived a few days later old forts were being brought into use and new houses built, so we weren't elbow-to-elbow among each other in the villages for long. I made sure the Ordovici warriors took part in raids alongside my own men, to foster fellowship, and to give them adventure after long years of nowt but guard duty and border patrols. I had the whipping post wrenched out and chopped up for firewood.

The wounded were my first worry. Tynos had broken ribs but the underlying lung remained sound and after a moon of rest and willow-bark tea he was fine; Mocco was a much harder task to save. He didn't surface from his wound, for certain, until the leaf-buds were unfurling on the trees. Ordovicos, Catuvellaunos and I secured his life that first evening but it was Rhian, patient as a fisherman, who nursed him through the skull-burning fever, when the rest of us were called to other work. I held a feast in Mocco's honour in the spring and wasn't surprised when

Mocco and Rhian took the opportunity to ask for my permission to wed. I agreed, with all my heart.

We held the hand-fasting just after Beltane, when I'd received Mathona's consent and when Tyllan's new harp was also ready. It gave us a bright shaft of sunlight to look forward to in what had been a dark year.

Kynbel was as joyful as anyone at the wedding. He gave the bride and groom a gold arm ring each and a brood mare from his own stable, and I had never been prouder of him.

The amity between the two lads was all the more pleasing to me because – healthy as a weed though I was – we were of course at war, and minds turned to who would now succeed me if I did die in battle. Kynbel had been my known heir for years, given my daughter was green as a pea-pod, but we were in a new land, with its own prince, and Ordovicos, for one, would not let me forget it. He cornered me, again, at the hand-fasting feast, when the couple were dancing at the heart of the yard.

'Mocco is the younger of the two, by five years,' I countered. 'Not much has changed for him – not for the worse, at least. Look at him – is he resentful?'

Gorfan huffed. 'He's just grateful to be loved. For now.'

I rolled my eyes. 'Wouldn't you be? If you were him?'

'The succession will bother him when *other* concerns pale.'

Well, maybe.

I swigged back my beer. 'Given all of us are in blood-soaked battle with Rome day by day "succession" might prove meaningless – leave it to the Gods to decide. That's your own favourite saying.'

He pursed his lips, and I departed back to the feast.

The Fourteenth Legion took most of the old Cornovi lands that summer as we'd thought they would. They built the fort by Uricon's old seat that we'd thwarted before. The Gemina tried to push further, but with our forces now strengthened the Ordovici mountains proved a sturdy gate. Scapula might have tried to get through the Deceangli land again too but my look-outs did their work. I sent Hedros up there, with his wife and a loyal force, to keep an eye on the weak points, and to trade with Blodau's Gangani cousins in Eire. I asked Camulora to go with them. On the face of it she was just a sort of cuckoo-mother to Blodau, an older, wiser head, but she had her own secret orders too. Whether time away, in Blodau's own land, and a bit of power and responsibility would help the couple . . . well, I couldn't know. I felt it couldn't hurt.

By late summer the Legion had stopped advancing. They'd gained a few more fields for their wretched empire but nothing like as much as they wanted. Ha! *Gods be praised.* All the while it rolled over in my mind: What if they withdraw? There could be a crisis elsewhere, it's happened before. Scapula could die . . . The Emperor could die . . . The Emperor could be murdered . . .

If we can just hold on.

I did get news, late that year, albeit not quite what I hoped for.

It was one of those bright, crisp days that makes you feel good. I'd just got back from a raid so Machan asked me to talk to our youngest set of warriors, at the practice ground, young Coll among them, about our success. I was bringing the tale of our daring escape to an end when I saw Nes running down the path to us, our daughter and young Eithinen at her side.

Nes waited for me to finish, and to get out of earshot of the rest, then announced 'Visitors!' with a smile.

'Venutios?'

'No, but a message from him, from Dillyn, so the next best thing.'

'Dillyn herself?'

'And Cam, because she came that way. They're exhausted so I told them to wait by the waterfall while I fetch you.'

'They've put their feet in the water so they don't smell,' Gladsia added, with a burst of giggles from Eithinen.

I raised my eyebrows but in truth it was a joy to see. 'Well, I might join them.'

Nes and I walked up the path hand-in-hand, Creegan ahead, and the two girls scampering among the rocks and twisty trees like squirrels.

'Does anyone know Dillyn is here, apart from the children?' I asked.

'No. That's another reason I asked them to stay at the fall. They camped in the wood last night and hung around until they spotted us picking rose-hips.'

'*Can* anyone else know?'

'Better not. Dillyn was supposed to visit the Deceangli and go straight back – Cartimandua thinks she is delivering a message for *her*.'

We reached the waterfall, where the two women were lounging on the mossy rocks, their feet in the water, as Gladsia had said. They sprang up at the sight of me but I put them at their ease. Nes and I joined them, while the girls splashed about and shrieked.

Dillyn confirmed what Nes had said. 'The Brigantes' queen thinks I'm her loyal servant,' she added, 'I won't last two breaths in that household if she starts to think otherwise.'

'Who was her message for? Not me, surely?'

She shook her head. 'No sire, for my "native queen". Scapula has offered Blodau a queenship – a hollow husk of a queenship – in return for her lands, as a bridge to you, and he's used the other queen he has in his pocket to offer it. Like taming a wild horse with a docile one.'

My heart jumped.

'What did Blodau say?'

Dillyn's nose creased with laughter. 'She said to tell her to shove her offer up her arse until she chokes.'

Nesica's jaw dropped. 'Blodau said that?'

Cam smiled. 'Word for word.'

I tipped my head back and laughed. 'Good for Blodau! ... You know I thought Scapula would try to go that way again. Does he plan to attack in the spring?'

Dillyn frowned. 'Sorry sire, difficult for me to say. I was sent out to fetch something and when I got back he'd gone.'

That raised a flag in my mind.

'Do you think Cartimandua guessed you understood their words?'

'I – I don't think so, sire. When she told me what she wanted me to do, later, she told me, in British, some of the things he'd said while I was still in the house. . .'

Hmm . . . that could just be a counter-move, cleverness on her part.

I must have looked as suspicious as I felt. 'Venutios said he'd get word to you as soon as they start to move,' she added.

'Does Scapula visit the queen often?'

She shook her head. 'Not often. Enough to keep her rich.'

Bribes now, great. A cool wind shook the trees and I wrapped my cloak tighter about me. 'So, what's she like?'

Dillyn's eyes sparkled. She leant back, spreading out her legs like someone corpulent, or knackered. 'Dillyn, *Dillyn!*' she called, in a nasal whine. 'Bring me my pillow! All day, all bloody day, with sour filthy dogs. Why can they not be content?!' She flicked her hair over her left shoulder, staring into the distance with a long look down her nose. 'Vello! *Vello!* Have them flogged in the morning! Just bring me more wine.'

'Who is Vello? Friend or enemy?'

Her black brows lifted. 'He was her husband's shield bearer until he started bedding her. Now he says he's her shield-bearer but everyone knows what's really going on.'

Nes and I swapped glances. *Poor Venutios.*

'Yet the people remain loyal to her?'

'Half of them do.' Dillyn shrugged. 'She and Vello are strange but she's made a lot of them rich – and there's the permanent guard Scapula left, hanging around. Briganti's skull still hangs on the gatepost. No-one dares say a word.'

'Not even Venutios?'

'That's the other thing he wanted me to tell you – he doesn't plan to live at home much any more. He will go north, to his brothers, so when a messenger comes they might be Carvetii . . . I wish to go north with him, my king.'

I sucked in a breath. 'I can see why *he* would want to do that . . . but you? You are doing good work where you are now. You said you thought Cartimandua didn't suspect you – '

'Not yet, sire.'

Not yet.

I turned to my wife, who was giving me one of her most dubious looks. 'You can't send her back to that woman,' Nes said.

Dillyn smiled. 'Don't worry, my queen – while she dotes on me, I'm safe. If she turns on me . . . well, I can give as good as I get.'

'Then why go north with Venutios?' I pushed.

She went red to her ears and Cam suddenly looked to the ground.

'Because . . . because we are close, my king.'

By the Gods.

'Oh Dillyn, it's a dangerous game you are playing.'

She nodded. 'I know. . . It wasn't my plan. We just sort of fell into it.'

Nes sighed, shaking her head. 'A secret like that – you're not going to be able to keep it. Not for long. Once his wife finds out, you'll be lucky if she just poisons you.'

Cam picked a burr from her dress and threw it into the pool. 'You need to watch out for other jealous women too – a man like that, an unhappy marriage like that, she won't be the only woman you've replaced in his bed. As soon as one of them finds out they'll use it as a weapon.'

Dillyn went still redder. 'Well I don't know of any others.'

Gods help her.

Creegan had stood up and was looking towards the path, sniffing the air. 'Machan will be bringing the young warriors home for their meal. You two need to disappear,'

I warned. 'I'll come along to your camp with you, so we know where to bring some food out later.'

Nesica shook her head. 'No, I should do it. I told everyone I was going out to pick rose-hips and I haven't got two dozen yet. You take the girls home.'

I sighed as I hugged her. *How suspicious have we become?* Sensitive to every twitch like a spider to its thread.

Gods help us.

Later, by our own hearth, Nes told me more. She went over to Gladsia's little bed and made sure she was asleep before coming to sit beside me.

'Camulora talked with the Gangani traders, alone, as you'd asked,' she said, in a low voice. 'They said they couldn't promise, straight-away, but the ship will return in the spring. They will have an answer then.'

I held her hand. 'That's as good an answer as we'll get for now, I suppose. I'll still gather all the treasure I can, in readiness. I didn't spend as much on the grain for the people as I feared I might.'

The fire spat and fizzed and Nes flicked a look at Gladsia lest she'd woken. 'When do we tell her?' she whispered.

'We don't, not until the boats are pulling up on the shore. We shouldn't tell anyone until the deal is set – don't say a word, not even to Alwona and Airdinna.'

'Airdinna's baby will be born by spring. Everyone's starting to think Rhian's expecting too.'

'I know. I don't want anyone's hope to be raised too much, in case the Gangani say no.'

Nes squeezed my hand, looking up into my eyes. 'It's not just that, is it?'

No, not just that at all. 'It can't look like we are giving up – if I show fear, or doubt, then we *will* lose. I make it happen. And sending all the children away . . . well it reeks of fear.'

'It's no worse than sending a child to be fostered. We might have done that even if we weren't at war.'

'All of them? To the same place?'

'Are you changing your mind? Because if you can't stand to send her away then I certainly can't.'

I took a deep breath. 'No.' I looked over to Gladsia, her blanket gently rising and falling as she slept, Creegan curled at her feet.

Nes was looking the same way. 'She is going to hate us for this, isn't she?'

I felt my throat tightening. 'Maybe, for a short while, but I know as furious as I was at being sent away it was still better than seeing my parents' heads hanging from a palisade . . . Some of the things we have seen, and heard, these last few years – we can't let it happen.' My voice cracked. 'We just can't.'

Thirty eight Last Farewells

I received word from Catuvellaunos, just after Samhain, that Siluri had succumbed to her lung-sickness and joined the Gods. I shed no false tears but I felt no joy in it either. Better news was that he said he was sending an older Initiate south to the Silures, to 'assist' Branadain, and I knew he had come around to my way of thinking that Brana should be the Silures queen once her brother, too, went to the Land of Youth. Catuvellaunos had been unconvinced, I feared, when I'd come clean with him earlier on.

The woman stopped a night with us on her journey south. She was an odd-looking creature at first glance. Her attire was the simple black of any druid but her hair had been divided by dozens of glass beads so that it poked out from every side of her head like a teasel. She had a flight of birds tattooed around one wrist and a herd of deer circled the other. A swarm of bees were tattooed across her face where freckles might have danced. She grinned up at me with big white teeth.

'Were you a great pupil of the last Siluri?' I asked, trying to keep the dread from my voice.

'Oh no,' she said.

'No?'

'Oh no. I never liked her, but I like Branadain. When Britannios said he needed someone to go to help her, I offered myself. He knew I would.'

'You know her brother, the King, is very sick . . ?'

She nodded. 'Oh yes. Brana told me everything, while we were at holy Mon. I'll help her, where I can.'

Nesica brought over a bowl of stew and the lass grinned at her, too, with a flash of teeth.

'I'm sure you will help her,' I said. 'These are dark times. We know the Romans are trying bribes where the sword doesn't work. What would you do, if they tried to sweeten you with a shipload of gold?'

She laughed, a great snorting laugh like a pig. 'Oh I'd melt it all down and send it back to them, shaped as a big gold fist.'

My wife and I shared a smile. *Well chosen, Catuvellaunos.*

I gave her an escort and put her on her way.

The escort returned before the Winter Solstice and brought Corbennog with them. I was on the palisade with a cup of dried blackcurrant tea to warm my hands, watching sick-green snow clouds roll in to coat the mountains, and I knew, to travel in days like this, what news they would bring. Corbennog had tears in his eyes as he bowed to me.

'Did he pass gently, at the the end?' I asked.

He faltered, just a blink, but I knew. 'Sire, I would like to say yes . . .' I stopped him from saying more with a gesture of my hand. 'His mother, the queen, did,' he reassured me. 'She followed him, within the day.'

I sat back upon the nearest fence. 'Gods speed them both to the Land of Youth.'

We stayed still, with bowed heads, until the first flakes of snow floated down and melted upon our flesh.

Remember you are a host.

My first meeting with Mathona sped into my mind, the generosity Gwyfina and I had met with. I took my old friend to the great house and shared memories with him all evening over a fine dinner. Only when our talk turned to the future did our spirits sink low again. He told me that the Valeria meant to turn north to join the Gemina, in the spring or early summer, to hunt me out. All the watchers were sure.

I leant back in my seat and drained my cup. 'And if the Hispana turn west at the same time then we are truly pinned with our backs to the sea. If you Silures come north to help us then the Hispana will move on you, or the Valeria will turn back.'

'Many of us will come north, sire. Enough to be of use. The new Queen held a council last full moon and asked us – there was no lack of warriors offering, sire.'

'I can well believe it. The Silures have always been brave, and loyal.' I poured us both another cup of beer. 'How fares Melistia?'

'We all thought she'd disappear, sire, after the funeral, perhaps go back to her Dobunni kin, or come north to you, but she was knelt there swearing her loyalty to the new queen with the rest of us. I was surprised, sire.'

'You are her kin now. Give her work. She would want to be busy.'

The lines about his eyes creased in a smile. 'The new Siluri said the same, sire, they have plans – they're all on fire with hatred of Rome. It feels like we have lost one she-dragon and gained three.'

I smiled back. 'The Empire will learn to regret their threat to the Silures.'

Never did I speak truer words.

A new spring came upon us quiet as a curl of smoke, but with promise of the flames to come. Kynbel and Airdinna's youngest was born while the spring winds raged, just like his paternal grand-sire, so they named him after Tog, which pleased me. They wanted me to do the naming ceremony, but I let Ordovicos do it, and kept the peace.

I spent my days riding between the villages, keeping our warriors watchful and our defences strong, Nes and Gladsia traipsing about the land with me, overnighting in a succession of new huts. All my most trusted people were doing much the same. Our raids into land under the Roman heel continued too, but not as often – there was less opportunity, by then. The enemy forts, neat and repetitive as honeycomb, sprang up all over our lost lands like lesions on a diseased face. I began to realise that they were not only stepping stones to assaults on us, they were intended to keep us *in*.

314

Our sturdy gate was becoming a stockade.

As the celandines faded for another year I received word from Camulora: the Gangani said yes.

I made my way back to Arthewin's old seat and called a council. By the time everyone else made it back it was the eve of Beltane Eve. None thought it strange, by then, that I kept the door shut, despite the warmth of the day, nor that I asked young Tarn and Elid's daughter to take all the older children gathering blossom until dinner – no doubt they thought I just wanted peace – but Nes and I knew.

Once everyone had squashed into the house and found a perch I started. 'How are we off for weapons?' I asked my brother.

'Plenty,' Dran said, with a firm nod. 'But in the long run we'll lack iron. We've copper and silver, in our own mine and Blodau's, but not much iron.'

'The Silures have it, though, in their southern reach. We can trade with Branadain as long as they can spare any.'

Dran's head tipped to the side. 'Yes. If they can.'

'I know, but all the signs are that the legions will come straight for us next.'

Camulora, near the door, caught my eye. 'I don't trust Rome not to try something sly,' she said. 'Be careful, Caradoc.'

I spread out my hands with a laugh. 'You're absolutely right, but am I *not* careful?'

'Perhaps *too* careful, Uncle,' Kynbel said.

Airdinna shot a sideways look at her husband. There was a slight gasp from all around, loud enough for me to hear.

Kynbel sat up a little straighter. 'I just mean . . . every time we've taken them on, well, *we've* won. We can't back west forever – we can't. Surely it's time we threw everything at them?'

He cast a look around for agreement and found little but I could tell Mocco, on his other side, next to his own wife, was warm to the idea. I opened my mouth to speak but Colleos got in before me.

'Prince Kynbel, that is *exactly* what the Romans would want.' He looked to me for reassurance and I motioned for him to go on. 'Look, I'm no prince and perhaps I speak out of turn but think of what happened to my own born people. The only successes we had were with stealth . . . and Vercingetorix had far more warriors than we.'

Machan, too, was looking at the two young princes with a sharp look in his good eye. 'You two are only sat here today because the King has saved both your necks. Don't be in such a rush to throw your lives away.'

Mocco raised his hands. 'I know, I know – no-one is more grateful than I. A battle on the flat would be a risk, I know that too. But we're also told that the hilltops are no barrier to them, that the Romans break forts like topping a boiled egg – what *are* we going to do then?'

I could see Airdinna was now biting her lip.

'Speak, Airdinna.'

'I – I won't be trapped inside a besieged fort again.' She shifted her baby to her other arm. 'Neither will my children.'

Her voice was soft as ever but her words had the weight of an axe falling. I saw heads dip, and Kynbel put his arm about his wife.

'There, listen to someone who knows the sound of the bolts when they come.' I took in a good breath. 'Look, you are all right, in your own ways. We are not toothless. We have warriors and we have allies. If the Brigantes rise again behind the legions then that *may* be a good time to push forward – but we must pick the spot well. We have our own missiles – ' I looked to Dran. 'The trick is knowing where to put them, to do the most good.'

Dran nodded. 'I think I know a good place, if we can lure the legions there.'

I smiled. 'If we bunch up all our forces and threaten them they'll attack us all right, no more lure required. If we could be sure help was coming from the north then I'd be keener.'

No-one argued with that. I took a sip of water and looked about the house again. 'Listen, there is another reason why I called you here today. I have an offer to share with you that could keep all our children safe and, well, given what we are about to face, I urge you to think about accepting it.' I told them the fosterage agreement I'd bargained with the Gangani leader, the price we could pay and the number he would take. 'As soon as we prevail we can fetch the children back,' I said, my voice firm – firmer than the doubt in my heart supported. 'What do you think?'

There was silence a moment, everyone looking to the floor. I saw tears rolling down Dag's cheeks.

Alwona spoke first. 'My two eldest boys died in battle with Rome and the horrors we've seen and heard of these last years have robbed my sleep. I, for one, would gladly see our youngest fostered somewhere safe, my king. He's too young to join the warriors yet.'

Machan gripped her hand and there were murmurs of agreement all around. Kynbel, though, looked uneasy.

'Why not just move the children to Mon, for the battle season?' he asked.

I spread out my hands. 'I wondered the same, but the Legion got within sight of Mon when they attacked the Deceangli . . . I'm not sure how long it could be defended, if we were to fail.'

There was a sharp intake of breath at that. Ordovicos looked like he was whispering a prayer.

'But what do we know of these Gangani?' Kynbel pressed.

'Not that much, I admit. If there was time I would go there and see for myself, but if I leave then the people will fear I leave for good. They are kin of Blodau, if you look back far enough, and allied with her, and us, no friends to Rome. . .'

'Decanglos speaks highly of their chief druid,' Cam added. 'He'd not say a good word about anyone cruel.'

Her eyes turned to Ordovicos, just a little, but I saw it. He saw it too. 'Watch your tongue,' he snapped. She laughed a mocking mirthless laugh but let it go.

Rhian had sat quiet throughout, her left hand across her swollen belly as if to protect the child within, but she now turned to the druid herself. 'What do the Gods advise about this, please, Ordovicos? I've seen nothing in my dreams.'

'The Gods demand that a fostered child is treated as a born child is,' he said. 'None of you need fret about their welfare whilst they abide there. *My* prayers will be more concerned with the sea crossing.'

The room tensed up like a harp string at that. *Thanks, Gorfan.*

'The Gangani cross the sea easy as we would a puddle,' Cam scoffed.

'We'll choose the calmest day,' Nes added.

Dran met my gaze. 'I want both of mine on the ship,' he said. 'I was orphaned in battle time and I sit here now, alive, and Eirian always said any free life is better than being a slave.'

Leon, to his right, nodded at that and so did Airdinna, across the room.

I put my arm around Nes. 'If we are all agreed then Camulora will take the message north tonight.'

Colleos was resting his head in his hands and Dag now comforting him. 'When do we tell the children, sire?' he asked.

'I leave that decision to all of you. With our daughter we expect her to resist. We will tell her as late as possible.'

Thirty nine Defiant

When the day came 'resist' was not a strong enough word for it. Gladsia howled and screamed like she hadn't for years, tearing up her bed and throwing her clothes. Nes tried to hug her and was punched for her trouble.

'No, no, no!'

'Gla-Gla, darling, ease yourself,' Nes soothed. A shoe flew across the room.

'No! I won't go!'

Nes slumped to a stool. Tears were flowing down both their faces. 'We don't *want* you to go. We're just trying to keep you safe.'

'I'm safe with you and Dada!'

I sat down on the edge of a bed and drew her to me. 'Listen,' I said, looking into her eyes, fierce as a caught cat. 'You are a Princess of the Catuvellauni, and my daughter. I need you to show the others a good example, can you see? You're older than Tyllan and Tog and Albucos. Even Temlyr and Eithinen and little Caradoc look up to you. Today, of all days, I need you to be a princess, do you understand?'

She kicked the bed. 'No!'

Nes threw me a look. 'She's only seven summers . . .'

'You were born royal, so was I – would we have got away with this?'

Nes conceded that, and I ended up putting Gladsia over my shoulder and taking her to the beach to burn out her temper, kicking and screaming the whole way, lest she start off every other child. She'd already set off the dog.

The sun was setting by the time she calmed. She came over and plonked herself down by me on the sand and carved channels about her feet with her little hands. I stayed quiet until she wanted to speak.

'What are the Gangi like?' she asked at last.

'Gangani. They are like us, but they live by the sea and have good boats. You like boats, don't you?'

'Yes.'

'And you like swimming?'

'Yes.'

'Well, you may like it there then. All your friends will be there, and Auntie Airdinna, maybe Auntie Rhian, and Retta's mama with her boy and little Albucos, so you won't be on your own.'

'Will you and Mama come to see me?'

Gods help me. Don't let this be a lie.

'Of course, as often as we can. We go to see your cousin Tegwyn, don't we?' I realised my mistake as her eyes narrowed. 'And Tegwyn is almost a grown man, he's busy. He doesn't need visits so much.'

I wasn't sure I got away with that. I saw she was starting to shiver, Solstice Eve or no, and she let me wrap my summer cloak about her.

'Come and have dinner. Let's not have this last evening together marred by strife.'

She wiped her nose on my cloak but I let it pass.

'Should I say sorry to Mama?'

'Yes you should.'

I awoke at dawn to find Leon shaking my shoulder.

'Sire!'

'Leon? Are you all right?'

'Yes sire, but Hedros is here. A messenger has arrived from Prince Venutios – his brother, another Carvetii prince. He says it's urgent, sire.'

'Here?'

Leon shook his head. 'No sire, at your seat. Hedros met him near the Deva river. He took him to your seat.'

Of course. All of us with children for the boats were bedded down in herder's huts for the night, near the beach, about as royal and luxurious as it sounded, but convenient for the morning. I glanced over at Gladsia, still asleep and snuggled on the other side of Nes, near the wall. 'How urgent? Did he say?'

Another shake of the head. 'He wouldn't tell me or Hedros anything, sire. He asked that we fetch you straight-away.'

Could be another assassin.

'How does the sea look? Is it calm?'

'Like a pond, sire, and not a cloud in the sky. Apollo has answered our prayers.'

We can't delay then, the boats will be here soon.

'Where's Hedros now?'

'Taking the opportunity to say farewell to his little brother, sire – I said I would wake you.'

I threw on my shirt. 'I'll see my daughter off and *then* ride. Half a morning won't hurt, or he'd have insisted on coming with Hedros.'

Many of the children were keening like the gulls as we readied ourselves but our daughter was quiet – too quiet. She allowed Nes to wrap her in a ludicrous quantity of clothes, on the strength of cold winds being inevitable at sea, without a word of protest, and when the sails were first spotted on the horizon I expected a resurgence of ire, but it didn't come. Instead she slipped her little hand into mine and walked down to the shoreline with me when I greeted the Gangani.

'All well?' Nes mouthed to me as we walked back to the others. I nodded and we both cast Gladsia a furtive look. She peered back at us from under her woolly hat. I couldn't read her mind, but I felt I could see it working.

I changed the subject. 'Three boats, for safety, as I asked. They said they'll have breeze enough once they get out from shore. It should be an easy crossing but they won't hang about.'

We all filed down to the shoreline like a funeral procession and the Gangani waited for us as we said our farewells.

Nes forced herself to smile even though her eyes were red and wet. She handed Gladsia a nettle string bag stuffed with food.

'You'll be a good girl now, won't you, Gla-Gla?' she said, squeezing the life half from her and squashing the food. 'I'll always be proud of you.'

I dropped to my knees and gave my daughter a good hug myself. 'Always remember,' I whispered, 'be brave, be kind, and you won't go far wrong, whatever happens.'

I got to my feet again and saw the same heartache on the beach all around. Kynbel was crying as he clung to his own wife and children; Coll crouching in front of his eldest as he talked to him; Rhian grasping onto her husband's tunic as she sobbed into his chest. Gladsia saw it all too. Her lower lip began to wobble.

'Dada, I don't want to go.'

'I know, but we must keep you all safe. This is the only way.'

The head of the Gangani traders was waving at me. 'King Caratacos! We must go now if we're to get beyond the worst by nightfall!'

'Come now, be a good example,' I said to her again, and lifted her into the first boat. All the others followed, the three adult women dividing themselves between the three boats as I'd asked, to keep the children calm. Colleos, Machan, Dran, Mocco, Kynbel and I helped to push the boats out into the current then we watched as the sailors pulled at the oars. I tried to keep up a smile as I waved. I kept my eyes on Gladsia's little pale woollen hat as long as I could.

Manawydan, please, I beg you, please keep them all safe.

The sails unfurled as the boats got further out and I could see Gla-Gla's hat no more.

Nes held my hand. 'We're doing the right thing, aren't we?' she said.

'Yes, yes I think so, however much it hurts.' I gave her a quick kiss. 'I should sing a Manawydan prayer, I said I would, but I think my voice will go.'

'I'll sing the words with you, as an echo.'

We did this, everyone joining in. We'd almost got to the end when Mocco's shout rang out.

'There's someone in the water!'

We all followed his gaze. *There's nothing. Is he seeing things?*

Kynbel had scrambled up the nearest rock. 'There!'

Oh Gods. Please no. To be honest my first thought was that Rhian had jumped, but then I saw the white hat.

Nes started to scream.

I felt my hands up at my mouth. 'Oh Gods, oh Gods, please no, please no.'

The waves seemed so much bigger now. I saw her an instant, then she disappeared, then the white was there again. Was it her? Was it just the hat?

'She's swimming!' Kynbel yelled, scrambling back down. 'She isn't drowning – she's swimming! She's swimming back.'

'It's too far!' Nes screeched.

People in the boats were shouting now, waving, pointing.

I felt a grip on my shoulder and my brother was there. 'We'll form a chain,' Dran said. 'All of us! A chain! Lightest, shortest at the back, tallest and heaviest at the front!'

I obeyed. Everyone obeyed. The water seemed ice cold as I waded in behind Dran. *Oh Gods . . . my daughter.* The waves swelled and I got a mouthful of salt.

'Caradoc, you still there?'

I touched Dran's shoulder. 'I'm here. Can you see her?'

'No . . . yes! Further left. Everyone further left!'

We all did as Dran ordered, forcing ourselves through the waves, my left hand on Dran's shoulder, Kynbel's hand on mine, until even Dran, tall as he was, had to tread water. 'Grasp hands now,' he said. 'We'll lose grip.' He was right. The waves were becoming stronger. I did as he said and passed down the message. Dran raised his free hand. 'Gladsia! This way!'

'Can you still see her?!' Nes shouted from further back.

I couldn't, I could only see Dran and what looked like endless dark water, but Dran yelled back yes. 'She's still swimming!'

'How far?'

'Not far now.'

The newest wave swept her even within my sight-line and Dranis reached out and grabbed her, by the back of her clothes. He meant to pass her to me but the weight of the wave meant it was more like a throw. She slammed into my chest. I felt her hands grasp onto my tunic.

'Got you. Got you. Thank the Gods.'

We started to scramble our way back through the waves until we were back on the beach. Nes and I clasped onto our shivering child. We were so soaked ourselves we couldn't warm her.

'Here – I was at the back. Have my cloak,' Dag said, and we stripped off all Gladsia's sodden clothes and wrapped her in this. After a little while, thank the Gods, she stopped shaking.

Dran had been checking everyone made it back out of the water. 'The Gangani are waving – I think they want to know if they should try to come back,' he said.

I looked to my daughter. 'No,' I said. 'Let them go.'

He waved them on and the sails unfurled again. They soon disappeared into the distance.

Dag had run over to our things and brought back a leather bottle which Nes now held to Gladsia's mouth. 'Water, here, wash the salt from your mouth,' she ordered, and Gladsia did as she was told, spitting the first mouthful onto the sand and then gulping the rest down. Her face was red now, but she looked a lot better. 'Why did you do it?' Nes asked, her voice a squeak. 'Why would you do such a stupid thing?'

Gladsia drew herself up a little straighter. 'I wasn't stupid Mama. I knew I *could* swim but when the sails went up it would be too late.'

Yes. Too late to get off and too late for them to easily turn and come back too.

'You planned this from early on, didn't you?' I bellowed down at her.

She said nothing.

'You could have died!'

Gods forgive me but I almost hit her.

Gladsia stamped her little foot on the sand. 'I don't *want* to go!'

All the others were looking at us and I saw a flash of amusement in their eyes then. 'She's your daughter, Uncle,' Kynbel said. 'What did you expect?'

I was in no mood to laugh right then but I let out my tense-held breath. 'Come on, let's get back, see what the Carvetii prince has to say.'

I held out my arms, gathered Gladsia up, and carried her all the way to the horses.

I arrived back in my own house to find our guest at the centre of it, tucking into a joint of wild boar, one of the serving women on his knee. He got to his feet as soon as I crossed the threshold, pitching the woman towards the hearth.

'King Caratacos! How pleased I am to meet you!'

He held out his arms as if to embrace me but I didn't bite and he turned it to a handshake, tossing the joint of roast meat to the nearest dish and wiping his hand on his ornate tunic. He had the same rumbling accent as Venutios, the same height and the rich red-brown hair, but not his breadth.

'Prince Lugrako arrived wracked with hunger,' Ordovicos commented, from the side. 'I hope you don't mind us starting without you.'

'Of course.' I nodded over to Tyllan and Tynos too, sat with the harp, awkward as owls in the noon day light. 'Thank you all for keeping him entertained.'

It had been a bloody long day but I managed a smile. 'Welcome, Prince Lugrako. Did Prince Venutios give you something to prove yourself friend?'

He blinked. 'Oh. Yes. Yes he did.' He plucked an object from his belt and handed it to me, a terret ring with coral inlay, a piece of blue wool tied round three times in simple loops. It wasn't my original wool, of course, nor a sophisticated use of it like the one before, but it was blue, and three loops.

I smiled again. 'Thank you. Please sit back down. Let's eat.'

He did sit back down, but without the confidence of before, and I had enough decency in me to feel a twinge of guilt. I sent the serving woman for beer and sat myself opposite my guest. 'Is your brother well?'

Lugrako nodded. 'Yes, very well, but he couldn't travel west himself this time. He's watched too closely, but – '

'Even when he's in his own Carvetii lands?'

I'd interrupted, but he didn't look annoyed. 'The borders are watched,' he added. 'But he wanted me to come in his stead.'

I smiled. 'You've managed to get through, despite travelling openly as a prince.' I made a tiny gesture to the embroidered edge to his cloak and the heavy torque at his throat and he blushed.

'I'm one of many princes,' he said. 'They can't follow all of us like dogs.'

I don't believe that for a moment.

Nes had been seeing to the horses but now she came in, flanked by Gladsia and Creegan, and I kicked myself. I should have told them to go over to Alwona's. *Too late now.* I introduced Lugrako and while he was chatting and making swift work of his beer I sidled over to Tynos, keeping my voice low.

'Do you know Brig, the young warrior from the north?'

'Yes sire.'

'Go and fetch him, please, tell him who's here, but keep it quiet.'

I returned to our guest and touched cups with him, inviting him to sit again. 'Did Venutios send you here for safety or to get word to me?' I asked.

He swallowed back another gulp of beer. 'Both, King Caratacos. I am to tell you everything he wanted and then stay and help with the battle.'

'The battle?'

Lugrako nodded. 'Five cohorts of the Legio Hispana auxiliaries are marching west to join the others. Scapula has had word from the Emperor – your defiance has gone on too long. They are to hunt you out, whatever it takes, as fire flushes the deer from the forest.'

'That leaves the east of the Isle more vulnerable to us than it was . . . '

'That's what Venutios said.'

I saw Tynos come back in, Brig by his side, and they both went over to sit with Tyllan and his harp. Brig got a good look at Lugrako. Lugrako took no notice of him – there were plenty of people coming and going from the house, after all – but the fact that my attention had wandered didn't escape him.

'There's something else,' he said, leaning forward. 'Scapula is sick. We can all see it, when he visits. Venutios says it will push him into a reckless attack, because he's scared of being sent home ill and disgraced. Venutios said that when the legions march west, our people should rebel again, behind them.'

I put my beer down and called a servant over to refill Lugrako's cup, to give me a moment. On the face of it all the man was saying was good news, the sort of news I'd wanted to hear, but that worried me, for a start. Something niggled me. He *did* have the blue wool token . . . as far as I knew only Venutios and I knew about that, and I hadn't told anyone.

'Excuse me one moment,' I said, with a smile. 'Eat, drink, my friend. I must speak with one of my warriors who has just returned from a raid – I'll be back in a moment.'

I went over to Brig without delay. 'Do you recognise him?' I asked.

Brig had a crease between his brows. 'I think I do . . . but I'm not sure, sire.'

'He *says* he's Prince Lugrako, which would make him your uncle. Do you have an Uncle Lugrako?'

Brig's eyes went round as moons. 'Aye, I do, sire.'

'Is that him?'

'I haven't seen him since the royal wedding . . . that was ten years ago. He was fostered, with the Dumnoni.'

Damn.

'It *could* be him. I was a boy and so was he. I'm sorry, sire.'

'Is there anything only the two of you would know? Some childhood memory?'

He shook his head. 'Nowt that any boy in the village wouldn't also know – but that torque he's wearing, that's a royal torque. It's the one my grandmother, his mother, used to wear.'

'Could he have stolen it from her? Taken it from her body?'

Brig shook his head again. 'No sire. She passed six years ago, from lung fever – nowt to do with the Romans.'

I turned back to Lugrako, who was eating again and chatting with Tyllan as he played. He'd shown a bit of nervousness, but well he might, given he was in a strange place, with strangers. He had the three loops of blue wool, the torque . . .

I'm inclined to believe him.

Forty **The Loyal**

I rode east, with Dran, the next morning. Just the two of us went for now, with a bodyguard, but I left orders with Kynbel for the army to be readied. Hedros was to stay with his parents for the time being and ride north again with news of the coming battle once I gave the word.

Lugrako wanted to come with me, I'm sure of it, but I housed him with his nephew and set the two of them the task of making sure all the Brigantes warriors who were with us were armed and ready to move. He accepted that with good grace – how could he not? – but I suspect he knew I was testing him out. No-one came forward to expose him as an imposter, so my suspicious heart was eased, a touch.

Dran had told me much of the mine before we left and whilst we rode, but when I reached the site with him and saw it for myself I understood why he liked it so much. The rocks stood out above the flat land to the east like an island. Behind us, in the distance, were the Ordovici mountains; ahead, beyond the plain, were the forts of the old Cornovi lands, Urikon's among them. When we'd got past the mine workings and climbed to the top there was a view the Gods wouldn't sniff at.

'We'd certainly see them coming,' I said, to Dran, with a smile.

Dran grinned. 'More than that. I was here for two moons, in spring. It rained all the time and those two rivers down there flooded. We'll be up here, so the good ground is all ours.'

I looked down at the nearest of the rivers. It was a gentle, sparkling line on a day like this, blue skies stretching as far as our eyes could see. We'd not had the warmest of weather for midsummer but it hadn't rained in almost a moon. 'I don't think there's much chance of them flooding again before the legions get here, Dran ... and bigger rivers than that haven't stopped them.'

Dranis shook his head. 'I know, but the ground down there is porridge-soft. They'll struggle to move the ballistas – or anything – while we'll have ours on platforms solid as you like.' He kicked his heel back to the nearest rock for effect and I smiled.

'And our ballistas are near here anyway? You built them whilst you were overseeing the mine?'

He nodded. 'Right down there. With enough men we could move them all into position in a morning.'

We passed a grand old ancestor tomb and started downhill again towards where the miners ate and slept. Three of Dran's copies of the Roman *ballistae* sat there in a line with another, half-finished, beside a hut. Some resourceful peasant woman had anchored one end of her washing line to it.

'Perfect.' I slapped him on the back. 'I'll send two of the lads back to give word and guide the army here. We'll stay and get everything ready – you can get that one finished. Well done, brother.'

He waved it away. 'Plenty to do yet.'

By the time Kynbel arrived at the head of our army plenty had been done. The Ordovici miners stopped mining and set-to moving the ballistas into positions we chose for them, and shoring up those positions with strong walls. There wasn't much woodland hereabouts so we used rocks to build walls as palisades, too, wherever the slopes looked easiest to climb. I would stand under these walls, throwing blunt spear-shafts upwards, until I felt the rampart was high enough. The local peasant children were collecting stones and pebbles for our sling-bearers and they thought it was funny, how I threw sticks at my own walls, but their parents knew what I was up to well enough. Once each peasant family had gathered a pile of sling-shot the height of their eldest child they moved west, out of danger, on my orders.

Dranis finished the fourth ballista with time to spare and got on with preparing for our army's arrival. The miners' hill top village was big but there'd never be enough room for all our warriors so most would have to camp in the hills behind until the actual day of battle. Dran made sure there was food and camp-sites waiting for them and a miserable lack of bridges, duck-boards and clear passes for our foe.

I was up on the ancestor tomb, eating my breakfast and watching for the legions, when I heard the cheer go up and knew our army had been sighted. Dran waved to me and we both went down to greet them as they came in.

'Any sign yet?' Kynbel called from atop his mare.

'None. Short of thick fog we'll see them a good half-day ahead – come and see the view for yourself when you've settled in.'

He grinned. 'I believe you.' Kynbel looked over his shoulder. 'Mocco's not far behind me. Let's wait for him.'

He was right. Mocco rode up soon after, at the head of thousands of Ordovici warriors, hair spiked and roaring to go. Ordovicos, by his side, looked no less joyous.

'The Gods' signs are good for the battle!' he declared.

Well I hope you'd say that even if it wasn't true in front of thousands of our men, was my thought but 'Welcome!' was what I said. I looked about, behind him. 'Is Elidoros with you?'

He shook his head. 'Coming tomorrow, some trouble at home.'

I raised an eyebrow.

'Nothing I couldn't sort out after dinner once I felt so inclined.' He slipped from his mare, rubbing the small of his back, and looked up towards the ancestor tomb. 'I've come here most years, at harvest, to bless the miners. It's early, but I may as well, while I'm here.'

'Be my guest.'

He raised an eyebrow at that. I stayed by the gate to greet Machan, Colleos and all the others as they rode in, a sight to bring joy to any king.

Those I met with at the tail end were less welcome.

I watched Nes trotting towards me, Gladsia on her pillion, Creegan running along one side and Leon riding on the other, with growing fury in my heart.

'What are you doing here? I sent for the army – not you!'

Leon crumbled before me but Nesica's eyes flared.

'Doesn't the army need food? Clothes? Bandages? A bit of comfort at night?'

'Not so much that I'd see you all butchered before my eyes!' I swept my hand towards my daughter. 'You're as bad as she is!'

Nes swung down from her horse and gripped me by the front of my tunic. 'Look, if we're destined for the Land of Youth, then so be it. We all go together.'

'Nes!'

She shook her head. 'I'm not going back, I'm not, so don't waste your breath going on about it.'

I gripped her back, round her arms.

'All right then?' she asked.

'All right.'

We gave each other a good kiss, much to the cheers of everyone on the ramparts.

I put them to work, Nes and Leon setting up a healer's camp on the riverside hill to the west, Gladsia collecting sling-shot like the peasant children. I was watching over Gladsia, sat sharpening my sword on a whetstone and having a beer with Colleos, when Lugrako and Brig rode in, at last, at the head of their northerners, late that afternoon.

'They took their time,' I muttered under my breath.

Colleos shot me a look. 'You do not trust him either, sire?'

'Meaning you do not?'

'I – I don't know. It's just the only way we have of knowing his people *will* revolt is his word.'

'I know, but if I send people to check then the legions will be here, before I've heard back.' I looked out to the plain. 'Which could just be convenient in itself . . .'

'Or the truth.' He smiled. 'You've done what you must, my king.'

'I have.' I handed him the whetstone. 'Do you remember Leon's tale, about the Hot Gates? The Spartans were winning and then a traitor – I forget the name – led the enemy up a secret path.' I gestured about our position. 'There is nowhere like that here but still . . . '

'Do you want me to keep an eye on him, sire?'

'Yes, and when the battle starts your men can be with his northerners – the numbers make sense in any case. If he is fighting as fierce as the rest of us, fine, I'm convinced – anything suspect, get word to me, or deal with it yourself if you must.'

'Yes sire.'

Gladsia was on her way back to us, the fold of her dress loaded with stones. 'Look Dada!'

'Yes, very good. Add them to the pile.'

She did so then skipped back towards us. 'When we win the battle can everyone come home?' she asked of me, but then looked to Colleos. 'Coll said he'd teach me and Caradoc Harelip how to fight with a spear when he gets back.'

Coll's face lifted with silent laughter. 'Did he now? I'll have to have a word with him, then.'

I laughed. 'Don't worry, might be useful.' I shooed my daughter away. 'Go on, collect more. No dinner until the pile is high as your head.'

She huffed a bit but she did scamper off again. Colleos sheathed his sword and bowed his head. 'Thank you, sire, for getting my children to safety . . . but your daughter . . '

'She'll be all right,' I said. 'We just have to win.'

The Deceangli arrived whilst we were having supper. I went out to greet them. I'd expected Hedros and a few hundred but more like a thousand came marching in, Blodau riding at their head, proud as Epona. She had her torque on and a rich cloak but, with her hair braided up on her head, her sling and a sword at her belt, I knew she was there in more than just name. Hedros, dressed just as fine, was riding abreast with her and he looked unperturbed, so I resolved to say nothing. When Cam strolled up at the rear, though, leading her horse, she had a smirk about her face.

'Where those two go, *I* go,' she said.

I held up my hands. 'I didn't say a word.'

'Your face speaks for you sometimes.'

I nodded to the young couple. 'Are they all right?'

She did the so-so gesture. 'Getting there.' Cam tied the horse to a post and brushed down her skirt. 'Where do you want me to be during the battle?'

'Have you been attending warrior practice every day whilst with the Deceangli?'

That met with a roll of her eyes. 'No.'

'Well Nes and Leon are setting up a healer's camp. You can be of use there.'

She looked even more horrified at that, and now *I* laughed.

As the sun was setting I took a turn about the camps on Buanedd, Kynbel by my side, to check all the watches were in place and wish everyone goodnight. It was a beautiful evening, the red glow in the west turning every wisp of cloud pink as bramble blossom. Kites were soaring, just innocent birds, for now.

Kynbel, too, was looking west. 'My mother and sisters are far to the east, my brother on Mon, and now my wife and sons in Eire. I envy the birds that they can fly.'

I looked to the sky. 'I know what you mean – perhaps one day we will know what it's like, but I have the feeling, if I die in battle in the next days, I'm coming back as a fox.'

He smiled. 'I can see that – but you're not going anywhere. Don't talk like that, uncle.'

As we turned back I saw Leon outside a tent, treating a young Deceangli warrior. 'What's wrong, Leon?'

'Blisters, sire.'

Kynbel and I both winced and it brought a smile to the youth's face. 'I'll be all right, King Caradoc – *they're* coming to *us* any ways.'

We laughed with him, but I was pleased to see Leon had strips of sheepskin ready, nonetheless. I heard a horn blowing to the south and something occurred to me. 'Where's Tarn, Leon? I haven't seen him yet.'

'He arrives with Lord Elidoros tomorrow, sire. He just got married.'

I looked to Kynbel and my nephew nodded. 'Elid's daughter, Sula. I thought they might.'

My jaw dropped. 'I thought I knew everything around here.'

'Not everything. Did you hear that horn blast just now?'

'Yes. It didn't sound like a Roman one, but we should take a look.'

We rode up to the highest point and looked south.

Gods be praised.

The sight of my own army marching in had brought joy to my heart, this no less. A thousand Silures were striding towards us, their bright shields before them, their spears catching the last of the light. At the front their leader was riding on a fine bay horse. I felt a grin spreading across my face.

'Welcome, Corbennog!'

By the time I was crawling into our tent to sleep beside my wife it was crow-dark outside. I could hear Creegan and Gladsia snoring, cuddled up together, but Nes was awake. She patted the bedroll so I knew where to head for in the dark. Even so I still managed to bash into her feet.

'Ouch! I hope you've unstrapped your sword!'

We couldn't help it, we both sniggered like children.

'Shhh!' I warned. 'We'll wake Gla-Gla.'

'We're all right. She's tuckered out, bless her.'

It was good to get in next to Nes, so warm and soft. She'd been working like a dog all day but she still managed to smell of rose-water.

'Everything set for tomorrow?' she whispered.

'Yes. Nothing much more we can do but wait. Corbennog said the Valeria should be hereabouts by tomorrow afternoon, maybe sooner. A farmer told me the others are even nearer than that.'

Nes snuggled up to my chest. 'Are you glad now that I came here?'

'Yes,' I admitted. 'But when the battle starts, if our line breaks or you see any sign at all that the Romans are going to win, promise me you'll get Gladsia and get on your horse and ride like Epona – I know you can.'

I heard her take in a good breath. 'I – I thought the same, to be honest. That's why I didn't bring Gladsia's pony – I can go faster with the two of us on mine.' She moved even closer. 'What about all the others, though?'

I sighed. 'If Leon, Cam, Machan and all the rest can get away too, great. But if they stay to shield your escape then *accept* it please, love. Everyone has heard and seen terrible things the last few years. No-one wants that for Gladsia, and she won't survive on her own.'

I felt her breath on my skin. 'I promise,' she said.

Forty one **The Legion**

We heard the legions before we saw them, the mules braying, the horns, the steady thud-thud-thud of thousands of feet. The day dawned misty with drizzle in the air, quite the turn from the evening before, so we couldn't see them from the distance we'd been hoping for, but the sound was unmistakable. I was up with Dran, doing another run-through with our ballista men, and our eyes met.

'Well, we're ready as we'll ever be,' he said.

'Is Rhyddo back yet?'

Dran pointed over the plain. 'That looks like him.'

Rhyddo was indeed haring back to our lines, on foot given the roughness of the terrain, but hopping between bogs and boulders as if born to it. He grinned and waved up to us when he saw we were watching him.

'All right, Rhyddo?'

He arrived holding his knees and gasping but we got another grin.

'They didn't even see me, sire.'

'Is it the Gemina?'

Rhyddo nodded. 'Yes sire, but another column joined them outside the fort, like two rivers flowing into one.'

'Did you see the banners?'

'Yes sire, bulls on these ones, not the long-horned goat.'

I looked to Dran. *That'll be the Hispana.*

'Well done, Rhyddo. Go get some breakfast – and greet your friend Tarn. He just got here. The others are teasing him because he just got wed.'

'Sula? She's a canny one. He'll be all right.' He started up the rocks then turned. 'Sire, what does "*merda*" mean? I heard them say that a lot.'

I smiled. '"Shit."'

He laughed. 'That makes sense then – one of their cart wheels had hit a rock. What about "*mund-us ster-cor-is*" sire?'

'"A world of shit."'

Dran and I turned to each other again.

'Excellent.'

All the reports coming in were much the same: thousands of Romans were coming towards us all right, from east and south, but they were making hard work of it. 'We'll have time for a midday meal, at this rate,' I remarked to Elid, and Mocco overheard.

'Do you want us to launch a fast attack? Bite them while they flounder?'

I shook my head. 'No, our men will get caught out there just as well as they. Let them come within range of us, as is the plan.'

It was grim, though, to wait, while the noise crept nearer, relentless as the passing years. I asked Ordovicos to lead us in prayers and, when we grew tired of prayers, Tarn led us in songs. It must have been a fine welcome to greet Scapula once he'd dragged his miserable troops close: the hill spiked with warriors' spears, the rock walls towering and thousands of us singing out. I passed among each group of our waiting warriors and everywhere I went the songs turned to cheers.

'Can they go any slower?' Blodau asked with a grin as I reached them. She and Hedros were sat sleeve-to-sleeve behind one of the walls, next to a huge pile of shot, sharing Blodau's rolled up cloak as a cushion.

'Should make them easy targets for you, no?'

She snorted. 'Too easy,' she said, and all the men around her cheered, Hedros included.

Kynbel waved to me from up on the tomb. 'The scouts have reached the first marker.'

I got up onto the nearest rampart and watched as two of the scouts dismounted at the river's edge and poked at it with a stick. They must have known they were out of range of our sling-bearers but even so the third scout stayed on guard, peering up to our ramparts, shield in hand.

'Should I?' Blodau whispered. 'It's not as if they don't know we're here.'

'It's too far.'

'Probably,' she said, but she took a stone from the pile, loaded her sling and gave it a good whirl, whispering something to herself that sounded like a prayer. I raised my hand and urged the others to wait. We all watched with caught breath as the stone sped through the air. It lost height too early as I'd feared but it caught the nearest scout on the hand, hard enough even at this distance to see him smart, and there was a laugh followed by jeers as the three scampered back to their lines.

'Good shot,' I said, and patted Blodau on the left shoulder. For once she didn't flinch. Hedros was beaming at her with pride. 'Don't get cocky, though. Stick to the plan.'

I got a nod so I walked back to Dran. He was looking nervous, scratching at his arms like he used to. 'They still don't know about the ballistas,' I reassured him. 'In fact they might now get a bit cocky themselves.'

'It's all right. We're ready.'

Mocco was wandering towards us, his eyes on Dran's red arms, so Dran started to roll down his sleeves. 'It's not catching,' Dran said, and Mocco raised his hand in defence.

'I know, I know. It's just my wife does the same, but with her knees. Oats help, no?' He smiled and Dran calmed. 'Here, from cousin Nesica.' He handed us a cheese bannock each. 'She was asking Machan if your brother Adminios has been seen amongst the Romans at all . . ?'

I jolted a bit at that. 'No . . . no. I don't expect him, to be honest.' *Oh, Nes, do you still fear him? After all these years?* I thought of my brother trailing through the battlefield with the enemy, if they won, helping Scapula to identify the bodies, and felt a shiver run up my own spine. 'Is she back in the healer's camp now?'

'Yes.'

'Good.'

I looked up to the ancestor tomb as Kynbel caught my eye.

'They're coming forward!' he shouted.

Dran, Mocco and I went to the rampart. A fancy-clad general on a white horse was edging into the river with his sword high in his right hand. I couldn't tell what he was saying, from here, but I could hear the shrieking tone in his voice.

Scapula.

'Kynbel – come down from there now.'

Soldiers were surging behind Scapula, banners and standards held high, great curved horns blasting. They were massed so close behind their massive shields I could hardly see any feet. Thousands of them. Tens of thousands.

Cernunnos, Camulos, Teutates, Epona, give me the strength to protect our people.

I tightened my sword belt, made sure my sword was loose in its scabbard and raised my owl-eye shield for all to see.

'Not long now – everyone ready?!'

The shouts of 'Yes!' came back so loud they shook the very rocks we stood upon.

'Ballista men! You're up first! If anyone needs to relieve themselves, now's the time.' They laughed. 'Wait for Prince Dranis's signal, then give them all the fury of the Gods.'

Our men roared and slapped their shields. The enemy came nearer but Dranis let them, his hand still down. Only when the bulk of the line was abreast with the river's near side did he raise his arm.

'Winding,' he said. 'Winding now.'

The noise was hideous, like bones breaking, but the ballistas were strong and they held up to the torture. The Romans below must have heard the ratchets, seen the gorse-branch covers falling away from the machines, but still they surged forward. They reached the cracked boulder. *Third marker.*

'Release!' Dran yelled.

The first rocks flew. They did their work. The legionaries didn't stop, they didn't even hesitate, but each rock killed.

'Again!' Dran cried. The practice paid off – our men were able to release another load before they even had to change the angle, and now the front edge of the attack group was nearing range of our slings.

'Sling-bearers! Ready!' I yelled.

The Legion reached the dead hawthorn.

'Now!'

Slingshot rained down, thousands of stones flying swift as peregrines and hitting hard. Some met shields and armour but those that found flesh cut deep. There weren't as many Romans pushing towards us as there'd been a moment ago.

'Again!'

Another volley cut a swathe through the ranks and every sling-bearer reloaded and swung, without any further bidding from me. As yet not a single spear had come upwards to us – there'd be no point at that angle, but those enemy at the front who survived had now reached the base of the hill.

'Ballistas lower!' Dran ordered.

The wedges were knocked out to drop the ballistas and they reloaded, Dran helping. The rocks flew again, at a straighter angle, catching the mass of auxiliaries behind. The sling-bearers continued their harvest, the front rows of Romans thinning by the heartbeat despite their enormous shields. I saw Blodau, sweat on her brow, one foot on the rampart to get a better angle, casting shot like the Gods were behind her.

Where's Scapula? I saw the white horse first, riderless and racing up the river bank, then spotted Scapula himself down below still near the front, shielded on all sides by about six soldiers. I could hear his shrill voice shrieking out.

'Sling-bearers! There – get him! Aim for him!'

The sling-bearers nearest me all responded. The flock round Scapula did thin a bit but meanwhile a few outlying Roman spear-men were starting to streak ahead.

'Shields!' I yelled. 'Shields ready!'

My people snapped to it. I saw Hedros shielding his wife as she continued to sling. My fear was unjustified at that moment as it turned out. The hill and the rampart did their job. All the Roman spears fell short.

Not by much, though.

'Our spears! Ready!'

I grabbed a few from the nearest stash myself and we started to throw down, the hill and the drop giving us the advantage. The Roman front line was falling like wheat to the sickle. Still Scapula shrieked them on.

Was he prepared to let the entire front line die?

The answer came to my mind in an instant.

Yes he was.

I looked out upon the tens of thousands pushing towards us with new eyes and felt my confidence fall away like ice to the meltwater.

'Uncle – watch out!'

A javelin went over my head – a good hand-span too high to kill me but it woke me up. I grabbed another spear and cast it hard, getting a legionary through the throat, before someone grabbed my by the back of my shirt.

'Away from the edge!' Dran shouted.

The ranks behinds us fell back but Kynbel was still perched on a rock, chucking spears like Lugos himself. Down below the surviving Romans had all hunkered beneath their overlapping shields. I could hear the officers shouting 'Testudo! Testudo!' and see the 'tortoise' getting wider by the moment.

Then I heard one shrieking order that chilled my heart: 'The wall! Dig the wall!'

They are prising out the rocks.

Oh shit.

'Kynbel get back!'

I was too late. The rampart crumbled beneath his feet and for one agonised heartbeat he rode the falling rocks like a piece of driftwood rides a wave. I stretched out, grasping at any bit of him I could reach.

Thank the Gods his shirt was loose.

I threw him upwards and we both scrambled up the scree. The tumbling wall killed some of their own men but *still* they pushed on, fierce as beasts. Those of my warriors who fell with the rocks were cut down without mercy, like deer stumbling into a pit.

'Up!' I screamed. 'Up to the next rampart!'

I pushed everyone on, slinging my shield to my back for now. Spears landed to my left and right but the Gods' protection held.

'Up! Keep going!'

I glanced south and saw Colleos, Lugrako and their men were doing the same, pressed into the hill by the twentieth legion. Their rampart, too, was crumbling. The enemy actually had pick-axes. Pick-axes! *By the Gods.*

Dran grasped me by the elbow and hauled me up to the next platform, next to a ballista. The lowest of our ballistas was falling, crashing to the river bank in a burst of splinters. It took a good dozen Romans in its wake.

'You all right?' Dran asked.

'Yes, and Kynbel.'

My nephew nodded. He looked a bit white but he wasn't shaking, as far as I could tell. Behind him Hedros was helping Blodau up to the next rampart. She still had her sling in her hand. A Roman javelin missed her by a hair.

Get back to it.

Dozens of our spear stashes had fallen with the lower wall but I was in reach of another. I grabbed a spear and threw – getting the Roman nearest the couple's tail.

'Turn! Keep defending!' I ordered. 'Or they'll do the same with this wall!'

My men heard me, and they fought back like dogs. I've heard snide people say we fell into disarray as soon as our rampart went and that isn't true – don't trust all you hear from men who weren't there. We cut and stabbed and slashed with sword and knife and spear. But the truth is, however hard we fought, as soon as the legions closed the gap, my people started to die, like winter brings death to the flowers. I saw Elid disappear under a dozen auxiliaries, sword in hand to the end. Mocco, whom I had saved from death before, went west to join the Gods, as they willed it. Poor Rhyddo too, too young.

My tears fall, to this day. I have lived these moments a thousand times and still this is hard for me to write.

As they rushed us I drew the sword of my mother's kin and I killed many, I know I did, but it did not save us. The ranks behind me rallied as they saw me fight. I heard the yells, saw the blur of spears rush past my shoulders, and I think it may have been the shield-boss of one of my own that smacked me in the head. Wherever it came from the darkness was welcome, for I saw no more death.

That day, at least.

Forty two Bare

I smelled the earth first. Damp and mud in my nostrils, a tang of metal. I was on my back and my back was wet. My head throbbed. *Am I bleeding?* I tried to speak but a warm human hand was clamped over my mouth.

'Be still. Be quiet.'

Colleos?

My eyes were open but we were in complete darkness. I sensed Coll was holding his breath and he was behind me. Another human shape loomed to the right. I could smell damp wool and leather above the mud.

A sliver of light opened, quick but not in a flash. The light was coming from a crack, no wider than my little finger, above our heads.

We are inside the mine.

The light had revealed the other man's face. Lugrako. Eyes big, face white, mouth opened. He wasn't breathing either. He disappeared again as another shape moved across the crack. Pieces of grit came down to us like rain but we didn't move so much as a twitch. The light returned and I heard a snatch of voices above us, speaking Latin. I couldn't make out what they were saying.

The light was stable for a good long while before any of us took the risk of speaking again . . . but I couldn't resist forever.

'Did my wife and daughter get away?' I whispered.

'Sorry sire, I don't know,' Coll whispered back. 'They're looking for your body. We can't move until we're sure they've gone.'

Lugrako's gaze remained fixed forwards, I supposed to the entrance. My eyes had grown used to the gloom but I could see nothing there. *What had they closed the hole with?* I didn't risk asking. I strained my ears to hear dogs but I heard none, thank the Gods. The human voices grew fainter and, as the light changed, it became silent above us. True rain started to drip through the roof crack, when the light had almost gone, but no more grit came down.

'I'll check,' Lugrako whispered. 'You two stay here.'

He shuffled forward on hands and knees and pushed what looked to be a branch or shrub aside. A little more light fell inside and I could see we were in one of the smaller caves, not the biggest of the miners' dug-outs.

'It's all right,' Lugrako said. 'Come out.'

He crawled from our sight. I sat up and turned to Colleos. Coll's eyes looked wary, to me, and he kept his voice low.

'He saved my life, got me in here,' Coll said. 'I can't fault him for that . . .'

'But . . ?'

'But I wouldn't sing his praises as a warrior.'

'What about Brig?'

Coll's gaze dropped and he shook his head.

'Kynbel? Dranis?'

There was pleading in his eyes then. 'I couldn't say – there was chaos. I had to choose in a blink, hide or die.' He looked over my shoulder. 'He's coming back. We should go.'

We too crawled through the puddles to the outside. The freshness of the air was a relief in my first breath at the entrance but then I stood, and saw, and my stomach turned. There were bodies everywhere. The sun was setting in a pale grey gleam behind the rain clouds to the west but there was light enough to see the bodies. The rainwater glistened – but only on bare flesh. All the shields, spears, swords, helmets, torques, armlets, rings, even cloaks, were gone. Every last thing was gone. There was a silence, with no metal for the raindrops to bounce off. Even Morriga's crows hadn't arrived yet.

'I should look for wounded,' I said, my voice choked, when at last I could speak.

Lugrako shook his head. 'There won't be any.'

There was a hard edge to his voice and I nettled.

'They were going around, putting a sword through the chest of anyone too bad to walk, when we took the chance

346

to drag you into the hole,' Coll said. 'If they hadn't had trouble getting the torque off Prince Mocco I dare say they'd have looked up, and we wouldn't be stood here now.'

I took in a good breath. 'Thank you, my friend.' I flicked another look to Lugrako. 'Thanks to both of you.'

The Carvetii nodded. 'We're not out o' the woods yet. Come on.'

'I must find my family.'

He side-eyed Colleos, right in front of me. 'Look, there's no-one here alive. Don't fool yourself.'

'Remember who here is king,' Coll snapped, and Lugrako actually kicked a stone like a little boy.

'*King*? We're all dog-meat if he wanders into Scapula's arms.'

I sucked in a breath, waving the two of them down. 'Easy. Calm down. I'm not stupid – I'm not going to give myself up to them. But you can't deny me the chance to look for my family. A dog wouldn't deny a wolf that.'

Lugrako pushed back his thick hair. 'Look, I understand, but they're not far away, someone could come back any moment – can't you smell the camp fires?'

I *could* smell the camp fires, but we did as I said all the same, heads down and furtive as mice. I ran from body to body, heart racing, saying prayers and closing eyes as I went, the guilt pressing down on me with more weight with every body I found. When I saw Blodau, crumpled beside a ballista, without torque or arm-rings, a sword wound through her chest, I stopped dead.

Gods forgive me.

I had no cloak to cover her with and her own cloak had been ripped off. *Please Gods help me. What more can I do?*

Colleos was near me and put his hand on my shoulder. 'Hedros isn't here,' he said. 'They might have taken him captive.'

'We haven't found Kynbel or Dran either.'

Coll nodded. 'Take heart, my king. They have value.'

Yes, whilst I am free and the rebellion in the north rages on. If the Empire wins then they just become more prisoners to feed.

We crossed the western river and climbed up to the healer's camp. The sun had set and the moon was scudded by clouds but we started finding bodies there too, from the start. Roman bodies, first.

'They haven't even finished clearing their own dead yet,' I remarked, to Coll, but it was Lugrako who answered.

'We need to get away, to get to Venutios. I keep telling you.'

We ignored him, and kept searching. I didn't find Nes or Gladsia, thank the Gods, but each body I found was another knife through my heart – Machan, the patch still over his eye, a circle of dead Romans round him; Leon, across the body of a warrior he'd been bandaging, by the looks of it, a sword wound through the back of his neck; Cam, oh my Cam, slumped not far from Leon, her fist still curled about the handle of a weapon that had been forced from her grasp. She didn't have a mark on her, at first glance, until I straightened her out and found the dark stain of blood on her back.

'May the Gods curse Rome and grind it to dust,' I spat. Coll reached out to comfort me once again but then stopped, looking behind me. He drew his sword. I whipped round – a black shape was looming up from the river.

'Caradoc?'

If the Gods loved me it would have been my wife who emerged then from a riverside hidey-hole, my wife or my daughter, or both, best of all. Gods forgive me but I looked back at Ordovicos dumb as a fence-post, without so much as feigned joy.

'I hid,' he said. 'I hid, then I thought I heard your voice.'

'Did you see what happened to my wife and daughter?'

'No.'

Of course. You hid, whilst Machan, Cam, Leon and all the loyal fought to guard their escape.

'What are you going to do?' Ordovicos asked, and I felt a bit sick.

'We're going north, to Venutios,' Lugrako cut in. 'We have to.'

Coll shot him a glare. 'There's no "have to" about it. Corbennog isn't among the dead we've found – we could just as well go south. A *lot* of our people got away – you yourself told them to run, did you not?'

All three of us looked to the Carvetii like crows at a corpse but he didn't wither.

'And the legions will be chasing them at first light,' was his retort. 'We won't do any good if we blunder into them and get captured.'

'My wife will head for my seat,' I said. I looked to Colleos. 'Tyllan and Tynos will help her – they'll all go to Mon, I think. Mon could be defended.'

Gorfan nodded. 'The Gods defend Mon, apart from all else.'

'Yes, and the sea. For enough time for us to get there, I think.'

Lugrako snorted. 'And then do what? Another last stand?'

His rudeness was grinding my nerves but he wasn't wrong, to be fair. I saw his expression soften.

'Look, if we get to my brother and join the rebellion it can only be t'the good. Even if he's been driven back then there are vast wastes in the north where we can all hide out – warriors are plentiful as sand on the beach. We could storm these legions from the north and rescue your people!' His arms flared out like a storyteller. 'But there's absolutely nowt, not a spit or a piss when the house is on fire, that the four of us can do on our own.'

He's right. Gods forgive me but he's right. I remembered Gwyfina and I taking on the slavers, just we two against twenty, and felt ashamed. *But Rome . . . the mighty empire of Rome, crushing all before it like a landslide. It's not the same.*

'All right,' I said.

Our progress was slow, in the dark, and on foot. We skirted well wide of the Roman camps but at one point we could see the grassy hillside where we'd corralled the horses. It was empty, as I'd feared.

'Perhaps our own people took them, when they fled,' Colleos said.

Epona let it be so.

We moved on, before anyone on the opposite side of the valley could see us. For a while we had enough sight of the stars to know we were going north but when the clouds thickened up again and it began to pour we called a halt and sheltered under a wide oak until it passed. Summer or not it was still cold and we had to huddle together beneath the two cloaks we had between four.

By day break it was clear how little territory we'd covered. I could see one of the Cornovi forts in the east, one where I'd stayed before on my travels, and the dawn light was brightening the Ordovici mountains to the west that I knew well. It felt like we'd walked forever, but if we'd had horses it would have been a short ride.

'We need to find some food, or we'll get slower and slower and it'll be autumn before we reach the north,' I said.

Coll nodded. 'Can we risk asking a village for help though?'

Ordovicos frowned. 'I am a druid, in druid robes – no loyal Ordovici or Cornovi would refuse me.'

'Loyal is the problem, though, isn't it? We've no way of knowing who is loyal and who not as things stand this morning.' Bitterness had edged into my voice and I curbed it, kicking myself. *Don't show any more weakness. This last night has been bad enough.* 'We'll find berries, at this time of year. I'll fashion a sling and bring down a pigeon. There are fish in the streams – we'll make do.'

No-one looked over-convinced so I went off to find decent bark to make a workable sling from. I wished, with hindsight, that I'd picked one up from the battlefield, but too late now. I had my sword, thanks to Coll, who'd grabbed it along with me, but a simple knife would have been handy too. The enemy had stripped out a lot but we could have taken a bag-load of stuff from our camp if I'd thought of it at the time. *I was in grief, I was trembling,* I told myself. *Don't berate yourself.*

The sun was climbing and its warmth was welcome on my damp clothes and seeping into my cold bones. I felt a little naked without my cloak, my owl-eye shield, Buanedd by my side. Even my torque was off for now, tucked inside my shirt, in case we ran into someone. I rubbed my empty neck. *We start our lives naked and we make a go of it from there. Be strong, it's not over yet.*

I crested a rise and saw the last thing I could ever want to see.

Lloergan, Nesica's horse, lying on her side by a stream's edge.

Fifteen arrows embedded in her chest.

Forty three Naked

I have criticised him often but it was Ordovicos, my oldest friend, who saved me then. They must have heard my howl and they all came running but it was Gorfan who held me tight and calmed me down.

'They're not here,' he kept saying. 'The horse is dead but there's no other blood, no bodies – they must be prisoners. If they're alive they can be rescued. Have faith in the Gods my friend, remember your faith in the Gods.'

It worked, may the Gods bless him. I let Gorfan lead me out of sight while Coll and Lugrako hunted around. They found tracks going off to the south but no other sign. At least forty cavalry soldiers, Coll said, and my heart plummeted still further. *They could be at their fort by Uricon's by now or half-way to Glevum.*

We returned to Lloergan, pale and sad in the morning light. I touched her flank and found her cold. Her bridle was still on but the enamelled silver decorations had been torn from it. We too took things away. We took off the saddle-cloths to make rough cloaks for Coll and me, who were without. Nesica's saddle-bag was there too. It had been ripped open, presumably to check for gold, but the Romans had left the needle and thread, the half-eaten bannock wrapped in a dock leaf, the little food knife and Nes's fire-flints, so we took the lot. I think Epona would have forgiven us for carving meat from Lloergan's body, too, given the straits we were in, but I'd no sooner have done that than carve up Nes herself, so we said a prayer over her and left her for the wolves.

We carried on north, with me drifting like a ghost. I kept thinking Creegan would run out from a thicket or Nes and Gladsia would see me pass and call out to me from their hide-out. I remembered Vedica hidden in her tree and peered up at every branch we passed under, but nothing happened. The land was silent. I knew I was fooling myself.

If Nes had had even a snatch of time she'd not have left the knife. I'm not sure even Gladsia on her own would have left it, green as she was.

By the third day hunger had hardened my soul again and I came back to my senses. We'd avoided people, as much as possible, but we ended up earning two good meals apiece from a young father for helping to thatch his new house, somewhere in northern Cornovi land. I think he and his wife knew damn well who we were but they didn't give us up. Neither did an old bandy-legged woman who gave us a crock of milk from her goats, or her grandson who took us to the quietest pass north, and gave us a bundle of food as we parted. None of them had news, either, though.

As we passed into the southern Brigantes land Lugrako seemed to relax, like a leaf unfurling.

'Do you actually know where Venutios is?' I asked. 'We can't risk stumbling into Cartimandua's people instead, or a cohort of the Gemina.'

He laughed. 'Don't worry, I know. If the rebellion has gone well he'll be at his southern camp, he likes it there. If he's had to retreat then he'll be at his northern seat, so it's further. So we'll start with the nearer camp. See how we get on.'

Coll raised his eyebrows. We were sat on the north side of a big river – Lugrako had called it the Mor – roasting a duck I'd brought down with my sling earlier. Up till now he'd busied himself with the fire, but I knew he'd heard all.

'I suggest we watch the southern camp the night before and wait, before we go in,' I said. 'To be sure.'

Lugrako spread out his hands. 'Of course.'

Ordovicos had been saying a prayer at the water's edge but now wandered back to us. 'It's still a very long way,' Lugrako said to him. 'Make sure you eat plenty.'

One roast duck between four isn't going to go far.

'Did you see any fish?' I asked.

Gorfan looked back at me, exhausted. 'What? Oh, yes. Yes I think I did.'

I went down to the river again myself and headed upstream a bit until I found my quarry. It took me a while and I got my feet wet but I was able to return to them with a well-tickled trout to supplement our supper.

'You're very handy with all these peasant skills, aren't you, for a king?' Lugrako said, with a smile, as I came back.

A few days earlier I would have nettled, a moon earlier I might have blushed, but then I let it go.

It took us another three full days and nights to be in reach of this 'southern camp' of Venutios. Avoiding settlements didn't help, meaning long detours, and we tended to skirt along the coast a lot. On the last day, as the sun was in decline, we came to an enormous estuarine bay, bathed in golden light. Beautiful, if I'd been in better mind.

'Not far now,' Lugrako assured us.

'We should go down to the beach, have a wash and rest up a while, until the sun is fully down,' I said, but Lugrako shook his head.

'There will be peasants hunting for shellfish at this time – and the flats can be dangerous. Besides, we'll be seen from the fort and we don't want to be seen, as yet.'

We bowed to his local knowledge, but I would have liked a wash. I'd taken the chance to have a good look at myself days earlier whilst I caught the fish and knew I was even leaner than usual, hair like a bear and no doubt filthy. Venutios would lend me the means for a wash and a shave and give me clothes, I was sure, but I was uneasy about what impression I would make when I first walked through the gate.

We cut through some gorse scrub, scattering sheep, and plunged into a birch thicket. Where this dwindled to broom and juniper we came across three huge boulders, lined up like guards on a palisade.

'We can stay here until dark,' Lugrako said. 'No-one comes out this far by evening.'

He wasn't wholly right – a boy passed us, late in the day, driving a small herd of cows with a stick, but he didn't see us at all, lost in his own thoughts. We relaxed in the lea of the largest boulder whilst we waited out the light.

'Do you think Venutios will have any news?' Coll asked, as soon as Lugrako went off to relieve himself.

'Little, I fear. If he's hiding out here then supposedly his revolt has gone well, but I doubt he'll have heard how our people fare until we tell him.'

Coll was biting his lip. 'Sire, do you have a mind to stay a few days or so, then try to get to Mon? Or do you think we'll have to stay longer?'

It was a fair question and I wish I knew. It had crossed my own mind that we could probably get a boat to Mon from here. Lugrako was coming back so I couldn't say any more but I wasn't sure what I *could* say in any case. It all depended on what Venutios wanted, what he had planned.

You will see your family again, my friend . . . whatever I have to do to make it so.

Ordovicos took off his shoes and stretched his sore feet. 'What are you all looking forward to most? I have a desire for a bowl of porridge – I never thought I would miss porridge.'

Lugrako smiled. 'I think my brother will be able to manage a little better than that.'

'If he's there,' Ordovicos said and the Carvetii shrugged.

'Well, yes. And pray he is or it's another three days' trudge at least.'

Gorfan groaned, and I had to stifle a sigh myself.

'This is already the furthest north I've ever been,' Coll said, to nods from Gorfan and me.

'I always wanted to come up here, though,' Gorfan added.

Lugrako looked at him aghast. 'Why?!'

The druid laughed. 'Well, to visit Briganti, most of all. I'm so sorry she's dead. I was terribly sweet on her when I was eighteen summers old.'

'You? Really?'

The words left my my mouth before I could think and I felt my face redden, but he just threw me an amused glance.

'Yes, *really*. She hardly ever came to festivals so I didn't see her often but I remember I was to sing a Morriga prayer at a mid-winter festival and I *knew* she was going to be there so I asked Modwyc – Decanglos, now – for one of his tame ravens, to sit on my shoulder whilst I sang, to impress her. It was *tame* enough, but then it shat all down my robe, just as I hit the best note.' He laughed. 'I wished I was dead.'

Lugrako was shaking his head. 'She'd have sucked the marrow from your bones my friend.'

Gorfan's eyebrows shot up. 'Did you know her any better than I?'

'Maybe not, but I can't imagine her hankering for anyone.'

Gorfan's lips pursed. 'I never said *she* was sweet on *me*. The Land of Youth be good to her.'

Colleos was looking far away. 'I don't remember what I ever did to impress my wife,' he said. 'It feels like we've been together forever.'

I smiled, remembering the shy girl in Calleva who seldom wandered from her uncle's side. 'You were her crock of gold at rainbow's end, my friend. You didn't need to do anything to impress her but be.'

The sun had sunk below the horizon and the stars were coming out.

'Lets move a bit closer now,' Lugrako said. 'To the outer wall at least. It's dark enough.'

We followed his lead, heading cross-country towards this 'fort', avoiding the main path. It was small for a fort, more of a watch-point, but well-ringed by walls as Lugrako had said, and with a fine view over the bay. I could imagine Venutios and Dillyn spending a pleasant moon here, clear of his wife, given the chance. Lugrako had never mentioned Dillyn, so I'd never mentioned her myself, just in case, but I was hoping I might see her, if we had a stroke of luck.

We ducked down behind the outermost wall, close enough to smell the cooking fires drifting from each house but far enough not to set off the dogs – yet, at least. I couldn't see anyone on watch but a man of middle-years was humming a tune as he chucked scraps to some pigs, over to the left.

'Do you know him?' Coll whispered, to Lugrako, but he shook his head.

A girl came into view, leading two horses into a walled paddock up against the secondary defensive wall. She was clicking her tongue. It wasn't Dillyn, worse luck, but the horse on the right struck me straight-away.

'That's Caboledd,' I whispered, with a smile. 'I gave him to Venutios as a gift when first we met.'

Lugrako looked to me in surprise. 'I should still go in first, though – to be sure. No-one knows where I've been except my brother.'

'What will you tell them, appearing here at night like a phantom?' Ordovicos asked.

Lugrako shrugged, slicking back his hair and easing his torque back on. 'I'll tell them I went to our western shrine to pray. They'll think I've been off to see my woman, but if I say I've been to pray they won't give me stick.'

The druid rolled his eyes and Lugrako laughed.

'Aw, you can't play that with me now, we all know your secret.'

He straightened his cloak and he was off, striding up the path with his lanky legs. The dogs started barking as he got near the gate and I saw the pig-feed peasant put his bag down and call out to someone inside. The gate swung open and Lugrako disappeared.

I ran my fingers through my hair a bit in place of a comb, but probably made it worse. I put my own torque back on.

'There he is,' Coll whispered.

I looked up and saw Lugrako, now on a platform to the right of the gate. He had a cup in one hand and waved to us with his other.

'It's all right! Come on in!'

I grinned to Ordovicos. 'Looks like you'll get your porridge.'

He got up, rubbing the small of his back. 'First I should say a blessing prayer for them all, or they'll never respect me.'

We walked up the path to the cheerful barks of the dogs. I could smell the food even stronger now. *Don't let my stomach rumble as I greet Venutios . . .* I tightened my sword belt and saw Coll do the same.

As we passed through the gateposts I felt the rush of air behind us. I heard the gates slam.

How could I have been so stupid?!

We were ringed by spear-men, at least a dozen. They sprang from the shadows. Coll and I drew our swords but it was useless. I saw a spear go straight through Coll, through his back and out of his stomach. Ordovicos screamed. He made a leap towards the gate platform. He too was skewered by a spear but he clung to the edge of the walkway. The man beside Lugrako leant forward and shoved a sword into his neck. I slashed out at the nearest enemy mad as a she-bear but it was no use. I was beaten to the ground with spear butts, punched and kicked, my sword kicked away.

'Alive! Remember we need him alive!'

Lugrako's voice.

I raised my bleeding head to see the man beside him, Gorfan's murderer, nudge the druid's body from the platform so it fell back into the yard. He wore a torque so big it made his head look small.

'Tie him up,' this man said.

I fought, using all my weight and strength to throw the men off of me. I almost got to Coll's sword when someone kicked me under the chin. Someone else stamped on my hand.

'Alive! Curse it!'

This time a female voice.

My arms were forced behind me. I felt the rope going on. Two men sat on me and roped my knees together. I squirmed and wriggled but they shoved me down again. I fell close to Colleos's face.

He was still alive. Blood was seeping from his mouth but I could see from his eyes he was still alive.

'Cernunnos take you my friend. The Land of Youth awaits,' I whispered.

The woman was out of the doorway now. She was in silhouette but I could see she was gnawing on something, maybe a pork rib.

'What did he say?' she asked.

May the Gods curse these filth for such an end to Colleos.

'May the Gods curse you until the end of time! May your ash mix with the dung! May your children forget you forever!'

She laughed, throwing the rib to one side. 'The old Gods hold no sway here.' She nodded to the men behind me. 'Let's get him inside.'

Forty four Lies

I strained to look back as they hauled me to the doorway but I couldn't see if Coll's eyes had stilled. Someone pushed me in the back and I fell to my knees only a hand-span from the hearth. I got up but Lugrako and the big-torque man shoved me back down.

'Check him for knives,' the woman said.

They patted me down and found Nesica's little food knife tucked in my belt. They took my sling too and yanked the torque from my neck. The big-torque man was foolish to get his hand so close to my mouth. As my teeth sank into his wrist he squawked and Lugrako punched me in the face. I tasted blood flood my tongue and felt one of my side teeth loosen.

The big-torque man took a step back, waving the torque in my face and smirking. He was a ghost-faced, wayward-haired, Samhain-night of a man but as Lugrako stood beside him a moment I thought I could see some resemblance between them.

He was watching me watching him and I saw him bare his teeth in a laugh. 'You're working it out, aren't you?' He reached over to Lugrako and pulled him nearer, into a hug. 'You see he's not Venutios's brother. He's *mine*.'

'And who are you? Some unwanted babe thrown out and raised by polecats?'

The woman snorted a laugh, somewhere behind me. 'That's not too far from the truth, dear Vello.'

Vello went to whack me with the torque but I twisted just in time. He laughed it off, squeezing the torque onto his neck, above the other one, as if he didn't value breath.

'Oh no you don't, sweetness,' the woman said. 'This one's mine.'

Maros, Mathona, if you see this from the Land of Youth, ask the Gods to give them piles.

The woman came into view to take the torque from him. She was fat, but tall enough to carry it well, with wavy, honey-coloured hair down to her waist. *This is Cartimandua.* I remembered Venutios saying she was pretty.

'Where's Venutios?' I demanded. 'Have you killed him?'

Cartimandua sneered. 'Me? No, I haven't killed him. He's alive as a frog pond in the spring, maddeningly so. Of course, if he comes riding out of the woods to the rescue then I might be able to remedy that particular problem.' She smiled, trying to lift my chin with one finger. '*Then* I'll hand you over to Scapula. Or before. I haven't decided yet.'

I spat out my bloody tooth onto her Roman-style dress.

She grimaced, leaping backwards, before recovering herself.

'Gag him,' she said.

I was locked into what appeared to be an empty granary. No food, no water, no warmth. It was still summer, even up here in the north, so I didn't fear for cold, but as the night wore on the need to relieve myself grew and grew. My hands were tied behind me and try as I might I couldn't loosen them. I rubbed the knot up against the walls, every knot in the posts I could find, but it wouldn't budge. The gag at my mouth grew wet with sweat and saliva as I struggled. It stopped me from shouting for help, but I decided I would have to, muffled or not.

After an age of howling like a mournful dog someone eventually came.

'What?!' came a man's voice from outside.

'I need a piss!'

'What?'

I repeated myself. He must have got the gist, muffled as it was.

'Well just piss yourself then!'

I recommenced my mournful howling and heard the man swear.

'You'll keep the whole village awake all night like this!'

Like I care.

Moments later he was back and it span through my mind that if it was just *one* man I might be able to free my legs and feet, once my hands were loose, perhaps knock him out and make a run for it, but he wasn't alone. Two guards came with him and when they'd freed my hands I had to relieve myself by spear-point. Once I was done the original man – I recognised the pig-feed man from earlier – threw an empty bucket into the granary.

'There! Now let us get some sleep or you'll lose another tooth!'

They bundled me back into the building, knees and feet still tied but hands not, and re-fastened the door. Now I *was* quiet. I had got both the things I'd wanted. With my hands now free I took the gag from my mouth and got to work on the other knots. They were tight, and I was in darkness, but I got there. I listened at the door a while for signs of someone posted outside. Nothing – no cough, shuffle, sniff, nor a scratch of his arse.

Either he is the best guard ever or there's no-one there. I tried the door. No such luck.

No matter. I got to work on the bucket. It was strong and I soon gave up trying to get one of the metal bands off. There was no way I was going to do that by strength alone, not without noise, but I did get the handle off. I turned to the roof next. It was a granary, so I could reach every part of it without stretching, except the point, and I could get to that if I stood on the upturned bucket. The thatch had been done well, though, I couldn't feel any gaps or soft patches, so I just chose the biggest section between strakes and rafters I could find, on the side opposite the door.

I put one end of the bucket handle under my foot and bent it more or less straight then used this like a needle to poke and waggle through the thatch. I got it about a hand-span in then hit a stop. *Two layers.* I'd expected it, but my heart sank a bit nonetheless. *Well if it takes all night* . . . I kept at it, pushing and pulling with my 'needle' until

I loosened the straw, one or two strands at a time. By the time my arm muscles were aching as much as the rest of me smarted and throbbed I'd got a good pile of straw at my feet and reached one of the hazel spars. I waggled at this until it fell out, then used this, too, like a lever in one hand, while I kept wriggling with the handle in the other.

When I first saw the sky the stars were still out.

Thank you, Gods.

I kept working, faster now as the gap widened and the thatch weakened. The sky was turning to deepest blue when I first poked my head out: quiet. There was smoke seeping from the house roofs but no-one was up yet. *It won't be long, though.* I waggled out a bit more straw, stood on the bucket, angled my shoulders, and hauled myself through.

I crouched on the roof a moment, still as a watching crow, waiting for the first bark of a dog. Nothing. Again I thanked the Gods. I kept myself low, slithering down off the roof and crab-walking between the houses. I saw the secondary wall straight away, but it was high there so I scuttled left, away from where I knew the gate to be – even if it wasn't guarded by man or dog the strong beam was too heavy to move in silence – to a section of wall with a log store up against it. I was up on the shed roof and over the wall in a heartbeat.

I landed, jarring my bruises and had to stifle a yelp. I found I was in the walled paddock we'd seen earlier. *Joyful Epona!* The two horses raised their heads at my sudden appearance but they didn't make a sound.

Should I?

Up to that point my plan had been to escape on foot but now I was torn. Caboledd knew me. If I could get him out of the gate without noise then I could get a lot further faster than on foot. There were at least a dozen warriors here, not counting everyone else. I didn't know the country. Venutios could be anywhere . . .

I decided to go for it. As I moved towards Caboledd though I saw beyond the other horse and my heart nigh stopped –

I wasn't alone with the horses. The girl was still there. She was sound asleep on top of a pile of hay but getting the gate open and Caboledd out without anyone noticing had just boiled over in difficulty.

Shit.

I looked to the gate. It wasn't much of a gate, more just a rectangle of wattle in a frame, but it was massive. To move that without waking the girl . . .

I looked to Caboledd. *You've done jumps before my friend . . . that's not much of a wall.*

I stayed low, moving towards Caboledd with big, slow, movements. I didn't dare speak, but I clucked my tongue, holding out my hand for him to sniff. His eyes looked wary but he did take a few steps nearer. As he let out a gentle neigh I felt it was a welcome rather than fear but my heartbeat leapt.

'Oh no, shhh, it's all right, you know me,' I whispered, and swung myself up on his back. I patted him as I steadied myself. The wall was a bit too near so I urged him back a few paces to prepare for the jump. I turned to check the distance behind me –

The girl screamed.

She was on her feet beside the haystack and screaming like a banshee.

Nothing for it. I urged Caboledd back another pace then forward for the jump. He made it over the paddock wall with ease, Epona bless him. We reached the outer wall and I think he would have made that too but the girl's scream had done it's work. A sling stone landed to our fore, a spear to right and left.

Caboledd reared, with a terrified neigh, and I was thrown.

I landed in the dirt with a thump but I wasn't giving up yet. I scrambled to my feet and ran straight for the wall, but the Brigantes were pouring from the gate now and dozens of spears rained down around me. They'd been ordered not to kill me though and I came within a handspring of making it when the rope caught round my neck.

I fell backwards, the pain from the rope burning like a fire up my skin, and three more spears landed round me like a cage. The warriors weren't far behind.

'Bind him! Now!'

Cartimandua's voice. She was there, coming through the gate, in little more than a shift but with a man's cloak thrown over. As I was held down and the ropes forced back on me I saw her grasp the pig-feed man by the hair. Her hand was like a claw.

'Look!' She forced his face towards me. '*Look* how far he got! Have your brains been swapped for shit?'

I was dragged back into the yard and bound to a hitching post. To be honest when I saw Vello come out of one of the huts with a whip I thought it was me he was going to humiliate but it was the pig-feed peasant who was strapped to one end of a lathe and flogged. The villagers were all herded out of their houses to watch. Vello didn't hold back, but the queen stopped him before the man lost consciousness.

'He stays till noon, then you can cut him down and treat him,' she ordered. She pointed to me. 'No-one speaks to this prisoner. No-one! No-one brings him so much as a crumb of bread unless I tell you to.' She pointed back to the flogged man. 'Remember what I tell you. Now get back to work.'

As everyone drifted away I turned to the flogged man in so far as I could.

'I'm sorry,' I mouthed.

He looked back at me, blood dripping from his lip where he had bitten down on it. 'No you aren't, ' he said. 'But if you were as shit as they are, you would have strangled her.'

I realised he meant the horse-girl, and this thought quieted me for the rest of the morning.

Forty five **Hopes and Chains**

I never was flogged, in Cartimandua's camp. My punishment was of a more subtle kind. I had all morning to sit there, thrice bound to the post, stewing all the ways 'Lugrako' had played me, all the ways I could have thwarted him and saved the lives of my friends. I had no choice but to see it as their bodies were hauled to the seaward wall and thrown over like rubbish. I would have wept but I knew I was watched and I fought the tears back.

At noon the flogged peasant was freed as Cartimandua had determined and not long after an old woman left the largest of the houses, flanked by two guards, with food and water for me. I wasn't untied for that, she fed me like a baby, but they did untie me long enough to relieve myself, at spear point, as before. The same routine was repeated as the sun dipped below the horizon and again the next morning. The village got on with their work as if I was insensible as the post itself.

Every now and then Vello, 'Lugrako' or Cartimandua herself would leave the house and stand in the yard, looking out upon the surrounding country as if waiting for something, and I got the impression I was being dangled there like a worm to a fish.

It rolled over in my own mind that someone might come to my rescue – Venutios, Dillyn, even some of my own men who happened to have fled the same way – and I scanned the land too, in so far as I could. *Storm this place in good force,* I willed, *there are more warriors than it appears. Gods protect you.*

We were all disappointed. By the third morning Cartimandua appeared with Vello and her fat, miserable dog by her side. She took another look at the fields. Rain clouds were rolling in from the sea. The land was quiet as a tomb.

'Curse it to Castor,' she said. 'Let's go home.'

The journey to Cartimandua's seat took three days, I think. I was in a closed cart, bound and gagged and knew only the bumps and rolls of the terrain. I was so exhausted by that point I sometimes slept. When I was removed from the wagon to relieve myself I could see we were in hills or mountains, but with no knowledge of the country, it could have been anywhere.

Any hope I had of rescue on the journey was already fading when I heard the blasts of two or more carnyx and guessed we'd arrived. I heard the driver groan a prayer as we pulled up. He jumped down, into a puddle, and swore. I thought I would be bundled into a building but I was left in the wagon a good while, listening to the dogs bark and rain patter the roof, before some guards returned. They added a blindfold to my fetters.

'Put him with the others,' I heard Cartimandua say and I was dragged out like a sack. I sensed we were going through mud. I could hear a smith hammering and someone chopping wood to the right. As soon as we stopped I heard a door unbolted and they pushed me inside. I heard gasps all around, female gasps I thought, but my blindfold, gag and ropes were only removed once a shackle had been locked onto my ankle. I heard more gasps as the gag and blindfold fell.

I opened my eyes, squinting against the light of the fire, and realised I was among friends. Dillyn, young Vedica and her mother were all there. The only one I didn't recognise was the man to my right. Dillyn was opposite me, on the other side of the hearth, bloodied and bruised, chained at one wrist to a chain wrapped around the house-pole behind her. She was also, clearly, at least five moons gone with child.

'Oh Dillyn . . .'

Her head dipped and it was Vedica's mother who answered: 'Nothing is sacred to that bitch.'

Vedica's gaze met mine. She was a little older than the last time I'd seen her of course but her hair still hung in two braids. 'Look what they did to her teeth,' she said.

Dillyn pulled back her upper lip and I saw she was missing her two front teeth. My stomach turned.

'Venutios will avenge you. He'll come to break us out,' I said, and the chained man turned to look at me. He was bruised too, and naked, apart from under-breeks and what looked like a woman's cloak.

'Well he hasn't yet,' he said.

'I'm sorry, who are you?'

'I'm Prince Lugrako. Venutios's brother.'

We had ample time to share our stories as we sat there in our chains. A succession of servants – never the same one twice, I noticed – brought us food and tended the fire a few times a day but most of the time we were alone. The guards on the other side of the door could no doubt hear what we were saying but by that point I was past caring.

Dillyn was caught first, I learned, some two moons prior. She'd realised her game was up and was sneaking off into the night to make her way to Venutios's camp in the north when discovered and captured. They then tortured her for what she knew, and she knew a lot. Far too much. I would still call him my friend to this day but I could curse Venutios for ever telling her about the three loops of blue wool.

Cartimandua and her pack then moved upon Venutios's northern camp themselves. Venutios himself wasn't there as he was off hunting, further north, but Vedica and her mother, his guests, were captured before they knew what was happening. Lugrako returned from the hunting trip early, on Caboledd, nursing a head cold, and found himself ambushed. It was then, it appeared, that the plan to trick me had been concocted.

'It worked,' I said, shaking my head, 'because almost everything the false Lugrako told me was true.'

Lugrako nodded. 'Scapula *is* ill, the legions truly were on the march. There was even going to be a rebellion right here, as he said there was, if Cartimandua hadn't moved first.' He rubbed at his neck. A pale line showed where the torque used to be. 'With every day that passed we were hoping you'd seen through it.'

I hear you. Gods forgive me.

'Is there any plan now?'

Lugrako raised his chain. 'What plan can there be? These can't be picked apart in the night.'

'No, but there must be something we can do.'

I looked to the chains themselves. They were all strong, long enough for us to shuffle to the bucket as needed but not long enough to get out of the door even if it was open. They were secured to the strongest-looking house-poles too, nothing we could pull free, alone or together. Maybe we could rush the servant and knock them down with the chains as they entered – but to what end? The guards would just flood in, fighting.

Dillyn flicked a look at the door and kept her voice low. 'You three are shackled at the ankle but young Vedica and me are chained at the wrist. I think I could squeeze out of mine, with a bit of butter or lard.'

'Have you tried before?'

She nodded.

I looked to the others. 'Is a servant due soon?'

Lugrako shook his head. 'Not again tonight.'

'Show me.'

Dillyn held her thumb to her little finger, tip to tip, and closed her palm like a flower-bud, trying to squeeze the shackle past her hand. It looked painful but she did come close.

'See – a bit of butter would do it.'

All the food I'd seen so far had been bread and soup. It didn't seem likely we'd get the luxury of butter. 'How about oil? We could ask for a lamp – I saw Roman lamps when they captured me.'

Dillyn's eyebrows lifted. 'Well you can ask . . .'

'It can't be me who asks – they'd suspect immediately. Who among you has complained before?'

Vedica's mother, 'old' Vedica, raised her head. 'Me, always me. We wouldn't be having three meals and the bucket emptied daily if I hadn't kicked up a fuss.'

'Good. We'll try in the morning then.'

Young Vedica had been copying what Dillyn tried and she now turned to us with a huge grin. 'Look!'

She was free, no butter required, and we all praised her, but her mother looked to me.

'What good does it do? Even if we *could* get her out I'm not letting her go alone.'

'No, I understand. But having people 'loose' could be useful. Let's get some sleep for now.'

I did sleep, lulled by the relative warmth and comfort, but I did not sleep well. I woke up long before the others and lay there, listening, studying the house. It was a thatched roof again, but this was no out-house, the angle of the roof was steep and high and the hazel spars were close together. There was no sign of a gap beneath the eaves, the white-washed wall went all the way up, and there was just the one door. A stout planked door. Nothing much was left on the hooks or shelves.

'Caradoc? You awake?'

I turned. It was Lugrako who'd whispered.

'Yes.'

'There's something you should know.'

'Go on.'

'My brother wasn't just hunting in the north – he was drumming support in the villages of the northern reach when I grew sick and left him. He was going on further – he might not even know what has happened to us yet.'

I sucked in a breath. It was as I'd feared, to be honest. 'All the more reason to get one of us out.'

He rolled his eyes. 'But Dillyn, five moons gone? Or the girl . . ?'

'They might be in less risk of their lives out there than in here.'

He conceded that.

'Whose house was this, before it became a prison? Do you know?'

Lugrako nodded. 'Briganti, the druid. That's why it was empty.'

'She might have left something useful, hidden . . . you never know. With Vedica free at least we can root around.'

'Old' Vedica set about our plan as soon as the first servant brought us porridge at daybreak. The serving girl's initial response was as expected: 'No, I can't. It won't be me who comes next time any way.'

Ved scowled. 'Well tell the others. That's simple enough.'

'What do you need a lamp for any way? It's light from the fire.'

'No it isn't! *You* try getting to the bucket in the night through all these chains. My daughter went flying!' Vedica was cuddled up, to hide her lack of chain, but her mother hugged her still closer. 'We are all royal – it is not unreasonable to ask for a *lamp*, for the Gods' sake.'

The girl retreated, muttering, but promising to see what she could do. I had been keeping my head down, eating my porridge, lest I give us away, but as the servant was let out I took the chance to have a good look out of the door. Just one guard now, that I could see.

Good.

I turned back to the room to discuss it with them but saw that Dillyn was crying.

'I only said it to persuade her,' Ved was saying. She leant toward Dillyn as much as she could. 'Besides, you *will* be royal, when you are his queen.'

Dillyn wiped her face with her sleeve. 'Will he even still want me without my teeth?'

'Of course he will,' Lugrako said. 'My brother isn't some wolf in the night.'

'Of course he will,' I agreed.

Dillyn forced a smile, still trying to dry her face. 'Sorry, all of you – I don't know why . . . I just can't . . .'

Ved stretched out and grasped her hand. 'It's normal. And the Gods only know you've enough to cry about.' She looked to me. 'What was it you wanted to say?'

I leant forward, keeping my voice down. 'Listen, I think they only have one guard at the door now, and if we remain quiet maybe they'll lose even that. Let's lull them into torpor – into thinking the chains mean all – then, if the oil works, there's a better chance for the two of you to get out.'

Lugrako frowned. 'Quiet is suspicious in itself, though, isn't it . . ?'

I nodded. 'Yes, so we should tell stories, play games, chat all the while, even if we're digging our way out with our nails.'

We did as I'd said for the rest of the day. The midday servant brought a small lamp of oil along with the food and 'old' Ved gave him just the smallest nod of thanks. I didn't even look up. As soon as he left, though, we all gathered round and Dillyn got started on her shackle.

'I looked out the door, when the servant left,' Lugrako said, leaning towards me. 'You're right – just the one man now, bored as a sheep.'

'Good.'

'There!' Dillyn showed us her bare wrist, triumphant.

We might have cheered but controlled ourselves.

'Should I start to root around then?' Dillyn whispered.

I shook my head. 'Wait until the last servant of the day has been and gone. Patience might serve us well – the spider doesn't hunt until she's built her web.'

The last servant of the day came, earlier than usual, by everyone's account. We noticed the dismissive, distracted air he had, though none of us remarked upon it until he'd gone. We saw the crude raw-hide mask, on leather straps, tucked into the side of his belt too. It put a shiver up my spine, to be honest, but when the music started, loud and rough, I started to understand.

'It's not Lughnasa yet, no?' I asked. 'I'm all spun round but surely not?'

Dillyn shook her head. 'No, but festivals come thick and fast here. I know of old.'

She was right. The noise became unmistakable, the music growing louder and worse as the evening wore on and the players grew drunker. By the time darkness fell it sounded like at least one chariot was being driven break-neck between the houses, to squeals and screams all around. Someone was vomiting their guts out a few paces away. I heard our guard swearing to himself on the other side of the door.

'Now's our chance, ' I whispered.

I set Lugrako, Ved and I playing a noisy game of 'Riddle' while Dillyn and Vedica began to hunt the house, single-minded as wolves. It didn't take long for the search to bear fruit.

There was a striped cloth, on a loom though it appeared finished, and none of us had thought anything of it until Dillyn moved it to one side. 'Damp,' she mouthed, holding her hand to the dark stain at the base of the wall. As she took her hand away a piece of limewashed daub fell.

There was a hopeful gasp from all of us.

'Carry on with the game,' I urged, beneath my breath. 'We can't arouse suspicion now.' So we did, though it was difficult not to keep looking while Dillyn and Vedica picked away at the wall.

'We can't get any further with our bare hands,' Dillyn whispered after a while. 'The daub is weak but the wattle's still too strong.'

I went over to try to help them, my chain at full stretch, but she was right.

'Maybe you could push the baking stone through it?' Lugrako suggested. 'If you leant it against the weak point and pushed with your feet?'

I wasn't sure that would work, but short of axe, knife or saw it was worth a go. I was surprised to see such a big baking stone in a small house and as soon as we'd managed to lift it we saw why. A small hollow was hidden beneath, full of Briganti's treasures.

'How did you know?' Lugrako asked me. 'I thought you didn't know her?'

'I didn't, but I knew she was in fear of her life, maybe for years, so it was a guess.'

A dagger caught my eye first, a slim, bright-bladed thing in a goatskin sheath, more suited for a small sacrifice than hacking through a wall . . . but the best we'd got. I chucked it over to Dillyn and she got started while we looked at the rest.

Another bout of vomiting from somewhere outside froze us all.

'How are we going to sleep tonight with all this noise?' 'Old' Ved piped up, as loud as she could.

Vedica exaggerated a yawn. 'I'm tired mama.'

'I'll tell you a story, as I used to,' Ved said, with a look to me, and she did, a good long story of magic and heroes, while Dillyn and I took turns to hack and saw at the wattle with the knife.

'Anything else useful?' I mouthed to Lugrako, but he shook his head. Just then another voice rang out, one to chill all our blood.

'Oi! What are you doing?!'

It was from the other side of the door. Our guard.

'But he can't see us,' Dillyn hissed. 'He's the wrong side.'

'I don't know, maybe it's not us.'

Another shout rang out: 'Leave her alone!'

We all looked to each-other in confusion. It was our guard shouting, but it didn't appear to be anything to do with us. In our sudden silence we could now hear a whimpering above the terrible music and chaos. It sounded like a woman or girl. Someone else, a man, was shouting back.

'This might be the best chance we get, while he's distracted,' Lugrako whispered. 'How's the hole coming? Is it big enough?'

Dillyn shook her head. 'Not for me.'

We all looked to Vedica.

'No,' her mother said. 'Not on her own.'

I sighed. 'Look, I understand you. But my daughter is half the age of yours and I would still want her free rather than in here. Who knows what they have planned for us tomorrow, or the next day?'

Lugrako nodded. 'The celebration they're having – I don't see that as a good sign.'

'Maybe Scapula has come back – that usually warrants a feast,' Dillyn added. 'You don't want Vedica in Roman hands.'

Ved looked to me with the eyes of a cornered animal.

'We could be discovered at any moment – now might be her only chance,' I urged her.

'All right,' she said at last.

Forty six   The Cage

I could see young Vedica shaking as she hugged her mother goodbye and I felt sorry for her but there wasn't much time. She had to take her cloak, over-dress and belt off just to wriggle through the hole.

'Here, have this one, it's better,' Dillyn said, rolling her own cloak, the one my Nes had made for her, and passing it through.

'You'd better have this too,' I said, passing the dagger. Dillyn flicked me a look as if to say 'Are you sure?' and I understood, but as things were Vedica was our best chance.

'The row outside is being broken up,' Lugrako whispered.

'Go! Run!' Ved hissed.

I watched the girl scuttle to the next building and disappear into the gloom, flattening herself to the wall. *Good, well done.* It was too dark to see any further but with every heartbeat that passed without a yell or scream I felt relief. There were yells aplenty in the *other* direction. Cartimandua's nasal whine was next to sing out on the other side of the door:

'Shove him in the lock-up for the night! I'm not missing the rest of the feast to deal with this goat.'

'Get back to your chain!' I hissed to Dillyn. There wasn't time to squeeze back into her shackle so she just wrapped it round her wrist and pulled her sleeve down. The door was being unbolted. I dragged the loom back across the hole and threw a cloth over the debris. The door began to open.

The stone. Shit – the stone.

'Lugrako!'

He twigged, thank the Gods, flipping it back down just in time, but Cartimandua must have heard the thump. I sat down, cross-legged, trying to look innocent, but her eyes locked with mine. 'What's going on?'

'We couldn't sleep so we were playing games.'

Cartimandua's eyebrows arched. 'I bet you were.' Guards came in behind her, holding a drunken wretch between them. 'This fool sleeps it off here tonight.'

She hasn't noticed Vedica is missing . . . by the Gods – how can she not have noticed?

Cartimandua turned back towards the door and took a step towards it. *Thank you! Thank you Gods!* She actually stepped across the threshold . . . but then she spun around. All the blood appeared to drain from her face.

'The girl! Where's the girl?! Guards!'

Men poured in, shoving us about, tearing up the house. They found the hole in a heartbeat. The queen's anguished yell might have cracked stone.

'You! This is *you*, isn't it?' She jabbed a fingernail into my chest. 'Guards! Find her. She can't have got far. Vello!'

The man appeared at the doorway, bleary from drink, a mask hanging limp around his neck.

'She's been gone all night, while you lot filled your bladders,' I lied. 'She'll be half-way to the sea by now.'

Cartimandua slapped me good and hard round my face but I just carried on looking straight at her, seething like a fox in a trap.

'Vello,' she said. 'Go to the camp. Wake Marcus – tell him I have a gift for Scapula.'

The queen smiled. I bared my teeth at her in return.

I don't know whether they recaptured Vedica or not. I beg Maponos not, but I don't know. I was moved that night. Vello's henchmen wrapped me in ropes and slung me in the back of a closed cart as before. I expected to be taken straight to Scapula but I was not. After the handover I was fettered in chains and put inside a sort of caged wagon, filthy with bear shit, and a whole succession of Romans, officers and men, came to peer at me, but Scapula himself was not among them.

We moved over the next few days, south, as far as I could tell, my cage dragged by braying mules. Every time we drew to a halt and someone came to pass food or water through the bars I would harangue them with questions. They showed surprise that I knew their tongue, but none answered me, so I took to shouting curses through the night, in both my language and theirs.

On the third night we were within the walls of a solid-looking Roman fort and it was a man of higher rank who came to me. I recognised the vine-stick tucked in his belt as mark of a centurion.

'So,' he said, 'are you going to let us sleep? Or shall I ask the *ursuarius* to restore the original prisoner of this wagon for the night?'

I had long since pushed all the dung out through the bars but the smell lingered and I knew what he was getting at, but it was an empty threat, and I knew that too.

'Where are my wife and daughter?'

His eyebrows lifted a little. 'Even if I knew I wouldn't tell you. Surely you know that by now?'

'You won. What do you profit by being cruel?'

He laughed. 'Look, if they were part of the same train we'd have put you all in together – we're not monsters. I honestly don't know. But if you keep my men awake all night again like a lovelorn cat then I promise you *will* know the meaning of cruel. Understand?'

'Very well.'

He smiled. 'How come you speak so well, anyway?'

'A girl taught me. Someone who was was drawn magpie-like to the shine of your world, for a little while.'

'Where's she now?'

Dead. With one of your swords through her back.

'Planning my rescue, I hope,' I lied.

Another laugh. 'Well, I wouldn't wonder, with your women.' He started to saunter back to one of their guard-houses. 'Remember,' he said. 'Quiet.'

I *was* quiet that night, though exhaustion had as much a hand in it as fear, and at daybreak men came with buckets to sluice out my cage. I confess I missed the bear smell, act of kindness or not, for it revealed how much *I* stank. When was the last time I'd had a chance to change my clothes? I was fettered at both ankles inside there so my breeks had to stay on but I began to remove my shirt on the warmest days, to let it air, and if it rained I would put my cupped hands through the bars to splash water upon myself rather than waste the drinking water.

I was in that fort five days, for no apparent reason. Scapula still didn't come. If someone on the outside did plan my rescue then I heard no tell of it. I heard plenty of other things, but nothing of use. After a while they stopped peering and pointing at me and just got on with their tasks. I heard endless talk of sprains and aches, rations and girls. I got the distinct impression my food was not much worse than theirs, if at all, and I could not in all honesty say I was ill-treated, then, apart from being caged. No-one befriended me though and no Briton was allowed near. I never saw the original centurion again. The next place we stopped at for a whole twenty-three days – for no reason that I could see – and the same pattern played out there.

It may be madness to say it but when we got moving I was relieved to be moving south again, even if it was to my doom.

One late-summer day we pulled into Verlamion.

I recognised it, though Roman buildings had sprung up all over. I pressed myself to the bars, craning my neck to see someone I knew, and it was the first time, in this lonely moon, I felt the people were craning to see me. Whispers built with the thunder. I heard our word for 'king', more than once, and 'Caradoc'.

'Let me speak to them,' I asked of the nearest guard.

'No way.'

'Please – I just want news of my family.'

'No.'

Right.

'Please! My people!' I yelled. 'If you have news of my kin speak now! We don't have much time!'

There was a rumble through the crowd and then an old woman cried out from near the back: 'Princess Verla lives!'

One of the guards started to push his way through to her but the crowd shifted. 'Lalga with her!' another woman shouted.

'No prisoners through here this year before you!' an old man chipped in.

I doubt a single one of the guards understood what we were saying but they were looking scared. They started pushing the people back, javelins side-on. . . for now.

'Thank you!' I reached my hand through the bars. 'Camulos, Teutates, Cernunnos bless you my people!'

An officer whipped round with a spear and whacked it on the bars, I had to snatch my hand back.

'This was a mistake,' he snapped to his comrade. 'We should press on to Londinium.'

'It'll be dark by the time we get there.'

'I don't care. Let's get out of here.'

The mules were thrashed and I felt the wagon jolt beneath me. As the town disappeared behind us I thought I heard the cry: 'Gods bless you, our king!'

Night had fallen by the time we stopped. I could hear horns, and the march of hundreds of feet, and smell a dank, brackish smell. I couldn't see it but I guessed we were near the Tamesis. The cage sped through a gate flanked by watch-towers and almost as soon as it was through I heard a deep voice shout, 'Get him out of sight!' and I was bundled out by four men. We rushed through into a building, or a succession of buildings. It was dark and seemed to grow darker still as we charged on, like Leon's tale of Orpheus. There was a pleasant smell of roses for a blink and then the muddy smell again. I heard a woman: 'And what in the name of the Emperor are we supposed to do with him?'

A man answered: 'Lock him in the shrine room, that's the best place,' and I was propelled forward again. There was sudden light and I was in a large room lit with lamps. Men of every age in life were scattered around the room, some on ladders, painting and drawing upon the walls.

'Keep him here,' the first man ordered and he came into my view. A grey, rough, burly fellow, like a badger-made-man. He swung a hand out towards the painters. 'You! No-one talks to this man! No-one goes near him! I'll be back.'

Good to his word I was soon dragged from the room, the painters all open-mouthed. Before me was a new cage, forming the front 'wall' of a curved niche. I was shoved inside hard enough to hit the back wall and I rounded on him like a poked bear, but he slammed the cage shut.

'There, spend a night with our Gods,' he said, turning the key, 'and may your fingers and toes fall off if you get up to no good tonight.'

The guards trooped out behind him and I was left in near darkness. I could see the Gods he meant: garish idols with their hard, staring eyes, posing on plinths against the blood-red wall. One was Mars, I think, grasping a head in his right hand by its hair. To start with I could hear the painters in the distance but the house grew quieter. I had no lamp, no fire, no water, not even room to lie down. I felt my mouth parch and my stomach start to rumble but no guards appeared until they escorted the painters out. I asked for water and no-one answered. They just hurried the painters on, and now I was alone. Just me and the idols.

'Leon,' I whispered. 'These are your Gods too, I think. If you are with them, as I pray you are, then pray for me.'

Thunder was my answer, another thunderstorm rolling overhead.

'Zeus, I am not your enemy. I fought only to protect my people. Don't take my fingers and toes.'

The thunder grumbled on through the night, a hungry, lonely night with not a moment's sleep, but I kept all my fingers and toes. The next morning, as the painters were marched through, one near the back whispered 'Christos save you' and chucked a small packet through the bars. I caught it, and I saw one of the guards clip the man round the head, but the soldier made no effort to get the packet from me and said nothing.

I waited until they'd gone before I unwrapped it. A fist-sized hunk of bread and twelve hazel-nuts, roasted and shelled – a feast to my rumbling stomach.

Thank you Leon, thank you Christos, thank you Zeus.

I confess a smidgeon of vindictive pleasure when the 'Badger' man was torn off a shred later that morning. I was newly chained inside a covered wagon and I could hear them.

'You left him his belt, you fool! He could have hanged himself,' the younger, shriller man extolled. 'Be thankful we didn't find a corpse this morning or it'd be *you* who faced the governor not *me*.'

The other huffed and hawed.

Malice is beneath you, I remembered.

'You can leave me my belt, I don't want my breeks round my knees,' I called out.

The wagon back-cloth parted and a young centurion, no more than twenty, stared at me. Another new face.

'You understood us?'

'Yes.' *Why are they all surprised?* 'I'd never take my own life. Scapula will get his prize.'

'Scapula?' he sneered. 'We're not taking you to Scapula – you're the prize of the Emperor himself.' He paused a breath – was he waiting for me to be impressed? 'We're going to Rome.'

Forty seven **The Emperor's Prize**

Despair did hit me then. Despair of rescue, despair of ever seeing my family again. I could no longer see our separation as an accident of where we'd been captured – I was sure I'd been singled out for Rome and the rest executed. I tried to remember what had happened to Vercingetorix's family all those years ago. I prayed and prayed with no sign my desires were listened to, let alone fulfilled, as a mad person chatters away to themselves. I cried whenever I was sure I was alone, the many losses of the last few moons presenting themselves to me like witnesses at a trial . . . my family, my dead friends, my horse, my sword, my shield, my torque. I lost weight and condition. I had no mirror to see myself in but I felt I aged a hundred years.

The Gods only know what I looked like when I was chained to a mooring post, at a port, the day I left the Isle. I was cold, and the call of the gulls did not soothe me as it used to. When another spectral figure drifted across my gaze I felt I recognised a kindred spirit . . . in more ways than one.

Adminios.

By the Gods.

My brother was tall and scrawny as I remembered but age had made him gaunt. His hair and beard were more grown out than I'd ever seen before and he was wearing a bizarre striped head-band that didn't suit him at all. He didn't see me watching him for a long while, leading a small child by the hand, appearing to tell the dawdling child the names of things, as they drifted about the quay. When he turned my way at last and I saw the shock of recognition in his eyes, for a heartbeat I thought he was going to walk onwards, but he didn't, he came over.

'You look terrible,' he said.

'You look rough as a donkey's arse yourself.'

Adminios burst out laughing – the last thing I expected. 'Do you think, under the circumstances, we might remember we are kin?'

The echo of Cunobelin in his words chastened even me.

'Be my guest,' I said, and to my surprise he sat down on the quay beside me, gull shit and all. The boy plonked himself down too.

'Is this your son?'

Adminios cast a glance at the snot-crusted child. 'I – I don't know. I promised his mother he wouldn't starve.' He shrugged.

'Did you know I would be here?'

'Me? No – they don't tell me anything, not these days.'

'I thought they'd make you a king.'

He snorted. 'Well I am, king of a few villages stinking of fish. My villa's just up the road there, I shouldn't complain, but Veriko's son did better out of it all than me, really. I may as well have stuck with Father.'

I wasn't sure what to say to that.

Addy laughed. 'But at least I'm not in chains.'

Thanks. There's my old Adminios.

'You wouldn't free me even if you could, would you?'

Addy cast a look at the fifty or more soldiers just west of us near the ship. A gaggle of them were seeing how far they could spit into the water. 'They'd cut us both to dog-meat before you so much as got off the quay.'

'That's not exactly what I asked, brother.'

He coloured scarlet as I knew of old. An *optio* I'd seen going into a shop earlier now came out and started barking orders at the spitting men. He turned towards us and shouted at Adminios for 'fraternising' with the prisoner.

'An interesting choice of words,' I said, and smiled, but Addy was getting up to leave.

'I know you can't do anything for me,' I said. 'But if you see Nes brought through here, or my daughter, if they are alive, brother . . . please.'

He snorted again. 'I'd help her still less than you.'

384

Misery added venom to my words. 'You know, if we should meet in the Land of Youth, don't bother telling the Gods that we are kin. There must be ten dozen people in this land I'd claim as my kin before you.'

Addy started to stride away, the boy trotting behind him. *Will I ever see him again?* I remembered Mother spitting on a cloth to get the blackberry juice off his cheek when we'd all got back from picking; his impish scowl as she used to ruffle his hair.

Malice is beneath you, I reminded myself.

'The emperors destroyed our family,' I called out. 'And they started with you.'

Addy had made it to the steps up to the path but now he turned.

'If they bring her out through here, I'll tell her you're alive,' he said. 'I'll find a way.'

He disappeared from my sight.

The journey through the old Gaulish lands took a long time and I used it well. I resolved to eat every crumb I was given, however vile, and I exercised my muscles as much as I could in the confines of my new cage, stretching and straining myself against the bars. I used rainwater to wash and the sun to keep my skin the colour of the living. Not for the first time did I feel gratitude for my boyhood among the druids. 'A druid is never bored' old Drysfal used to tell us. During those moons, for the first time in my life, his teachings came to fruit. My cage could be sat in the same mucky lane for two days straight and I would entertain myself naming all the birds I heard singing. I could meditate for days on the smell of flowers in the air.

The soldiers started to show curiosity about me again. They would gather about my cage and ask for stories, so I obliged them with the most blood-curdling stories of Britannia I could fathom. They did not tell me anything of the other British prisoners but I began to believe that they didn't know, and I chose not to hold it against them.

As we moved south the days grew shorter but the air stayed warm. I could see the trees turning colour but many of the trees were unfamiliar to me.

'Is it Samhain Eve yet?' I asked one of my more amiable guards when he brought me soup that night and he shook his head.

'Tomorrow.'

I haven't missed it.

'Might I start having a lamp? Now the nights are drawing in?'

'Don't see why not.'

As darkness fell on Samhain night I retreated to a corner of my cage. I could hear the Gauls among my captors telling tales in the distance, none wandering far from the fire.

Cernunnos, Camulos, Teutates, Epona, as I have ever been your loyal servant help me now. Show me what has befallen my kin.

I tore three hairs from my head and burnt them in the lamp. 'Please,' I whispered. 'If you are dead, come to me in a dream. I'm not afraid. I just need to know.'

I settled into the corner to sleep, but of course I could not sleep for an age. I grew cold, waiting, listening to the troops tell their stories.

I awoke on a slope of short grass. I could hear a stream somewhere behind me and feel the warmth of sunlight right through to my bones. It was such a pleasant feeling that for a moment I didn't want to move. I thought I felt a hand shake my shoulder but when I looked there was no-one there.

'Get up, Caradoc.'

It was a man's voice, but not a man I knew. Not even Cernunnos, who I might have expected to see. I did as he'd said and turned around, towards the stream. There, on the opposite shore, were two young men. One had golden eyes and golden skin, hair that shone like starlight. His clothes were made of fresh green leaves – I could smell them.

The other, well he looked like me.

I felt my breath catch in my throat. He had freckles over his nose like Nes and a copper tinge to his hair but his bones were all me. *O Gods . . . thank you.* The lad held out his arm, smiling just like Epaticos used to and I stepped forward a pace but Maponos gently eased him back.

'Look, look what he is showing you.'

The boy swung out his arm and I looked but there was no-one else there. The grassland stretched as far as I could see. There were saplings, their leaves trembling in the warm breeze, and swallows swooping through the air, but not another human soul.

Of course. Nes would be here. Gladsia would be with her.

'Thank you.' I bowed.

Maponos bowed in return, the hawthorn blossom of his crown blooming as he moved.

I smiled at my son. 'It was good to meet you. I think I will be here with you soon.'

I awoke with a start – to find myself back in the cage. The thin morning light was taking the chill off and my guard was pushing a bowl of porridge through the bars.

'Eat up,' he said. 'We're on the move again today. Should be in Rome in about ten days, all being well.' He went red to the roots of his hair. 'Not that you'll be pleased about that, I suppose.'

'It's all right,' I said. 'I'm ready.'

We arrived on the outskirts of Rome on the tenth day as the guard had said we would. I was still in a cage-wagon so I could see the people as much as they could see me. I expected to have things thrown at me to be honest, at least harsh words, given I was an enemy and must have taken the lives of many of their soldiers over the years, but they just seemed curious – as I was about them. Some of the field-workers were slaves, I was sure. The soil looked good, the trees healthy, but the people subdued. As the light failed and we neared the city I saw less living people by the roadside and more tombs.

I thought I would get my first sight of the city Addy had always bragged about but almost as soon as we'd entered a gate between massive walls we stopped. The wagon was driven as far as possible under a portico and the driver and guards started to unharness the mules. I could smell a sort of fishy soup and hear a strange mixture of someone singing and someone else screaming.

'You are one lucky bastard.'

I turned – it was the friendly guard's taciturn pal, shaking his head from side to side as he eased the poles to the ground.

'Am I? Enlighten me.'

He just rolled his eyes but the friendly one now appeared in my sight. 'He just means we've been told to put you here – it's better than normal.'

'Prisoners like you go to the pit, it's always the pit, but the pit's full they say,' the grumpy one continued.

'Is that because my family are already there?'

'Could be.'

The friendly one shot me a look. 'Could be anyone. I've never heard of women or little'uns going to the Tullianum – don't torture yourself.'

I nodded backwards to the sound of screaming. 'No need, by the sound of it.'

He laughed. 'It's not torture – you're next to the hospital. This is the *Castra Praetoria*.'

'Probably one of these cocky work-shy peacocks with a dose of the clap,' the grump said and his friend shushed him like mad.

'The praetorians will sort you out with a meal and a bucket for tonight,' the amiable guard said, to me. 'You won't see us again – I'd say keep your mouth shut and your head down and you might get to stay here. . . y'know, till the time comes.'

The other scoffed. 'Nothin' to do with how *he* behaves. Posh folks want to gawp at him – can't have them traipsing through the drains can we?'

He was shushed again and I couldn't help but smile, despite everything. 'Thank you,' I said, to both of them.

The friendly guard waved it away. 'Not to worry. Fortune smile upon you.'

My new home for the next moon or so was indeed this praetorian 'camp', or my own two-pace-wide patch of it. By night these elite soldiers would wander over from the barracks for tales, as before. By day it tended to be the walking-wounded from next door, who would come for a chat, and a whole parade of assorted other people, who did not. These others, men in milk-white togas, arrived in small groups, escorted by one particularly puffed-up tribune, and were not allowed to get too near. I would hear my name, or their version of it, 'Caratacus', and other tantalising mentions of words I knew: Silures, Britannia, Camulodunum, but never word of my family, and none came within reach.

Until one.

I did not recognise him at first but when the man detached himself from the group and walked my way there was something familiar about him. He stared at me and I stared back. It was a rough, sun-tanned face of middle-years.

'I know your face,' he said.

'And I yours.'

'You saved me from being kicked in the head – the battle by the river.'

I remembered him then – the purple-clad general my brothers-in-law had almost captured.

'You did well,' I said. 'Your men clearly loved you.'

He smiled. 'The same could be said of you. You know I have told that tale many a time at dinner but I had no idea it was the great Caratacus I encountered.'

'And what is your name?'

'I am Gnaeus Hosidius Geta.'

I wasn't sure quite what to say so I nodded, as to a fellow warrior, and he smiled again.

'Your fate will be decided by the Emperor himself tomorrow or the next day . . . but is there anything I can do for you? Are you well treated?'

Shall I be honest? 'I have not been ill-treated for some time,' I admitted, 'but I have never been so filthy in all my life. I have been washing in rain-water. These are the same clothes I was captured in. Please, let me go to my death clean even if it cannot be as a king.'

His eyes looked into mine. Steady eyes, like a dog. 'I understand. I'll see what I can do.'

Good to his word that evening I was visited by two men 'from the household of Geta' bearing a basin of hot water, razor, shears, comb, clean clothes and towels. They did a good job and my limping audience remarked upon the change. It was a new visitor the next morning, though, who was most astonished. He stood a good few paces out, flanked by two guards, staring at me open-mouthed.

'This won't do at all!'

I was eating my breakfast and irked by the intrusion so early in the day in truth. 'I beg your pardon?'

The man ignored me, turning to his guards. 'He could pass for a senator! Where's our barbarian?!'

'Oh, I'm sorry. Perhaps I should paint myself blue and dance round a fire?'

One praetorian just looked back at me blank as a cloud while the other stifled his laughter into his hand.

The toga-wound cockerel spun on his heel, barking 'Sort it out' to the two soldiers, and that afternoon I lost my new tunic and gained a pair of checked breeks, though not my original ragged ones. I gained a torque, too, and a 'tattoo' of random swirls across my chest in some sort of paint.

'This isn't my torque,' I said. One of the praetorians preening me nodded.

'We know. It's from a dead Gaul – he won't mind you borrowing it I dare say.'

He took a step back to admire his work.

'Will I do? Or should I put the dirt back under my nails?'

He smirked. 'You had to pull Narcissus's tail. You should have known better.'

How could I?

I'd been chained at the ankle again as soon as the new breeks were on but now they moved towards me with hand-shackles. I hadn't been tied at the hands for a long time and I flinched.

'Don't get lairy now,' the praetorian warned. 'We'd have offed you months ago if that'd been our orders.'

They put me in a covered wagon and I heard the horses nicker as it pulled away. There were hoof-beats of a different horse and a man said 'See you at the Martius'. It meant nothing to me but I remember *This is it* flashed through my mind.

Gods, I know you will welcome me. I know my kin and my ancestors wait for me and I'm not afraid, but please help me keep my dignity.

There was noise all around and it got louder as we moved. People, dogs, chickens; music, shouting, banging. When we stopped and they pulled me out I could see – just – that we were in a field by a river. The view was masked by thousands of people. I had never seen so many people apart from on the battlefield. There were soldiers but others too, women, children. There was much gasping and pointing when they first spotted me. I could see a line of buildings behind them all. Huge temples but humble huts too, perhaps market stalls.

'Up here now,' one praetorian said.

An open cart was in front of me, pulled by two dun horses. They, like me, were painted in blue swirls. The soldiers had to help me into the cart because my hands and feet were tied and one young praetorian hopped up beside me to connect my ankle shackles to two chains.

'I'll be driving and I'll go steady,' he said. 'Try to stay on your feet.'

'So I am a better target for the mob's missiles?'

'No they won't. Not if they want to keep their hands.'

I could see what he meant as we set off. There were praetorians on all sides of the wagon and high as I was a thrown egg or clod was just as likely to hit one of them as me, however well aimed, at least on its way down. We had got a few spear throws along when we joined a massive column. I could see more praetorians, some on fine horses. The armour was gleaming in the afternoon sun. It shone off cart loads of treasure too. I could see shields, swords, carnyx-heads piled high. Hundreds of people in chains walked ahead of them.

As we moved forward I could see two more carts like mine being driven towards the column too from the other side.

In one a flaxen head. Head and shoulders above all else. *Dranis?*

'Dran! Dranis!'

Dran turned towards me but so did the hundreds in chains. There was a roar like a river's rush and then they all started to chant: 'Ca-ra-doc! Ca-ra-doc! Ca-ra-doc!'

The praetorians nearest my cart were looking worried. . . and furious.

'Let me speak to them,' I pleaded.

'You have got to be joking.'

'No. I only mean to calm them down – I want no excuse to have them slaughtered. Please. There must be some among you who can speak our tongue and will know if I lie.'

'I had a Morini nurse,' one piped up. 'I'll know if you throw us over.'

They drove my cart towards the hordes of slaves and the roars got louder.

'My people!' I yelled. 'It gladdens my heart to hear you! We waged war for years and we waged it well. Long will our fame last in the minds of Rome! But now I go to my death and I want the Emperor and the people of Rome to see the dignity we have. They call us barbarians! Let them see the quiet dignity of those who have faith in the Gods. Be at peace my friends, for I have seen the Land of Youth and I am not afraid. Keep your heads up, but keep your words for the Gods.'

Quiet fell, like a noisy household slumps to slumber.

'Well done,' the praetorian with the Gaulish slave said.

We got going, my cart near the back, but I could see Dranis and Kynbel clearly now.

O thank you Gods!

They looked pale and rope-thin but they were alive and they were together. *Perhaps they were together the whole time? I hope so.*

'Look!' Kynbel yelled. 'Look who is ahead of us!'

He eased Dran to the side and I saw what he meant. A woman and a girl in the further cart, clinging to eachother, facing back towards me.

'Nes! Gladsia!'

Forty eight Triumph

'Caradoc!'

Nes waved at me. It looked like she was only shackled at the ankle. Gladsia was hanging onto her, buried into her dress, like a child half her age. They, too, looked thin and white and ragged but I couldn't see any bruises, from this distance at least. Tears were running down both their faces.

O Gods, where is my bold Gladsia . . ?

'Keep your heads up!' I yelled to them, in our tongue. 'Don't let them see us as weak.'

'Easy,' the driver warned. 'Don't rile them all up again.'

'I'm just trying to comfort my wife and daughter.'

'Fair enough.'

We went over a bridge and the narrow pass made the whole snake of column bunch so I was nearer Nes's cart. There were hundreds of people lining the streets to see us, slowing the procession down, and the praetorians were trying to hold them back. Nesica was reaching out to them.

'Mercy,' she pleaded. 'Mercy for my daughter . . . *please*, I beg you, ' but she was saying it in our language so I doubt many understood. They saw the tears, though, and a child of eight summers clinging to her mother. Some of the women by the roadside were crying themselves. I started to hear shouts of '*clementia*'.

Dran and Kynbel looked back to me.

'It means mercy!' I yelled.

They took up the cry. '*Clementia! Clementia* for the girl!'

I almost joined in . . . but stopped myself. Not all the crowd had tears in their eyes. There were soldiers and men who looked to be old soldiers. Old people whose sons might have died fighting our forces. People with missing eyes and scars on their faces.

I was their enemy . . . and begging wouldn't help.

Stay as you are.

I felt Cunobelin and Epaticos were at my back. I straightened to my fullest height and raised my chin, riding that cart like a chariot, looking anyone in the eye who looked in mine, silent as an oak. We entered a vast oblong area that looked like a parade ground, again flanked by thousands of people, and there were cheers – *cheers* – as I came into their sight.

The praetorians were smiling now.

We passed among tall buildings that I supposed were temples, their steps and platforms thronging with thousands of people, and the cheers and calls for mercy continued. As we entered an impressive gate set in thick walls there was something familiar about the buildings surrounding the long, flat yard and I had a sudden realisation – we were back in the *Castra Praetoria*. It was an area I hadn't seen before, though. Another building that looked like a temple sat at one end, festooned with banners. As we drew nearer I could see people up on the platform within, including a man sat on a throne. There were enormous wooden models on either side, depicting the ocean, gods and sea-monsters. Piles of stolen loot sat in giant urns. Dancing girls, dressed in blue and green, flitted about like butterflies.

'Victory over the ocean!' an extraordinary helmeted figure announced. 'Victory over the Tamesis! Our Emperor Claudius vanquished Britannia herself!'

The carts bearing Dran, Kynbel and my wife and daughter drew up and we were all helped down. Praetorians on either side escorted us up the steps – Dran and Kynbel first, their heads hanging low, then Nes and Gladsia, who were still crying. I wanted to reach out and comfort them but my hands were still tied. The ankle shackles were making the walk up the steps difficult and the praetorian to my left put out his hand as if to steady me.

I shook him off. 'I need no encouragement to meet your Emperor,' I said, 'I've looked forward to it,' and I lifted my chin again.

The praetorian grinned. 'You are one tough son of a bitch.'

I think the Emperor heard us. I saw his lips turn up in a smile as he looked down at me from under his crown of leaves. He was an old man, with heavy-set eyes, big, low ears and a tapered chin. His crown looked odd on him, like a child with his father's torque.

'I had heard that you speak our language,' he said.

'I do, and I will speak in our defence if you will let me, Caesar.'

Claudius turned with a delighted smile to his entourage. A curly-headed woman sat a little apart, but on a chair equally rich, and she had her own crown.

This must be his queen.

I saw her give a little nod.

'Woe to the conquered!' the Emperor said. 'Our legions have conquered Britannia by skill and valour – nothing you say can remedy that, esteemed prince. Britannia will be the jewel of our empire forever. But we can spare a moment to hear what you have to say.'

Now's my chance. If I am to end up murdered and thrown out like rubbish then I've nothing to lose.

I kept my back straight and spoke with a level voice, but loud enough for all to hear.

'If I had been more cautious early on, as many of my rank and nobility were, I could have come to this city as a friend rather than as a prisoner of war and you would have welcomed me, rich as I was. I had horses, men, riches, wealth – more than the rest of them, truth be known. Are you surprised I didn't give them up willingly? That I fought for my land and people? Wouldn't you? If you want to be masters of the world, do you expect the world to just *accept* slavery? My present state, degrading as it is to me, this is glorious for you!' I tipped my head back towards the city. 'If I'd just rolled over like a coward eight years ago then there'd be neither tears nor cheers for me today, but there'd be less glory for *you* too. If you execute me then the moment will pass, the people will forget, but if you allow us to live then I will be a lasting example of your clemency.'

I don't feel it was my most eloquent of speeches, more of an impassioned outburst, and all those on the platform looked back at me in stunned silence. Nes and the rest of my family were looking at me too, perhaps just catching the odd word, but shocked nonetheless.

Gods, if I've made it worse then forgive me, but I'm not sure how I could have.

Then I saw the Emperor's lips turn up in another small smile. 'An example of my everlasting clemency, you say? If you speak like that then, by Mercury, I think you could be.'

'I could sing your praises till my beard is as white as Apollo's teeth, Caesar.'

Claudius grinned, twisting to look at his backers. 'Our rebel king is an orator!' He turned, getting to his feet and throwing a loose bit of his toga over his arm. 'I have spoken before of transferring to this city all of conspicuous merit, wherever found. I have told the Senate that we should look to our own Romulus and not to the Spartans for knowledge on how best to treat defeated foe. Which of our cities thrives best now?' They all laughed and I wasn't quite sure what to make of his words, but now he turned back to me. 'It seems I have been the physician to treat my Senate and now I am required to take my own medicine.' He looked to my family, his eyes resting for a heartbeat on Gladsia. 'A pardon, by Jupiter. I grant you all a pardon.'

What? Can it be true?

The strange helmeted figure on the plinth looked to us and then to the Emperor. Claudius gave him a small nod. '*Clementia!*' he exclaimed. 'Our renowned Emperor is as merciful as he is wise!'

The Praetorians all around erupted into cheers and I – well to my shame I fell to my knees. Nes and all my family followed me like barley to the breeze. 'Thank you, Caesar,' I blurted, my voice choked. 'May the Gods bless you.'

I struggled to my feet to bow again and then we turned to his queen and bowed to her too. This raised a titter of laughter through the throng and put a knife through my heart.

Oh no, what have we done wrong?

The queen got to her feet with dignity, throwing out just the slightest flash of glare – not at us. 'Cloaks,' she snapped. 'Bring cloaks to comfort the pardoned.'

Servants scampered to it and within moments we were all wrapped up. The others looked cleaner and healthier in an instant, and I understood the sense of what she had done.

As soon as our bonds were freed Nes ran to me, throwing her arms round my neck. Gladsia too hugged herself about my waist. The praetorian troops behind us cheered again.

O thank you Gods. If I were to live a thousand years I could not repay you for this moment.

'Come,' the Emperor said, his right hand held out. 'Come inside and sit down.'

We followed him, me carrying Gladsia shoulder-high and the four of us adults arm-in-arm.

'What's going on?' Kynbel whispered to me as we went up the steps.

'The Emperor has granted us a pardon – after that I don't know. Are you two all right?'

Kynbel flicked a look at Dran. 'We've survived, but could be better.'

Dran still hadn't said a word.

'I'm not sure what we will face in here,' I whispered. 'Let's just stay quiet and grateful, and see what tonight brings.'

'Do you think they'll let us go home?' Kynbel asked.

Gods help me. 'I – I doubt it, Kynbel, I'm sorry.'

My nephew squeezed my arm. 'We were expecting to be strangled in a cell tonight – we were shown what was going to happen. Don't apologise.'

That evening was one of the longest of my life. There were speeches – by the Gods there were speeches! They made most of my own efforts seem bald statements. As each toga-wrapped dignitary rose to his feet my heart filled with dread that they were furious at the clemency Claudius had shown and might persuade him otherwise. As the night stretched on, though, they did not and I could breathe again. They did talk at great length of the Emperor's wisdom and the fallen kings of the past. I, at least, could understand most of what was said, baffled as I was by many names, but my poor family were at a loss. We sat in a row, Gladsia curled on my lap, trying to show interest and keep up a look of quiet gratitude.

By midnight we were all trying as we might to keep awake.

It was the Emperor himself who came to our rescue. He wandered our way at the end of the latest speech, his arm about a young boy, a few years older than Gladsia, with bags under his eyes.

'Our Britannic guests must be tired and hungry, Britannicus.'

'So am I, Father.'

Claudius laughed into his chest. 'I know, but we are obliged to stay when citizens are praising us. Have another sweetmeat.' He looked over to a young praetorian on guard near the entrance, who looked just as weary as we. 'Titus!'

The lad brightened to attention.

'Go with Narcissus, young Titus, get some keys. You can take our guests to their house and then retire for the night.'

Claudius turned to me.

'Thank you again, Caesar,' I said. 'You have been most generous.'

He shot me a lop-sided smile. 'Well, the divine Gaius Julius Caesar wasn't right about everything,' he muttered, 'or he wouldn't have ended up with a knife in his ribs.'

Indeed.

Young Titus led us through the dark streets at a quick pace, ignoring all the beggars and drunks. 'It's not that far,' he reassured us, but it was the furthest I had walked – or had a chance to walk – in many moons and I could feel it in my legs. I lifted Gladsia and carried her.

We entered a quieter street and Titus stopped dead outside a dark, cold-looking house. He brought out an enormous iron key from his tunic, unlocked the door, then gave the key and a small scroll to me.

'This house is yours, a gift from the Emperor, for as long as he sees fit,' he said. 'Go on in.'

We entered the gloom, feeling the crunch of dry leaves beneath our feet, and then suddenly we were outside again. Four columned walls surrounded us but up above I could see the sky. A small tree at the centre of the court was shedding its leaves in the cool night breeze.

Titus was looking around, confused. 'Two slaves come with the house,' he said. 'You'll need more but those two should be here.'

He clapped his hands and two tiny people appeared as if sprung from the soil, a man and a woman, both grey. He was weasel-thin, she round as an acorn.

They looked up at the pack of us in sheer terror.

I had been holding Gladsia on one side and was hand-in-hand with Nesica on the other, but now I put my daughter down and raised my hands to them. 'Be at ease, we are just people, as you are. For now, I am the only one of us who can speak your tongue. I am Caratacos. What are your names?'

The two looked at each-other and then the old man answered. 'I am Glyptus, sir. This is Primula, sir.'

'How long have you served this house?'

'I was born here, sir, in the fourth bedroom, when the Emperor Augustus was still alive. Primula was brought from Syria ten years ago.'

'What befell the previous owners of the house?'

The old man and woman looked to each-other again, the fear back in their eyes. Glyptus bit his lip. 'I – I'm sorry, sir, but we're not allowed to tell you.'

I wasn't sure how much Nes understood but she now looked up to me, worried. 'I'll tell you later,' I said, in our tongue, and squeezed her hand again.

'Please,' she said, to the couple, 'is there somewhere warm? Where we could have a drink?'

I translated and Primula's old brown face creased into a smile. 'We have wine, and chicken stew, in the *culina*,' she said, to nods from Glyptus. 'Come, rest yourselves.'

Titus slapped me on the back. 'I'll return in the morning, with some money. Sleep well.'

There were enough rooms in that big, draughty house to have had one each to sleep in if we had wanted. That first night we just asked Glyptus and Primula for blankets and all bedded down together in what turned out to be the dining room. No matter. Niceties such as bathing could also wait for the morning. First we had to eat our fill in the *culina*, the only warm room in the house, all seven of us sharing our sad tales and more than a few tears, well into the night.

I woke first, with the morning sunshine streaming in, kissed my darling wife as she lay sleeping, and went for a wander. By the time I found Glyptus, loading a brazier full of charcoal in a gaudy painted room, Gladsia had found me, and slipped her little hand once more into mine.

'Good morning sir. The soldier has arrived, he is waiting in the atrium.'

He was, sat on the edge of a stone-built pond with a bag of money on his lap.

'This is your stipend for the quarter, from the Emperor,' Titus explained. 'Are you familiar with our money?'

I remembered the foray of Atrebati and I into Gesoriacum. 'Not much.'

Titus clucked his tongue. 'I should come with you today or you'll end up blowing the lot.'

He was treading a fine line between rude and kind but I accepted his help. I had just time to teach Glyptus the British for 'Back soon', lest Nes fright to death, and we set off, at a smart pace again, behind the soldier.

The streets were noisy, smelly and bursting with people, the tall buildings shading the streets and adding to the crowds. I held my daughter's hand very tight. Titus pointed out buildings as we went.

'Those are the baths,' he said. 'You'll like the baths. Everyone does.'

I tried to be polite but it looked little better than a giant whorehouse to me.

We entered a marketplace loaded with bolts of cloth, of every colour imaginable, men shouting their prices. There were trays of fruit and sweets, cages full of ducks and chickens. Women tried to tempt Gladsia with stuffed dates.

'It's all right,' Titus said, 'they're good.' He parted with a small coin of our money and bought us a little basket-full.

'King Cunobelin used to like these,' I said, and he smiled.

We turned a corner and were confronted with cages of another kind. These were loaded with people, chained and solemn, with plaques around their necks. I heard Gladsia gasp and pulled her to me. A trader up on a platform was pulling about a boy to show his muscles. It looked like the boy had chalk on his feet.

'Let's see what's available,' Titus said, and marched forward. I felt my stomach turn. I could see what was available. A fair quarter of the men there that day must have been British. I felt a hush fall over the sea of heads as they recognised me.

When a pair of big hazel eyes met mine, near the back, I felt tears spring to my own.

Hedros. Oh no.

The nearest trader saw me looking at him. 'You, up,' he said, flicking a cane under Hedros's chin. His loose tunic

402

was dragged off of him so he stood there in loincloth and chains. I could see his plaque:

Healthy

British

Quiet

23 years

'Careful,' Titus warned.

'I *know* him.'

'I know. But you can't buy him.'

'You said we could buy slaves!'

'Not British ones.'

I sucked in a breath. 'Who would know?'

'Everyone,' he said. 'And I would know.'

I looked back to Hedros. 'I'm trying, my friend. I'll try to get you out of there.'

The trader shot a suspicious look at me. 'You speak Gaul too? He'd be a good purchase for you then – he's thick as boiled fish but strong. Good teeth – '

'He can learn,' I snapped, and the man nodded away.

'Oh yes, given time.' He laughed, waving his hand about. 'But with so much choice . . .'

'What will happen to him Dada?' Gladsia asked and I threw a desperate look at Titus.

'The gladiator trainer will be round this morning, sweetie, he'll get bought,' the trader said.

I know what you're up to you scum.

'He knows we want him, he's trying to push the price up,' I hissed to Titus.

'You can't buy him, even if he was one *sestertius*. I can't let you.'

I shook my fist up to all the marble in anger. 'You have all this wealth! Yet you send thousands to slaughter to steal our huts? And now this?!'

Titus bit his lip. He threw a look at Hedros and then back to me. They were about of an age. Hedros looked sad as a whipped dog but he hadn't said a word.

Maponos, help me again, I beg you. I have to do something.

'I'll buy him,' Titus said.

'Two thousand *denarii*,' the trader said.

Titus sneered. 'Nice try you bastard. I was born here – think again.'

Hedros was settled into the household of Titus's father by the end of the day. I saw him walking into the villa with the other slaves with a heavy heart, but they appeared healthy, and were kind to him, and I reassured myself it could be worse.

Titus walked me back to our house and shook my hand as we parted. 'I have to get back to the *castra*, but may I offer some advice?' he said, and my heart sank again.

'Of course.'

'The Emperor is fond of you, *now*, but emperors can be gone in the morning or last thirty years – there's no way of telling. I would say be cordial, if he is cordial to you, but be neither enemy nor friend. For the friends of one are the enemies of another. The money may not even last – make some investments. Ask around. But above all else keep your heads down.' He looked into my eyes. 'You do not mind me saying this to you?'

'Not at all.'

Forty nine   Post Scriptum

I heeded the words of young Titus. We settled into life in Rome without another squeak of discontent after my outburst that day. I did make a few trips to the Palatine, as it turned out, at the Emperor's request, and we got on well. He even loaned me books, but I would not say we were ever close. I was glad none of us were anywhere near the place when he was murdered a few years later.

Sometimes I would wonder if I did the right thing in pleading for our lives. *What will the Gods think of that when the time comes?* Perhaps like Vercingetorix I should have remained defiant to the end? Then I would see Nesica braiding my daughter's hair under the tree in the yard, hear them chatting and laughing, and I would think 'no'.

The money did dry up, of course, as soon as Claudius and Narcissus were dead, but by then I had bought some land south of the city and the horses we raised there and fruit we grew kept enough money coming in, enough for food in our bellies. They stopped watching who I associated with after a while and I was able to purchase a few Britons to run it for us and live out their days with easy work and sunshine.

Dranis and Kynbel got work themselves, once they'd mastered the language, with an Alexandrian horse-trader down at the *Circus*, and they flourished, but Kynbel had a dream of earning enough money to pay for passage on a ship – or a dozen ships – to Eire, and one summer he left his job and made a try. He never got beyond the port of Ostia. The soldiers there recognised him and they turned him back. We welcomed Kynbel home with tears of joy and sadness, the old Egyptian gave him his job back, and none of us ever spoke of it again.

In time we grew to love the house, with its little walnut tree in the atrium and the chamber with murals of pear trees and frolicking deer that became Nes's and my own. I would say a Cernunnos prayer each morning and imagine myself out in the forests of home. There was another garden too, towards the back, and Nesica soon had it full of herbs and pottery bee-skeps with Glyptus and Primula's help. They became fond of us, I think, and we of them. They found her a cat too and a skinny starving dog from the street to love, though Creegan still held a place in her heart.

My darling Nes saw her fifty-second year but it was her heart that failed her in the end, despite my best efforts. She saw our Gladsia married to her soldier but I will have to greet our first grandchild without her. The child is due in the autumn, before Samhain we think, when the grapes are ripe. Some people are surprised that I would let Gladsia wed a warrior of Rome, but he is a decent man and after some of the horrors of men I have seen here I am content with that, as was Nes.

I am old now, and I sit on the atrium ledge feeding crumbs to the birds, and I find there is one robin who will get closer than all the rest, sometimes eating from my hand. *I know you will always be with me my Nes. Gods bless you.*

So, my tale is done. I am going to roll this last scroll up now and hide it in the dry spot in the *tablinum* wall with all the others. I don't know if I have one moon left to me or a year or ten years – who does? – but I am pleased I've got it done before my eyesight goes. Everyone I ever loved is preserved in these pages. I am often told, in the market place – or even dining in my own hall – by men who have read their 'Campaigns of Julius' and think they know us, that we 'Celts' are warlike unto death. I listen, I smile, I am a good host. I keep my head down and do nothing that will endanger my daughter. They may try to draw me out on one side or another but I am old and my fighting days are done. I am done with it.

All the news I have heard of Britannia of late has been bad. I worry for those we left behind, but I fear the little I can do I am already doing, and I am tired, and I have realised, after all these years, that there is no better way to spit on your enemies than to die in your bed.

Author's Note

All of the Caradoc trilogy is a work of fiction woven around a framework of historic truth and with Rebel King this is truer than ever. Readers familiar with the relevant passages in Tacitus's Annals will recognise that I have followed Tacitus closely, if not to the letter. Some characters and incidents were inspired by archaeological finds.

The following characters in Rebel King are all real people who appear in the Roman histories: Caradoc himself; Adminios; Venutios, Cartimandua, Vellocatus; Ostorius Scapula and his son Marcus; Gnaeus Hosidius Geta; Emperor Claudius, his wife Agrippina and son, Britannicus, and his assistant Narcissus.

The following people who are mentioned in Rebel King are also inspired by the Roman histories: Cunobelin, Epaticos, Togodubnos, Veriko, Prasutagos, Boudicca (Bouda in the book), Aulus Plautius and his wife Pomponia. Tacitus mentions that Caradoc had a wife and daughter and 'brothers' in addition to Togodubnos and Adminios – whether biological or metaphorical brothers is unknown, and that Venutios had at least one brother and other 'relatives', but I have given all these people names.

Some characters, Saenu and Aesu of the Iceni, and Eisrig Boduocos and Coriona of the Dobunni, were inspired by fragments of names on the coins of their tribes. Young Vedica of the Cornovi and her father Uricon were also real people.

In the story Caradoc never knows whether Vedica makes it or not but I can tell you that yes she does. She lived to be thirty years old – a decent age for those days – and we know this because her tombstone was found in Yorkshire. On it was information on her father, her tribe, and even a carved portrait.

Just about all of the locations in Rebel King are real places. In truth there are far too many to list here without this 'author's note' becoming a book in its own right, but perhaps readers who are familiar with the archaeological sites of Britain will recognise them. Check out my blog on Goodreads to see the definitive list.

At this late stage of the trilogy I have to confess to a mistake. I have used the word 'harp' throughout all three books but evidence for true harps – with a triangular profile and enclosed string terminals – does not predate the 8h century AD in the British Isles. The instrument Tyllan plays is actually a lyre – with a flat bridge and visible tie-off points for the strings. The earliest evidence for lyres in the UK is the fragment of a lyre from 300BC found on the Isle of Skye. Like many unmusical people I am guilty of using 'harp' and 'lyre' interchangeably and did not discover my error until it was too late.

On the whole I hope I have done Caradoc and his people justice. It has been a great joy for me to bring this story to life and I hope reading it gives you pleasure.

Caradoc – The Rebel King,

book 3 of the Caradoc Trilogy

Aknowledgements

I continue to be hugely grateful to everyone who has helped and encouraged me. Thanks to Ann and Nathan at Pendown for doing such a great job and infinite friendly assistance.

A big thank you also to Dulcie Durman and my Mum for their helpful comments on the draft text.

Many thanks also to Dru Durman and other members of Dumnonika for useful conversations on weaponry and Iron Age life.

The realistic 1st Century AD Torc, on the front cover - was hand-made by Dru, copying a real example.

A huge thank you to my Dad, my husband Mikel and all my friends, family and colleagues for their continuing encouragement.

Thank you for reading

Caradoc – The Rebel King,

book 3 of the Caradoc Trilogy

**We hope you enjoyed it and will feel able to put a
review on Amazon or Goodreads – or both.
Reviews make a big difference to authors with
independent publishers – thank you for your help in
letting other readers find a good book when they are
looking for one.**

This book is also available in eformats from
Amazon and PendownPubishing.co.uk

Also by Sally Newton

Book 1 - Caradoc - The Defiant Prince
ISBN 978-1-909936-18-8
Book 2 - Caradoc - The Druid Heir
ISBN 978-1-909936-21-8

For news about her writing and publications follow
Sally Newton on

Twitter @SNewtonAuthor

or Like her page on Facebook

www.ingramcontent.com/pod-product-compliance
Lightning Source LLC
Chambersburg PA
CBHW050859250626
47155CB00001B/34